Now & Then

Also by Jacqueline Sheehan

LOST & FOUND
TRUTH

Now & Then

Jacqueline Sheehan

AVON

An Imprint of HarperCollins*Publishers*

"At Sea" by Wendy Mnookin on p. 7 from *The Moon Makes Its Own Plea*. © BOA Editions, 2008. Reprinted with permission.

HarperCollins books may be purchased for educational, business, or sales promotional use. For information, please write: Special Markets Department, HarperCollins Publishers, 10 East 53rd Street, New York, NY 10022.

FIRST AVON PAPERBACK EDITION PUBLISHED 2009.

Designed by Diahann Sturge

Library of Congress Cataloging-in-Publication Data
    Sheehan, Jacqueline.
        Now & then / Jacqueline Sheehan. — 1st Avon paperback ed.
            p.   cm.
        ISBN 978-0-06-154778-2
        I. Title. II. Title: Now and then.
    PS3619.H437N69   2009
    813'.6—dc22   2009012851

09   10   11   12   13   OV/RRD   10   9   8   7   6   5   4   3   2   1

Harry Francis Sheehan
1906-1959

At Sea
By Wendy Mnookin

At the end of the jetty.

Where the boats come in. Where the boats go out.
   At the pile of rocks that swallows the sun at the
   end of the day.

At the turn of the trail. At the last dune.

In front of the hot-dog stand. At the door to the pub.
   By the shanty, the shipbuilder's yard, the discarded
   yellow boots, the smashed clam shells.

You thought I'd give in to despair.
But today is today, everywhere I look. And I look
   everywhere.

Chapter 1

The castle docent led the group along a roped path through a cold room. The early September air had already taken a turn, but it was doubtful that the stone castle ever warmed comfortably. Castles were expensive to keep up; the taxes were dreadful, and owners had to bear the humiliation of opening their homes to a weekly stage show of tourists if they expected to hang onto the family estate.

Anna didn't like walking through living rooms with family photos on the end tables. She had been hoping for a bawdy ghost, a sense of Renaissance people gulping honey mead, their fingers greasy with smoked fish on wooden planks, bristle-haired dogs stretched on the floor surrounded by a pile of bones. She did not want to be the dreadful price that the present owners had to endure.

After silently counting them with her eyes, the guide led them through the library. One wall was filled with books—flat leather-encased pages—and, on the opposite wall, paintings.

"And here," the docent pointed with her arm, "this shred of cloth is all that remains of the Fairy Flag."

The castle held the tattered remnants of a banner. The faded fabric was framed in glass and hung on a north-facing wall to protect it from light.

"What type of fabric is it?" asked a woman who had not said one word until that moment.

"Silk. See how it shreds? Linen, which would have been the other choice, frays in a bolder pattern and the dyes tend to take more of a toll on linen," said the guide. "No one knows exactly where the flag comes from, but the story that has been handed down is that it had the power to save the local clan from destruction. And like all good tales, there was a catch; it could only be used three times. So you can imagine that they saved it for only the worst disasters, when invaders were at the gates and the clan had no hope of escaping a massacre. Then the Fairy Flag was flown."

The guide was a good storyteller, and she paused, knowing that the story begged for questions. She let the tension build, until she was prodded by the inevitable. A young boy with a Red Sox baseball cap shot his hand up.

"Yes?"

"Did they use it up? Did they use it all three times?" asked the boy.

"We know it was used in 1490 and again in 1580, but we are not sure if it was used again. In those years, clans fought each other as well as invaders from the sea. Life was perilous. I rather think that it was used again, that we wouldn't be standing here in the castle if it had not been used. This castle has remained in the same lineage for over seven hundred years." She looked at her watch and extended her left arm to the door. "Let's move along to the bedchambers."

Everything in Ireland was so unimaginably old, unlike the

United States. People in Ireland referred to a day seven hundred years earlier the way Americans talked about the Eisenhower administration. Disagreements that had taken place in a village in 1251 were remembered as if they had happened last week. Time bent and folded like a piece of string looped around a stick. Since the divorce, Anna felt time slow down with a dark, rotted sludge clogging her every movement. Since she quit her job at the law firm, she sometimes forgot what day it was.

Three times, the flag was good for three times. Had Anna been good for three times? The first time was not the worst because Anna didn't know there would be a second and a third time for miscarriages. She thought the first was a fluke. Anna and Steve each worked seventy hours a week at law firms, eighty if needed. They saw each other for a chaotic morning of shower, coffee, and dress for Boston's legal world and then not again until evening. The first time she was pregnant, she told him by texting, *Preg.* That's all she wrote, after peeing on the little paper strip first thing in the company bathroom.

She had been exactly three weeks pregnant. By six weeks, she told her mother, her brother, Steve's parents, and her law school buddy, Jasper, who had emailed back.

"You have my permission to name the baby Jasper. Boy or girl, doesn't matter to me. Are posting the birth on YouTube?" he asked.

"You're an idiot, even for a lawyer," replied Anna.

Jasper had fled Boston right after he passed the bar and now specialized in entertainment law in LA.

"How can you take entertainment law seriously?" said Anna.

"How can you take contract law seriously?" said Jasper. "Go have a baby."

At two months plus, her uterus twisted with seismic cramps, stripping itself of the baby-to-be. Anna was shocked by the decisiveness of her body, the bloody torrent that woke her and Steve at 4:00 a.m. on a Sunday morning.

She sat hunched on the toilet crying, while Steve crouched next to her, wearing only his blue Man Silk underwear. He pressed his forehead to her thighs, leaving the two of them wordless.

That had been the first time. Six months later was the second time. This time they only told her mother. The miscarriage, a word that Anna hated, like a miscarriage of justice, happened when Steve was on a case in Atlanta. She phoned him.

"It's OK," he said into his cell phone at the Marriott. "We'll try again." She'd heard a spray of voices in the background and a high peel of laughter, like crystals rising in the air.

The third time, six months after that, she'd been driving from Boston to Greenfield to visit her mother when the familiar eviction by her uterus began. She was on Route 2, going west into the sun and it was hard to get off. No place seemed right, not Fitchburg, not there. She hung on until she pulled into her mother's driveway. She'd driven the last thirty miles with a dark gray towel stuffed between her legs.

Anna beeped the horn and her mother came out with a flutter of high school math papers in her hand. Anna beckoned her to the car and watched the smile dissolve from her mother's face as she felt her own crumble.

"I've just miscarried. Why can't I do it? Why can't I have a baby? What's wrong with me? What's wrong with all of us?"

Anna opened the car door and felt another tight cramp that made her chest cave in.

"Let's get you inside and call your doctor. We can tackle the esoteric questions later," said her mother, placing a firm hand under Anna's elbow and pulling her up.

Anna ducked for the castle exit, desperate to shake the images of failed pregnancies. The rest of the group followed the guide to the bedchambers. She was anxious to be outside, not inside with the poor castle all trussed up like a Disney exhibit. She felt uneasily like one of the invaders who must have been thwarted by the Fairy Flag. Tourists did not impale the locals on spiked poles, or pillage the castle, but they did break up the continuity of a place with gawking and pointing, eventually bringing big box stores to the edge of town, there to suck the life out of the tiny villages with their ancient family businesses. Anna didn't know how her friend Harper made a living bringing attention to otherwise quiet locales so that they could be infested with visitors and digital cameras.

But she had been grateful that Harper had invited her on a trip to write about Scotland, Wales, and lastly Ireland. Anna was thirty-four and her life was a wreck.

She walked outside to the soft northern sun, leaving the relic behind. She strolled along the dirt path to the parking lot.

"Psstt."

Anna turned her head toward a juniper tree but caught only a flash of color—a bright woolen hat knit of blues, pinks, and purples, and all the colors that permeate the hills, rocks, and fields. She walked around the tree and saw a small woman.

"Do you mean me?" Anna asked. At home she might have

ignored a stranger who *psstted* at her, but here in the land of unrelenting civility, she responded.

The woman's white hair was held by a clip at the back of her neck and she wore clothes that people might have worn in a *National Geographic* magazine about charming Ireland twenty years ago. The sweater was buttoned up and the skirt of well-worn plaid stopped just at the bottom of her knees. She held a yellow-and-blue plastic carryall bag.

"Here, dearie. I thought you'd never come out. I've got a bit of something for you."

The woman had not been in the group of culture seekers from the castle. But she was clearly Irish, too full of culture to be seeking it. Law school and a few miserable years of law practice had made Anna suspicious. Her last research with corporate law had been about English contracts with the Irish during British occupation. Judging from the age of this woman, she had lived through the years when Ireland had clawed itself out of a wretched economy, not unlike a third world country. But on this trip Anna was practicing beating back her law school demons; she was done with law.

The woman tilted her head to one side and took a good look at Anna. "I saw you when you came in. You're not nearly as tall as I was told. For an American I mean, not so tall for an American."

"Are you waiting for someone with the tour?" asked Anna.

"Oh, no. Not them."

"You might have me mixed up with someone else," Anna said. "I've noticed since I've been visiting here, that people tell me that I look familiar to them, like a cousin or a sister, their friend from school. My family is from Ireland but we weren't very good at keeping track of that sort of thing. Not a genealogist in our whole family." Anna looked back at the entrance to the castle to make sure she didn't miss Harper when she came out.

"No, I've been waiting for you, waiting longer than you could guess. It must have made things worse in America, with so much time going by, building up a steam of misery. I thought of going there myself, but dreadful things happen to the likes of me when we travel over water. Don't let me talk all day now. Your friend will be out the door in a few moments."

She dug around in the plastic carryall. "Here it is." She pulled out a small bundle wrapped in brown paper, taped neatly just the way all the shopkeepers did in Ireland. It was soft and about the size of a deck of cards. She placed it in Anna's hands.

"Take it now. Here, put it in your pack. You'll be needing it. There's nothing else for you or them now," she said and reached up to put her cool palm on Anna's cheek. "I shouldn't say more, but I didn't know that you would look so poorly, so filled with misery. Love will force you to make a frightful leap straight through the terrors. You can walk away from the call, but you'll be left by yourself. And that would be the pure pity of it."

Anna froze to the spot, unable to break the trance.

Harper yelled from the gate of the castle. "I'm coming, I'm coming. I had to stop at their gift shop. You wouldn't believe the stuff you end up with for these travel articles."

Anna turned to see Harper with a small pile of bundles— more woolen fabric, no doubt, and a few books. Suddenly Harper tripped on the uneven stones and the packages scattered before her in a lava flow of souvenirs. Anna ran to help, looking back once to the old woman who had turned away and walked with an agile step along the path to the parking lot. Anna collected a few packages as Harper dusted her pants off.

"Thanks," said Harper. "Let's put everything in your pack. We'll sort it out later."

"That woman just gave me a little package," said Anna.

"Happens to me all the time when people find out I'm a travel writer. Tonight is our last night, I can't believe it. Let's dump this stuff back at the inn and head out for some good pub food and a few pints. Our flight leaves in the morning."

Chapter 2

In the cattle car section of Aer Lingus, the plane rocked as it was slammed by ever-stronger winds. Harper, who sat in first class, had come back to tell Anna in urgent whispers that the pilot was gambling on beating a storm to Boston. He had seen it on the radar, a giant swirl heading from upper Michigan, picking up speed across Pennsylvania and virtually following the Mass Pike to Boston. Landing at Boston under the best of conditions was congested. The approaching storm could cause hell.

"Remember, we're safer in a plane than we are in a car," said Harper.

"Thanks for the tip," said Anna.

Seat belt signs blinked on and the flight attendants scooped all remaining beverages into black plastic bags, holding onto each seat back for support as they claimed they were thirty minutes out of Boston.

Two men in front of Anna began to vomit, first one and then the other, when the plane seemed to fall out of the sky and then catch itself. She handed three vomit bags from her row, hoping this would be enough to contain what sounded like an extraordinary event. The smell made others start to wretch. Once, when the plane rolled violently to the right and then just as violently to the left, she was sure they would roll over if they went even one inch farther in either direction.

Passengers pulled out cell phones to call spouses, children, and friends, despite the admonition from the flight attendants to keep cell phones off. One of the baggage compartments burst open and two Lands' End backpacks flew out, followed by a plastic bag from the duty-free shop. Anna and the two passengers in her row gripped each other's hands and squeezed hard. One was a man named Robert, from Glasgow, who was going to visit his cousin in Boston. He had a very large hole pierced through his earlobe, into which a silver plug had been inserted. He was dressed in black leather. He had immediately announced to Anna that he was gay, and then he'd speculated on which American actors were gay. Now he gripped Anna's left hand and the hand of the older woman from Vermont on his right. Anna wished that she had gone to the bathroom earlier because she was afraid, for the first time since she was a toddler, that she was actually going to wet her pants right there in the seat.

She did not want to die in the Atlantic five months after a divorce. She couldn't believe there was that much unfairness in the world. But then, she had been pretty sure that nothing could feel more unfair than Steven leaving her. If Steven had wanted to hurt her more, he could not have.

He chose their favorite Thai restaurant in Boston to tell her. Anna picked at her shrimp and lemongrass stir-fry. She cleared her throat. Anna had suspected something for months.

"When were you going to tell me?" she asked.

Steven's eyes darted to the door as if calculating his escape.

"There aren't many reasons for asking that question. How did you find out? No, that isn't the point. The point is, I'm seeing someone else."

She put down her fork. "Seeing someone? As in dating? You can't date someone else. You're married. To me."

"I'm sorry, there's no way I can be anything but the bad guy here. I don't have the right to ask anything of you, but could you please not turn into Anna the lawyer?"

She pushed her plate away, bumping his water glass. His hand shot out and grabbed it. She looked down and saw with frustration that her hands were shaking.

"Did you meet her while I was in the hospital with the first miscarriage or was it the second? The third? Is this a Henry the VIII decision on your part? Don't tell me she's pregnant?"

Steven looked down at his mound of rice.

"Oh. She is pregnant," said Anna.

Anna fell back against the padded seat of the booth. The blaring truth of Anna's miscarriages, her one non-negotiable failing, had caught her unawares. She fell hard into a pool of bitterness and stayed there.

Three was a horrible number of miscarriages, a triumvirate of miscarriages, of fetuses begun but unable to hang on, hanging onto a cliff of a uterus, tumbling off, and washed away in a monsoon of blood and betrayal. There was nothing anyone could say after each miscarriage. There was nothing right to say because miscarriages came from forces unknown or at best, unstoppable, like lighting. But at night when she slipped from waking to sleeping, she saw the unfit part of her, the place inside where babies of all sorts refused to grow because she had produced a space that could not love a baby. Was that the family legacy, played out by the men, felt with exquisite pain by the women?

Anna saw baby spirits pondering an entry into life, selecting a mother and a father, shopping around for reasons indecipherable. And when almost-babies chose Anna, they soon saw their mistake and pulled the escape hatch. Steve had fallen away, not unlike the almost-babies, falling in love with the fertile delta of Rita, the receptionist at their dentist's office, who already brimmed with life. An almost-baby had landed in a perfectly, color-coordinated uterus and was strapped in for a full-term ride aboard the Rita mother ship.

"Bloody hell!" said Robert. He crunched her hand as they were tossed about in the shaking plane. "I don't want to die in America! Oh, I'm sorry. Nothing personal about America, but I'd just as soon die in Scotland, thank you."

He must have seen something terrified in Anna's face, something that broke through all his leather and body piercing.

"Look here, nobody will die today. Not us. We've got a big life to live," he said.

She looked down and saw a watery stream of vomit under her shoes. She picked up her feet.

"Flight attendants prepare for landing."

The landing gear opened with a familiar sound. She leaned across her two companions. "I just got divorced," she said as loudly as she could to be heard over the racket. "We have to make it." And more than anything, she wanted to believe that was true, that the worst had come and gone.

Since the divorce, she had lived in Rockport, a seaside town one hour north of Boston. She couldn't afford a place right on the water; her house was a half mile inland, but during the months immediately following the divorce, she stationed herself on the immense gray slabs of rock that separated land from ocean. Her mother had said that tranquility was genetically out of the question with her, but she discovered that the roar of wind and ocean could temporarily scour the pain of divorce and for that she had been grateful. Stormy days had been her favorite, zipped up in a Gortex jacket, hood pulled tight, rain pants repelling all downpours. She sat on the unyielding mountains of rock and faced the ocean, squeezing her eyes to slits to keep out the driving horizontal rain. This had been her brand of therapy: harsh, punishing, and exacting. She used the rocks for everything. She even used the rock to file her nails, taking them past the bloody quick. She had wanted to exfoliate her pain, patting it with tinny placations. For every person who tilted her head and said, "I know how hard divorce can be," she counted the seconds until she could run to the rocks, lay prostrate on its fat hard tummy, and take what the ocean and wind had to offer.

Anna said good-bye to Harper who had a slim thirty minutes before her connection to Chicago.

"You're going to be fine. Anyone who can do a triathlon around Boston will survive divorce. I have great pictures of you jogging all over Wales and Scotland. Maybe I should use that as my theme; *Running with Anna.* I'll send you the first draft," said Harper as she headed for her gate.

As the excitement of the flight receded, Anna felt an uncontrollable urge to sleep, which she did—deeply—for thirty minutes in the chairs near the Starbucks, with her feet on her luggage. She then had to drive another hour north to Rockport once she located her car in the labyrinth of the parking garage. The rain was fierce, and she realized that Harper really had been right; the greatest danger was driving her car in the rain, rather than flying in the storm. Many more things could go wrong in her car. Traffic was snarled hopelessly.

When she pulled into her driveway in Rockport, the house was dark and empty. She had known that it would be empty, but since the divorce there were moments when she longed for lights to be on, footsteps thudding down the stairs even though this was not the house she had shared with Steven. The mail was piled high on her entryway table. The cat was at her neighbor's house, and it was now too late to go get him. It was midnight, almost time to wake up for a good cup of tea in Ireland.

Anna peeled off her clothes and tossed them in the direction of the bathroom hamper. She pulled out a length of dental floss and wrangled the mint flavored string between each tooth, followed by a thorough brushing. She turned on the overhead fan to circulate the stuffy, warm air and slid naked between the sheets that had been changed three weeks ago, the day before she'd left. Her body jerked violently as if she had fallen from a mountain; then she dropped suddenly to sleep, and slumber took her into its grasp.

A voice broke into her consciousness, prying her out of sleep. Confused, she looked at her clock radio—12:40 a.m.—and wondered who could possibly be talking at this time. Then she heard, "Anna, you must not be back yet and I hate to leave this kind of message for you. . . ." It was her mother's voice, deep and rich, but something was wrong; disaster poured into her house as if a dam had burst. The phone must have rung four times without Anna's hearing it. She scrambled to reach her bedside phone.

"I'm here. What's wrong?"

"Oh. You are there. Did you just get back? Anna, your brother has been in a serious accident. I'm already at the hospital in Hartford. He's still in surgery. This is looking . . . complicated."

When Anna arrived at the hospital in Hartford, she was aware that one layer of her was jet-lagged and sleep deprived. Another layer had lurched into overdrive when she'd heard that Patrick had been critically injured. She regretted every lapsed visit with him, regretted everything ever said to her older brother about how he treated his son; she needed to make a full list of her misdeeds because she didn't want him to die. She wanted to argue with him about music, food, and politics. Anna had thought she'd have the rest of her life to joust with Patrick, to be criticized by him for being a low-life lawyer. They weren't done yet. He was six years older and had hacked his way through childhood with a machete, battling with their father as the enemy. Anna had hated to be in the same room with them, had hated to see her mother reduced to tears again and again. Her father had bristled like a dog whenever Patrick had walked in the house.

The only good thing about the drive from Rockport was the fact that she had missed the commuter traffic flooding into Hartford. It was 4:00 a.m.

Her mother looked suddenly smaller; hospital waiting rooms did that. They shrank people until the only thing left was fear and skin and hearts that beat too fast. Anna wrapped her arms around her mother and sniffed her hair, breathing in a mixture of vinegar and almond. Her mother felt damp, as if her skin had been weeping.

"Pretend that you can't smell me, Ma, I haven't bathed in two days and I stink like an airplane full of pukey people. What happened?"

Her mother, wearing chinos and a long-sleeved cotton shirt over a tank top, patted Anna and pulled her into a chair next to her. "We only know that they had to use the Jaws of Life to get Pat out. They aren't sure that he is going to make it. That's not exactly what the doctors said; they said with head injuries, things can change quickly, that we had to be prepared for things to go either way."

Her voice shook and she stuttered over "head injuries" so that it sounded like, "hey-hey-hey-hey-ed injuries," as if saying *head* was too terrible. Anna felt a brown caustic juice descend from the top of her head and it filled all her soft places in her throat and stomach. Every inch of her intestines threatened to dissolve her from the inside. Anna looked around the waiting room and noticed Alice, her mother's best friend, standing outside the door. Alice pulled a piece of paper from her back pocket.

"Just when you think things are horrible, remember that they can get worse," said Alice. "Your brother was on his way to pick up Joseph. Your nephew is in jail in Newark, New Jersey. They said it was the Essex County Detention Center. We wouldn't have known if I hadn't gone by Patrick's house to get insurance information. I listened to his phone messages. There was one that said something like, 'Where the hell are you, come get your kid.' Anna, someone needs to go get your nephew."

Alice and her mother had been friends for over thirty years, since they'd started working together at the high school in Greenfield, where Patrick and Joseph lived. Alice taught Latin and Anna's mother, Mary Louise, taught math. Both were approaching their sixties, but neither one of them was interested in retirement. Alice was long and lean, tan from daily tennis over the summer. Mary Louise had what she called a peasant body—short, close to the ground, and steady, with good wide hips.

Anna stopped short when she heard her nephew's name. She had not been able to have a real conversation with him since he was about ten years old; now he was sixteen, had a bad haircut and pimples, and seemed to practice squinting his eyes to look evil.

"Why is he in jail?"

Mary Louise, who was a militant supporter of her only grandchild, said, "They said he stole a car with his friend Oscar and got as far as New Jersey. The state police claimed that they may have found drugs. They're threatening to put Joseph in jail with adults. You'll go get him, won't you? I am not leaving this hospital. I am not going to the parking lot, the restaurant, or the bathroom until I know how Patrick is. And you've got to tell Joseph about his father."

There was not room to negotiate. Anna wanted to do both things, but more than anything she wanted to be with her brother, to act as his advocate with the hospital. She knew he would want that, and she knew that he would guard her like a pit bull if she was unconscious in the hospital.

"Do we have to post bail?" asked Mary Louise.

"Not as long as they're treating him as a juvenile," said Anna. She had twisted her hair into a knot and held it in place with two chopsticks. The bamboo sticks were gradually loosening and her hair bulged in an auburn bundle at the back of her neck. She felt one stick dangling perilously. She dug in her bag for something else to bind her hair. Alice handed her a coated hair tie, the kind she bought by the dozen in the drugstore.

"I'm not leaving until I see Patrick. Joseph is not the most important person in this scenario. Other than being scared shitless, he's not going to be damaged if I get there a couple hours later," said Anna, with her hair tightly tied back. "Although he might advance his newly found criminal career by being in Essex County Detention Center."

If she left immediately, she'd be there in about five hours, maybe six, considering the fact that she was going to be hitting peak rush-hour traffic. She had only unpacked a few things from her trip and had grabbed the small backpack as she had charged out the door: it had a change of clothes and a toothbrush in it. But the boy would need to wait until Anna learned more about the fate of Patrick before she would leave.

After two hours, a surgeon came into the room where they sat. "Mrs. O'Shea?"

Mary Louise stood up slowly, as if bracing for a catastrophic blow. Anna noticed that her mother's umber toenail polish was perfect. She was particular about her toenails and went every two weeks to have them done. She had always said, "I want something to be perfect in my life and if it's only my toenails, then so be it."

The surgeon stood with his feet wide apart and his hands held together in front of his pelvis. Anna stood up and held her backpack in front of her torso. Alice, who had not sat down since arriving at the hospital, sank slowly into a green, vinyl chair. She brought her knees together, leaned forward with her elbows tucked into her thighs and held her head in her hands, fingers pointing up to her eyes.

"Patrick is stable for now. We had to alleviate the bleeding in his brain. We do that by making a hole in the skull."

Mary Louise made a noise like air escaping from a balloon, whizzing into the atmosphere.

The surgeon, dressed in sky blue scrubs, continued. "We were fully able to set his leg; because it was broken in three places, he may end up with a shorter leg. And his pelvis was broken as well. But the bones will mend. We almost wish for broken bones with car accidents because we are so damned good at fixing bones . . ." He faltered for a moment, uncovering his pelvic area and bringing his hands together in front of his chest like a prayer. "Brain damage is unpredictable. For now, we will keep him in a medically induced coma and we will wait and watch. But he needs to be transferred to Boston as soon as possible." He brought his hands up to his face so that his two pointer fingers pressed against his broad, soft lips, tapping them. "He's young and strong. Patrick is in great shape. That goes a long way in my business. Does he have a wife, kids?"

Anna looked over at Alice; Mary Louise swiveled her head to look at each of them. They were conspirators now, agents of Patrick, to do his bidding while he was unconscious.

Mary Louise straightened her spine. "He's a widower. His wife was killed in a fall from a horse twelve years ago. He has a wonderful son. I have a wonderful grandson, Joseph. He is out of state at the moment. We are making plans to bring him home."

The surgeon nodded. "Good. Anecdotally, if there is a child in the picture, I have seen parents fight harder to come back from injuries like this. They have a reason to come back."

Later, when they filed one by one into the ICU to see Patrick, Anna did not recognize him. His face was swollen and deeply bruised. She was most unnerved by the tape that held the intubation tube into his mouth. He was taped like a package, or something broken: a cup, a child's toy, or one of the glass panes over her kitchen sink that she had been too preoccupied to repair. She had taped one pane, and it looked awful. So did her brother. She looked for one place on his body that she could touch. She peeked under the sheet; his right foot looked puffy but unbroken. Anna looked out the door to see if any of the nursing staff was nearby. She tentatively placed the palm of her hand against his foot and imagined a current running from the molten center of the earth, up through her body, and into Patrick. She would never in a million years have done this if Patrick had been conscious and she knew she would never tell him when he recovered. When, not if, not yet thinking about *if.*

"Are you family?"

Anna startled, and she straightened the sheet that covered her brother's feet. A young woman stood at the door. She wore scrubs with cats and dogs on them.

"Patrick is my brother."

"I'm sorry about his accident. I was on duty when he arrived and one of the paramedics told me that he said something to him in the ambulance. He thought it might mean something to you guys. Your brother said, 'Mind the coin.' Does that mean anything to you?"

Anna flashed through any possible connections and came up empty-handed. She shook her head.

"Just that? Nothing else?"

"With brain injuries, it's very hard to know what's happening. It could just be a cacophony of images racing through his head and weird electrical impulses. Or he wanted to say something. Anyhow I thought you might want to know. I almost forgot about it and I was headed for my car when I remembered. Good luck," she said, hoisting her purse over one shoulder and leaving.

Anna met her mother and Alice back in the special ICU waiting area, a pale yellow room that contained all the terror and sadness from past visitors. A TV was anchored to the wall and a cooking show was on; the host demonstrated a way to make fresh chicken sausage.

Mary Louise said, "We need to tell your father. You have to tell me if you've heard from him, you have to tell me."

So this is what it takes, thought Anna. *It takes a burr hole in Patrick's head and a brain that might never be the same for her father's name to be brought into the mix.* Her father had left twenty years ago and he had never returned, had not sent birthday cards, or called on graduations or births. In fact, her father knew nothing about the family since his leaving, at least not that Anna knew about.

Anna had hired a detective after she'd passed the bar exam to find her father. That was seven years ago. He was in Thailand, teaching English. Charles O'Shea, director of English studies in Bangkok. Anna held his address for days before she used it, finally firing off an email that said, "Your son, daughter, and ex-wife are living stellar lives without you. But I know where you are. Dad, how could you? I loved you."

She recalled the last time she saw her father and Anna felt like she was fourteen again, coming home to the sirens, police cars, flashing lights, and ambulance. As Anna ran into the house, her heart pounding, her father, face bloody and sweaty, pushed past her to leave the house.

"Daddy!" she screamed. "Come back."

Patrick had been twenty. It looked to everyone as if Patrick and his father had tried to kill each other. Each one was beaten bloody. Patrick was fully grown, and could finally fight back.

Anna's mother came out of Patrick's bedroom, her forehead tight, a bottle of medication in her hands.

Anna took a broom and began sweeping the broken glass, too afraid to do anything else, despite her mother's warning about getting cut by the shards. Anna wanted to clean everything up. She scooped four dustpans of broken glass and dumped them into the garbage can on the porch.

The overhead light in the kitchen, hanging on a chain in artful swags, now hung crooked over her mother's head, over her mushroom-bobbed hair.

"Is he okay?" asked Anna.

Her mother set the prescription bottle on the kitchen island.

"The broken nose and ribs? Bones mend. It's the rest of him that I worry about. I should have been home."

"The next time that Daddy does this I'm calling the police," said Anna, closing the door to the porch, to the people in her neighborhood who had seen the ambulance, the flashing lights, and to her friends at school who would know all about this.

"There won't be a next time. Come here, sweetie," said her mother, patting the stool next to her.

Anna smelled something worse than the musky feral scent left behind by the fight, something reaching for her.

"Your father won't be coming back."

The wobbly legs of her existence began to shatter, the molecules exploding from the inside out. Her balance went first. That's what happens when a father leaves.

Money appeared in Mary Louise's account from the early withdrawal of his pension.

Anna stared at her mother in the waiting room. "You think Patrick isn't going to make it. That would be the only reason to contact Daddy. You think he deserves to know." She didn't mean to say Daddy. It sounded like she was little again.

The furrow between Mary Louise's eyebrows was deep. "You two children only had one set of parents to choose from. Patrick needs his father right now. I don't so much care about what Charlie needs. You know how to contact him, don't you?"

"Yeah, I do. I sent him an email once. I'll do it when I come back from retrieving our wannabe gangster."

Chapter 3

Anna waited in the reception area of the detention center. Juvie Hall, that's what kids called it. That's what her brother's friends had called it when they'd been teenagers and had organized like guerilla fighters to avoid getting caught for their petty crimes of vandalism. Patrick had never been caught for any of his misdeeds.

Metal detectors lined the doorways leading to the interior of the building. Why had Joseph broken the law in New Jersey? Nothing about this was going to be easy. New Jersey apparently hadn't thought about painting this place in a long time. The walls of the reception room were light blue. The color was probably intended to be calming, cooling down the raging spirits of adolescents. Anna didn't know exactly what her nephew had done, and part of her was holding tightly to the hope that his crime was the most minor, or that a mistake had been made.

She hadn't truly slept in two days; her eyes were dry from staring down the highway for five hours, driving from Hartford in the rain and fog. Her stomach echoed in dark fear every time she pictured her brother's swollen and bandaged head, the respirator forcing breath in and out of his broken body, and the chorus of blinking machinery that echoed in his room.

Her nephew didn't know that his father wasn't coming for him, or that he had been in an accident. Anna had asked to speak with the director of the detention center. It was 11:30 in the morning and the director wasn't in yet. The correctional officer at the desk said that nothing was going to happen until the director arrived. She would have to wait until after lunch when the caseworkers returned.

Anna approached the desk, with its shoulder-high barrier between her and the officer.

"My brother was on his way here to get his son, Joseph O'Shea, when he had a very serious accident. That's why no one showed up yesterday. My brother is in the intensive-care unit in Hartford right now. Could you please just release Joseph to me so that I can bring him home?" asked Anna. She had already produced her driver's license. "Here's the phone number of the hospital. You can call to check and see if he's there."

The correctional officer listened with an expressionless face. "I worked the graveyard shift, so this is a double for me. I don't know who you are, and this kid was taking drugs across the state line, in a stolen vehicle."

He did not add, " . . . and I'm sorry about your brother." The officer had a small television set tucked under the counter and clearly intended to continue watching it. On a better day, Anna would have understood, she would have known that this guy was at the end of his graveyard shift and that his circadian rhythms were screwed up, making him out of sync with everyone else. She would have known that this guy had perfected an invisible shield around his heart that got him through the worst times at 2:00 a.m. when coked-up kids came screaming through his waiting room. But right now she didn't want to care about him.

Anna looked at the clock. 11:45. She sat down and scribbled a note, came back to his counter, and pushed the note toward him. "I'm going out to my car, where I am going to try to close my eyes for an hour or so. Please give this note to the first supervisor or caseworker who comes in. Tell them Joseph O'Shea's aunt is here to pick him up, that I am acting on behalf of my brother. And I'm a lawyer." The officer pushed the note to one side of the counter and nodded slightly to her, as if he was conserving energy.

She pushed her car seat back as far as it would go, rolled the car windows down one quarter of the way, and hoped that the shade of one asphalt-strangled tree would hold for an hour. Was there any danger in sleeping in the car? Was she safer in a parking lot of a detention center for kids, or less safe? Would gun-carrying officers notice and come to her if someone reached their hands into her car? Anna closed her eyes, but like a cat, she kept her ears alert. She drifted, half in sleep, half crouched at the ready.

Joe had been born with an expectant look on his face, as if to say, "I'm waiting," as if he had heard the beginning of the story and was prepared for the ending. Patrick had uncharacteristically insisted that Anna come to see his newborn. It had been her first year of college, only a month before final exams, but she'd been intrigued by her brother's sudden insistence. She'd used her boyfriend's frequent flyer miles to fly from Chicago to Hartford. Her mother had picked her up at the airport and driven to Greenfield, Massachusetts, where Patrick had lived with his new wife and infant. He'd never told Anna where he'd met Tiffany, his tiny, pale wife, who liked to read by the hour curled in a corner of the couch. Oh no, thought Anna, too delicate; she'll never last with Patrick.

Patrick and Tiffany had lived in a 1950s ranch-style house that had not changed at all since it was built. They'd lived two miles from the center of town, with the other last poor houses.

Anna and her mother had pulled into the muddy driveway.

"They could use some gravel," her mother had said as she'd turned off the car.

Tiffany had opened the hollow-core door looking pale and exhausted. Anna had hugged her and felt like she might crush her new sister-in-law, as if Tiffany's bones had been filled with air and that only her shoes had kept her from levitating. Tiffany had brushed her thin hair from her eyes and offered a smile.

"Come on in, he's in the kitchen with Joey," she'd said.

Anna had prepared herself, as she always did, for the unpredictability of her brother, the chance that she might say or do something that would cause an explosion. With her mother's guidance, she had purchased a jersey sleeper with little blue lambs on it for the baby. She'd followed Tiffany to the kitchen, then remembered her gift.

"Hey, I've got something for the little guy . . ." she'd started, but she'd stopped at the sight of Patrick in white T-shirt and jeans with the infant in his arms. The baby had looked straight up at his father with dark marble eyes. Patrick had placed his forefinger near the baby's hand and the baby had latched on, holding onto his father's finger with his entire fist. Anna had never seen anyone hold Patrick like that; everyone else had been afraid to. But this baby boy had not yet known his father, so he'd grabbed on and offered Patrick the elixir of complete faith. Patrick's face had softened.

He'd looked up at his sister and mother and said, "I love this baby." Anna had never heard Patrick say that about anyone.

The height of the sun and the heat in the car woke her from her reverie. She had not been asleep, not the nourishing depth of sleep that she craved, but her eyes had been closed and they no longer burned with fatigue from the night drive. She popped the seat back up, closed the windows, and went back into the detention center.

She figured they'd be on the road by three o'clock. Four hours later, Anna finally saw Joseph, after a mountain of paperwork and phone calls finally released him into her custody. There were charges of auto theft in Massachusetts, and, if the substance that the troopers had found tested positive for illegal drugs, they would have to return to New Jersey for court.

The first thing that she noticed was that he hooded his eyes with disdain. His running shoes had been stripped of laces. Had they imagined that he was a particular risk for suicide, or was it general policy that everyone had to hand over their shoelaces? Anna didn't know; she had never been inside a prison, or even a juvenile detention center, until this morning. She hadn't been that kind of lawyer. Contract law was not about detention centers.

She watched her nephew as he walked between two guards across a black paved walkway. His shadowed eyes looked at some unknown horizon, ignoring the men on either side of him but keeping them on a short leash in his peripheral vision. Anna could see that Joseph was terrified to walk between two armed, uniformed guards and that a perfectly reasonable choice was to walk with an attitude. One guard pressed a button on the external door, and a man at the front desk hit a button that opened a loud metallic door with a shattering clank.

Anna had already talked at length with the intake supervisor about Joe and his father's accident. The state of New Jersey was glad to be rid of one more child car thief. Joseph was going to be transferred to Massachusetts courts and released into Anna's custody. That is, if Anna didn't kill him first.

Joseph raised his eyes to scan his aunt for two seconds, then turned to the guard on his right.

"Why is she here? Where is my father?"

The supervisor pushed a large Ziploc bag toward Joseph. It had, among other things, his shoelaces, matches, a few wadded-up dollars, and a pocketknife. It was late afternoon, the hottest part of the day, and the window air conditioners clattered and hummed a guttural dirge. All the staff by now knew that the boy's father had been in a car accident on the way to get his son.

Joseph seemed to sense a shift in the immediate atmosphere. One of the guards put a hand on his shoulder and said, "Good luck, son."

Joseph walked into the waiting room with his plastic bag. The tongues of his shoes flapped open, tangling with the shredded hem of his pants. At three years old, he would have run to greet her and clung to her legs, pulling her by the hand. At ten he would have needed thirty minutes of warming up, but at sixteen, he kept two arm's lengths away from her. She hadn't actually touched him in several years.

"Come on," she said, stuffing papers into her day pack, wishing for her more professional briefcase. "Let's get out of here."

Joe pushed open the double doors and let them slam on his aunt, not looking back. Anna sighed. They stepped into thick September air, a fetid pool of humidity and air pollution.

"I need to talk to you about your father," she called after him, making him pause on the sidewalk. "But let's get in the car, I'll turn on the air conditioner as we talk."

He was already close to six feet tall, taller than his father. He folded into her green Subaru. He reached down with his right hand and found the lever to move the seat back. Anna started the car, rolled down her window to release the boiling air, and turned the air conditioner full blast.

"Your father was in an accident on his way here," said Anna.

She chose the direct route in a crisis; facts were important to Anna, and she wanted him to have the facts. She was not a good hand holder. But the jolt that ran through the boy shocked her. His neck turned crimson in scattered blotches as the red tide marched up his neck and across his cheeks. The car was too small to contain the body slam that the boy absorbed.

Anna rushed in with more information. "He's in a hospital in Hartford. That was the closest hospital, but he's going to be transferred to Boston. Your grandmother is with him. He's had a head injury and a broken leg. I got here as soon as I could. I just got back from my trip." Anna waited for the boy to speak. Then Joseph slammed his fist on the dash.

"I told him to slow down when he was driving! I told him to be careful," he shouted.

"Grandma talked to the state cops. They said he went into a slide when someone made a sudden stop on the highway. He did a one-eighty into oncoming traffic and then went into the median. He flipped the truck and hit some boulders."

Hearing more details gave Joseph something to focus on.

"Where? What boulder? We've driven that road a hundred times."

Useless questions, really; it didn't matter which boulder had crushed the truck. But Anna was glad just to have the boy in her car, belted in, and talking. She pulled out of the detention center parking lot. She had written down the directions on a scrap of paper, and now she tried to figure them in reverse. She propped them on the ashtray.

"Is he going to die?"

The picture of Patrick's swollen face, blackened eyes, and the breathing tube taped over his mouth made for a convincing picture of someone who was going to die. She remembered what the doctor had told her: head injuries could go either way. People made stunning recoveries, or things could go haywire.

"Your father is in the intensive-care unit. They've induced a coma to control the swelling in his brain," said Anna as she pulled the car onto a four-lane road. She searched for road signs. She decided against telling him that they had drilled a hole in his head to relieve pressure.

Driving with her nephew, she didn't know how much teenage boys understood or what was most important for Joseph to know. Her head throbbed over her left eye. Lack of sleep made her brain feel like crushed rock. She reached up to unclip her sunglasses from the visor. It was 5:00 p.m., and the sun struck her left side as she pointed the car north.

"Auntie Ann, this is my fault, isn't it?" said the boy.

He had not called her Auntie Ann in years. She chanced a glance to the right, and for a moment he looked familiar again. His curly brown hair was soaked in sweat around his brow, just like it used to when he ran with the neighbor kids when he was eight. She reminded herself again to call him Joseph, not Joey; he had recently insisted on the change.

"We're going to call first thing in the morning to find out how he is. Then we'll go to the hospital. And Grandma will have left us a message on my phone."

"Why don't you have a cell phone? Everyone has one. Cell phones are made for times like this," he said.

"I had too much cell phone and too much Blackberry when I was a lawyer. I'm trying life without one. Possibly a mistake. Hey, your dad said something after the accident. One of the nurses told me. He said, 'Mind the coin,' or something like that. Do you have any idea what he was talking about?"

The boy shook his head.

They drove past Newark and tangled with the worst traffic of the day. Anna considered pulling off the highway, huddling under the arms of a gas station, and waiting until the last of rush-hour traffic subsided and dispersed into the agony of Newark. But this was an emergency and the chemical change of disaster propelled her forward. She smelled the acid scent of crisis on her breath; she had to keep driving. So they crawled for hours, willing the thick traffic to move along.

She had forgotten to eat, but she remembered to ask the boy if he had eaten. Joseph was famous for eating not one hamburger but two or three, for gulping not one glass of milk but two. He declined. The inside of Anna's car crackled with shards of his fear.

"What happened? About the car, I mean. Whose car did you steal?" she asked as they crept along. For the last hour, anger had started to boil in her throat. Car theft? Drugs? Was this the beginning of the end of Joseph? Was he lost already?

Joseph shrugged his shoulders and folded his arms across his chest. He tried to slouch, dipping his right shoulder slightly lower so that he pointed his body away from Anna. "I don't know. Nothing," he said.

"I just sprung you out of jail. 'I don't know' is the wrong answer. And when did you start taking drugs?"

"We didn't steal the car. It was Oscar's grandmother's car. He said she wouldn't notice. He said she didn't drive it anymore." He spoke to the passenger side window.

"And who is Oscar?"

"A friend. He's my friend."

The lawyer was seeping back into Anna. "But Oscar took the car without asking the owner? Is she going to press charges?"

Shoulder shrug. "I don't know. His parents came and got him right away. Isn't there anything in the law about family members not pressing charges against other family members?"

"No, there is absolutely nothing in the law that stops people from doing that. Lawyers live off the inclination of families to do bad things to each other and have each other arrested. What about the drugs?" Anna tapped her fingers on the steering wheel as she stared at the back end of a semitrailer.

"Two hits of X but we'd already taken them. I didn't think

Oscar had anything else in the car. When the cops stopped us, they tore the car apart and found something in the glove box. My father is going to kill me."

"Your father will be unable to kill you for some time. He's going to have to get a lot better before you need to worry about that," said Anna.

The traffic started to move.

Chapter 4

"Why are we going to your house?" said Joseph. "You're like three hours from Greenfield?"

It was ten at night. They had steadily run the air conditioner since late afternoon, and the sudden silence in the car without the iced air startled her.

"Because my house is closer to the hospital in Boston. Remember, he's going to be airlifted there. Besides, I swore to keep you in my sight. The only reason I was able to get you out was that I promised to be responsible for you." Anna rolled down her window after shutting off the AC, letting in the air that had finally softened under the fall of night.

Joseph rolled his window down too. "My father's truck has automatic windows. Did you have to special order these?"

Anna overlooked his sarcasm. She shifted into third gear to drive up the abruptly steep road leading to her house. She turned at her mailbox, parking in front of the garage, which had developed an unfortunate tilt over the past year. A motion-detector device splashed light over the drive and the walkway to the house.

"Let's go call Grandma and let her know that we're back."

* * *

She had had time to do little more than pop open some of her luggage and let the damp scent of Ireland and the ocean expand into her house before she'd gotten the disaster call from her mother. With a wince of sadness she remembered the smooth foam from a dark beer and the slick coolness from the stone walls. She let the strange combination of odors carry her on a reverie far from intensive-care units and monosyllabic nephews. If she could run away, that is where she would go, back to Ireland.

"So where am I supposed to sleep?" said Joseph.

It had been years since the boy had begged to sleep over at her house, to ice skate on her pond with his friends, to watch cartoons on Saturday morning. They did not even speak of these times. Anna thought his adolescent self was embarrassed that he had ever crawled on her lap, yanked on her hand or made cookies with her.

"You know where the spare bedroom is. I'll put a towel in the bathroom for you. We'll leave around seven in the morning. I'll wake you." She paused, looking up at her nephew, who must have grown four inches over the summer. But he was riddled with anger. She saw it in the way he held his hands, tight and hard. And in the way he spoke to her without looking at her. *Oh please,* she thought, *not Joseph, don't let this happen to him too.* God damn Patrick, God damn her father. She refused to think about her father; there was only so much room for catastrophe in her brain.

Joseph had not cut his hair in the nearly shaven style so popular with the athletes at his school. She had popped into his wrestling matches when she'd been in the area. In fact, his hair was longer, rolling into curls, swishing along his collar and hanging in his eyes. He had the same dark hair as his father, as if his mother's genes, with her golden hair, had not been added to the mix at all. But if the ability to be hurt, to feel crushed by sharp words, could be genetically traced, then he clearly had the sensitivity of his mother.

Losing his mother had been devastating for a boy of four. She prayed that Joseph was not going to lose again.

"Goodnight, Joey." She let his boy name slip out, and for a moment he brushed his hair from his eyes and let his glance fall on Anna. He remembered, she knew he remembered the old days, when he'd smelled like Milky Way bars and boy sweat and she had kept a special supply of toys for him at her house.

Anna reached back in time to when she had last slept. Maybe an hour or two when she'd first arrived from Europe, before her mother had rung her into the mouth of Patrick's hospital room. She had stayed awake for the entire flight from Ireland. And she had slept badly on the last night of her trip; she always did before a major flight. She tossed a towel into the bathroom in hopes of encouraging Joseph to shower, either now or in the morning. Why didn't teenage boys bathe more often? When Patrick had been a teenager, and she'd been an admiring kid in grade school, her mother had given Patrick gentle yet consistent prods about showering, yet never when their father had been home. Their mother had been vigilant about never pointing out anything that could have been construed as Patrick's shortcomings when their father had been around. For as long as Anna could remember, their father had seemed to wait for any failing in the boy, and then he'd pounced and shamed him with taunts of "Stupid!" "Idiot!" "Useless!" Anna had watched in horror as her father had turned on Patrick like a relentless hyena, hanging onto his prey with iron jaws. Every bit of the horror show had poured into Anna and she vowed to protect herself from wanting to be loved as much as Patrick did.

Joseph closed the bedroom door before she could say anything else to him. She turned out the light in the kitchen, took one desperate look at her upended luggage in the living room, and turned off that lamp too. Wrapped parcels, gifts for family and friends, poked their heads out of her large suitcase. She could not imagine finding a moment to open any of them. She went into her bedroom and closed her door. She dropped her pants and blouse to the floor, stepped out of her underwear, and unhooked her bra. Anna needed one caress of comfort, and she didn't care where it came from. She pulled open the bottom drawer of her dresser and pulled out her ex-husband's large T-shirt and a pair of his silky boxers that she had once teased him about. The brand—Man Silk— had been good for months of ribbing. She took a breath of safety from his underclothing.

When she had first learned of the affair, her friend Jasper had told her, "He wasn't right for you. He was never enough for you, believe me. Come to California." But right now, she had never felt more alone and she longed for the shreds of relationship that she and Steve had. The bed was damp with late summer humidity, as if even the sheets had been weeping. As soon as her head hit the pillow, she plummeted into sleep.

Chapter 5

Joseph lay on top of the bedcovers. This was the worst day of his life, and he didn't know how he could possibly survive one more minute, one more hour. But he had to be strong for his father, he had to help his father get better. Then he would take any punishment that his father would dole out; he just wanted him back again, well again.

He'd never seen his father sick or hurt, not really hurt. His father's hands were constantly raw and calloused from the stonework that he did, but now that he had hired a full-time crew, his father was free to do more design work, and his hands didn't even look so bad anymore. He pictured his father the last time he had seen him, two days ago, when they had both been eating cereal in the morning. His dad, absorbed in thought, had wrapped his hands around a cup of coffee, and the morning sun had hit his hands for a moment, illuminating the dark hairs that sprouted along the fingers, the cracked fingernails. Joseph had looked down at his own hands, thin and as yet unmarked by labor. Would his hands be the same as his father's? Was that how it went?

He pulled the pillow over his face and wept. He did not

want Anna to hear him or try to comfort him. And it was not like Anna was all that great to be around anymore. Why did people freak out when they went through divorces? Anna used to be fun when he was a little kid. She was the one person who knew how tough his dad could be, and he'd been able to talk to her. Then Uncle Steve and Anna had gotten divorced a year ago and she'd left her job and she was just miserable to be around. Or maybe Anna didn't like him anymore; he was sure that his father didn't like him half the time. He wiped his face on his soiled shirt.

Joseph slid off his jeans and shirt and pulled the sheet up. His feet hung off the end of the bed, forcing him to fold up on his side. How had everything gone so wrong so quickly? He had been too afraid to sleep at the detention center, and he fell asleep within minutes in Anna's spare bedroom.

Joseph dreamed that he was a tourniquet around his father's leg. "Doctors," he said to his medical dream characters, "we've got to slow down the artery." When he woke up, sweating in his aunt's house, it took him a full minute before he understood where he was. He felt suspended in air with no familiar objects in view. Then the realization of his father's accident crashed in on him. The long car ride with Anna back to Rockport, and the terror of Juvie Hall, where they had taken away his shoelaces, trickled in last. He closed his eyes again; sleep had to be better than his real life.

He dropped immediately into the dream again, fell through the floor of his waking life, back into the dream with his father and the doctors. This time he stood by his father's bed and he offered his father a blue vase to hold all his blood, but his father, oddly uninjured, refused to take it. Instead, his father held out a math book to Joseph, and it flew open to a chapter on Absolute Values. His father became his true self, his absolute value, without anger or hate, cruel words or open-fisted slaps. His father's eyes were warm brown marbles, softer than Joseph had ever seen. His father pointed to something in the book, a photo of something fluttering like a moth, and Joseph wished he could see it better. "Open it for Anna, Buddy. We all need it now," said his father.

Joseph broke through to wakefulness with a gasp, like a fish desperate for water again. He woke with the belief that something could save his father, and he let himself be led to it without thinking.

Chapter 6

The noise scratched her eyelids and her soft brain. Sleep had sucked her deep into the crevice of exhausted, motionless sleep, muscles paralyzed, and brain flitting uncensored. The noise lassoed her ears and pulled her up and up, dragging her reluctant consciousness along. She heard, then recognized, the sound of the plastic zipper on her suitcases being opened slowly. She had left the door ajar, unlatched, and a long knife of dim light pierced her room.

Joseph; why was he awake? The sun wasn't up yet. She rolled to her side and with her left arm pushed up and slid her legs around. Anna's feet hit the cool wood floor. She stood up, and the floppy shirt flowed to her thighs. She considered the jeans on the floor but decided against them. The sound of paper crumpling and expanding came from the living room. A glance at the clock radio revealed the ghastly hour of 3:48, still hours from daylight. Every sound in the house was amplified at this hour: the hum of the refrigerator, the creaking floorboards, and crushing paper. She stepped into the doorway, looked out, and saw that the beam of light came from the hallway to the left leading to the living room.

What was he doing? He probably couldn't sleep. She could let him wander the house, no danger there. So why was she afraid; what was wrong? She had to be careful, as first responses were deceptive, based on not enough information. Yet the charge of alarm was already racing through her blood. She heard paper rustling again, and the inability to picture what he was doing, what the boy was wrapping or unwrapping, finally pushed her down the hall. She followed the glow of light and there was Joseph, his hair askew from being slept on and pushed up on one side. He was bent over her suitcase, rear end pointed up in Anna's direction, white underpants beaming. Anna stopped; he hadn't heard her yet because he was totally engrossed in his task. He stood up with a small brown package in his hands, one of many such packages, neatly wrapped, secured with tape.

Anna walked soundlessly toward her nephew, watched his shirtless back, not yet broad but with promises of muscles making triangles from the points of his shoulders to the protrusion of his shoulder blades. Joseph had grown so suddenly. Should she wear only a T-shirt and underwear; would she embarrass one or both of them? But this was a crisis, a time on the brink of death. Patrick hovered in time, touching death and life, tethered by a respirator forcing in breath. She felt her place between her brother and this sprouting nephew, and saw memories of Patrick in the untapped strength of the boy's back, the grinding fear for his father that no doubt kept the boy from sleeping.

"Joey," she said, in a moment of tenderness, saying his

toddler name and at the same moment reaching out and touching his shoulder. He leaped and jerked away, gawking at Anna, looking like a trapped animal. Anna jumped back.

"I'm sorry, I didn't mean to startle you. Are you OK?" she asked and then stopped short.

He had whirled around, and in his hands he held the half-opened package with a bit of fabric erupting from the confines of paper. What was he doing? Not Joseph, not the boy she'd taken swimming in the summer, the one who'd presented her with his first art project from day camp. Had the world shifted and he had become lost, popping Ecstasy in stolen cars in New Jersey?

"What are you doing?"

"I woke up and I knew I had to find something. My father told me to look for something in my dream and I just came out here. I was dreaming . . ." Joseph suddenly looked shocked, glanced down at his own hands as he stood in the sea of Anna's sprawled luggage. "It's not what you think, Anna . . . "

The days of sleeplessness met with the nausea she had swallowed upon seeing her brother in the ICU and driving to New Jersey to retrieve Joseph from the detention center. The collision of all these points was cataclysmic. Thunderclouds exploded across Anna's brain, lightning crackled in her skull. She grabbed the boy by the arm.

"Why are you going through my luggage? Have you lost your mind?" She couldn't stop. "What's wrong with you!" From a distance she saw his eyes grow large and young. He had something of hers in his hands, a piece of cloth that flowed like water; she grabbed at it and they both held tight.

As soon as both of them held the cloth, Anna heard a roaring sound and something immense extracted the air from her lungs. Tidal wave, tornado, terrorist bomb attack all ran through her head for the three seconds before complete darkness and speed overcame all other sensations.

Chapter 7

When Anna imagined what dying would feel like, or more to the point, the moment after dying, she pictured flinging from one time to another, shooting outward, going past the arc of the earth's atmosphere, becoming a tendril along time, rippling and snapping until she plunged into the circumspect future of existence without form. She had taken Ecstasy in college once—well, twice—and maybe not just Ecstasy, because she had truly felt the moorings come loose from her body, which is exactly why she didn't want her nephew taking drugs. You could come apart and never return again. You could feel like you were dying, and Anna didn't want that to happen to Joseph. During her voyage with drugs, something had lifted off her and taken flight, ricocheting off harmonic lights. So maybe it hadn't been just Ecstasy alone; she'd never found out what the drug had been that had temporarily fragmented her into particles. But she had thought that dying would be like that.

She'd never expected the fish, the way she could breathe under water, that it was water, not air, but sound and water that were the transport system. Clever, very clever.

She tried to look at her body to see if it was still there, and with the greatest effort, with supreme concentration, she turned her eyes down and to the left, where her hand should be, and very far away, she saw a persistent memory of a hand tangling with an aspiring hand. The effort was exhausting and worked against everything that was happening, against the schools of fish, the operatic whales, and the suddenly obedient sharks. If she was dead, why could she still see her body? This was something else.

Was she skimming the bottom of the ocean? From somewhere in between the small spaces of her ribs, she let go and went forward, outward, and down. *I'm dispersing*, she thought, *like the pellets from a shotgun blast*. But she had not come alone. She and Joseph had been plucked together; for one moment she had seen him as he had whipped past her. She was not shooting down this hole alone. They had been at her house and had struggled. And before her thoughts flew away from her, she reached as far in one direction as she could to find the boy and felt nothing.

This is time travel, she thought. She recognized it not because she'd ever experienced it before, or knew anyone who had slid down the corridors of time. It was the fish and because there was no other explanation.

Anna choked and felt the gush of water leaving her lungs, mixed with the salt and acid from her stomach, as she spit out the water she had just swallowed. Her belly was scraped raw from being dragged by the tides, flipped by the waves. Was any part of her broken? As she lay sprawled on her side, she heard the thunderous roar of the surf, as loud as a jet engine. Her eyes stung from the salt and sand, but she let the lids open and waited for the world to come into focus. She was wedged between two slick rocks dressed with seaweed that looked like huge dark green lasagna noodles.

It was the wind blasting and howling that created the overwhelming noise. When she was a child, she had gone with her family to Hammonasset Beach, and a storm had hit the coast of Long Island Sound. The wind had not allowed her to speak; she had experimented and even screamed as loud as she'd been able, but she hadn't heard her own voice because the wind had grabbed any sound and swept it away, shattering it.

She tested this wind and made a sound. "Hello," she croaked. Only the vibration along her upper palate let her know that she had uttered a word. Anna pushed up to a seated position and began to check her body, running her hands down her torso. Good, the essentials were here: head, torso, and arms. Was this night, or was her vision impaired from the abrasive salt water? Whatever the reason, she could barely see her own body. She ran her hands down her right leg. Good, now the left. Bare thigh met icy cold hands, and as her hands slid below the knee, they were met by an eruption of skin and another vibration of sound that would have been heard as a scream had it not been for the cursed wind. An electric shock sizzled up her leg. She bent her head as close to her left leg as possible, and a deep gash stared back at her with shocking exposure; the leg was cut to the bone, a jagged lengthwise cut. She dove into her own memory; surely there would be a recollection of this. Nothing, only fragmented thoughts of fish and college recollections.

She tested her other leg with renewed urgency, knowing how much depended on at least one good leg. The toes were bloody from being scraped along the shore but nothing else. Anna felt her chest again. She had on what used to be a white T-shirt. All that remained was the ringed collar and one strip of cloth, enough to cover one breast. She touched her waist and felt what had to be boxer shorts, or what used to be boxer shorts. This was part of her ex-husband's underwear. The waistband remained, shredded of its cloth covering in all but one thin strip the width of her palm. She protectively pulled the bit of cloth around to her front. Oh God, someone had to find her like this.

Whatever thoughts she had had the moment she'd been wrested from her home were gone now. Had there been an accident on her flight from Ireland? Her memory was pock-marked with bolts of bright scenes uninterrupted by continuity. Accident, yes, her brother, the terrible accident. And her nephew. She startled, fear helping to clear her head. Joseph, she had picked him up in New Jersey and they had driven forever until she'd thought she'd scream from lack of sleep. Where was he? She stood up, the thought of her nephew grinding into her chest. She put all of her weight on her right leg. "Joseph," she screamed, cupping her hands around her lips. The wind slid greedy fingers around the name and blew it miles away.

As her eyes adjusted, she saw the dark outlines of more rocks, a beach, a gray light that could have been either dusk or dawn. She picked up a long strip of seaweed and wrapped it around her calf, tucking in one end as best she could. Regretfully, she glanced down at the remains of her clothing and knew that one or both pieces would have to be sacrificed to her injury. Could the world of women be divided between those who would choose to be rescued wearing only a piece of cloth covering their breasts and those who would choose to cover their bottoms? No, the world of women could be divided between those who chose to survive and those who chose to cower in vanity. She pulled the remains of the T-shirt off her neck and secured the seaweed bandage, pulling as tight as she could bear.

She began to climb her way over the rocks, and as she did, she picked a direction, keeping the ocean on her right side for this journey to find help. Anna knew two things: she could die from hypothermia or shock, and Joseph (if he'd survived the assault of the ocean landing), could die as well. She had to find him.

After painfully slow progress, she stopped walking along the shore, with the cold driving deep into her bones, and considered that this could be a dream, since she had no logical explanation for her circumstances other than a hazy thought about dying and time travel. If it was a dream, perhaps it was a lucid dream, given the stunning reality of it. Her roommate from college had continually read books about dreaming and had said that the ultimate was lucid dreaming, being fully conscious in the dream. She looked down at her feet in the dim light, and the bluish tinge on her legs and feet was decidedly undreamlike. If this was a lucid dream, she could change any of this, she could fly, change scenery; too quickly, she knew this was not a dream. The rocks and the shore were slick, and she fell, with the greatest shock to her tailbone, which had smashed into an unforgiving rock. The jagged pain that shot up her left leg from the ugly gash hammered with a nearly audible throb.

She rounded a corner of a rocky point and headed to a more protected bay, still seeing no one. Could it be that there were simply no people who lived on this stretch of the coast? And which coast was it? An inexhaustible force drove the wind, and Anna grew progressively sleepier. The rocks called to her as a perfectly reasonable place to sleep. She remembered hiking in New Mexico once, near the Mescalero Apache Reservation. When they'd gotten above ten thousand feet, Anna had felt her eyelids descend with an urgent demand to sleep. She'd said to her companions, "I'll stay here and nap in this meadow while you go on. Pick me up on the way back." And it had been sweet and pleasant. Perhaps it would be sweet and pleasant again here.

No! That had been altitude sickness and was nothing like now. She shook her head, her hair heavy with salt and sand. Rocks slick with rain and salt water were not good places to sleep, and she could too easily slip into shock if she allowed herself to rest. If she died, there would be no hope for Joseph.

She kept moving one foot in front of the other. The land had a bit of a rise to it and then grass was underfoot. That was the good news. The bad news was that the slim ribbon of light she had seen pierce the clouds was not dawn but dusk; darkness galloped in to ensnare her. Anna had never been this afraid before. She began to shake uncontrollably. Her body was trying to warm her.

Anna had taken a winter outdoor survival course in northern Vermont last January. There had been something that the instructor had said again and again, aside from the basic mantra of *Stay dry, at all costs, stay dry*, which had already gone by the wayside. Now would be the absolute best time to remember the rest of it. Yes! Every victim that they had ever recovered had had one thing in common: dehydration. That was it; dehydration was nearly as deadly as hypothermia. How very interesting. She needed water.

She continued to climb upward and away from the ocean, leaving the pounding waves at her back. And hallucinations; both hypothermia and dehydration could cause hallucinations. What part of this was a hallucination? If she'd been back in her winter survival course, she could have raised her hand and asked that very question of her polypropylene-clad instructors. And now would be a good time to ask that question, because Anna saw two lights bouncing erratically—and they were coming closer.

As she pondered this question, she noticed that she was now on her knees. She couldn't recall how that had happened, and she knew that it couldn't be good for her leg, which she had wrapped with a good stout strand of ruffled seaweed. Anna fell forward and was eye level with an engaging rock that had a slight indentation filled with water. She was flat on her belly, a position that allowed her to lap at the rock with her swollen tongue. "Water," her instructor had said, "will save you."

She heard a voice breaking through the wind.

"Here's one. Do you suppose more have landed on shore?"

Anna's left cheek pressed into a pocket of wet sand. She knew she should rise up to greet her rescuers; that would be the proper thing to do. And she wanted so much to thank them for finding her. But more than anything, she craved the moment that their hands would touch her to confirm that she was alive. Soon they would touch her and she would be saved. The first hands touched her shoulders, and she heard a moan slip from her lips.

"This one's alive. As cold as death, but still alive."

Every word sounded different and the same. Their words turned and curled where hers were straight. They spoke English, but they were clearly from another country, visitors from Ireland, or the British Isles. Hands, one on her hip and another on her shoulder, turned her over, face up.

"Jaysus and Mary! Cover the woman."

Anna's eyes closed as she gave herself to warm hands.

Chapter 8

She had not been sleeping. Anna didn't know what she had been doing, but her head was too thick, her eyes too hot, her skin prickled with sharp points of pain everywhere. And now there was something on fire in her leg, in the bone. Her tongue was huge and dry.

Blinding light came from a window and blue sky filled the entire vista. She squeezed her eyes shut. What was left of her thinking brain, the large chunk of frontal brain, registered high fever, sensitivity to light, and skin painful to the touch. Where the hell was she?

She rose up on her elbows, and black dots filled her vision. She felt a wool blanket on top of her. Anna sat up and swung her legs around. As soon as her feet hit the floorboards, a howl tore out of her and she crumbled, collapsing like a Tinkertoy with a missing piece.

There was a deep chill to the floorboards, and Anna's fevered skin sucked in the coolness like a tonic. Despite the burning pain in her leg, she pressed her face gladly to the floor and spread her palms broadly to soak up fresh cool. *Exchange*, she thought, *this will be an exchange of energy*, and

Anna took in the cold and gave back the fire of her fever. This is what she was thinking when she heard the clatter of footsteps, the metallic slide of the door latch, and the draft of air rushing along the floor to greet her.

"Here now, there's no call for that. I'd have been here in an instant if you needed to get up," said a woman, clearly from somewhere else.

Anna, still facedown on the floor, tried to push up with her hands so that she could see something other than the woman's shoes—boots really. She pushed and rose slightly, as if she'd been arching her chest up into a yoga pose, the name of which escaped her . . . lion, lotus, cobra, something. Only she wasn't rising.

"I can't get up," said Anna, more startled than anything.

"Of course, dear. Tom, come in here and help me get her up. She's fallen to the floor."

More footsteps; a sharper, longer stride. Two hands gripped her armpits and helped her float to an upright position, and they half dragged her, half lifted her to the bed. They sat her on the bed, and the woman reached down and lifted Anna's legs onto the bed. A hot poker of pain shot through her leg again and she cried out. She gripped the wool blanket and squeezed her eyes shut. She needed to anchor herself. Where was she? Had there been some disaster? Was this a Red Cross disaster center? She clearly lacked a point of reference.

She had been at home with her nephew. Her nephew. Anna's eyes flew open. "Where is Joseph?"

For the first time, Anna looked at the woman and the man standing beside her. With subtle turns of the head, they exchanged worried glances. The woman's dress was long, loosely fitted at the waist. Her sleeves were rolled up and her hands were chapped and red. Anna was terrible at judging ages, but she guessed this woman might be in her thirties. Her reddish hair was pulled back from her face, and it hung down along her back. The woman turned to the man at her side.

"She's not from here, Tom. And if that midwife doesn't get here soon, she won't be with us long. Will you bring her a whiskey? I'll get more wet cloths and try to bring down the fever, although it might have gone beyond cooling."

Anna sank back into sudden exhaustion. A doctor—she needed a doctor, not a midwife. Didn't they know that she wasn't pregnant? Yes, a doctor would fix everything. She could go back to sleep.

This is what Anna dreamed. An army of men dressed in black was on a mission to cut off her leg. Her brother appeared in his swimming trunks and he was his younger self, ten or eleven. He held out his hand to her. "Take the dots, Annie," he said.

Anna woke. For the first time in she didn't know how long, her head was clearer. The difference was dramatic. She didn't move, but she thought about things on her To Do list: balance the checkbook, go through her mail, call her mother. . . . Oh no, now she did remember. The accident. Her brother.

She sat up and remembered the room that she had seen before. The chalky white walls, massive by the looks of the windowsill.

"Hey," she yelled. "Hey, is anybody there?" She looked around for her clothes after peeking down at the white sack of a sleeping gown. She pulled back the covers and started to swing her legs around. But there was a damp cloth on one leg and she pulled it off. She stopped and stared. Large black dots, six or seven of them, lined either side of a nasty slice on her leg. She reached down to brush them off. They were soft and warm. They moved in response to her prodding and pulsed slightly, just like one might expect with leeches. Leeches.

"Get them off! Get them off me!"

The door flew open. A familiar-looking woman came in and rushed to her bedside.

"All right now. There's no need for screaming. The leeches have done their work for you. Tom, bring a candle, no, the lantern. We need to take off the leeches even if they aren't full to bursting."

Anna had pulled herself up to the edge of the bed. She pulled the front of her nightgown out a bit and peered down to scan her body to see if there were leeches anywhere else.

"Are there leeches anywhere else? On my back?" Her entire body felt as if it had been covered with black leeches, sucking away at her.

"No dear, only where they were needed. Now be still and we'll have them off."

This is what happens when you lose your mind. You wake up floating in the ocean, and then you crawl along a rocky shore in the shredded remains of your ex-husband's T-shirt and his blue Man Silk underwear. Oh, and you wrap thick, slimy seaweed around your leg because that's gashed open. Then you wake up and leeches are sucking blood out of your leg. The leeches are removed, presumably because they have done their job. Then you get dressed in a long linen skirt and blouse and you stand outside and you suddenly get it; this is madness, because you don't know how you got here or where you are. Everything is wrong.

Anna looked out the window. The thatched roofs were wrong, the man hitched to the plow was wrong. She was pretty sure this was Ireland, given the accents and the landscape, and that was very wrong. And it wasn't now, not Anna's now.

She surfaced for a brief moment. Rohypnol, the date-rape drug; that was it! She'd been drugged and kidnapped by back-to-the land isolationists. She could integrate that possibility, but it included the possibility of the present. That was still now.

It was time to get up and get a better look at the surroundings. She limped out the front door, past the three children who lined up behind their mother as if Anna was going to eat them. Anna kept one hand on the door frame and took in the stone walls, the fields, the barn behind the house, and the rutted lane in front of the cottage. The woman, who'd said that her name was Glenis, had also said that fresh air would be good for her.

Anna went back to the house through the tiny door. "Glenis, could I talk with you for a moment?"

"Aye. Michael, go help your father and take the two little ones with you." Glenis was wearing an apron that covered as much of her dress as possible. The children backed out the door eyeing Anna. Glenis looked expectantly at Anna, taking the pause to dip her fingers into a piece of lard and rubbing the grease into her red hands.

"I don't remember how I got here, and I don't know where I am," said Anna.

"You've had a terrible fright. We think there was a shipwreck somewhere along the coast; that happens too often for me. We're always finding bits of wreckage along the rocks. And when they found you, you were near cold as iron. I wasn't sure we could warm you, if you know what I mean. I thought the Archangel had you by the toes."

Anna didn't answer. No, she thought, I was not on a ship. I was not shipwrecked.

Glenis went on. "And if I may ask, where are you from, where did you start out?"

What could Anna possibly say when everything was so wrong and when she had tipped over into madness? Maybe she'd had a stroke; she was only thirty-four, but it was still possible. Maybe she wasn't really hearing what people said. Her vision could be affected also. She blessed every minute of law school that forced her to read a situation for all possibilities.

"America. The United States. Massachusetts," she said.

Glenis let a sigh slip out, and her shoulders dropped a bit lower. "America, that explains a lot. And you've not been sent by the British?"

Anna thought of possible reasons why Glenis would lead her down this particular path. The British?

"Glenis, where are we? What town is this?" Anna felt a buzzing in her head like crickets. She gripped the back of a straight-backed chair.

"We're not in a town as such, but we're most near Kinsale. The village is down the hill. Does that help?" asked Glenis.

"And the date, could you tell me the date?" asked Anna.

"The back end of summer, as you can see. Coming into second potato harvest, September," said the woman.

"No, the year, tell me the year." Anna's stomach turned over and she headed for the door. As she did, Glenis called after her.

"Well, it's 1844, such as it is," she said as Anna made it to the door just in time to heave all over the stone steps.

* * *

Anna weighed her options. She could look at the situation from two angles and think thoroughly about each one. If these people were an isolated, fundamentalist cult who wanted to believe it was 1844 and had for some reason drugged and kidnapped her, that was one thing. If she'd been kidnapped, it had been a seamless event, marked with so much perfection and coordination that it was as if Anna had been plucked like a goldfish from a pet store's fish tank. What did she last remember? Driving to New Jersey to pick up Joseph from the detention center, the long, miserable drive home, collapsing in bed, then waking up and seeing Joe in the living room. What then?

To ground herself, she made herself slow down to remember each detail of her house. New stainless-steel fridge with double doors, a stack of mail and newspapers, her espresso machine that she rarely used, the stove top and the oven, butcher block counter space, the sink with the arching faucet, and her garbage disposal, also rarely used. Yes, all the appliances, all the electricity running through her house behind the wall boards, in between the wall studs; electricity and outlets where the electricity exited to her appliances.

Electricity was everywhere in Anna's house. Anna looked outside and saw no power lines. Then she sat on a bench outdoors for hours and heard no planes, no hint of engines anywhere. But if these people were throwbacks of some sort, people who wanted to prove they could live naturally, without electricity, without the gas-powered compromises of daily life, then there was an upside to all this. She could eventually escape. It would only be a matter of time. In fact, she could test this theory out and tell Glenis that she was going for a walk.

The other possibility was that this was the past, that she had looped back 164 years and she was standing, flesh-bound, amid people, sheep, houses, birds, and smoke from a time before. Just as Glenis insisted, this could be 1844.

Anna had read every issue of *Discover* magazine since she was a teenager with their scientific sound bytes of information. She had tried to understand string theory; what she'd come away with had been a sense that time undulated like a ribbon. And hadn't she wished as a child that she could step into the past or float into the future? As a teenager, she had wondered about going into the past wearing very cool clothes from the present; would people twenty years ago perceive that her clothing was innovative and brilliant, or would they treat her like a painted bird? Would they gawk and turn on her, plucking out her eyes and her bright feathers? There were tests for everything, and Anna could test out her options.

She walked to the front door, where Glenis sat braiding a child's hair. Glenis sat on the front step, and the child squatted on the ground between the folds of her mother's long dress. The girl had taken her father's dark hair, not her mother's thick, reddish hair.

"Glenis, I was not alone on the ship. I traveled with my nephew. I need to look for him."

Glenis tied a piece of yarn around the child's braid.

"Would that be Joseph? You talked about him when you were sick. Seems the lad was in a bit of trouble. And you're only now asking about him? I'd say your head is still in the worst of fogs."

"No, my head is beginning to clear. I'd like to see where I was found. Can you take me to the place where I was found?"

"You've only been up for one full day. You're pushing it if you think you can walk all the way to the beaches and the cliffs."

Anna wanted to protest; she felt the weight of her mother, her brother, and her missing nephew press hard on her shoulders, and she knew she needed to look for Joseph immediately. She needed to assess the situation, look for shreds of information about him. That's what she was thinking when the ground rushed up to meet her.

"Tom, she's down again! You were right; it was too soon for her to be up."

And Anna felt strong arms lift her and carry her back into the cottage. They returned her to a bed, where she sank into a troubled acceptance of time.

Chapter 9

Taleen was there when the boy was brought in, fresh from the ocean, naked and sweet. She'd never seen a boy so lovely and smooth. She took him to be not yet a man; his shoulders hadn't broadened, and the hair on his face, although darkening, was soft and thin.

John Carrol, a master cooper, had found him on the long stretch of Tramore's beach. He'd said that the fairies had rallied him from a perfectly good sleep, chattering around his window until he'd gotten up, lit his lantern, and walked the two miles to the sea. When he was later asked why he'd walked directly to the shipwreck beach, as it was called, he couldn't say, but when he'd gotten there, he'd found the boy rolled like a seal in broad bands of seaweed, with his white skin gleaming through. The boy had been deathly cold and would not waken. John Carrol had taken off his coat, placed the boy in it, and carried him like a child until he'd gotten to the Mitford estate, because Taleen's mother, Deirdre, worked in the kitchen and everyone knew she was the most heralded *liaig* in Waterford County. She could save a calf who had not taken a breath, and she could save a mother whose blood had all but emptied out in childbirth. She would know if this boy could be saved.

John Carrol unlatched the kitchen door and was himself ready to drop from the weight of the boy. A pot still hung over the banked fire. He knew the master of the estate was away; all the Irish knew when he left, and they sighed a collective breath of peace when he was gone. But even if he had been home, he would not have heard John Carrol call to Deirdre, for the master slept two levels higher than the world of the servants. John Carrol placed the boy on the table, and the coat fell open.

"Deirdre, come quick; this one's about to die from cold and the cursed water!"

Deirdre appeared at the door followed by her bright-eyed daughter Taleen. The pair came and stood in the doorway, looking at the naked boy with the gleaming skin and the dark hair. Before the woman could say a word, Taleen, a thin rail of a girl, walked straight to him and placed her hands on the soles of his water-wrinkled feet. The boy shuddered and gasped like a fish taken from the ocean.

Deirdre's hand flew to her heart. She said, "Oh darling, I wish you hadn't done that. It's too soon for you. But now it's begun."

Taleen was five years old when she'd first heard the word "sight." She'd overheard her mother say, "The child has the sight." She'd wondered who her mother had been talking about. What was this thing that another child had, and could she ever have it?

After their supper of brown bread and butter, Taleen had asked her mother about sight.

"What is it? Can you wear it or eat it? If it's to be eaten, does the child share some with other children?"

Her mother had wrapped a good quilt around the girl. The spring had been wet and cold, and the part of the house where they lived took all summer to warm up; the warming had not yet even begun. They lived off the grand kitchen of Master Mitford, deep at the bottom of the house. Their sleeping room was close to the kitchen, and Taleen's dreams were filled with scents of hard sauces and stews and every sort of potato and the game birds that simmered all day after a hunt. Even wrapped in her quilt with her Mum squatted next to her, Taleen smelled the essence of a full day of cooking that hung off her mother like a gentle cloud.

"You're old enough now," her mother had responded. "You'll remember what we talk about. The memory sets in good and strong at this age. It's you I was talking about, it is you, my dear child, who has the sight."

Taleen had pulled herself to sit upright, and the quilt had fallen off her shoulders. "I've got it? But where is it? Is it packed away?"

"No, not except that it's packed away in you, waiting to be practiced like a fiddle. Do you remember when you told me Sunday that the egg man wouldn't be coming because he'd taken ill with the fevers? That's the sight. Or when you knew that two pups from the wolfhound's last litter would be born still and without breath? That's the sight. Not everyone can see those things. You get to see them first before the rest of the folks. Although I'll tell you, I've never seen the point of it. Sight passes from mother to daughter—to the seventh daughter exactly, and that is who you are. When people know you have the sight they're after you day and night to tell them this or that: will he love me, will the babe survive, and will the crop be overflowing or disastrous this year? We get to see what's happening a bit before the rest of them. If only they'd wait, they'd see it too. People don't want to wait."

Taleen had listened intently, for the tone of her mother's voice had been altogether different than it had ever been before.

"Do you mean to tell me that every other person couldn't tell about the dead pups in the litter? They couldn't see the sad eyes inside the mama's belly? And you're saying it's only you and me that see such things?"

"Yes, that is what I'm saying, and there's more, little one, even though I would give my best boots to not have the sight on some days. My sight comes more with the body, and that is how I can tend to the sick ones. The lungs and the stomach, the aches in the muscles, that's where my sight has settled. We must wait and see where it settles for you. The sight will settle in its proper place when you are older." And Deirdre had wrapped little Taleen back up in the quilt and let her newfound knowledge soak in.

In the weeks after the revelation, Taleen had asked her mother about everything, to figure out which was sight and which was how all the rest saw the world.

Does Miss Fiona see that her back tooth must come out? No. Did Master Mitford know that his best horse would lose a shoe on a journey to Limerick? No. Did the farmers know that this crop of potatoes was plump and abundant? Aye, oh yes, they did.

And so it was, ten years later, that Taleen was dressed and waiting and the fire was ready when John Carrol brought the boy, plucked from the sea as if he had been a creature spurned by the ocean and spit out. The kitchen was warm; a chicken broth was already prepared, and there were two quilts to wrap him in. After the boy began to breathe again, jolted by Taleen's touch, Deirdre ordered two men to lie next to him, one on either side, to wrap their arms around him and draw out the cold.

Taleen stood at the boy's feet. She laced her fingers between his toes, a thing that she had never done before, but she knew that she should, that she could tie him to this place, twine her fingers around his toes to bind him to her so that he could never leave her.

Chapter 10

Wherever he was, it was not the Essex County Detention Center, and it was not home. Miracles did happen; he had wished and prayed in the detention center that something would save him from the wreck of his life. Never in a million years had he imagined that he'd have ended up in a jail in New Jersey. Everyone at home would know; he'd get kicked off the wrestling team and his father would kill him. Wait, there was something else about his father. What was it? And something about Anna. But before he could fully remember, those thoughts rushed to the back corners of his brain, where they turned dark and quiet, humming a sticky tune that lulled him back to sleep again. He dreamed of the gravel base that his father had put in the trench of new stone walls, then the meticulous layers of rocks wedged into each other as if they had waited all their life to go together. Buried like the gravel, no rubble, that's what his father had called it.

When he awoke, he smelled food and heard the murmur of voices. A rough blanket rubbed his neck. He ran a quick hand down his torso and realized he was naked. With a firm grasp on the blanket, he sat up. He was in a bed of sorts, a scratchy, noisy bed, as if the mattress was stuffed with, wait a minute, straw or corn husks. In front of him was a small fireplace, where a smoky fire smoldered.

The voices came from the next room. Joseph stood up, wrapping the blanket around him, and tiptoed to the door. He pressed his ear against the door in an attempt to hear what the people were talking about, but a sudden dizziness took hold and he fell against the door, which clattered on the hinges. All the conversation on the other side of the door stopped. Joseph caught himself and pushed away from the door. He stepped back and prepared for the worst: more trouble, even if this wasn't jail or home.

The door creaked open and he was hit by a gust of air that brought the full scent of warmth and light. As he breathed in the smell of food and his lungs expanded, his chest felt hard and fiery all at the same time, and he coughed a dry, painful bark.

"You breathed in half of the Atlantic, lad. Your lungs are going to feel like they've been torched by fire pokers for a few days. But you've cheated the devil, deprived him of one more soul, so he's off sulking in the bogs, waiting to catch the next poor bloke."

Joseph stopped coughing. He rubbed his chest, as if it would help, and stared at the man who'd spoken to him. Joseph took in the accent; the man was like a guy in the movies. The clothes looked different—even Joseph knew they weren't right. The shoes; the shoes were wrong. No running shoes. This guy wore leather shoes, and they had a buckle. A woman with a long dress and an apron stood behind the guy. Next to the woman was a girl who had the biggest eyes he'd ever seen, blue eyes rimmed with dark lashes and a half smile, like she knew a joke or a secret. She was thin, swimming around in her long dress like a trout. If Joseph just walked across the room, he could pick her up in one arm, he knew he could.

The woman turned to the girl. "Taleen, you're needed upstairs. We'll look after the lad."

The man moved toward him. "I'm Finn. I'm not the one who found you, that was John Carrol, but I'm the one who made sure you could stay here with the best woman in the country to look after you."

The woman sighed. "For the sake of us all, give the boy some clothing. He can't come in like that." She picked up a pair of trousers and a shirt from a chair. The chair clattered on the stone floor. Stone, he didn't know anyone with a stone floor. Except once when he'd gone to work with his father. . . .

"Here," she said. "These will have to do."

Joseph had gone to Sturbridge Village with his grandmother. She was a teacher, and every birthday had been a trip to someplace like Sturbridge, a reconstructed early American village, or Mystic Seaport, or the Science Museum in Boston. The last time he had agreed to go with her was when he was thirteen. He wondered if he had somehow landed in a reconstructed village, but that didn't make sense.

The woman pushed the clothes into Joseph's hand, the one that was not desperately clutching the blanket. "I'm Deirdre. You just saw my daughter Taleen. Can you speak? Have you a name?"

"Joseph, my name is Joseph. Where am I?"

Finn tipped his head to one side. "You were plucked from the ocean, found along the beach of Tramore, nearly drowned and frozen. You were the color of death, and the devil had his grips in you."

"I was in the ocean?"

Deirdre and Finn exchanged quick glances. She ladled a steaming hot liquid from a pot hanging across the fire. "Aye, and you breathed in too much of it. That's why you have the cough. Go put your clothes on, young Joseph, then come and have this soup. It'll draw out the last of the ocean."

He went back into his room, closed the door, and dropped the blanket. There were no underpants in the pile of clothes Deirdre had given him. He shrugged to himself and pulled on the pants. No zipper either. He buttoned the pants and paused, then pressed gently against the door, placing his ear lightly on the wood. He heard Finn say, "He's not an Irish lad. We have to tell Mr. Edwards now. And he'll want to tell Colonel Mitford. He'd not be interested in an Irish lad, but this fellow is from America. I know the accent from the sailors who come into Cork and Tramore."

Joseph pulled the shirt over his head, buttoning the last few buttons near the top. The sleeves were long, but not long enough for his arms; the cuffs stopped a few inches from his wrists. Didn't these people have T-shirts? That was all he needed. He was barefoot and saw no shoes in sight. What was her name, Deirdre, she's the one who'd given him the pants and shirt. He opened the door to the kitchen because she had told him to come and eat the soup. Joseph sat down in a straight-backed chair and sniffed the bowl of soup. It smelled OK, like something weird that his grandmother might have made. Right now, he didn't so much care who'd made it. His stomach felt hollowed out, like someone had suctioned out his guts. He stuck his spoon in the thick soup, finding chunks of potatoes. This would have to do for now until he could load up on pizza or a sandwich.

So where was he? He'd already considered Sturbridge Village. Or maybe a reality TV show, a survivor kind of show. Sure, that was it; people had signed up to live for a year in olden times to see if they could take it. Very realistic too. He liked the big fireplace, the iron pot hanging over the fire, the mountain of potatoes piled in the far corner. Oh no, this was too gross; a headless chicken with all its feathers still on it lay on a table.

Whatever this place was, he was going to try very hard not to get in trouble until he could figure out what to do next. He already had enough problems, like a police record.

Deirdre returned to the kitchen from a stairway on the far end of the room. She had a pair of boots and something that looked like knee socks, the kind girls wore.

"I don't know if these will fit properly, but they were the best we could do. While you were mending I happened to notice that you have quite large feet. You spent three days sleeping and shivering. You ate the soup just fine, I see. You're ravenous, no doubt, all lads are, but you've had nothing but a few sips of water for the entire time you've been with us."

While she talked, Deirdre slowly circled him, as if she was scanning him all over, taking an X-ray, searching for something that she couldn't quite see.

"Your soup was good. Thank you," said Joseph, trying to remember every rule that his grandmother had taught him. Say thank you, say good-bye when you leave, offer to help clean up, carry groceries, and open the door for others. What else, what else should he do?

"I don't know where I am," he blurted out. "What are you all doing here? I mean, why are you dressed like that?"

Deirdre stopped circling the boy. She had dark hair, spun

with a streak of white near her temples. It was pulled back and wrapped intricately around her head, but her skin was smooth and fresh, making Joseph think of a peach.

"Finn thinks you're from America. Is that so? But Finn here is a butcher, and they know carcasses better than people. Were you on one of the ships? We've had more ships run aground and splinter onto the islands than you can imagine."

Joseph suddenly realized that he could play this like a computer game, the fantasy games that his friend Oscar always had running at his house. Oscar always created his characters with a strategy in mind. Joseph needed the advantage here, and he needed to accumulate points. He needed time to think, to figure out what was happening. Was his mind playing some weird kind of trick? But he didn't want these people to know where he was from, not yet. He didn't want them calling his father, or the police.

Anna had told him once that it was sometimes easier to tell people you were from Canada when you were traveling, or at least that she had been tempted to do so. Why did that suddenly pop into his head? Make a move, tell Deirdre where he's from, but don't make a mistake.

"No, not America. Canada," said Joseph, looking Deirdre dead in the eyes.

He saw something flicker across her face as if the woman could see something clear into his mind. But he didn't dare switch from one story to another; now that he had made his choice, he had to stick with it. Deirdre turned and picked up his bowl to refill it.

This is what Joseph decided in the amount of time that it took for Deirdre to serve him another bowl of soup: he had to run away from home and never go back. It would be better this way. His head cleared more and more as he ate. The soup warmed his entire body. He needed a plan, and this time it had to be a good one, not a half-assed plan like the one he and Oscar had cooked up when Oscar had called and said come on over, I've got two hits of X and the keys to my grandmother's car, let's drive to fucking New Jersey. That had turned out great. Jail. Oscar's parents had come and gotten him within hours, and he had cried like a third-grade baby when he'd been released. But not as terrified as Joseph had been when he'd been left alone.

The people here, wherever he was, only knew his first name, and he was going to keep it that way. He didn't want to get sent home. He needed time to strategize, that's what his wrestling coach had always told him; you had to think three moves ahead of your opponent. And you had to make the first move so fast that the opponent didn't have time to think. And lastly, never, ever give up, even when hopelessly pinned to the mat. But who was his opponent?

Deirdre left again through a hallway at the far end of the room. He put on the socks and boots that she had given him. The socks didn't stretch enough; they were more like some kind of wool, which he hated because it made his skin itch. But as soon as he put on the boots, he was glad that he had the cushioning of the socks. Could they possibly have given him less comfortable shoes? The clothing gave more weight to the idea that this could be that old dungeons and dragons game, where everyone dressed up crazy and took on a character.

Deep, resonant voices from the stairway brought him to his feet. Finn and another man appeared.

"Joseph, this is Mr. Edwards, the house manager for Colonel Mitford, the lord of the manor that you're standing in.

I've told Mr. Edwards that you don't yet recall how you came to be floating in our dear waters," said Finn, who turned to Mr. Edwards and stage-whispered, "his mind has had a shock, that's all, give him time. He's quite muddled."

Mr. Edwards was dressed much finer than either Finn or Deirdre. He wore a vest beneath his jacket and a tie around his neck, wrapped like a scarf. Joseph guessed he was a few steps up the rungs in importance.

Mr. Edwards stared at the boy, regarding him from head to toe. "Finn tells me that you're an American. Is that so?"

"No, I'm from Canada."

Finn looked at Deirdre and raised an eyebrow, which Mr. Edwards couldn't see.

Mr. Edwards's face illuminated with interest, and his mouth formed a silent *oh*. "The colonel has a particular interest in Canada. He has land holdings there. He'll want to see you. He has no love of the Irish, so if you'd been an Irish lad who washed up on the shore, you'd be no concern of his. Follow me."

Joseph had a moment of panic at being taken away from the people he'd met. Neither one of them had done anything harmful; in fact, they had fed and clothed him, and now he was being taken somewhere else.

"Could you tell me first where I am?"

Mr. Edwards nearly skidded to a stop and twisted his head around at the boy, scowling. "You're between Waterford and Tramore," he said.

"And where is Waterford and Tramore?"

A plump silence filled the large kitchen, blossoming out until it began to pulse.

"Boy, this is Ireland."

The incongruity of being in Ireland jolted Joseph, and he began to rock, ever so slightly, back and forth. His feet moved into a fighter's stance, with his weight distributed evenly, knees flexed, body poised, pulsing with boiling energy from head to toe. First one foot, then the other, rocking. He was in Ireland, someone was lying, and he was not going anywhere with this guy who looked like the high-school vice principal. Something was more wrong than anything had ever been wrong before, even when he'd been in jail in New Jersey. He gauged which one of the men he'd have to take down. The one with the tie wouldn't be ready, even after he ducked his head and brought down Finn. Joseph began to pull his energy into the center of his body.

Suddenly he felt a hand on his arm and Deirdre was in front of him, filling the space between him and Mr. Edwards. Her hand was small and hot, and it was latched firmly to his wrist. The entire side of her body was pressed against his right side.

"Should we reconsider this arrangement? The boy has a befuddlement that I've seen before with seamen after the ocean has shaken the sense out of them. Let's get this lad a breath of fresh air, give him the rest of the day to calm his nerves before you present him to Mr. Mitford. I don't think he'd take kindly to the boy vomiting like a sick dog, or worse yet, sick with the scutters. I've got just the thing for him— warm breezes, a bit of hot whiskey to settle his stomach, and a good walk about in town," said Deirdre.

Joseph stopped rocking. Mr. Edwards backed up, putting an entire body length between himself and the boy. He cleared his throat.

"This evening, then. Do whatever it is that you do," he said

with a mocking tilt to his head. He spun around and made
for the stairway.

Deirdre released her grip on Joseph. She turned to Finn.

"Go get Taleen and the night cooks. Tell them that I need
them in the kitchen now. The lad and I are going out. He
needs to see where he is," she said.

Joseph's legs relaxed and he let himself be led out the door,
following Dierdre as if he'd done so all his life. She spoke
to him over her shoulder as she opened a heavy door to the
outdoors.

"Get ready, boy. You have much to see, and I pray to God
that your brain cools down. Hotheaded lads do poorly here,
whether they are from Canada or Tramore."

Brilliant sunlight poured over Joseph, and he automatically shielded his eyes.

"Come this way," commanded Deirdre, "and see what's
about."

For a small woman, Deirdre moved quickly, dodging
clumps of moist horse manure as if she'd been a dancer. Joseph's muscles felt suddenly limp and disconnected, and he
struggled to keep up with her, his legs skidding out from
under him on the unpredictable cobblestones. A high garden
wall marked their path on the right, blocking his view. Joseph
turned around to see where they'd come from, a chance turn
of his head. He pressed his backside against the wall, letting
his body sink against the tightly fitted rocks.

"Wait a minute," he said. "Is that where we just came from?
It looks like a castle, or almost a castle." He rubbed his eyes
with the backs of his hands. "Tell me again where we are?"

Deirdre double backed to him and regarded the boy,
searching for something in his face.

"Give me your hands," she said. She examined his palms, the backs of his hands, and his mostly clean fingernails. She rubbed her thumbs quickly over the palms of his hands before releasing them.

"This estate is Glenville. Take a good look; it's one of the finest manors in Waterford County. I've worked for this family since I was a child, which is longer than you can guess. Taleen is my youngest child and my final one. You'd not believe how many children I've brought forth, so I won't tell you. How old are you, lad?"

Joseph normally didn't like it when women talked about bearing children, leading to horror stories of birth and unmentionable things, but Deirdre's voice had a musical lilt to it, and he willingly traveled on her words, riding them and eating them up like cotton candy.

"How old am I?" he repeated, blinking in the brilliant daylight. "I'm sixteen."

There should be no harm in telling her his age; indeed, there was no point in trying, since she was someone's mother and they could always figure out how old kids were. But he must remember that he was from Canada. He had to stick to that story. Montreal, Canada. He'd been to Montreal once.

"Sixteen years old," hummed Deirdre, as if she was ready to burst into song. "You don't work, you're not a stable hand, no shoveling, pitching, chinking, chopping, none of that for you. Your hands are without a whisper of callus."

"No. I'm in school, that's why. In Montreal."

Three men walked by them, dressed in pants that ended oddly, several inches above their shoes. Their leather vests were deeply stained in dark splotches. One carried a tight bundle of splintered wood; one carried a cloth bag brimming with tools, a handsaw and other things that Joseph couldn't recognize. The third man carried an empty wooden bucket.

Deirdre nodded at them. "Stop at the kitchen door and tell them I said you all need to have some of the soup I made. Tell them so."

The more he looked around, the more he thought of Oscar and his computer game, which had looked just like this place. Oscar was addicted to The World of War Craft. Joseph had tried it, and he'd liked it, but it hadn't grabbed him by the throat the way it had with Oscar, who'd dove into the game for days and weeks and had had to be hauled out of his room by his father for both food and showering. Oscar had created his own avatar, a character on a quest who had helpful powers like restoration and the ability to freeze people into statues. Perhaps the people he was seeing here could be so crazy about the game that they all dressed up like their characters and talked in accents.

And then a sharp needle of memory pierced his skull and he remembered the water and being pulled with a fearful velocity through it and having to breathe, feeling his body turn inside out with gut-spinning certainty. And Anna, he'd gone somewhere with Anna and they'd been ripped apart when the loud sucking sound had tried to crush his eardrums.

He looked back at the manor, now about a football field length behind them. The walls of the building glowed golden, illuminated by the late-day sun. The manor seemed to go on forever, four stories in some places.

"So this isn't like a hotel, is it? This is one family's home?"

"Yes, one family swimming in wealth," said Deirdre. "Can

you walk more, or are you going to swoon on me? If we walk down into Tramore, it may settle you and give a notice of your bearings, which you have clearly left in the ocean."

Joseph rubbed his fingers along the stone wall. The rough grit of stone felt real along the pads of his fingers; Deirdre's hands had been real; the smell from the horse manure had been real.

"I'll follow you," he said.

And they walked and walked, and it was not until they emerged onto a rutted lane about thirty minutes later that Deirdre let them pause.

"We've just left the boundary of Mitford's estate. Now, let's step lighter, with the weight of labor lifted from us, and bring you to the village."

Joseph smelled the salted air that rushed up to meet them. He wanted to call Anna, just to let her know that he was alive. He wanted to ask Deirdre if there was a cybercafe, if he could borrow a cell phone, but already the words felt wrong and he chewed them before they could leave his lips. He looked up at the sky and already knew that there would be no contrails, no jets overhead. It was the silence from the sky that most alarmed him.

Only once, when he'd been just a kid in third grade, had he ever seen the sky go quiet. It had been his father who'd pointed it out. For the three days after the World Trade Towers and all the rest of that stuff, no planes had been allowed in the sky.

"Joey, come out here," his father had yelled from their blacktopped driveway. "Remember this. Remember how screwed up everything is when the skies go silent."

And that is just what a sky was to him without the distant hum of engines propelling planes in steady arcs over-head. There were no planes, jets, none of that. He followed Deirdre, letting her stay a few steps ahead of him, until she stopped, hands on her hips, and said firmly, "Keep up with me. I don't like someone walking behind me. Come on now."

They walked side by side, staying to the rutted land, cross-ing a field along a well-worn footpath, coming out into a grove of trees, following a path through the woods that felt to him like a tunnel. Deirdre was small; the top of her head came to his shoulder. Like her daughter Taleen (who had already come to his mind twenty times on their walk) her hair was very dark, not brown, but a deep color, like old fur-niture. Deirdre must have been old, as old as his father, but she didn't move the way old people did, hauling their bulk around like weary cows.

Once they were through the woods, they had to cross a stone wall. Deirdre startled him by trotting up to it and jumping over it, lifting her long skirt just enough so that Joseph could see the tops of her boots. She jumped like a deer or a cat, as if gravity didn't affect her and she could leap straight up. She seemed to have forgotten his presence for a moment, but after her gazelle leap, she turned to him with a shy smile.

"Ah, the small pleasures are the most satisfying. Come on, the village is not but another mile."

And then they were on tiny streets, some curved, some with cobblestones. Joseph heard the buzz of the place, as if some-one had turned up the volume: babies crying, horses clipping along, a man sharpening an axe head on a circular grind-ing stone, which he moved by a foot pedal. Someone tossed a bowl of water out a side window. Suddenly they were in the heart of it, and below the town, he saw the port, crammed tight with ships of all sizes. He looked as far as he could to the left at the massively long beach, then to the right, then back where they had come from, and he let his gaze run out past the ships again.

Joseph didn't want to ask Deirdre the date, although he could think of little else. He wanted to see it written down. Something had happened when he'd been with Anna, somehow they had been sucked into water and then they'd been pulled apart. But he knew exactly where he was; a boy in a shitload of trouble, arrested, caught with a stupid hit of Ecstasy in the car, thank you very much Oscar, and Anna, he remembered reaching for her, grasping at her as she'd turned into something like air.

"Is there a newspaper I can read?" he asked.

Deirdre tilted her head and considered. "We do love the word, and we've newspapers. But there are newspapers and then there's trouble. Which do you want?"

Joseph did a quick tally of everything he knew so far. Given his evaluation of the situation and the silent skies, he said, "I'll take trouble."

"I thought as much."

She led him along a smaller street and came to a door above which hung a sign that read Book Bindery: Thomas Fitzgerald.

Deirdre opened the door and stepped inside. She greeted a man who was hunched over a table, his arm pressing down hard with a stamp. Deirdre spoke to him in another language, the sound of which jolted Joseph. Was it German, Dutch? What was it? All he could tell was that the man stared at Joseph and shook his head no. Then Deirdre spoke in a smooth persuasive manner, leaning over the table and laughing and talking more until the man stopped bristling. He unlocked a drawer, pulled out a newspaper, and handed it to Joseph.

"Read it here, lad," he said angrily, then quickly reconsidered. "Excuse me manners. If you are here with Deirdre, that should be good enough for any of us. But you must read the newspaper here in my shop. It's the *Nation*, and as such some British look upon it as near to treason."

Joseph had almost no idea what the man had said. He'd never heard of a newspaper called the *Nation*, not that he read newspapers very much unless forced to or unless his high school wrestling team was mentioned. But he was impatient with the long lead-in; he wanted the front page, the date. He took the newspaper, and Tom Fitzgerald pointed with his head to a plank bench along the far wall.

"Keep in mind it's over a month old. Takes that long to get here, and the print is all but dragged off the page by so many eyes by now."

Deirdre glanced over at the boy, then said to Tom, "Come outside with me, man; there's sunshine, and you look as moldy as the dark side of a tree."

Tom's chair scraped along the floor and the two of them stepped through the small door to the street. Joseph peeked from a window and saw that they were hovering near the door. He unfolded the paper with a snap and looked immediately at the top of the border. *The Nation. August 12, 1844. Published in Dublin.* So this must be about September 12, 1844 if what the man had said was true.

A brittle reality rattled into place, clinking like tin in his gut. Only a small bit of him had latched on to his first theory, that this was a computer game or a reality TV show prank or anything but this. The part of him who'd reached for those beliefs was a child, and in an instant, the child vanished. If Anna had been here, she could have figured all this out, but there was no sign of her.

Not knowing what else to do, he began to scan the newspaper for any additional information, but it was dense with political stuff, the kind of thing that was so boring it made his eyes roll back into his head. But he knew he had to concentrate; he couldn't be a baby about this.

The words *home rule* jumped out at him several times. That's what this newspaper was all about, wanting home rule. Maybe this guy would let him take the newspaper back where he and Deirdre had come from if he promised to return it. Joseph popped his head out the window, which curiously had no glass in it. Instead it was bordered by shutters on the inside and another set on the outside.

"Can I borrow this? I'll bring it back."

Tom and Deirdre looked stunned. Tom looked accusingly at Deirdre, then to Joseph. "And take it where, back to the Mitford estate? Are you daft?"

What had he said wrong? Wait, Deirdre had said something about trouble. He really didn't want any more trouble.

"Sorry, I only wanted to study it more. And I really only wanted the date. That's where I was so mixed up. You see with the accident, being hauled out of the ocean, I lost my sense of time."

He felt ridiculous talking to them through the window, so he pulled his head back in and came around to the door. He handed the newspaper to Tom. As soon as the newspaper hit the light of day, Tom startled again, stiffening like a dog, alert, fur raised. He pushed Joseph back inside again. He squared off with Deirdre.

"I was having a perfectly lovely day pressing letters into the page and now I'm jumping like a fish. Let's put the bloody newspaper aside." He slid it under his workbench, beneath a wooden tray heavy with tiny blocks of letters.

He turned to Joseph. "You're not from here, I can hear it in your voice, lad, so you're not to blame. And Deirdre tells me you hail from Canada of late and that our fearsome ocean spat you out."

Joseph gulped, preparing to ready his tongue for another go at this lie. "Yes, Canada. I don't recall much else before I was rescued." For the first time it occurred to him to ask the obvious. "Did you find any others on the shore?"

Tom looked expectantly at Deirdre, giving way to her for the answer. As a shimmer of light from the door ignited Deirdre's eyes, Joseph noticed for the first time that they were greener than anything else he had ever seen. Something as green as that didn't look right—at least he had never seen anything this green on a person. Deirdre moved out of the light, closer to Joseph, and her eyes went from emerald to blue-green again, less dazzling and also less distressing.

"Every time someone is washed ashore, dead or living, we search the coast in either direction for miles. The current is ghastly strong; you can't imagine how far something buoyant can be carried. But no, the word was sent out fifteen miles each way, to be on the lookout. It was only you. And no ships were heard to have accidents." She paused. "Of those ships that we hear from. But some ships sink, the sea pulls them under and there is not a bloody sliver left of her. " Her green eyes flicked once in Tom's direction.

"Right. Well, lad, your people must be sick with worry," said Tom.

Joseph needed time to formulate the rest of his story; he had to be careful. This was where Oscar's game training might actually come in handy. He needed to create his own avatar, a personality and history and maybe even a quest. The weight of this pressed down hard on Joseph, sagging his bones.

"Of course you'll be wanting to write to your people to let them know of your mishap," said Deirdre.

"Yeah, of course," said Joseph. What he didn't say was, Whose name should I make up? What fake address should I use? Not that it would matter. He remembered that he had to think harder than he had ever thought before. This wasn't high school; he couldn't doodle in his notebook, text Oscar, fall asleep in history class. This had to be more like wrestling—being light on his feet, knowing the opponent's move before they knew it, being decisive and fast with his strike.

They walked back to the Mitford estate, the land steadily rising beneath their feet. Joseph was different on the return trip, filled with a knowing that ricocheted inside him, chattering around each cluster of synapse, neurons, rearranging the design until he was exhausted from the effort. A sudden longing for his family tightened his throat. Did this mean he would never see his father, his grandmother, and even Anna again? Wait, why hadn't his father driven to New Jersey to get him? As he kept pace with Deirdre, a sudden dread about his father stopped him as surely as if he had crashed into a stone wall. He dropped to his knees and held his head.

"What is it?" Deirdre was at his side, squatting next to him. She placed a cool palm to his forehead. "Here, sit back on your arse, now put your head down. You don't have a fever, but you are unwell."

"It's my father, something is wrong with my father." The words wrenched out of him, each one jagged along his throat. He sat up and wiped tears from his face, turning away from Deirdre as he did. "I know something is wrong, but I can't remember, I can't see it."

Deirdre waited for him with her arms wrapped around her knees. When he cleared his throat and tried to right himself by wiping his hands down his shirt, she stood up. "You'll recall everything that needs remembering. Sometimes not remembering is a sweet thing, rocks us like a baby until we are right and strong again. I've got my eye on you, and some people would say that's a great shame and others would say it served them well. We'll see which way it goes with you."

They had come up the steepest part of the road and they both looked back, out to the sea.

"Colonel Mitford will be returning at sunset from riding with the dogs. Hunting," said Deirdre. "If I could keep you from him for one more day, I would, but as soon as he hears word of you, he'll want to inspect you, see, like you were a bird from a Spanish ship, or a monkey from the coast of Africa. We had a wee monkey running about the manor once; it was a horror to watch. The loneliness of the creature was near too much for me to bear. And then one day, the thing was gone. I don't know if the colonel wearied of his toy or if the wretched thing escaped. If the monkey ran off, we have more than enough hoodie crows and sea eagles to kill it."

There was nothing about this tale that Joseph found reassuring. Must he somehow be offered up to the lord of the manor, if that's what he was called, as if there was no escaping? Would he end up like the monkey, tossed away and torn to shreds by birds?

They had entered the tunneled path through the woods, and slim strands of light from the late-day sun made it through. He heard only his own footsteps and the slightest sound from Deirdre, as if she did not fully make contact with the earth. They emerged into the open space of the meadow and Deirdre quickened her pace.

"I know you're ready to drop, lad, but now's not the time to linger."

When they returned to the vast kitchen of the manor, she pushed him into a chair. The fresh and bloody carcass of a deer had been gutted, and its hindquarters now hung above the side tables.

"Eat this," she said, pushing the last of the soup in front of him. "Finn, get a slice of ham for him. I'd forgotten how quickly food burns through lads."

Finn opened a door that looked like a closet, and he disappeared for a moment, returning with a hunk of meat. Joseph felt a rush of saliva in his throat and a welcoming yelp from his belly. He'd never understood the girls in high school who'd been vegetarians. *Rabbits*, his father had called them. No, Finn wasn't the only other person he remembered. Taleen, where was she? He scanned the kitchen for her.

Finn pulled a foot-long knife from a drawer and sliced off an end of the meat. He handed it to the boy.

"Could you put it on a plate, man?" sighed Deirdre.

Despite Finn's smile and his gentle eyes, Joseph caught the hint of disregard in the final shove of the meat.

"Why do you trust him?" asked Finn. "Why did you take him in as if he was John O'Connell himself? We know nothing of him, and he's seen far too much of us."

Deirdre was already tying a fresh apron around her. "The speed of gossip makes my head spin, truly it does. What great mouth told you where we had been and who we spoke with?"

Finn shrugged, looked sideways at Joseph, and said, "What does it matter who brought the word?"

Joseph bit off a piece of the meat and began to chew, glancing up at Finn and Deirdre. The meat was dry. He dunked the next piece into the soup, hoping to soften it.

"He's not British, we know that much, and he's just a lad, and if ever someone needed a hand before being dumped into the lap of our Colonel Mitford, it's him," she said.

"Lovely," said Finn. "And suppose, just suppose that your unappreciative sentiments that you so openly stated are repeated to our lord? What then? I've never known you to lose your caution, never. And to put so many at risk. The boy's not Irish, can't you see?"

Joseph stopped eating and looked at Deirdre. He wanted to let her know that he'd never say or do anything that would hurt her.

"I get it," he said. "Deirdre took me into Tramore to see if I could remember more about what happened when I was washed ashore. I looked at the ships in the port and I didn't recognize any of them. Then we came back. That's all."

Without comment, Deirdre tipped her head to one side and looked at Finn.

"He's quick and he has some sense about him, but bless us all, I hope that's enough," said Finn.

As if on cue, the door that led up the stairs screeched open on its rusty hinges and Mr. Edwards emerged, stepping only as far into the kitchen as necessary.

"Come along, lad, the lord of the manor is riding in at this moment and you shall be the first thing he sees when he returns. It is your good fortune that it was a bountiful hunt."

Joseph pushed his chair back, peering up at Deirdre as he did so. She nodded slightly and stood aside to let him pass. He thought he heard her say something as he passed by, or perhaps she had simply coughed, clearing her throat; he couldn't be sure. But if she had said something, it had been, *"Caution."*

"Follow me," said Mr. Edwards.

Every aspect of the manor grew in size as they moved further and further from the kitchen. The doors grew wider and taller, the wood planks broader. The windows went from glass to stained glass. Joseph followed his guide through paneled hallways and rooms that seemed to have no purpose other than displaying oversized portraits. They paused finally in a vast entryway. The floor was cut from huge slabs of stone, and rich carved molding ran up the walls. A huge painting greeted them, a scene from a hunting smorgasbord. The hunter stood with polished boots amidst his pile of bounty: dead pheasants, a huge stag with bloody tongue protruding at an unlikely angle, ducks of all varieties, and a small mountain of rabbits piled up in the killing frenzy of the hunter.

Even as Joseph began to feel smaller and less distinct in the massive entryway, he heard the sound of a loud, rumbling voice, the snap of hard-soled boots, and the self-congratulatory air of men who had accomplished something together. They approached from a hallway to the right.

In walked four men in riding gear. The aroma of oiled leather and horse rushed ahead of them. They stopped abruptly when they saw Joseph with Mr. Edwards.

"What's this? Have you caught a thief, Edwards, one more bit of Irish riffraff plundering our estate? The timing is perfect; we've not finished shooting for the day," said one man. His sandy hair was slicked back, tucked behind one ear. The three other men erupted in deep belly laughs.

Mr. Edwards made a slight bow. "This lad, who is not Irish, sir, was found barely breathing, washed ashore. I knew you would want to see him immediately. He is from the Province of Canada, sir, a well-schooled, proper lad."

"From the Provinces? Get him out of those rags then. What must he think of us, offering him tatters from the Irish. Tell me your name."

Of course the lord of the manor would want to know his name. Why hadn't he thought more about this? Joseph's mind raced to news reports, television news bytes of England. Suddenly his brain was blank, as if he had never heard about one English person in his entire life. Then he remembered the one name he could associate with England.

"Joseph Blair, sir, and I'm very pleased to meet you."

Chapter II

Joseph awoke to the elevated status of honored guest at Colonel Richard Mitford's estate, and it went beyond his wildest expectations. That he had been sucked into a time other than his own caused him little discomfort when balanced with the advantages. He had slipped into a life of privilege as if it had been designed for him.

Mr. Edwards delivered a pile of clothing, cinched in to fit his slim hips, his long legs and arms. Joseph wore a waistcoat of finely woven wool, a vest beneath that, and a starched linen shirt close to his skin. His host had supplied him with knee-high boots that glistened ebony black. A manservant had polished them and left them in Joseph's bedchamber, and he'd assisted in pulling on the boots that very morning. The colonel had said they would go riding in the afternoon.

Joseph, who had been served in the dining room at a massive table, finished a meal of slightly overcooked pheasant, potatoes in cream seasoned with herbs, and bread that was moist, rich, and so deliciously explosive on his tongue that he experienced an erection. The main course was followed by unrecognizable berries with a sauce that tasted somewhat like vanilla ice cream except lots warmer. And this was a midday meal.

While he was looking out over the formal gardens from his seat at the table, a boy came in to check the fire. He looked to be about Joseph's age.

"Good morning, sir. The colonel wanted me to check the fire for you, although it seems altogether too early for a fire. Not that I'm assuming anything about the colonel's choice, but the day is warm," he said.

Joseph had never been called sir before, and the weight of it hit him unpleasantly. He pushed his chair back and stood up, moving to the fireplace. He held out his hand.

"I'm Joseph. What's your job here?"

"Con is me name. Short for Connor, but nobody calls me that. You're asking what I do? I tend the fireplaces when the cold weather is upon us and I work with my father, the stonemason, whenever I'm able. Can I do anything for you, sir?"

Joseph was eager for the company of another boy.

"Could you show me around the estate? I'd like to see the stables and the hounds."

"Aye. I'm headed to the stables. Come on then."

The colonel had fussed and gushed over him, making sure that he had all the proper clothing and boots. He had indeed promised his guest a tour of his land, but Joseph wanted to know the estate in a way that would bring him to Taleen; he had seen her walking with a large dog and had heard dogs elsewhere.

The two boys left the manor and walked left along the long drive, heading to the back, where the stables took up nearly as much space as the manor itself.

"These dogs are as old as Ireland, that's what Deirdre tells us," said Con, opening the door in the stables. "She said they truly did keep us free from wolves, kept the wolves from tearing through our sheep and the wee calves. But the wolves are long gone."

The door hinges creaked. Everything creaked in Ireland, Joseph was sure of it. Maybe it was the salt air taking a constant nibble out of the iron hinges, biting out molecules, making bumps so that the metal screeched on metal.

"The colonel fancies everything Irish except the Irish. He wants to have twenty wolfhounds on his estate, castle guards, you see, because he learned that the old Irish nobility had twenty dogs on each estate. But the dogs don't want to breed for him, or not often. Deirdre thinks the wolfhounds are leaving Ireland, as if they decided they were finished."

Joseph followed Con through the back of the stables, past the bulging-eyed horses, who tossed their heads as Con walked by, spreading their nostrils to pull in the scent of visitors.

"We had a litter in early summer. They're coming out all wrong, and the litter was small, not but four. One was stillborn and never took a breath. Another took on the cough and stopped suckling. She wasted quickly. Another did not fare well . . . " Con paused and seemed to consider saying more.

Joseph heard rustling, a scraping sound.

"We've kept the runt. The colonel said to drown him, but I could not. I brought him to Deirdre. As soon as Taleen saw him, it was settled. Taleen takes care of the runt. She's out here every chance she gets, and the runt has taken to her."

If Joseph had been interested before, he was fascinated now.

"This is Taleen's dog?" asked Joseph.

"'Tis. As much as anything can be ours on the colonel's

estate. If it weren't for Deirdre talking her way around the colonel, making it seem like it was his idea, the pup would have been food for the gulls."

Con slid open the door to yet another section of the estate, where three gray adult wolfhounds rose their heads to look at the humans with unfiltered appraisal. The stare took Joseph by surprise; the unblinking seriousness of the eyes made him wish he'd never done anything wrong. A charcoal gray dog stood up, and Joseph was startled by its sheer size. For her part, the dog stepped lightly; gravity did not dare pull at her, didn't grab at her mass, and she seemed to float, the pads of her feet bouncing off the earth.

Before the gray had crossed the yard, another, younger dog bounded into the center and leaped at the older animal, tasting her neck in one gushing tongue lap, ricocheting off her and prancing to Con and Joseph with his big paws plopping on the earth.

"This is the runt?" asked Joseph, laughing for the first time since skidding along time. He dropped to one knee. Seeing an invitation to play, the oatmeal-colored puppy placed both paws on Joseph's bent leg.

No sooner had the puppy occupied Joseph's full attention than the three adult dogs silently surrounded him, looking slightly down at him. Their fur was coarse and stern. At the shoulder, the dogs had to be three feet tall, and at the head, four feet. Joseph felt a sudden urge to stand up.

"Don't."

She sounded exactly as he had imagined she would. No, better, one hundred times better, as if her voice formed crystals in the air. He didn't know where Taleen had come from, but he decided that obedience was the best course of action.

"Don't move just yet. They need to smell you and look at you. They want to know what you're all about."

Oh no. He hoped that they couldn't really tell what he was all about. The three monstrously sized dogs closed in on him, while the puppy, oblivious to the seriousness of the inspection, licked his face. They sniffed at his clothes, his hair. He cautiously held out one flat, upturned palm, which the animals sniffed. It was the eyes that unnerved him, the overly long stare from their amber eyes.

"Now stand up," said Taleen.

With exaggerated slowness, he stood up, trying to calm his twittering nerves. First the male—his gender having been obvious from Joseph's previous position—then one of the females stuck a businesslike snout into his crotch. Joseph prayed that his dick smelled just right, whatever that was.

"They're giving you a special sort of sniff. They're trying to figure out where you're from. Give them a bit."

Joseph submitted to the extended crotch exam. Suddenly the male stood up on his hind legs and with amazing gentleness, placed his front paws on Joseph's shoulders. The dog was taller than he was. Joseph got the message loud and clear about who was bigger. He had never seen dogs that were this huge. The male dog dropped back to the ground. Each of the three adult dogs gave a solemn wag of the tail and returned to his or her resting place.

"This one is Madigan. In old Irish that means 'little dog.' Fitting, don't you think?"

Joseph nodded. Somehow this was all he could manage with Taleen. His tongue dried up and his brain felt far away. He could not depend on the words that fell from his lips.

"The colonel and I are going riding today," he said and immediately regretted it. He sounded stupid.

"Well then, off with you. Don't keep him waiting," she said.

As he walked away, Taleen stood next to Madigan, her hand resting easily on his head. For such a large dog, Madigan, still a puppy, managed to look remarkably goofy and not at all serious, like the adult dogs. Joseph managed a wave that might have looked as goofy as Madigan.

Joseph was sixteen, and he had never kissed anyone except his grandmother, his aunt, and his favorite second-grade teacher, Mrs. O'Connor, with whom he'd simply fallen in love. The kisses from female relatives had been cheek pecks, compulsory and embarrassing. He'd mostly hated the moments greeting his grandmother and aunt, though his aunt didn't seem to want to peck his cheek anymore and so wasn't much of a problem. She had probably given up on him. But his grandmother was different; he mostly believed that she loved him, and he did like the way she smelled. Besides, she was always there, as she promised she would be.

Mrs. O'Connor, his teacher from second grade, had sent Joseph into delicious spasms of seven-year-old delight. During the first half of the year, he'd forgotten and called her Mommy when he'd finished his addition so quickly. Two boys in the front row had heard him and teased him at recess, but those same two boys, Alex and Jeremy, had called Mrs. O'Connor Mommy the following week, so the score had quickly evened out.

His teacher had been more beautiful than anyone else he had ever seen, and he'd imagined that he would marry her someday. On the last day of school, Mrs. O'Connor had knelt down and given each child a hug. Some of the kids had kissed her cheek; Joseph had been one of them. Her cheek had been so soft and her hair had smelled so delicious that he'd wondered why tigers and bears didn't just eat Mrs. O'Connor. If she ever went camping, bears would surely think she was candy and break into her tent. She'd written a long note on everyone's progress report for the year, and she'd said that Joseph was a fast learner and good at everything he tried.

Joseph's father had never said anything about the progress report, but he'd left it on the kitchen table, as if reading it had been enough. Joseph's grandma had found it and whooped with delight, reading it in senatorial tones again and again. But it hadn't been quite the same, for he'd been hoping to hear his father say, "Good boy."

If his mother had lived, everything would have been different. She would have loved him totally. He was never sure if he remembered her, or if he just remembered the stories that his grandmother and aunt had told him. He could recite all the details of her death. She had broken her leg when she'd fallen off a horse on a simple trail ride, something that should have healed in six weeks. Riding horses had been her pleasure from childhood, and Patrick had surprised her with a trail ride on her birthday. A clot tossed off by the broken femur had raced to her brain. Not a common injury, everyone said. Not common, just life-changing for Joseph.

Even so, he had not hesitated when the colonel had invited him to go riding. This was where he had meant to be all along.

Chapter 12

Here are things that Anna could have used in 1844. Duct tape. Why couldn't she have been transported with a fat, gray roll of duct tape? She could have wrapped it around her shoes, which were now split wide open. She could have mended a hem or fixed a splintery gate on the fence. Anna had no duct tape, aspirin, antibiotics, tampons, lemon juice to pump a bit of vitamin C into her diet, and no dental floss, although she had already tried sliding thread between her teeth. She'd puzzled her hosts by brushing her teeth with a well-chewed stick. She had no fleece. What she would give for a lightweight fleece jacket, and zippers and deodorant. For everyone.

All that remained of the twenty-first century were two odd and useless pieces of clothing—the shredded waistband of her ex-husband's boxing shorts and the neck and one shoulder of his T-shirt. These were the things Anna had been wearing when she'd fallen through time and had emerged puking salt water.

Glenis had kept the shreds of cloth, but she did not reveal them to Anna until the fourth day that Anna could walk without passing out from the shattering pain of her still oozing leg. Anna could now get out of bed by herself to limp around the cottage and barn. That was when Glenis slid the boxer-shorts remnant out of her pocket and said, "Tell me, dear, just what is Man Silk?"

Anna saw the stamped tag still attached to the waistband. Her hand shot out to grab the cloth, a sudden connection to who she was, where she wanted to be. She pulled the cloth to her face.

"You're missing your family, I daresay. And no wonder. I don't know how I would fare if I'd been hoisted up naked and half drowned from the sea. We'll get you back where you belong," said Glenis.

"Not until I find Joseph. That's the most important thing. He must be terrified, wherever he is." She slid the shredded fabric into her pocket.

"Right. Tom and I are going to send word out to be on the lookout for him. A lad, you say? American, like you of course? And tell me again about the ship you were on."

"Joseph is just sixteen, and he's never traveled before. He won't know how to make his way. And he's very worried about his father, my brother, who had been in a terrible accident . . . " Anna paused; she wanted the story to make sense, to fit with the time of no radio, no telegraph. Why would the two of them have traveled to Ireland if Patrick had been injured? She had to remember to slow down; the world was much slower, no instantaneous messages. She rubbed her lower leg to give herself more time to think.

"How's the leg coming along?"

"Better, but I had a sharp pain just now, and I think I'll sit for a moment." Anna leaned her backside against the fence rail. "Our destination was France. We were coming to get my brother after we had received word of his terrible accident. He's a lawyer and has lived in France for two years. We got a letter saying that he had fallen, I don't know how and they didn't say, but he was in and out of consciousness. We booked passage immediately to be with him and bring him home," said Anna. She put both her hands over her face in startled embarrassment; she was crying. Not over the fabricated story that she was telling Glenis but at the sudden image of Patrick, ghastly, swollen, bruised beyond recognition, attached to plastic tubing and electrical impulses. Was he still alive?

"Stop now, you don't need to tell me the whole bit. Pull yourself together. You can't help your brother or the young fellow until you get stronger," said Glenis. She reached over and rubbed Anna's hand with her rasping, callused palm.

Anna took in the first tender touch that had been offered to her in the face of Patrick's calamity, despite the lie and despite the truth that Patrick did not yet exist.

Anna took stealthy expeditions each day to get the lay of the land. And she pumped Glenis about geography.

"What is east of us? How far is it to Dublin? Where is the largest port? Have you heard about any other survivors of shipwrecks?"

She was careful to avoid references to the twenty-first century, but it was very hard. It was easy not to use words like *email, webpage, computer, car, cell phone, jets,* because there were constant visual clues about the nonexistence of electricity and internal combustion engines. But she slipped now and then when words of her time fell out of her mouth, like when she announced to Tom that she was off to the bathroom.

"Excuse me, but where might that be?" he asked.

Anna stopped breathing for a moment. "Oh, that's an American saying; it's what we call the outhouse, er—the privy."

Glenis chimed in from the doorway, "Well, it's the last place I'd care to bathe."

She didn't know what would happen if she told them about the future. Did the Irish believe in witches? Did they stone people who were aberrant? Or would they think she was mad? And what was the fate of someone who was mad? So far she had covered all of her mistakes and oddities by coming from America.

The last time Anna had washed her hair, it had been in a shower with hot water and shampoo that had smelled like lemon and tea tree oil, and bubbles had flowed down her breasts, over her hips, tangled in her pubic hair. She had shaved her legs; it had been summer, and Anna had liked the smooth gleam of her legs after shaving them. She had turned off the shower and dried herself in a fresh towel, slightly scented from some form of chemical from the dryer. She had oiled and lotioned her legs and arms, smudged deodorant along her armpits, put sunscreen SPF 15 on her face, and scrunched a bit of styling gel into her brown hair. She didn't know how long it had been since she had skidded to a stop on the beach of Kinsale, Ireland. Glenis had said she had been delirious for five days. Anna had been keeping track of time since she'd started walking again; that was another eight days. So Anna had not washed her hair in two weeks.

She knew that there were more pressing issues at hand, lots more, like the whereabouts or the very life of her nephew, but washing her hair suddenly became the most important thing on her mind.

Tom and Glenis's house did not have water indoors, but it had a well outside. Anna felt her hair; she realized that somehow they had rinsed out the salt, but she truly needed to wash it now. Her tresses had sectioned off into oiled clumps, so she desperately pulled her hair back as tightly as she could. She asked Tom for two pencil-sized pieces of wood, which she scraped and scraped with a knife until they looked like chopsticks. She then wound her hair up into an oily bun and used the sticks to contain it.

Glenis watched her and said, "Why, that's such a simple thing you've done. Is that a fashion in the colonies now, or in France, do you think? I've never given one thought to hold-ing my hair with sticks."

"Here," said Anna. "I'll show you how to do it." Anna untied Glenis's hair, which had been held with yarn, then wound it into a tight mound at the back of her head, placing the two sticks so they marked an X.

"Lovely," said Anna, admiring her work. "And now could you give me some idea of how to wash my hair? I mean, do you have a type of soap or something that I could use? I'll haul the water and heat it by myself."

Glenis looked stunned. "Why would you be wanting to do that? Did you spill something on your head? I told you that we got the salt out of your hair. Sea salt will eat right through anything, cloth or hair, if you leave it."

Anna had grown up washing her hair every other day.

During a particularly fastidious period in high school, when she'd been shocked at the smells that her very own body had been able to produce, she'd washed her hair every day. And then there had been the hair products. Conditioners applied immediately after shampooing, with a citrus scent, grapefruit, organic, overpriced. And in her bathroom at home were several plastic bottles of hair gels, crèmes, and pastes containing clay, alcohol, glycol, paraffin, dyes, scents, inducements, and hopeful promises.

Anna thought about what she could use. "Could you spare some ashes and the smallest bit of cider or vinegar? I think I can mix up something with that."

"And you won't mind me watching you, because I've never seen the likes of this."

Anna hauled a bucket of water from the well, took it inside, and heated half of it over the peat fire. She carried the kettle of hot water and the wooden bucket of cold water outside. She had a handful of ashes and a small bit of vinegar. At the last moment, she looked around and scooped up a handful of gravel, then placed that near the ashes. She dunked her long hair into the bucket, getting it as wet as possible. Next she rubbed a bit of water into the ashes and rubbed this into her hair, scrubbing the long tresses from end to scalp. Anna used the small, sandy pebbles to rub even more vigorously, hopeful that the sand could scour off the accumulated body oils and dirt. She had fretted terribly about lice at first, but no one in Tom and Glenis's family had lice, and Glenis had been rather put out when Anna had revealed her concern. "We've had bedbugs, but never lice," Glenis had said with a twinge of irritation.

After Glenis watched Anna go through the sand scouring part of the hair washing, she offered to help.

"This is a job for two women. You'll never get all that sand out by yourself," she said, rolling up her sleeves.

Anna could not remember when someone else had washed her hair, except when she'd paid at a salon, back in her other life—or ahead in her life, where a beacon of longing pulled at her ribs.

Glenis poured the cold water over Anna's hair, scrubbing and fluffing as she went along. The last rinse was a watered-down mix of vinegar and more water.

"Where did you come up with this concoction for your hair?"

Anna paused. Where had she come up with it? Chemistry class in college, an assignment that had required her to know the pH levels of everyday substances—the one really useful piece of knowledge from a semester of suffering. The young professor had tried to make the class relevant to the students by asking them to invent their own body and bath products using what they knew about pH levels. Anna and her room-mate had created a makeshift version of shampoo that had somehow made its way into her long-term memory.

"In school, I learned about this in school," Anna replied as Glenis doused her with one last blast of cold water.

Later in the evening, when all three of the children were as satiated as they could be on a supper of roasted potatoes and buttermilk and the parents were putting their feet up at long last, Glenis told a rousing story of washing Anna's hair that made the children laugh.

"And then, when I'd blasted her with a bucket of cold

water, she was as happy as a sky lark, tossing her wet hair about," concluded Glenis. Anna shrugged her shoulders in a helpless gesture.

"We are very peculiar in America," said Anna. She hoped that foreign peculiarity would continue to provide a cover for her.

Tom made a walking stick for her that was dotted with small burls, giving it a human look, as if the stick had been a long arthritic finger. He smoothed the top knot for her so that her palm fit it perfectly; he cleverly carved an indentation so that she could comfortably wrap her hand around the shaft. The oldest boy, Michael, had helped by initially scraping off the bark. All in all, the walking stick had taken four days to make. On the last day, Tom carved the letter *A* into the side of the stick.

He presented the stick to her and said, "This should keep you from falling down until your leg gets better. And after your leg is properly healed, you can use this stick to cross the moors and the mountains. It's that good, if I do say so."

There was something different about the passage of time when there were no wristwatches, no minute-by-minute schedule to maintain. No meetings at 10:00 a.m. sharp, no deadlines at precisely 4:00 p.m. Instead, Anna gauged time by watching her leg heal, limping from house to dirt lane to field, then coming back again, exhausted, allowing her brain to mull over the preposterous situation that she was in. Yanked into the past where she could be of no help to her family, she fought to see a purpose, some logic to what was happening. She was not a believer in random chaos; Anna looked for the strands of connectivity that could provide an explanation for time travel. Law school had taught her to look for the issue in any given situation, and then the rule. So far, she could find neither. What was the issue when one was transported to the past? Was it random, or was it specific to Anna and Joseph?

She checked with Tom and Glenis each day about any word of an American boy who had been found in similar circumstances. They had said that they would send out word to neighbors and let the question pass from village to village.

"Surely someone would have noticed a boy who was clearly not from here. Have you heard anything today?" she asked again after returning to the neat cottage with thick thatched roofing. Late fall flowers still erupted along the rutted lane that ran into Kinsale.

"And surely we would tell you if we had heard," said Tom. He still had on his thick leather apron that protected him from the white-hot embers needed in his blacksmith shop. She heard the irritation in his voice, the weariness from forcing stubborn metal into convenient shapes: door hinges, horseshoes, wheels. She caught Glenis glancing at him, tilting her head to one side in a silent language between husband and wife. Anna was sure that it meant, *Hey, lighten up; she's just worried and you're tired and hungry*. But then again, nothing that Anna was sure of was holding up too well.

By October, the leg stopped oozing, the flesh having pulled together. Anna imagined the molecules of muscle and skin beneath the surface growing stronger again. The scar was raging red, and she doubted that it would ever be a subtle scar. No, this was going to be a racing stripe that could be viewed from across a dimly lit room. But for now, Anna was the only one who saw the scar, shrouded as it was by her long dress.

Part of Anna's daily walk to a nearby meadow and back had been designed to build up her strength again. One day she asked Glenis to take her to the coastline so that she could see where she had been found. Glenis agreed to hitch up the horse and drive the cart to the shore where Anna had been found.

On the designated morning, the mist was thick, and Anna at first worried that the drive to the coast would be out of the question.

Glenis laughed. "If we let go of everything due to fog, we'd stay in our beds all day long. This will blow off by midday or sooner."

Anna could not tell if they were going south or east or west, because the roads curved and turned, and even when they approached the sea coast, she was still confused by where exactly they were. Glenis set the brake on the cart and swung down when they found an agreeable spot with cliffs in sight. Anna grabbed her walking stick and eased herself down, still keeping most of her weight on the good leg. She followed Glenis through closely shorn ground cover with hints of sheep nearby: Bits of sheep wool clung to stickery bushes, and round scat dotted the ground.

"This is where it began," said Glenis. "The farmers who live closer to the cliffs saw the lights from a ship, and they knew right away that it was too close to the rocks. We need a good lighthouse here, that's what we need. There have been too many swollen bodies tossed ashore with their eyes eaten out by the fishes."

Anna flinched. "Glenis, please! My nephew was with me, and I don't like thinking about him without his eyes." She had learned that Glenis was unblinkingly honest.

Both women faced the Atlantic, and their dresses blew against their legs. A path led down the cliffs to the shore.

Glenis pointed to the left. "That's Kinsale there with the ships and the smoke from the port town." She nodded with her head for them to continue walking.

"If he's dead, he won't be needing his eyes. The fish might as well have them. Then, of course, we eat the fish . . ."

"Glenis!" snapped Anna. Then she reconsidered. She needed Glenis to help her. "Look, I'm sorry. Where I come from in the city, we don't see death every day like you do. I don't have sheep, or cows, or even chickens. But I am desperate to find my nephew. I know he's alive, I know it. And I'm responsible for dragging him with me on a trip that he didn't willingly go on. And my brother is so badly injured. Can you see why I can't rest until I find him? Wouldn't you do the same?"

"Aye, I'd want to set things proper. I'd want to know if the sea had taken him or not."

Glenis was younger by a few years, a fact that had shocked Anna when she'd learned it. Glenis was twenty-eight, six years younger than Anna. Aside from the three children that Anna knew of, another had died in childbirth and a fifth had died of pleurisy in his first year. As if Glenis had been reading Anna's thoughts, she asked, "You've no children then?"

Anna knew this inquiry could go down a slippery slope. She spoke with caution, trying to see ahead of each turn.

"I had three miscarriages and then my husband left me. Not just because of the miscarriages, but it was part of it. He left me for another woman. We were granted a divorce," she said, knowing that the divorce part was going to be the show-stopper. Divorce had only become legal in Ireland in 1997.

"They do that in America? So you're free to marry again, free to go your own way? You're not Catholic for sure." Glenis cocked her head toward a turn in the path leading to the ocean, and they continued along it.

"We are Catholic, but in an irregular sort of way. We don't attend often."

"And is that because of you being divorced? Were you banned from church?"

"No. It's because I wanted to try other churches when I was a kid. And then I decided that I could figure out my own relationship with God." Anna stopped herself from going on about the Catholic Church; it would have nothing to do with the moment in time where she and Glenis stood. What would Glenis think about her friend Jasper, who was gay, or women who demanded more power in the church, the right to conduct services?

"Could you now?" Glenis put her hands on her hips. A gull swooped up on an obliging air current and floated in space, surveying the two women.

Anna did not want to debate religion with Glenis because she felt inadequate with the particulars of religion and distant from the Catholicism that her own parents had abandoned.

"Will you show me again where they said I was found? Let's walk down the trail until my leg howls."

Anna followed Glenis along the hairpin footpath, giving weight to her walking stick, sucking in the charged air off the ocean. Glenis looked back to judge Anna's ability.

"I grew up on these trails, so they're no different to me than walking around the cottage, or down the lane to the neighbor's for trading milk. But you're not going to last long. Remember, it's not just the walking down part; we must come back up again, and I'll not carry you."

Anna was already sweating with the effort of keeping her full weight off her injured leg. Streams of sweat ran down her back and collided with the waistband of her skirt. Getting to the beach looked insurmountable; getting back up again looked impossible. They were on a level stretch of the path, a plateau before the next corner and descent. She placed her feet into the well-grooved path, followed for hundreds of years by people and animals.

"You could be right. Could we stop here and rest?" asked Anna.

"We'll stop here and rest and be grateful to get back to the top again."

Anna looked up, and the top of the cliff already loomed far away. She found a soft spot among the rocks and sat down. Glenis did the same. Anna's leg throbbed.

"Why would someone have been looking along the shore when I was found?" asked Anna.

"This is part of the major shipping lane that connects our Cobh to England and France. Ships often anchor a mile off the shore and send smaller vessels to take off passengers and freight. In storms such as the one that you were found in, ships can go aground. All that is found on the shore from their wrecks is fair for the taking. And we are all raised on the sea—we know the rhythms of her, and some of us can tell when she has spit out something that needs saving. Such as yourself."

"After I was found, did people look for other survivors?"

"To be sure we did. The beaches were scoured. Old Mr. Sweeney's wolfhounds were borrowed for the task and sent galloping along the shores for miles in each direction. If there was a scent of man to be found, those hounds would have picked it up. That was the odd thing. Not another person, dead or alive, was found, and not a bit of wreckage. Seems odd, don't you think?"

"Oh, I think everything about this is very odd," said Anna. She lay back on her elbows. When she did, she found Glenis's face silhouetted by the sun and her hair ignited in russet tones. But Anna thought she heard an edge, a place where Glenis was made of grit and scar tissue. Was Glenis suspicious of her story? Anna knew it would be best not to explain herself unless Glenis asked her a direct question. Endless police suspects had incriminated themselves over the ages by blathering on rather than just being silent. Nothing wrong with being silent. Anna, however, had been only partially successful. She sat up again, dislodging the cloak of the sun's shadow on Glenis.

"I've no sense of direction. How far is Kinsale?"

Glenis faced the ocean and pointed to the left. "That way, about four miles. Beyond that another fifteen miles is Cork, a mass of people if ever there was one. Cobh is the main harbor for Cork, a spit of an island sitting in the bay."

"Should we try to go back now?" asked Anna. "Thank you for making us stop here and not trying to get to the bottom of the cliff; I am exhausted by coming this far. You're wiser than I am. And thank you for tending to me and letting me stay with you in your home. I've never had anyone be this kind to me, not like this."

Glenis put her hand on Anna's elbow and helped her up. "Surely friends help friends. That's how we all get by. It's nothing. Come on now, we'll walk slow, like two old ladies all dressed in black." Glenis shook her head as if to dislodge the image she had just created. "No, let's not picture ourselves dressed in black yet. Let's not mourn anything on this fine day. Step lively, step as lively as you can, my friend."

They walked the path together. Glenis hummed a tune, but Anna thought only of Cork, with a mass of people where a teenage boy might blend in. If he was still alive.

Chapter 13

Joseph's first order of business, if he was going to travel about the manor at night, was to oil the hinges on his door and the six doorways that led to the lower levels of the kitchen. Through the kitchen were the servants' quarters. What would be most like 3-IN-ONE oil or WD-40? Whale oil was available, and lard could be easily acquired, but he worried that the entire house might smell like something had died.

To begin, he took a tiny bit of whale oil from one of the library lamps and persuaded a drop or two into the hinges of his own door first. His door was the most important one. Once his door was silent, he'd be free to work on the others. How did people sleep around here with these humongous doors screeching like bugles? He worked the hinge back and forth during the day until he was satisfied with the smooth glide of metal gliding on oil. Then he allowed two days for everyone to get used to the change from screech to silence when he opened the door to his guest chambers.

Several days later, he poured a small amount of whale oil from another lamp, this time from the gun room, and oiled the hinges of the door that led from the wing of the house

filled with bedchambers to the great rooms. The main doors
to the house were important. The hounds outside howled as
soon as the doors to the manor opened, so he had to work on
them when the full bustle of the day's activities distracted
the dogs. By the time he had worked his way to the main
doors, he had practiced on dozens of others, and he'd become
both efficient and fast. Joseph then worked his way to the
kitchen. By oiling one door every few days, he arrived there
three weeks after the start of his project. Now he could get to
Taleen without alerting the colonel or Mr. Edwards. Now he
could do what he'd wanted to do since the first day he'd seen
her. It was as if she was calling to him each night. He could
hear her voice in his head. No one had ever said his name the
way Taleen had the few times they had been alone.

Joseph found any excuse to talk with Deirdre, hoping that
Taleen would be in the kitchen. He had tried not to stare at
the girl, not to feel the heat of her narrow body, or let his eyes
linger on her white neck with the tendrils of black hair that
escaped from her hair cap. Each time she turned her head
and lifted her eyes to his, he thought that his body would
explode.

Joseph knew the way Taleen's hands would feel on him
before she ever touched him. He knew they'd not be all that
soft; she worked ferociously hard in the massive lower-level
kitchen, taking directions from her mother, Deirdre, who
was the almighty ruler of the servant realm. But he imagined the temperature of her hands, warm, as if they came
from bathwater.

When Taleen did touch him, his body suddenly remembered her touch. They encountered each other on the stone
stairway. He had been descending, clattering like the percus-

sion section of a band with his British boots. She had skittered up the steps in a birdlike way, not quite touching the steps. But that couldn't be; he knew she had to touch the steps. Or could she have been like the mallards on the pond that seemed to run along the water while their wings beat downward to keep them afloat? The two of them arrived at the narrow turn in the stairs at the same time. She reached her arm out, perhaps to stop him from crushing her, but she ended up with her palm pressed against his solar plexus. What had his father told him about grounding wires and electricity? He wasn't sure now, as that time of his life grew dimmer every day— except for the memory of the grounding wire, whatever that was, because that is how he felt when Taleen reached out and touched his suddenly vulnerable torso beneath the arch of his ribs. A current of alarming energy ran from her hand and galloped jagged lines along his spine, raised a huge ruckus at his penis, and then sped down his legs and out the soles of his highly polished boots. The moisture in his mouth had gone south as well, leaving his tongue thick and ponderous.

"Taleen," he managed to say, and he was richly rewarded when her slender face erupted in a smile. She placed her hand on his forearm and kept it there for ten seconds, then an amazing twenty, then he put his other hand on hers, and there they stood.

"I touched you once before, when they plucked you out of the sea. You were naked and cold. My mother set the men to banking fires. I placed my hands on your feet and started to warm you."

Naked? His twenty-first-century brain sat up. She'd seen him naked? A red tide began at his chest and, like the Nile River, ran north. He felt the heat of the blush rising, ignit-

ing everything in its path until it reached his ears. Suddenly
they heard more footsteps, coming from the top of the stairs
in a sharp rhythm. An outside force threatened to burst them
apart.

"The far garden wall tonight," said Joseph, two seconds
before Mr. Edwards converged on them. Joseph and Taleen
shot apart, he descending, she climbing upwards.

Later, when Joseph knew that the colonel had retired for
the night, he slid out of his room, boots in hand, and padded
to the end of the hall, through the next hall, then to the lower
level, through the two main rooms, then out the side door,
where he sat and pulled on his boots. All the doors opened
and closed in smooth, oiled silence. He had counted on a clear
sky because he'd wanted the full moon to be with them. And
because the entire universe was now turning in his favor, the
sky was indeed uncharacteristically clear. The full moon shot
buckets of creamy light along the garden path. He stayed
to the grasses and hugged the massive garden walls, built to
encourage the fruit trees by warming them. And there, at
the end of the old wall, was the new wall construction. He
had just visited the stonemason during the day. There, there
she was, and next to her was the dark outline of the dog Madigan, looking every bit like a small dragon, with his long
snout and impressive fangs.

Joseph had never been this close to another person before,
not in this way and not with this intention, so he had never
needed the words to describe the flush along his neck. If there
were such words, he had never heard them from Oscar or the
guys on the wrestling team. Did such words exist? He turned
shy so suddenly that he worried he might weep. Words fell
out of his mouth.

"I felt you once in my legs before I ever met you. I can't tell you how," he said. "It's like a memory."

Without hesitation, Taleen reached for one of his hands, then the other, until they faced each other with only a sliver of space between them. As if they had always meant to find this spot along this garden wall at this very moment, they pressed into each other. Joseph released a sigh from his old life and drew in a fresh, clean life layered with Taleen.

Madigan suddenly jumped up and flung his paws on either side of Joseph's shoulders, smashing the girl between dog and boy. Madigan's long snout was eye level with Joseph.

"Madigan, it's no trouble now. Get down. Here, come down," said Taleen with a laugh in her voice, pushing the hound off them.

"He's protecting you. That's good," Joseph said, finding the sweet spot behind Madigan's ears, rubbing with firm pressure.

"Is it protecting that I need?" asked Taleen. Before he could answer, she did the most extraordinary thing that Joseph had ever experienced. She stood on the tips of her toes and reached for his face, pulled him close, and rubbed her cheek along his, first one side and then the other. He had seen cats do the very same thing when they were marking something as theirs, leaving their scent.

The October chill did nothing to cool them. They sank to the ground, and their clothes fell off like leaves. Her skin was deliciously soft, marked by surprising muscles along her thin arms and legs. He touched her breasts and a puff of sound escaped her lips. When she touched his sex, everything that he had ever believed about himself changed, and he wept unashamed. He slid his hand across her hips and found the sweet mound of hair.

"Taleen?"

She answered with a press of her body. They made love cautiously the first time, absorbing the pain of newness. Taleen clasped him to her, and they found the pleasure of it again and again.

Madigan huffed to the ground, resting his head on his paws. From time to time, when Joseph would pull his face from the tangle of Taleen's hair, Madigan stared up at him with his amber eyes, as if to say, *So now it's the three of us.*

Chapter 14

Joseph ran his hands down one sleeve, where he met the confident cuff and the slight resistance of the wool against his fingertips. He inhaled the intoxication of love and power intertwined, pulling snug his young testicles, expanding his smooth chest. He was on top of the social heap here. He pictured a triangle of social importance, and he gloried in being at the pinnacle. The air on top was invigorating, and the advantage of being able to look down made him feel invulnerable. In high school, his body had ached from the weight of being so far down in the social heap, holding up the entire structure, just as the servants here held up the manor.

He didn't understand how groups formed so quickly in high school, how the coolest kids knew precisely where to stand, how to speak, who to speak to, what to wear. Everyone wanted to be with the kids who were casually clever, without blemishes, who walked with the ease of ownership, owning the very oxygen in the dank school halls. But there was room for only a predetermined few, and once the slots were filled, the rest scattered like drowning sailors and grabbed the first piece of flotsam that came their way, then paddled to any rickety port within their grasp: the football team, the skate-boarders, the wannabe Goths, or, in his case, the wrestling team. That had been his only life raft, and it had hardly been a reliable port. More like an emergency landing.

Joseph stood up and ran his hands down his jacket and the legs of his pants. He could already feel her breath on his face, could sense the quiver of his flesh rising to contract, pulling him tight like an arrow. He could think of nothing else. Taleen would be with her mother now in the vast lower level of the kitchen, where servants cooked for the manor. He walked past his bed and looked out the window, hoping to catch sight of her.

This is what made his flesh tingle, the thought of her hair, her wide eyes turned on him like searchlights. No one had ever looked at him like that before, illuminating his heart and belly.

He heard the colonel's voice trumpet downstairs.

"Where is my good lad? Where is our young Canadian?"

Joseph glanced at his image in the mirror. He buttoned the top button of his vest, pulled his spine taller than it had ever been, and ran his fingers through his hair.

"Coming, sir."

They were headed for a day of riding.

"Let me tell you about the Irish, lad," said the colonel. "They're difficult to manage. They're sly, clever in dark and thieving sorts of ways. And do you see how many children they have? They can't control themselves, nor can they feed their own lot. If it wasn't for the British, they'd perish."

The colonel rode a gorgeous chestnut horse, and right beside him rode Joseph, on a similar but smaller horse.

Joseph thought this line of reasoning sounded familiar, but he couldn't quite remember where he had heard it. He regretted every missed assignment in history class, every book that he had resentfully skimmed, every time his grandmother had wanted to talk about what had been happening in places like Ethiopia or Darfur, places that hadn't mattered to him. That was it—the colonel sounded like his great-uncle Elliot, who said that Mexicans were coming to America to take our jobs and have babies and go on welfare. He remembered that his grandmother had come unglued when her brother had staged a political debate at one Christmas dinner. She'd finally ended with, "Shut up, you sanctimonious idiot. I want to enjoy my family and the food that Mexicans have grown for us." Grandma didn't hesitate to speak her mind.

"Sir, what do you think the Irish people would do if the British went home?"

The colonel stopped his horse, and Joseph did too. He tried to do everything the colonel did. The older man turned slightly in his saddle to look at the boy, and the saddle creaked with the effort. The chestnut horse flicked his tail and turned his head to see what was happening.

"If we left? Why would we leave? Do you mean abandon our responsibility here, our right to govern lawless people who have no regard for the very value of life? What an absurd question. We've invested in this place; it's part of our empire, our destiny. You've only seen my estate, my well-managed estate that employs over forty Irish men and women to work it. You'd like to see what the Irish people would do if left to their own? You and I shall leave the estate and I'll show you what we're up against."

The colonel pulled the reins and his horse turned around.

"Come along, boy. We'll ride back now. We'll leave in the morning, head up to Clonmel. A good week in the country should answer all your questions."

He urged his horse on, and Joseph did the same. He had already learned that this horse responded to the slightest pressure from his legs, his wrists along the reins. This horse was better than driving a car. Not that he'd had all that much experience with cars, but the horse was definitely better. He gripped tighter with his inner thighs and tried to loosen his hips, letting his pelvis hinge freely with the horse. This adventure sounded like a camping trip with the colonel, and Joseph was ready to explore more than just the grounds of the estate.

When they returned to the manor, two groomsmen were waiting to take their horses. How had they known when the colonel would return? "Get the horses ready for an expedition," he said. "Tell the kitchen to prepare food for us to take for a week. You, you'll be coming with us to take care of the horses. We'll leave tomorrow."

Joseph dismounted in what he hoped was the way the colonel had—sharp and swift, a bit of a snap at the end when his highly polished boots hit the ground.

He didn't want to leave Taleen, nor the odd comfort that Deirdre provided, but the excitement of an expedition tipped the balance. After all, Taleen would still be here when he got back.

After a supper of organ meats and pork, Joseph a bit queasy, the colonel continued his instruction about the Irish even as he continued to stab at the meat with pleasure, popping dark hunks of it into his mouth. Con had lit a strong fire that beat back the late October chill in the vast manor. The heat from the fire made Joseph sleepy, and he wished for the lesson to be over. The colonel had to admit that the Irish had a particular way with horses; had an odd kinship with them, which had to do with the animal nature of the Irish.

"That makes them closer to the horses. They speak the same language, all grunts and snorts," said the colonel, emphasizing his relentless point.

Joseph had overheard two men speaking in the stables, and he realized they hadn't been speaking English. He asked, "What language do the horsemen speak?"

"While they work here, they'll speak only the King's English. We fight the Irish language day and night. It's the tongue of rebellion, disloyalty, and papists. There's no excuse. Thank you, lad, you're another set of ears for me."

Joseph didn't want to be another set of ears for him, but he was intoxicated by the sudden sense of privilege, the order, the ease of having cooks, men to select his clothes, to saddle and unsaddle a horse for him. It felt so right, as if he had been waiting all his life for this, as if he'd been born into the wrong family. The colonel liked and appreciated him, but Joseph didn't want to squeal on anyone. He backpedaled as furiously as he could.

"I think it was just their accent, I mean my accent. As you have noted, my accent is quite strong; you said so. They could have been speaking English. Yes, they were speaking English all along, and I couldn't get the accent."

The colonel put down his whiskey with enough force that the amber liquid jumped into a panicked peak.

"There's one way to find out. We'll bring them in and ask

them, not that they can be trusted one inch, but I've learned to detect their lies. They're like small children; they can't lie properly."

He rang a bell that rested on the table. "Edwards, call the stable boys into the manor. Have them take off their boots before they come in." He pushed away his plate of greasy meat, sending a small pool of oily liquid to the table.

Joseph began to sweat, and his fine clothes grew tighter around his waist, binding him. His prized boots locked him in place like anchors. He would rather have been anywhere than in the grand hall with the colonel as they waited for the unsuspecting stable boys. They were men really. Why was he calling them boys?

Joseph heard Mr. Edwards's shoes along the stairway from the kitchen. Behind him were the men from the stable. What were their names? Owen and Sean, their hats in their hands. The clean rich scent of the horses surrounded them, along with a burst of hay and leather.

The colonel gave Joseph a conspiratorial wink. "Good evening, gentlemen. Our young guest from Canada was wondering what language you speak. Could you explain to the lad?"

Joseph thought for sure that Owen and Sean would look at him, glare at him, accuse him, but they did not flick a glance in his direction.

Owen spoke. "It is your rule for all of us to speak English. And that is what we speak, just as we are now, and just as we should. But there are small moments, between men, when the old language serves to let us speak of those who have died, our grandparents, who spoke only Irish. Surely that is what Mr. Joseph heard."

Mr. Joseph? Owen was a well-built man who looked to be somewhere in his early twenties. Joseph was suddenly embarrassed to have an adult call him Mister anything.

The colonel turned to Joseph. "Do you see how long-winded they are? Could you hear an answer to my question in that papal sermon?"

Joseph cleared his throat and prayed that his voice wouldn't crack. "After hearing them speak, I can see that I was mistaken. This is exactly the sort of English that they were speaking when I heard them. I can't understand everything that they say, that's the problem. But honestly, I heard only English. I made a mistake."

The colonel proceeded as if Joseph hadn't said anything. "Edwards, could you tell our guest what the penalty is for speaking an outlawed language, a language of traitors?"

"Yes, sir. For speaking Irish, there is immediate loss of employment on your manor. If the offender rents a cottage on the manor, they shall be evicted." Mr. Edwards spoke to an invisible audience, directing his voice to the vastness of the room.

"Have I not been lenient at times?" said the colonel. He flicked something from beneath his fingernail.

"Yes, sir. You have been most lenient at times."

"Would you say I exude a sense of royal benevolence to those in my charge?"

Joseph was not sure what benevolence meant, but he did know what royal meant, and he thought the colonel was sucking for compliments—something that was completely unnecessary, since he was the man. Joseph fidgeted in his tailored clothes and hoped that someone could bring the conversation to an end.

"You are very much in the manner of royal benevolence, sir. And may I say that your charges are loyal, due in large part to your firm hand and your benevolence," said Mr. Edwards.

This guy is good, thought Joseph as he looked at Mr. Edwards with renewed interest. For the first time, Joseph understood that Edwards was working the system—he just didn't know what system.

"You are all dismissed," said the colonel. "And let there be no further incidents of speaking Irish on this British soil."

There, there he saw a twitch come across Sean's face. It ended in his fists tightening. Mr. Edwards displayed nothing, a perfectly studied nothing on his face.

Chapter 15

"She's just the sort who could be a British spy, sent to see if we are stashing shillings under the mattress. They'd think we should feel sorry for her and that's the way she'd wheedle into us," said Tom.

"I think not," said Glenis. "It's as likely that she's a bit daft, imagining some grand life, working with the uppity ups. She's just a lass with soft hands and remarkably white teeth, but a lass none the less. Her family could have turned her out."

Anna had stopped breathing, with her back pressed flat against the side of the barn beneath the open window. She'd been sitting in the sun, stretching and contracting the muscles of her leg. She couldn't let them know she was there.

"Do you think that's why she hasn't tried to get word to them?" said Tom.

"Aye. If they don't want her, that would be reason enough. But she's lost Tom, that's true enough to see."

"Lost or not, she's got to earn her keep. And if people see her working, they'll stop their yammering about her being a British spy."

Anna heard light footsteps in the barn, and then the sound

of a door hinge squealing as the barn door was closed. She quickly tiptoed behind the building lest Tom and Glenis come to the side. It had not occurred to her until this moment that she was putting them at such risk. She had only been thinking of herself and they had shown her nothing but kindness. They had saved her life. Anna felt a wave of shame sour her stomach, curdling the breakfast of buttermilk and potatoes.

Worse than the curdling was the gap that Glenis had found in her armor, her ability to out-think, out-negotiate anyone, her law review, golden-girl regalia. Glenis said that her family had turned Anna out. This worm of truth crept along Anna's ribs and like a tropical parasite, found its way into her heart. Steve left her. Her father left her.

Anna thought hard about what she had to offer Glenis and Tom. She asked if the children might like a tutor. The two oldest children—twelve-year-old Michael and eight-year-old Mary—were her first students. Their youngest, Nuala, was only four, and she cried bitterly at the exclusion. A third student arrived after the first week of lessons; young Phoebe hailed from an hour west of them. Phoebe was ten years old and a neighbor's child. Anna was surprised at the designation "neighbor" since she lived so far away, she was also surprised that the child was allowed to walk by herself.

Anna didn't have any direct experience with teaching, but growing up with parents who were teachers had exposed her to the idea of lesson planning and presenting new information in small increments. The children each had a piece of slate on which they practiced their numbers and letters. A teacher had previously come to the area once a week for families who had been able to pay him, but he had been missing for months without explanation.

"You can't believe how hard we must work to get our children a proper education. The Catholic children are allowed in the schools now, but they're treated like slop. It's the ones who've gone over to the Church of England that get the good treatment. We would just as soon have the bairns go to the hedge schools than have them treated like rubbish," said Glenis as she watched Anna prepare for her weekly tutoring session.

On the very first tutoring session held in the front room of the small cottage, Anna announced, "We'll practice writing today. I will show you a letter that I must write to my family in America, telling them where I am, and asking for them to write back as quickly as they can. You can all write a sentence to them as well."

The children practiced on pieces of slate until they had perfected their achingly polite sentences. Anna caught a glance pass between Glenis and Tom at the beginning of the lesson that looked like a sliver of relief.

Anna quickly saw that Michael was keen for numbers. She began to present him with rudimentary math, which he swallowed as if numbers had been the missing chinks in his brain. Everything about numbers made sense to the boy. Anna could nearly see his neurons galloping around his head, doing happy back flips as he chewed and savored numbers. It was on a day when both Anna and the boy had soared past long layers of addition, subtraction, and division and she'd seen through her scholar's eyes that he was ready to launch into algebra that they heard Tom calling for his boy with an edge to his voice. Anna startled, and a deep visceral strand in her gut tightened as she assumed an old role that was as natural for her as breathing.

"It's OK," she said to the boy. "Go out back, through the pantry, and I'll say that you weren't here. Go quickly, before your father gets here."

The boy looked at her quizzically. "I'll not lie to my Da," he said. "He needs me, and I forgot what I had promised him."

Anna's heart rate was going so fast that it stuttered. She had always protected her brother from their father whenever she'd been able. She'd placated, tiptoed, lied, thrown herself between them, whatever it had taken, however she'd been able to imagine. But there was little that had stopped the stream of venom that had spewed from her father to her brother.

And now she was suddenly to blame for causing young Michael to get in trouble with his father. She was gripped with fear. Having grown up in a house where father and son had battled nearly to the death of wills, she froze, as she had done so many times before, when she heard Tom's footsteps on the flagstones.

The door to the kitchen opened and Tom, his boots sticky with mud, held a bridle for one of their horses. "I can't grow two extra arms this day. When are you planning on joining me?" he asked Michael.

"Oh, Da, Anna was preparing to teach me the largest and strangest numbers I'd ever seen. I lost track of myself. I'm coming right now." The boy got up and grabbed a corner of hard bread as he left to join his father, whom he touched in an easy manner as he squeezed past him in the doorway.

Tom tipped his hat at Anna. "Sorry to drag off your student, but the horses don't know numbers from rocks." He smiled and gave a nod.

* * *

Anna did not remember her father ever touching her brother Patrick with anything other than an intent to hurt him. Even when he put his hand on Patrick's shoulder in what should have been a tender touch, Anna would see the bulge in her father's bicep, the deep grab of his fingers into her brother's thin shoulder, gripping bone and muscle in a promising threat. If their mother wasn't home, Patrick's mere presence would incite their father into a swift strike.

Somewhere stored in Anna was a cascade of memories of her dressed in footed pajamas with her cheek pressed against her father's stubble when he kissed her good night or swung her up on his shoulders. She never knew what was worse, the tender memories or the violent ones.

If she and Patrick were home together after school, her stomach clenched tight with the anticipation of her father's fresh delivery of anger. On such days, she watched Patrick attempt to become invisible so that his father would not see him and thus hate him. He became the blanket on the couch, rough and bumpy. But his boy scent would tip off the older bull of a man, who aimed his horns into the tender underbelly of the boy. Their father tore the blanket off his warm body and left the boy fluttering in the cold air.

"What are you hiding for? What have you done? What are you smiling about?" their father would snarl. And from that moment onward, there was no way to change the trajectory of events unless their mother stepped in the door. She calmed her husband like a drug. But if their mother was not at home, or if some delay took her protective force away from them, Anna knew that she was the only one who stood between her father and her brother.

Once when Anna was seven, old enough to see and hear everything, she watched in horror at the suddenly changed face of her father as he sat with his pre-dinner beer, waiting for Anna's mother to get home from the high school where she taught math. Anna looked at the clock. It was ten minutes after four. This was her mother's day to stay late for the math club, so she wouldn't be home until 4:45. That was too much time. She heard her father take three big gulps of his Heineken, an acceptable beer for the vice principal of the junior high school in the next town. The empty bottle tinged on the glass coaster.

"I asked you a question. What are you smiling at?"

Patrick was thirteen, skinny and hard. He had just walked into the house, only to be met full throttle by his father. To Anna, Patrick normally looked huge, towering over her when the two of them were home alone, arguing over the TV or who should get the last of the pizza. But in relation to her father, he looked like a stick, a milkweed that could be snapped in half.

Patrick tried to stand his ground, tried not to move his body in a way that would reveal anything. He clenched his backpack.

"I was thinking about school, about how Mr. Patterson said he liked my history project. That's all." He was in eighth grade and the very worst of things had not yet happened. Patrick took a tentative step toward the hallway to their bedrooms.

Anna looked at the clock. 4:20. Time had slowed to a tortuous crawl. She heard the living room clock ticking in a slow, watery drip. Patrick shifted his backpack minutely.

"I told you yesterday to clean your room. I don't suppose you remember that. I decided to give you a hand. Why don't you go take a look?" said their father.

Anna knew this was a trick; it had all the sounds of a trick, of a coyote making encouraging pup sounds to a housecat before it snapped its neck.

Patrick backed away from the living room and only turned when he was in the hallway. His footsteps quickened as he neared his bedroom. Anna followed him. At first she couldn't see into his room because Patrick's body blocked her sight. Then she ducked under his arm and saw.

All of Patrick's posters had been ripped off the walls and torn up. His soccer trophies from middle school had been ripped from their bases; everything, everything was piled high in the middle of his room, as if it had been a toxic dumpsite. Patrick's alarm clock was somewhere under the heap of his life. Anna could no longer see the time.

"I'll help you. I can help you fix it," Anna said as she grabbed his hand and pulled him into the room. She had to keep him in the room until their mother got home. Patrick's face reddened; the ruby tint started on his neck and traveled to his cheeks.

What else could Anna do? She could ordinarily distract Patrick or her father, but this was different, this was the first time that something had gone too far. She heard the creak of her father's chair and his crisp steps down the hall. Patrick and Anna stood on either side of the wrecked pile of her brother's possessions, the shreds of paper, the punctured soccer ball, the sheets balled up with a jumble of running shoes. Their father stopped in the doorway and leaned one hip into the doorframe. He crossed his arms and he smiled.

Anna worried that she'd freeze, as she did in her dreams when alligators chomped at her heels.

"So how do you like it? Next time I tell you to do something, do it. Don't make me go to all this trouble."

Patrick vibrated with rage. "I would have cleaned it. What did you want me to do? Make my bed? Pick up the clothes off the floor? I've seen you drop clothes on the floor."

And that was all their father had been waiting for—the opening, the excuse.

"Don't tell me about my clothes, my bedroom. Because this is my house and if I tell you to clean your room, you're going to clean your goddamn room."

"I'm not cleaning this," said Patrick.

"What did you say to me? What did you say?" Their father stepped into the room and grabbed Patrick by the front of his shirt. The backpack hissed to the floor.

"Daddy!" said Anna. "I'll clean his room."

But neither of them heard her. Their father lifted Patrick up against the wall until the tips of his running shoes dangled within inches of the floor.

"What did you say to me?" His face was unrecognizable, screwed up into a jumble of popping veins, red flesh and lip spittle.

Anna sprang on her father, pulling at his arm and with one powerful toss, Anna landed on the floor and slid into the baseboard. Thrown away, that's what it had felt like, tossed away.

Anna heard the front door open. A gust of air broke the vacuum seal in the bedroom. She pushed up and wiped tears off her face, a bit of snot from her lip.

"Where is everyone?" their mother yelled in her best teacher voice, trained to project to the farthest reaches.

"Mommy, we're here. We're in Patrick's room," said Anna, jutting her chin out at her father.

Their father released his grip on Patrick and turned toward his wife's clear voice. The presence of their mother had always been the determining factor, had always brought the father back from his train wreck of rage with Patrick. But the power of her presence was diluting with each new eruption.

In the year that Patrick entered high school, he grew four inches over the summer and into the fall. He grew so steadily and so quickly that Anna was sure she could hear him grow at night. She was sure his new size would crush the house with his height, with his size twelve feet, and the lower register of his voice. She no longer smelled the boy smell in his bedroom that was like the boys in her fourth-grade class. She felt the snake of fear travel across her neck with her brother's new scent. She had watched enough National Geographic specials to know what happened when a male came of age in a pack. The old bull, the elk, the alpha male, drove off the young buck. Their father needed no more excuse to drive Patrick out than to catch a scent of this new creature that had replaced the boy.

Anna had learned to bake cookies, and she had permission from her mother to bake them by herself. She was, after all, old enough to do such things. She would quickly throw together a batch of chocolate chip cookies, confident that the smell would drug her father and all of them into a sense of confused comfort. She would run to the basement and dig out the summer fan, plug it into the outlet near the kitchen door so that the sense of love and chocolate would be dense and powerful in every corner of the house.

She had to camouflage her brother, douse the house to cover the dangerous man smells that would eviscerate the last bit of safety that remained for Patrick. Then Anna noticed something strange; her mother began to cook also, stuffing her family with aromatic roast meats, bluefish, and French cheeses until even Anna could not force herself to take another bite. The mother and daughter worked in wordless tandem. Each night at dinner, the father would glare suspiciously at his son, his nostrils flaring to catch wind of something, then he would fall into the delirious pleasures of his food.

Patrick had stopped speaking at dinner and was in between sports so that he had no excuse but to be home. Fall soccer was over and wrestling season wouldn't start for two weeks. As they finished a calming bread pudding, dusted heavily with cinnamon, the phone rang. Teachers and principals took calls at all times; it could be for her mother, in which case it would be a parent of a student who was presently sobbing over her math homework. If it was for her father, it was a parent who wanted to negotiate about a child's suspension. Their mother picked up the beige wall phone and the family watched to determine which educational calamity was at stake.

"Alice? What's wrong? Oh, dear God. Yes, of course I'll come." Alice was their mother's best friend, another teacher at the high school. The family waited for the specifics of the bad news.

"That was Alice. Her husband has been in some sort of accident, she didn't say what exactly, something about the loading dock at the paper mill." She looked at her family, looked one second longer at her daughter. "Is everyone OK here? I've got to go. Alice is all alone at the hospital." She put on her coat.

Anna felt a prickle of fear starting in her knees. "Take Patrick with you, Mommy. He could drive. You look too upset," said Anna. And from the look on her mother's face, the pause, the dark cloud that ran across her eyes, Anna understood for the first time that her mother knew everything that happened when she left the house. That she was willingly leaving her daughter to be a waifish referee.

Her father clattered his knife to his plate. "He's only got a learner's permit, for Christ sake. Mary Louise, it's better for you to drive yourself. The kids have their homework. You don't know how long this will take." Who could argue with this?

Their mother had her coat on, car keys in hand, on her way to her best friend's urgent need, and Anna knew they couldn't stop her; she couldn't refuse to go. Her mother paused at the door.

"Charles, I'll call you from the hospital. I'll let you know how things are."

This was code for letting them all know that she was going to check on them. But it was not enough, not nearly enough.

Chapter 16

She wondered if they had been reported missing back in Massachusetts and what calamity had resulted from their disappearance. Who would miss her? Not Steve, her ex-husband. Her mother would, deeply and inconsolably. But not her brother, the coma patient; of all of them, he now had the simplest problem—he simply had to sleep. Even his breath was assisted by a respirator. Her friend Harper, her travel buddy, confidante, and late-night margarita drinker, might miss her, but she had gone directly from their Celtic trip to Peru. There was not a chance that Harper would give two thoughts to any calamity with Anna. Her other buddy from law school, Jasper, lived in L.A., specializing in entertainment law. So if he did miss her, there would be messages on her phone machine, curious at first, teasing, then petulant, then hurt. He would eventually take it personally and wonder if he'd done something wrong. Her friends knew that she had been traveling; they'd eventually think she had extended her trip. So it would only be her mother and Alice who knew that she and Joseph had fallen off the grid.

Anna was on her own to figure out something that appeared incomprehensible. She didn't know the rules of time travel. Is six weeks in the past equivalent to six weeks in her time? Could she get back to her time without anyone noticing because only five seconds had elapsed? Did time bend and whoosh round like a piece of seaweed pulled by the tides? She was beginning to think that what she had always understood to be true was only partly true or not true at all. She'd seen a five-year-old Joseph struggle with time concepts of today, yesterday, and tomorrow: she remembered him saying, "We're going to the park yesterday" and "Remember when I fell off my bike tomorrow?" She had been fascinated by the unnatural net that had had to be fit over the boy's brain to force him to grasp the generally accepted notion of time—that there is a past, a present, and a future, and they form one straight line. Everyone knows that. The past of twenty-four hours ago is yesterday. The future of twenty-four hours hence is tomorrow. The moment that we are inhaling a breath is now. Talking about a week in the past is preceded by *last,* as in *last week.* If it is one week in the future, it is preceded by next, as in *next week.* Once Anna broke it down for Joseph, she saw how hard it might be for a kid to understand. But she had never imagined that she would be the one who was completely wrong.

Stay on issue. Find the rule. Analyze. Then make a conclusion. This had worked so well in law school and later at the firm. But here, she found it hard to get past the issue. So time is somehow fluid, enough so that she and Joseph had tripped a switch and landed in the past, exactly 164 years prior to the time formerly and erroneously known as the present. She squawked at the lack of veracity. The how of it was the big question. And if this happened to Anna and Joseph, had it happened to anyone else? What had flipped the switch? And why Anna and Joseph, of all the unlikely combinations? Was the issue time, or was it Anna and Joseph?

Anna was having a hard time remembering what had happened immediately before the big time portal express. While studying liability in auto accidents, she had heard about retrograde amnesia: people often lost their memory of events leading up to an accident, often as much as hours prior to the accident. It was as if the brain short-circuited due to the trauma and erased memory banks right before an accident. Knowing what the memory gap was called was not particularly helpful to Anna, but it did ease her sense of knowing so little.

When she wasn't thinking about her life back in Massachusetts, her life in the future, her mother, her brother in the hospital, or the fate of her nephew, she was thinking about food. Anna was hungry; she had never been this hungry in her entire thirty-four years. She ate two potatoes in the morning, some kind of porridge midday that was potatoes mixed with oats, and when night fell on Tom and Glenis's cottage, they ate roasted potatoes. She had been here for more than two months and her gums had started to bleed when she'd scraped at her teeth with a sharpened stick in an effort to clean them. Her famously strong nails had begun to crack. And mostly, Anna craved protein. She fantasized about a filet mignon cooked rare, with a side of broccoli dripping with butter. An entire peach pie with lattice crust waited in the culinary wings. Without protein, a switch had turned deep in her belly, and she was howling for meat. One night she dreamed of meat cooking on a black, domed grill, sizzling, sending up curls of grease-scented smoke so delicious that it made her weep.

She had to get better nutrition. She wished that her life expertise had been more than political science, followed by law school. If her college friend Emily had been sucked back in time, she would have known how to search out herbs and plants to supplement her diet. What did Anna know about plants? Who'd had time to learn about anything else when they'd been on the fast track through law school, then to a coveted spot in a major law firm?

Think, think, she had to figure this out. She needed to stay healthy, she could not get sick in the past, where aspirin and antibiotics were still unimagined, where the idea of germs was unconsidered. What if she caught tuberculosis or the plague and died in the past? Wouldn't that erase the future, or at least her part of it? Would her death in the past cause a tear in the time space continuum and rip open the universe? What would happen if she was never born? What about those times that she had diverted her father's rage and Patrick had been spared a beating? What would have happened? Would Patrick have become even more damaged, less loved? Would her nephew have been born at all, would Joseph have braved a childhood with his fitful father without Anna latching onto him when he was a toddler, dragging him here and there, baking cookies with him, sending him books and paints and all that? What if he was never born?

This is exactly why time travel is a terrible idea, she thought as she walked the high fields around the cottage. Mistakes could be made anywhere, disturbing the order of the universe. What about the kids that she was teaching? She knew nothing about the history of math. What if she taught something that wasn't acknowledged or known in 1844? She felt sluggish and sad. She needed food.

Anna thought hard. *I need protein, and I need some goddamned green vegetables.* What did Emily used to drink? Rose hips tea, yes that was it, vitamin C, wild rose hips. The English hadn't made a law against rose hips yet. She could find those. And fish, and seaweed, whatever came out of the ocean was now going to be up for grabs. She was not going to die here.

Anna no longer used the walking stick, the *shillalah.* She trotted down the hill, testing her leg as she went. As she neared the house, she saw Glenis with Nuala on her hip.

"Glenis, can you show me where the wild roses grow? And you said you're ready to bring a load of seaweed up from Kinsale for fertilizer. I want to go with you," said Anna. "I'm going to make some seaweed soup."

Glenis squeezed her face up. "My Grannie made me eat seaweed soup. You're on your own with that." She wiped Nuala's runny nose with the tip of her apron. "Tom could use an extra pair of hands with the load of seaweed. He just said that it's time to dress the garden beds for the winter. And there are old rose bushes on the road into Kinsale, near the old monastery. What would you be wanting with those?"

"I want the rose hips to make a tea," said Anna, taking the young girl into her own arms so that Glenis could hang clothes.

The child looked fondly at Anna and placed a tiny hand on her cheek. "You are a lovely lady," said Nuala.

"Aye. Lovely and odd," said Glenis.

Anna's head ached from trying to understand the Irish language that people spoke to each other. No one seemed to expect her to understand the language. It sounded like nothing she had ever heard before plus German, which she didn't understand either. But she wasn't sure about the German part; perhaps it was a Slavic language. She was learning a few nouns. She liked the word for book—*leahbar*, rhyming with tower. And she liked something else about the language that dropped her deeper into the land, into the music of the place. Glenis, Tom, and the children helped her learns bits and pieces.

The structure of the language pulled her into a direct relationship with anyone she spoke with. If someone asked her, "Are you walking to the blacksmith?" she learned to answer by falling in step with the question and responding, "I am not walking there." As a lawyer, she was used to asking questions for which the answer was absolutely yes or no. Glenis told her, "You say yes or no like the English do, as if all the world fits only one way or the other. We don't think that way. You see, the hope can't be scratched out of us. There is always a place where a thing is mostly not, or tis, but only for a wee bit. We Irish are much more specific about what is and what is not."

But Glenis couldn't hide her amazement that Anna was learning the Irish language at all. Anna figured it had to be those years on the bassoon; their band teacher had told them repeatedly that kids who studied music also learned languages easier. Anna's mother had insisted that she study an instrument in junior high and high school. Her mother had agreed with the music teacher. "It's about your brain," her mother had said. "Musical training will develop parts of your brain that will help you learn languages, and possibly math too, but the jury is still out on that one." Anna had suffered with the clarinet until eighth grade, when the band teacher had said that they'd needed someone to play the bassoon. Anna had raised her hand and never looked back. She'd played it for the next five years.

Anna tried to explain to Glenis. "I studied music, which helps some with learning languages. I have an ear for them, that's all."

"Some people love that you're beginning to speak the language. But others are suspicious, and you can't blame them entirely. Kathleen O'Connell was heard to say that this is absolute proof that you're a British spy. But I said to her, when has an Englishman ever been able to speak Irish? They can't do it, it's not that they won't; they can't work it out. Anna's too smart to be English. That's what I told them."

"Thank you, Glennie. Will it cause problems for you if I keep learning it? I mostly learn it from the children when I teach them on Sunday nights."

Glenis flicked a bit of straw from her skirt. "I want my children to be more than beasts of burden. You keep teaching them and let them bring you along in Irish."

The two women walked arm in arm along the streets of Kinsale. Anna felt suddenly bold and playful. *"Is mise munteoir,"* she said, in what she hoped was a passable accent.

Glenis stopped and raised an eyebrow, looking up at Anna. "Indeed you are the teacher. A very odd-sounding teacher, but yes, my dear, you are the teacher."

Chapter 17

"Come along and meet the best horse in Ireland, or he is such for me," Glenis had said after the midday porridge had been served to Tom and the children. The two women and Glenis's daughters walked down the long road toward Kinsale. Mary and Nuala held hands and stopped at every beguiling fern or perplexing rock that called to them from the roadside. The cooler winds of late October had found even this southern coast of Ireland, and Anna had to pull a shawl around her shoulders when the chill sought her bones.

Both sides of the road were lined with hedge rows that nearly obstructed their view of the fields on either side. Glenis led them along a smaller lane that ran uphill to a freshly whitewashed cottage. A powerful horse galloped along the pasture, creating a chorus of trilling sounds from the girls.

"O'Connell, O'Connell. We've come to visit," announced Mary. Both girls reached into the fence with their small hands, and it was only the horse's accommodating bow that allowed them to come anywhere near his head.

"This is the great Daniel O'Connell," said Glenis, who also

reached out to stroke the dark mane that had flopped to one side.

"That's an odd name for a stallion," said Anna, who knew next to nothing about horses.

Glenis and the girls suddenly stopped speaking and erupted in laughter.

"Now you can't tell me that horses are so different in America that geldings and stallions look the same. O'Connell is a gelding. Just take a look," said Glenis with a tilt of her head to the horse's flanks.

Anna looked and nodded in what she hoped was a convincing manner.

"You do know that geldings are castrated, don't you now?"

"Well, of course I do," said Anna, putting that bit of equestrian knowledge into an almost blank file.

"And please don't tell me you've not heard of Daniel O'Connell in America? He's a champion of the Irish people; the only one who has worked his way into the British parliament and is a royal burr in their backside," said Glenis.

At some point Anna had stopped berating herself about her deficits in Irish history. She knew more than most people, but that was due mostly to Jasper, her buddy in law school whose first summer clerking job had landed him in the historical archives researching an Irish claim of genocide on the part of the English during the famine years. The claim was widely ridiculed in the law firm, but he'd been assigned to the grunt work in his first months with the firm.

He'd summed it up in one of his long emails. "Your people didn't just get screwed in the 1845 famine; they'd been screwed for hundreds of years before that. The convenience of an airborne fungus that wiped out their last remaining crop and one million Irish was just the icing on the cake. Another two million emigrated the hell out of there. Our firm dropped this claim like a hot potato. Get it?"

Anna knew the worst famine to ever hit Ireland would arrive with the first crop of potatoes in 1845. Yet here was Glenis, laughing with her two daughters at Anna's lack of common sense and general knowledge, unaware of the tsunami that would hit them within the year.

"There is too much that I don't know," said Anna. She reached down and picked up wiggling Nuala. "Even this little girl knows more than I do about horses and Daniel O'Connell." Anna gave the child a quick hug and put her back down again.

They said their good-byes to O'Connell and began walking home.

Anna let it be known that her primary mission was to find Joseph. But the complexities of what to do once she found him had to remain unspoken—not that she knew what to do other than find him and then find a way home. If they had time traveled one way, there had to be a way to travel back again. And she had to do this while protecting Tom and Glenis, and not interfering with their life any more than she already had. Teaching the kids on Sunday afternoons was as far as she could go; math and English would not change the course of the universe. Doing long division in 1844 had to be the same as doing long division in the twenty-first century.

There was a sweetness to the way of life that Tom and Glenis had, despite the backbreaking rigor of it. The couple was absolutely certain that they would be together forever;

that was clear. To survive, one had to be a member of a family, a "clan" as Glenis said. They knew every person in a thirty-mile radius—if not personally, then by association. A man in the desolate peninsula of Beara might never have stepped into the town of Kinsale, but Tom knew that his cousin in Cork was a mason of the first order. In this way, Tom was connected to the man in the windswept crags of the peninsula.

Anna longed for the familiarity of their world. She knew only one of her neighbors at home in Rockport and that was only because the neighbor's dog, a scruffy miniature poodle, had appeared at her door one day. Anna had scooped up the shivering dog and carried it to the closest house. Because of a lost dog, she knew one neighbor. Here in the world of Glenis and Tom, she already knew many more people, and people knew about her before they ever met her. She was knitting into their family, and she knew it from the hunger that wrapped around her and everyone else. Her belly was pulled in with hunger; she ran her palms over the expanse between the ridges of her hip bones, the knob of the pubic bone and the faraway ribs. The hunger wove her in with Tom and Glenis, their three children, and their yearning for each day's warmth of porridge, a slosh of potatoes, and buttermilk in a sea of water, extending it so each mouth received a full, hot dose of the elemental food source. Anna's insistence on seaweed soup did little to stem the constant hunger. The less they had, the more Anna felt like she belonged with them in their quest to live and eat.

As the rhythm of their life revealed itself more and more, she noted that people came and went, stopping to speak with Tom in his blacksmithing building. This did not at first register as anything but the normal drumbeat of life in a coastal village. That they were often men did not send up a red flag; of course men would cluster around a guy like Tom. He had an unflappable nature that would draw others to him, a sureness that resonated in him whether he was bartering for food, tending his potato patch, managing his other tenant farmers, or grappling with a sick calf. Of course a steady stream of men would stop by the local blacksmith, and yet . . .

Anna finally distinguished a pattern. Almost all of the visits were at night, which made sense in a hardworking community; they saved their recreation until the day's work was done. But it was the fact that the same faces appeared with the same regularity. And they never carried lanterns, never.

"Why don't your friends carry a light to guide them home?" asked Anna. Tom had just said good-bye to three solemn-looking young men. "I'd be afraid that I'd fall off a cliff without a light, especially on misty nights like this."

Tom looked first at Glenis, as if all his words had been used up. Glenis crossed the room to move to her husband's side. "They know the roads by heart, and lamp oil is dear. There's no need for a light," she replied.

The couple had pulled in tight, closing ranks, standing side by side with no room to spare between them, one finishing a thought that made the other weary. Anna envied them for their certainty. There was no question of their marriage lasting, there was only a question of surviving together. But Anna wanted to know what the two of them weren't telling her, because it was becoming clear that there was a subtext to life here and she wanted to know what it was. Any bit of knowledge that she could gather might let her find Joseph and find their way home.

"Of course they would know the roads by heart. What was

I thinking? And now it is time for me to go to sleep before I ask any other overly obvious questions of my two hosts." She felt a sudden fondness for the young couple. She headed for her tiny alcove of a room where her bed waited for her. On the way she kissed each of them on the cheek, as she had seen so many people do here. They were her only link to finding Joseph. They had promised that they would help her find him.

Several days later, as Anna headed for the door first thing in the morning, eager for fresh air, she was startled by an unusual sight. Anna was not a horse person; she was intimidated by their size and power, and the specter of her sister-in-law's death in a riding accident was ever prominent. But even she noticed that the chestnut mare that she had tentatively nuzzled behind the ears for weeks had been replaced by a speckled mare. The chestnut mare was gone. She heard Tom's footsteps on the flagstone steps, returning from an early morning milking.

"Tom, someone has switched horses on you," Anna said, knowing immediately how idiotic this sounded.

Tom said nothing. He set down the bucket filled with warm milk. She had started to adjust to the interminable pauses between sentences that people of this time used. No one talked over the middle of someone else's sentence. And they were profoundly good listeners, taking in a speaker's words as if they'd been tender and precious. She'd learned to count to thirty after asking a question; people needed this much time or more to collect their thoughts. No one was multitasking here.

The morning fog was raw, filtering into Anna's bones. She counted to thirty, and still Tom did not respond.

"Where is the other mare? I know I'm being too direct, too nosy, but I'm an inquisitive person and I can't help but notice things. It's what I do. When I went to sleep last night, the chestnut mare was here and now the sun is just peeking over the horizon and there is a different horse in its place that looks like she needs some fattening up. What happened?"

Tom took off his hat, ran his fingers through his dark hair, and put his hat back on again. She counted to thirty again before he finally replied.

"I can't legally have two horses. And I can't have one horse that looks too grand. If they see that I have one horse worth more than five pounds, then they have the right to take it from me. Oh, they'll give me the five pounds, but the horse would truly and rightfully be worth far more. So when I feed the mare regular and her flanks fill out, then we have to run her out to the high meadows and switch her off with my other horse that has to fend mostly for herself, eating off the hillsides. My cousin brought me the other horse last night and rode out with the mare you've come to know, taking her to the high meadows."

Anna's thoughts flew into legal hyper speed, stuck on the law about having a horse that was worth too much. She looked at the speckled mare, her ribs and pelvic bones showing clearly through her hide.

"So you cannot appear to acquire more than the British believe you are due."

"That's one way of saying it. The same goes for the value of our house. If we improve the condition by building on another room, then the value of the house goes up and we would be charged more, and in most cases far more than the house is worth."

"You have two horses but must appear to only have one. But what about O'Connell? Is he yours or your neighbor's horse? He seemed awfully fond of Glenis."

"Fond, you say? Those two are in love with each other. Glenis would some days sooner brush the gelding than cook our porridge. And you've rightfully discovered our third horse. We've had O'Connell since the day he dropped to the ground. We keep him at the good neighbor's to make it look like they own him. What can we do? We are Irish and we love the horses."

Chapter 18

"Cork is rich and fertile; anything can grow here, anything. But the Irish are an odd lot. They lack the spirit of enterprise, and it's a great pity," lectured the colonel.

The colonel, Joseph, and Sean, the stable hand, rode along the outskirts of a village. A herd of sheep was being walked through its tight streets, blocking the way. To Joseph's surprise, the colonel pulled his horse off the way to let the sheep pass, followed by a barefoot boy. Joseph had imagined that his benefactor would rear up his great horse and clatter over the sheep, roaring like a lion.

"It's not about dignity, lad, it's about commerce," he said, catching the look of surprise on Joseph's face. "There's an inn on the far side of the town, which is not far at all, and that is where we will stay for tonight."

After the sheep passed, they rode through the village and stopped at the Farmer's Arms. Sean slipped off his horse and made ready for the colonel to dismount. He took the reins of all three horses and led them to the stable.

As they walked up to the door of the pub, Joseph saw a flyer nailed to the door. *Parish Wrestling Tournament, Saturday*.

"Look, sir," said Joseph. He had easily fallen into the habit of calling the colonel sir, something he had never in his life done before. He noted how easy it was to change into someone else. "There's a wrestling tournament tomorrow. Will we still be here?"

The older man smiled. "They think they've invented wrestling the way they carry on. Big farmers with mud on their hands. In England, wrestling is a gentleman's sport."

The colonel pulled open the door, and the tang of a turf fire greeted them, laced with aromas of something like soup, followed by layers of men's sweat and pipe smoke. Joseph's eyes began to water as soon as he stepped into the pub. The air felt filled with tiny bits of gravel, all of which kept dropping into his eyes.

"Innkeeper," the colonel intoned. The hum of jovial voices dimmed and quieted. "Have you a proper room for the night, for me and the young lad?"

This didn't sound like a question, this sounded like a summons. The innkeeper looked a lot like Joseph's father, dark-haired with a dusting of freckles, dark eyebrows that formed a ridge, like a declaration. He wiped his hands on his pants and said, "A room, sir? Yes indeed, we have a room. Give us a moment while me good wife prepares the room for you. We've a fine brisket that's ready for eating. Sit down, eat a bit, and the room will be ready."

The other men in the pub looked at Joseph and the colonel, their eyes reading them only as long as they dared. Then they looked away. Joseph needed fresh air. He was still unaccustomed to rooms thick with smoke.

"I'll go and give Sean a hand, sir," he said as he bolted for the door and a release from the density of the pub. He gulped in fresh air and trotted off in the direction of the stables, where he'd last seen Sean. He heard the thrill of competition before he saw it, heard the timeless sound of people wagering, urging on others. When he came around the back of the pub, he saw two men circling each other, with crouched knees, intent looks of winning in each face, a crowd of people around them.

"Come on, lads, give us a show, give us a show," said one of the men in the crush of onlookers.

Wrestling. Right here, right now. Joseph suddenly felt anchored and real, not struggling to guess the right answers, as he so often did with the colonel. Joseph pushed his way to the front of the small crowd, sliding between people like a fish, slick and young. The late afternoon sun cast a warm glow over the two men who circled each other, knees flexed, arms loose and ready, eyes focused on each other. Finally, here was something that Joseph understood—wrestling.

One of the men looked like he'd been selected for his height and body mass. He must have been over six feet tall, maybe six foot two. The other man was more slight, a likely candidate for the 160-pound class, of which there had been few at Joseph's school.

One of the guys had to be the local champion. Joseph could see the confidence in his shoulders, his smile, and the open invitation that he gave his opponent. This wouldn't take long; the local champ was going to take this guy to the mat with the first throw. The champ had red hair, stiff and curly with the requisite thick neck. The late rays of sun played off the hairs on the man's arm, and for a second, he glowed golden. They danced slowly, walking around each other, each tapping the other's arm, circling and taking one million years longer than any wrestlers would ever take in high school. Then, like a pit viper, the champ struck, flipping his hapless opponent over before he even hit the ground, pressing both shoulder blades into the dirt, smiling a big toothy grin the whole time.

"That's the way," cheered the men and women who had gathered behind the inn.

Another contender, this time a larger man, bigger than Red, stepped forward, sure of his weight. Given weight or speed, a wrestler has the clear advantage with speed, and Red had speed. A few men from the crowd cheered the new challenger.

"You can take him John. Jaysus, you could crush him."

John was a big man, broad in shoulders and gut. He had lived a life of assuredness due to his size, but Joseph could see from his clumsy movements that Red could sidestep him and use the man's weight against him. John lurched forward like a bear, arms wide, and too much weight on the front of his feet. They grappled for a long bit, holding each other like star-crossed lovers. Then Red let the man fall and pinned him in three slick moves.

Joseph saw a tree full of birds, funny-looking crows that Deirdre had said were hoodie crows. They cawed to each other, as if evaluating the wrestlers, and then grew silent, gazing down in unison at the two men in the center of the crowd. Joseph looked up as if to say, Should I? One of the crows made the strange quacking sound that they sometimes made. Joseph took that as a sign.

When Big John got off the ground, slapping dirt off his pants and elbows, he shook hands with the champion. Joseph knew the feeling, the winner shaking your hand. It felt just like he was grabbing your balls and yanking on the short hairs. Joseph stepped into the crudely marked circle, a stick here, a rock there. He knew the boundaries by heart.

"I'll challenge you, sir," he said, attempting to lower the register of his voice.

Heads swiveled around. It was his accent. He knew by now that it was a showstopper, but there was nothing he could do about it except use it to his advantage, which is what he hoped for in this instance. Joseph gave the silence a few more seconds.

"I'm traveling and I'd be honored if you'd accept my challenge," he said, letting the words hang foreign and heavy in the alcohol-scented air of the crowd.

Big Red was thrown off for a nanosecond. Joseph saw it—the slight downturn of his mouth, just the beginnings, before his brilliant champion's smile returned.

"You're welcome to it, lad, but you best be warned, I'm the parish champion. Have you ever wrestled, wherever it is that you came from?" asked Red.

"Oh, just take him and be done with it," said a man from deep in the crowd.

Red offered a welcoming bow to Joseph. "Come forward, lad, and prepare to get your finery stained with our best mud."

Speed, balance, and surprise. Accuracy and persistence. This had been drilled into Joseph since the first day of wrestling. And he had the advantage of having watched Red's style for two rounds. That was all it ever took Joseph to read another wrestler.

Joseph walked into the circle and they nodded to each other. As soon as the nod hit the downward end, Joseph struck, foot placed, hand on Red's opposite shoulder, and slammed him to the earth, bouncing the smile off his face. Red struggled, and Joseph wrapped a practiced leg over him; with a sharp, persistent move that came from the core of his torso, he pushed both of Red's shoulder blades into the earth.

"Call it. He's down," said a man.

Joseph released Red and held his winning hand out to the loser to help him get up. He gave the hand an extra squeeze.

From the crowd, Joseph heard a familiar voice. The colonel.

"So, lad, you're a wrestler."

Joseph saw what looked like pride and admiration in the colonel's eyes. He felt a void deep in his chest fill with warmth.

"Yes, sir, I'm a wrestler."

Joseph knew that old people, like his teachers, had no idea what it was like to be a kid. Or they understood what it was like when they were kids, but they were clueless about being a kid now. How every rich kid in town had gone off to private school when high school had started, how the rest of the kids who'd been left behind had quickly closed ranks before Joseph had had time to figure out what group was his. And he'd been left on the outside of everything at school, along with the few other dazed kids who'd also been among the unaffiliated.

He had tried to explain this to his grandmother, who was the head of the math department at the high school. At least she'd breathed the same wretched air as he had, every day, in the same building, which had looked like a backdrop for that Charles Dickens book they'd had to read.

Joseph had been at the top of his class in science and math until high school had come along and he'd been left in the outer perimeters, until the heart of school had gotten ripped out for him. His grandmother had said, "Your grades have dropped like a rock. What's going on?"

He'd tried to explain to her. "Do you know when the kids are passing in the halls and some kids always walk together and look kinda happy and they're loud and talking to each other and stuff?"

"Yes."

"And do you notice how some kids hug the walls, keep their eyes down, and pray that no one says anything to them?"

"Perhaps."

"And there are the kids you don't notice, because no teachers ever notice them, not the teachers, coaches, or the principal. They're the kids who sneak up to you and say to Suzanna Emmons, 'Bitch. Ugly fat ass.' Or to the special ed-ers, they say, 'Retard, go home and bag groceries.' Or to me they say, 'Don't touch me, scumbag. Don't walk on this side of the hall ever.' But they say worse stuff too, but I can't say the swear words to you that they use."

His grandmother had stopped grading papers. She'd taken off her reading glasses.

"I'm on the outside, Gram, and it's not going to change," he'd continued. "This is how it will be all the way through high school. I didn't know my life could suck this much. There is no one who will even sit with me at lunchtime. I spend lunch in the bathroom or the library."

He hadn't told this to anyone before—certainly not to his father, and not to his aunt Anna, either. The world had turned such a miserable corner that he hadn't even known if he could really trust his Gram, but he had always trusted her more than anyone, so she'd been worth a try.

"Wrestling," she'd finally said.

"What?"

"You heard me. Wrestling. It was the thing that saved your father, as much as he could be saved. He loved the hand-to-hand combat that wrestling offered. And I think he liked the physical contact too. When he and your grandfather were going through their bad times, your father won most of his matches. He went to state finals one year."

"I told you that my life is torture and you think joining the wrestling team is going to help?"

"I think stepping inside one of these groups is essential; you can't go it alone. Why not wrestling? It's very unique, ancient and primal. And I know the wrestling coach."

That had sealed his fate. He'd gone to the wrestling coach's office the next afternoon, suited up after school, and gotten his face shoved in a wrestling mat. What his grandmother hadn't known was that on the hierarchy of sports in high school, wrestling didn't even reach the bottom rung. But at least he'd gotten on the ladder, and for that he'd been grateful. And like his grandmother had said, you never knew when wrestling might be useful.

Chapter 19

Joseph reveled in his new status as wrestling champion. A champion? Who would have imagined that he would be a champion anywhere? His coach had told him that he would move up in the ranks as he got better, but Joseph had never guessed that wrestling could take him this far. He was especially pleased that he could wrestle without the embarrassment of the tight Lycra unitard that announced every boner to the sparse crowd in the stands. No mats; this was strictly on the ground. And of course no headgear, nothing covering his ears. He worried that someone would take the chance and rip on his ears just because they could. Finally, here was something that Joseph knew about. No, not just knew about: he was fucking fantastic at wrestling compared to these local guys. Well, to be honest, the local guys from the past.

If the colonel had treated Joseph like a privileged guest before, now he was a rock star. True, there had been no rock stars in 1844, but if there had been, he would have been one. Once the colonel saw that Joseph could pin the parish champion as if he had been no more than a hapless honeybee, everything changed.

Over the next several months, Joseph competed in four wrestling tournaments and won all of them while barely mussing his hair. He had the benefit of an additional 164 years of science and study about wrestling. His opponents were strong men from the villages who called themselves wrestlers. They thought that hard physical labor from farming or blacksmithing or fishing should be enough to win at a sport like wrestling. But the colonel's young lad from the Canadian Provinces—Joseph Blair, as he was known—cut through the local competition with shocking precision.

Each match was the same. Joseph watched his opponent's feet; that was number one. The second thing he did was shake his rival's hand. So far, every wrestler he faced had been poorly trained. They went in for endurance grappling, circling each other to kill time, holding each other up and pushing hard into each other with their legs. Joseph had had two years of training from a hard-ass coach, whom he now silently thanked each time he wrestled a big, bulked-up Irish man.

Wrestling was done barefoot, which Joseph at first saw as a disadvantage. He'd always worn wrestling shoes, light and flexible, which had given him a grip on the mats. But barefoot wrestling on the ground revealed his opponent even more quickly. Most of the men stood with one foot pointing slightly at an angle. When this happened, Joseph knew the takedown would be swift. With one foot pointing straight ahead and one foot even fifteen degrees out from center, he could fake to the turned-out leg, then lunge for the straight leg (which took longer for the opponent to move), reach in behind the thigh and lift it up, flip the guy on his back, and let two shoulder blades smack the ground. Then he'd hold him and release. The guy never knew what hit him.

The added bit of information was in the handshake. If asked to explain it, Joseph would have had a hard time doing so. But he knew instantaneously, in one transmission of hand sweat and electrical impulses, if he could take down his opponent. It was a mountain of information that flowed from one person to another, and it happened in the two seconds that the hands touched. Joseph could tell each time that he was faster and more precise than every other wrestler that he met, even though his opponents were generally bigger and older. There seemed to be only the vaguest of weight categories.

Joseph had to harness all his energy in every muscle of his body for no more than five minutes. So far, it had been for no more than three minutes. His matches had been lightning fast; he'd had the advantage of surprise in his first parish matches against local champions. Now, his reputation was spreading out like a wet stain and he could no longer count on the element of surprise. He would have to count on his precision.

His last opponent had expected him to be fast.

"Give us a true match, lad, not your fast flipping magic," he'd said at the handshake.

But all Joseph had noticed had been the plea and the hesitation in the handshake, the vulnerability in the outward turn of one foot.

"Nice to meet you," Joseph had said before doing a magnificent fireman's throw. His coach would have said he was being too much of a show-off, but the euphoria of throwing a big man made him jubilant for days.

The colonel had quickly seen the advantage of betting on Joseph Blair, the strange lad from Canada, and he was pulling in more money than he had made on his last horse races.

He offered Joseph every luxury and squired him about like royalty. Joseph did everything he could for the colonel, earning him money on every match, and he drank in the praise of the most powerful man he had ever met.

This was what it was like to have everything, to be in love, and to be admired. As he walked through the village of Tramore, children pointed to him and stage-whispered, "Champion." Thoughts of home intruded from time to time, but if he saw the ghostly apparitions of the future coming toward him—his grandmother checking his math homework, his wrestling coach, Anna, his father—he batted them away like he used to do in T-Ball. His grandmother had been his T-Ball instructor, her baseball cap turned backwards, and she'd told him that if he had any troubles, he could make them go away by smacking that ball for all it was worth. He'd pictured the plastic bat sending all future thoughts into the air, far out over the ocean.

In order for him to fit in as well as possible with the people in general, he decided that the best thing to do here was not to take sides, because even someone who had faked reading his history book could see that the Irish and the English had some smackdown problems with each other. He wished he could tell the Irish that everything was going to turn out OK for them, that they'd get to be their own independent country again someday. But for now, he wanted to ride the wave of living in both worlds, because clearly there were some disadvantages to being Irish—being dirt poor, for example. He could remain the favorite of the colonel and still be friends with the Irish, or at least with Deirdre and Taleen, and if he had Deirdre on his side, there were no Irish on the estate who would cross him.

Only Con seemed less friendly to him. He didn't know why at first. Con was a boy just like him. Well, not like him. He was Irish and the stonemason's son. Joseph was Irish too, except it was different coming from the Irish and living in America; that's hardly Irish at all, and nobody here needed to know anything about it. Joseph slipped down to the kitchen level of the house to talk with Deirdre.

"That's Con's entire job, keeping the fireplaces lit?" he asked.

Deirdre was boiling apples for sauce, and she stirred the kettle with a large flat paddle. The kettle hung on a hinge that could be moved over the fire or back out again. She tasted the glaze of apple left on the wooden paddle and tossed in a pinch of cloves.

"There are nine bedchambers, one ballroom, the gun room, the library, the conservatory (well, that doesn't have a fireplace), the fine china room, several dressing rooms, the laundry room, and if you added all those up on a full and busy day when relatives from England are here, or when a hunt is in progress, Con would be up two hours before the sun rises and not entirely finished until long after the last person is asleep. That's the winter life for him. The rest of the year he's apprenticing with his father, the stonemason."

"How long does he have to apprentice, I mean before he could be a stonemason on his own?" Joseph sat hunched by the side of the fireplace. He had woken up chilled. Deirdre had given Joseph a mug of hot mead, and the odd warmth of it expanded his torso.

"Oh, I'd say five years if he is bright, which Con is. Then if he is to become a master stonemason, that's years more. But it's all up to the stonemasons themselves. Half the time they

speak their own language, not Irish, not English. I don't try
to get it, don't have room enough in my head, but they speak
the language of rock and the slow way that rocks move and
sigh. I only know this because me own husband was a stonemason. My first husband that is, back when I was young and
the babies were popping out of me like the seeds of a tree."

Should he ask what happened to her first husband, and
would that have been Taleen's father? He wanted to know everything about Taleen. And where was she? He got up from
his warm perch and walked the length of the kitchen, past
the wooden firkins of butter that had arrived yesterday, past
the barrels of apples that Deirdre had drawn from just this
morning. He opened the door to the garden courtyard and
gave what he hoped was a casual peek outside.

"She's not here this morning," Deirdre called to him.

Joseph jumped, irritated that his intention was so obvious.
When he looked across the long room, he saw that Deirdre's
back was to him. He shivered, knowing that she had seen
through his intense need to locate Taleen. If his friend Oscar
had been here, Joseph would have said to him, "I'm not shitting you man, Deirdre can see what you're doing even without looking at you."

Deirdre looked over her shoulder at Joseph.

"She's at the hedge school. She attends when the colonel is
gone. He doesn't see the need for her to attend school."

"What kind of school is a hedge school?"

Deirdre swung the kettle of apples away from the fire.

"You don't know much, do you, lad? I suppose in the
provinces of Canada, life is different. But here the English
wouldn't allow Irish Catholics to attend school of any sort,
so those who could teach set up in a meadow or lean-to or

a barn, and children go there to learn Greek and Latin and their computations. Not all scholars are good at teaching, but this one is."

Deirdre popped the top off a barrel and, with a frighteningly large knife, excised a hunk of lard, which she dropped on the worktable. She scooped a handful of flour from a bowl, plopped it on the lard, and began to push at it with the heel of her hands.

Joseph had seen the colonel's library, with its rows of musty books, floor to ceiling. But he was starting to get the picture of who could do what here, and he knew Taleen would not be permitted to touch the colonel's books. Joseph was already concocting a plan, already imagined leaving the library with a book or two beneath his coat, which he could present to Taleen.

The colonel was not due back for a week or so. A trip to London still held him. Surely Joseph could borrow books from the library without notice while the colonel was gone. And even when the guy came back, Joseph was sure he could tap into the abundance of entitlement that the colonel had cloaked him in. Joseph had even begun to ring the long cord that led to a bell in each room, which would bring a servant clipping to his call.

"Thanks for the drink," Joseph said to Deirdre, sliding the mug toward the wash table. He headed up the staircase to the main level of the house and went directly to the library, where he paused in midstep; he suddenly knew why Con was stiff with him now. He had wanted to hook up with Taleen, that was it. Con had had his sights on Taleen until Joseph had arrived. No one had ever been jealous of Joseph before, although he had been jealous of nearly everyone else in his former life as high school outcast. He stepped into the library and basked in the full glory of having everything.

He would do anything for Taleen. The first time Joseph had caught the memory of her scent on his skin, his heart had quavered and beaten faster. It had been something like being hungry and filled at the same time, air racing beneath his ribs, but unlike anything else he'd ever felt in his entire life. Where the sky had been pale before, now it was shockingly blue, scorching his eyes. If he closed his eyes, he saw Taleen and he wanted to know only her. He wanted to swoop her up and carry her away. This was the kind of love that lasted forever, and it was a miracle that he had found it.

If he concentrated enough, he could make his thoughts jump into her heart, he was sure of it. He ran his fingers along the backs of his hand, and a jolt of electricity shot through him. He could not sit; he could only pace with a rhythm that matched the strum of his heart. He constructed a list of reasons to see her, ways to avoid the too-watchful eye of the colonel when he returned. Joseph knew, absolutely knew better than he'd ever known anything before, that Taleen wanted him. He could feel her wanting him, could feel the gold cord that ran from the center of his chest to the center of her sparrow ribs.

The best thing to do under circumstances like these was wrestling practice, and Joseph had already agreed to practice every day. Every afternoon, the two stable boys, Sean and Owen, were assigned to Joseph as wrestling partners, but Joseph had to teach them freestyle wrestling before they would be of any use as practice buddies. Joseph didn't know how to teach, so the wrestling sessions were a series of sustained humiliations for the two boys, who kept getting pinned to the ground instantly by Joseph. The alpha status felt like a drug, like the one time he'd taken X and his heart had split open with expansiveness.

Owen and Sean hung their heads.

"You've got to give us a chance. We can't be your mates at this if we don't know the landscape," said Sean after being flipped to the ground and neatly pinned yet again.

Joseph fought with the impulse to keep using them as his guaranteed-to-fail opponents, because how often was he ever going to get that? He could demonstrate his mastery, strut his prowess. The absolute icing on the cake was that Taleen saw him winning every practice match. There she was, leaning into the fence, her slight frame resting like a dragonfly paused in flight, her wings glittering, her young dragon of a dog, Madigan, standing next to her.

She scanned the scene, watched Joseph pin first Owen, then a slump-shouldered and reluctant Sean. Joseph's penis sprang unbidden under her far-off gaze, but when he looked up to wave at Taleen and drink in her admiration, she was gone.

He dismissed Sean and Owen and trotted after her, wending toward where he thought she might go, back to the bustling kitchen, the underworld of her mother, Deirdre, and all the other kitchen and house staff.

"Hey, Taleen," he shouted when he caught sight of her. He picked up his pace and came even with her. Madigan took hold of his arm in his soft mouth, a special greeting reserved for Joseph.

"Taleen," he said, softer this time, wiping dog saliva on his pants. "Did you see our wrestling practice?"

She whirled around, her dark tendrils whipping across her face like seaweed. "Practice? Is that what you call it? Cruel is what you should call it. You're kicking those boys silly. They don't know what you're doing. They'd never wrestled once in their lives until you and your colonel came back excited as garden geese about you being the brilliant wrestler. Cruel, Joseph, that's what I call it."

Joseph did not sleep that night. He spent the hours trying to figure out how teachers taught something new. All he could think of was using his father's method of yelling, humiliation, scolding, slamming a few doors, and cursing a blue streak. Then he remembered the way his grandmother had tutored him in math. She'd taken things one step at a time, and she'd always served brownies at the end.

He talked to Deirdre the next morning. He explained how the extra food was a part of his training plan.

"Not every day, lad. We can't have that. Send them to the back door of the kitchen every other day after your wrestling matches. I'll find something for them," said Deirdre.

Joseph announced his new wrestling plan to Sean and Owen.

"Today, we're starting with the wrist hold. And we'll keep doing it until you can do it in your sleep."

Sean and Owen eyed him suspiciously. "Then you won't be grinding us into the dirt today?"

"No. See, there's no point in that. Prepare to learn the gentlemanly sport of wrestling," he said, as if it had been his idea all along.

Chapter 20

Deirdre and Taleen slept together on exceptionally cold nights. The small peat fire glowed, and the mother and daughter curled into each other. Both of them allowed their hair to be unfastened. Taleen's dark hair flowed into her mother's hair, which had only recently begun to sprout bits of white around her temples. They talked quietly to each other.

"There are good reasons not to use the sight," said Deirdre. "Aye, just as many reasons to use it as not to use it. It's always there, niggling at you. You can't throw it off, but there is always the choice of using it or not, or speaking of it. You don't think the sea eagle ever stops searching, do you? Oh, he must sleep and who knows what the sea eagle dreams. But sure, when he's awake, he never stops using that which he was given."

Taleen picked at a fingernail that had been bothering her all day. "How do I know when it's the sight that's niggling at me or only something that I want so very much?"

"That is my point, daughter. How can I talk with you about what you want without using my own sight? I see him all over you, your young Joseph. I see you wanting him. It shows on your shoulders and dances along your ears."

Taleen worried for the first time that too much sight raced around her and her mum, depriving her of sole access to her thoughts and desires. "I knew it the moment he was lifted from the sea and brought to us. All of my life was meant for that moment," she sighed.

"Oh, Taleen, you are so young, and a seventh daughter lives so long that all this will be hard to remember one day . . ."

Taleen sat up in bed. "No. This is not a child's love. You think it is, but in this way you are wrong."

Deirdre squeezed her eyes shut and tucked her lower lip under her upper teeth. "Young Con has the makings of a fine husband. Perhaps not now, but someday, when you are both older. And he is Irish. You can't cross the line. The colonel will never allow it. Joseph is not one of us," said Deirdre.

Taleen heard the pause in her mother's voice, the skip, some unnatural positioning of tongue and mouth.

"What do you see with your sight?" demanded Taleen. "There is something that you see that I cannot."

Deirdre sat up and crossed her legs.

"He is from across the water, true enough. He is from far away and he is strong and vibrant, the very makings of a hero. No wonder the colonel has taken to him even if he does use him like a racehorse, showing him off here and there, wagering on him all over Ireland with the wrestling."

Taleen had to agree with everything that her mother said. Perhaps her mother did understand; Joseph was a hero and he had come for her.

Her mother continued. "My sight tucks into the near

future and reads the past, mostly about the body. Yet I cannot see his days to come. It's as if they are shot out to the stars that we shall never touch. Aye, that far away," said Deirdre.

Taleen considered this, and the truth of it mingled with her skin and her breath, and the potent mixture confirmed the miracle of his arrival on their long beaches of Tramore.

"He is like no one else I've ever seen," she said, shivering at the memory of his touch.

"There is one thing that troubles me. The hounds have taken to him in the way they only treat our clan. These hounds are from our long line and they answer only to us. They treat the lad as one of their own. And this cannot be. This is what troubles me beyond all the rest," said Deirdre.

The next morning, the dense fog off the sea proved a harkening of the November weather. The cold began to settle on the land and work its way indoors. Taleen quickly disappeared outdoors before the onslaught of morning chores so that she could give in to the unstoppable thoughts of love. She and Madigan slipped into the stables and warmed themselves by the colonel's best mare.

The boy was glorious in his sweet skin and honey breath. Taleen had never seen the likes of him anywhere, not with the sailors strutting along the docks of Tramore and certainly unlike any lad here. Joseph had come for her, which meant that there was more magic in this world than even her mother understood. She could never leave the Isle, her mother had made that clear. A seventh daughter of a seventh daughter cannot leave, cannot cross water vast enough that the other side remains unseen.

So if something brilliant was going to happen in Taleen's

life, it had to be delivered to her. And with her sight, which had been passed down since the beginning, she had seen the boy coming like a brilliant wave reaching for her.

There had been no mistaking it when he had been pulled from the sea, splayed out naked and gasping for air, when she had woven her fingers between his toes. She had felt a ping low and deep start in her belly and travel between her legs, and she had seen something in the future such that she'd never imagined. It was something bigger than the Comeragh Mountains to the west and it was all about Joseph and her, about the two of them galloping off like Queen Maeve and her king. The vision was that grand.

"He doesn't know all the bits of what we are," her mum had said. "He thinks I'm a darling good cook and you're a stunning lass and he's fast in love with you. If you try for the likes of him, you'll be naught but a tragic ballad sung by drunken men and wistful women. He's a gentleman, or at least he is deemed so by the colonel."

Taleen returned to the kitchen and took over the preparation of morning porridge and puddings while Deirdre attended to several children from Tramore, one with terrible worms and the two with deep pleurisy. They had come to the kitchen door as her patients always did unless they were in such a state of suffering that Deirdre was called to go directly to them. Her mother always said that her sight was about the vessel of the soul, and if she lay on hands, she saw a dazzling map that showed inflammation and clogged bowels, hearts that beat too feverishly fast, big clumps of things that showed up in the wrong places like the kidneys or the liver. With some of the ailing people, Deirdre could lay on hands and remove the tangle of unhappiness (with the help of good herbs and hot drink), but with others, the affliction of bones in particular, the sideways curl of the spine, she could not but offer tender hope and prayer.

The sight emerges early with the seventh daughters, but in the young years, one could never be sure where the sight would settle. Some became strictly bone menders, others like Deirdre could lay on hands for the most frequent ailments, and others saw forward. These were the ones who parted the vapors of time and saw into the future. While they were the most sought after, Deirdre believed this was the most dangerous sight to have, because people were never pleased with the results. They wanted to know if they would find a husband or a wife. Would they have a babe? Would the crops be abundant, and would their favorite horse win the race? And when the truth was seen and revealed, happiness was not often the result.

Daughters with this sort of sight were better off learning to make butter or weave linen. Deirdre hoped that the sight should settle on something useful for Taleen. Just this morning she had told Taleen, "Come with me while I send the worms out of young Orla. It is a wonderful skill, and we'll see if you take to it."

"I don't want to heal those with worms. I truly do not. I want nothing to do with arses and worms. Here is what I see. I see Joseph riding home with the colonel and he has won another match and he is the champion and he glows a great gold color and even the colonel cannot deny the greatness of my Joseph. They are riding in the coach and they will here by dark, and I will be waiting for him."

Chapter 21

"It's time you saw more of our countryside, and, by coming with me, you'll be a great help to us. Tom can stay at home and finish his large order of barrel straps, and the children will be with him," said Glenis.

Anna perked up immediately, wanting to be useful to the kind couple. Anna had only just returned from her morning visit to the outhouse.

"Yes, I'll do anything to help. Where are we going and what are we doing?"

Glenis stood by the hearth and struggled with Nuala's hair, which looked like it had exploded overnight.

"We'll take a cart of thatch to a cousin in Skibbereen, if he is there. If he is, he'll continue on to Glengariff and you and I shall turn around and come home. If we've missed him, then you and I shall travel on by ourselves," said Glenis, pulling a comb through the child's hair. Nuala grimaced and braced herself by holding on to the seat of the chair.

"When do we leave?"

"Promptly. Before the morning is done with us. Tom has packed the cart and everything that will sustain us."

Anna obviously still missed a good part of what happened here; she did not know that their horse cart had been packed in the early morning as she had slept, or that Glenis and Tom had even talked about a trip to sell thatch. Nevertheless, she hurried to her bed and recovered the two scraps of fabric that tied her to home. Although she wished they'd been more meaningful or beautiful, she wanted them with her if she traveled. They were simply all she had of home. They left within an hour.

Anna and Glenis rode their one-horse cart, pulled along by the high-spirited O'Connell, a horse of unparalled persever-ance, or so Glenis claimed.

Anna's questions were innocent enough at first.

"You and Tom have a lot of cousins. We're carrying a load of thatch and you say it's forty miles to your cousin's home. Isn't that a long way to go to sell thatch?"

"Not so long," said Glenis. "And we use the term 'cousin' in a loose way. Let's just say we're related by blood some-where since the beginning of time. Excepting that Donal in Skibbereen truly is a cousin."

"And Tom thought it better for you and me to go?"

"Aye, he did think so." Glenis's rich red hair was pulled back and held by one of the sticks that Anna had carved for her. A cloud of shorter hairs had slipped loose, framing her face in thin ringlets that bounced in time to the wagon.

Anna's lawyerly brain woke up again, remembering the steady but overly casual string of visitors who'd come by Tom and Glenis's house in the last week. They'd arrived with fat satchels filled to bursting and left with far lighter loads, all of which had been covered by a smoke and a drink with Tom, the men helping with the second crop of potatoes, while Tom tended to the horseshoeing. No, this was commerce. Anna turned in her seat and looked back at the tightly bound thatch.

"We're not just delivering thatch, are we?"

Without looking at Anna, Glenis let the horse go on for a moment, the steady plop of the hooves strumming Anna's heart. Glenis pulled up on the reins and the horse snorted and stopped, flicking his dark mane and stamping his feet. The November sun was still warm, and the smell of the ocean reached them on a light breeze. Glenis wrapped the reins tightly around a polished knob in front of the bench seat.

"I told Tom it was just a matter of time before you added everything up. He said all you could think of was finding that nephew of yours, Joseph, that you had no eyes for anything else." Glenis took in a breath. "We're smugglers."

And as soon as Glenis said this, the bare spots filled in, like the thousand-piece puzzle of birds she used to do on family vacations to Vermont. Suddenly the picture emerged. It was not synchronicity at play when neighbors visited Tom and Glenis at night, just happening to have come with cloth bags filled to bursting and leaving with bags flattened and rolled tight. And once, just once, Anna had seen a look from Tom that she hadn't been able to identify. Anna catalogued everything, and Tom's sideways glance had been unmistakable; she had placed it under *not true*, even though she hadn't wanted to do so. Lies live in sideways glances.

The puzzle pieces floated into interlocking spaces and plopped into their rightful homes. The frequent visitors passing by to talk with Tom relayed more than idle men's gossip in his blacksmith shop, which camouflaged the chatter with the clanging of metal on hot metal. They were smugglers. It all made sense.

Glenis gathered up her skirt and leaped from the cart. "Come down, Anna, and we'll stretch our legs and let the horse rest his." She walked to Anna's side of the wagon.

Anna felt the shift in Glenis; an imagined membrane between the two of them dissolved. She pulled her skirt up with one hand, revealing far more bare thigh than Glenis had done.

"God in heaven! Must you open the garden gates all the way?" said Glenis when she saw the flash of flesh.

"Sorry," said Anna, jumping to the ground, joining the other woman as they stepped along a pasture, walking as wanderers do, without destination.

The Irish woman bent over to pick up a stone that caught her eye. She rubbed the smooth disk in her palm with her thumb. "We could not get by, none of us, with the old Penal Laws. The English strangled us with their embargoes; they've left us without the ability to sell what we make and grow, and they refuse to allow other countries to trade with us. So we trade goods in and out without benefiting England. We've done so for generations."

Anna sidestepped dried sheep turds, then stopped to face Glenis. "You're smugglers. And not just the two of you. Is every person I've met thick into the black market?"

Here in the land of mist and green, nothing was what it seemed to be. Even if Anna had been in her own time, it would have taken her at least this long to figure out that affable Tom was a prime organizer for the underground market. Of course; everyone who had any wits about them would strategize around sanctions against marketing linen, wool, corn, and anything else that looked lucrative.

Glenis gazed off to the right, as if she was picturing all her family and friends.

"Well, let's see," pondered Glenis. "With the exception of a few of our very old ones—Mr. Healy in particular, who said he had religious reasons for not smuggling—then yes, everyone you've met runs this or that through Tom and me. We take the goods first to my cousin, and then he splits the lot up, figuring where his best market is, then he does the rest."

"What would happen if the British discovered this lively enterprise?"

Glenis reached for Anna's hand and held it between her hot and urgent palms. "If they found us out, first it would be prison for both of us. They'd take the house and all we own. They'd burn it down as a way to stick a spike into our souls. Then, if they found the crime heinous, they'd hang us. Michael is twelve, so they might take him as well, leaving the two little ones to fend for themselves."

If Anna could have picked a sister, she would have picked Glenis. And if she could pick a friend, it would also be this sweet-faced smuggler, braving everything to take a risk with Anna.

"You're the first outsider who is not vested by blood, and you've caused a fair amount of consternation. We've taken a great chance with you. You could turn us in; half of County Cork is praying that you won't."

They walked on, holding hands like schoolgirls, until they found a suitably flat stone wall to sit on. Glenis glanced back at the horse, who seemed to be resting on three legs while he held one hoof to the ground like a ballerina on point. Anna opened her top buttons a bit and faced the sun.

"But why would the British put any worth in what I had to say? They are none too fond of Americans. We bested them in our revolution, against all odds, and countries have long memories," said Anna.

Glenis sighed. "You're as dense as a stone about some things. I didn't say *I* thought you'd turn us in. I said some frightful nervous ones said so. I know you won't. I've seen you teaching our wee bairns, better than any of the teachers at the hedge schools. They'll be bloody scientists by the time you're done with them."

Glenis stood up and kicked the heel of her boot against a rock to chip off some turf. "It's the smuggling, don't you see? You could help us. We trade with American and French ships, but we've recently lost our best American trader; he said it's too awful dangerous. You could help us find a new market in America, I know you could. When you go home, that is. I have a feeling about you that you could make the right connections. You said yourself that you work with lawyers."

Anna had explained to Glenis that she was a secretary of sorts to lawyers; she'd hoped it had been plausible. Now Anna wanted to laugh. Going home. Just how was she supposed to do that? She didn't understand how she'd gotten here, how she had spiraled through a watery conduit of time. The sudden mention of home turned her mouth sour with longing and choked off any laughter.

"Oh, Glennie, I would help you in a heartbeat, I swear I would, but I can't." Anna turned her palms up and shrugged her shoulders in a pitiful gesture not befitting the moment.

Glenis looked like she had been struck hard, then quickly brushed at the seat of her skirt.

"Aye, of course. I should not have asked. Yeah, well, let's be going on. The road to my cousin's house is a far way still."

What had it cost her to ask Anna for help? Anna pictured her standing toe to toe with Tom, convincing him that the American could be trusted, that she'd help them. Glenis had risked her standing with friends and family only to be turned down by the woman she had nursed back from the brink of death. Glenis walked off with a stiff gait. Anna jumped off the stone wall and rushed to catch up with her. She grabbed Glenis's arm.

"It's not just that I'm from America . . . ," started Anna.

"No, but that's why I asked you, because you're from there."

Glenis was red in the face, her lips tight, her brow brewing dark.

"Listen, it's not that at all. I'm going to tell you something that you'll probably not believe, but you mustn't tell anyone else. Will you promise?"

Glenis nodded.

"I want you to swear on something. Swear on your children, your husband, all that you hold dear," said Anna.

"Right. I swear that what you are about to tell me shall remain with me. I swear on my three sweet wee ones and all those to come."

All the moisture in Anna's mouth evaporated, and her tongue was dry and useless. She had longed to tell someone, and the one person she'd wanted to tell was standing directly in front of her. This moment would change everything, and Anna had no road map for how it would go. She popped a smooth stone into her mouth and sucked hard on it to get some saliva going.

"I'm not from this time," she began. "I'm from the future, so far into the future that you could not imagine. That's why ... that's why I can't help you. I don't know one soul back in America as it is right now. I'd be as lost there as I am here. That's why there has been no answer to my letter."

Glenis softened first in her eyes, followed by the spreading of her overtaxed brow. Her lips relaxed and gradually parted.

"I never meant to tell you," Anna continued. "I thought I could see my way out of this without having to tell you because I know how insane this sounds, how preposterous, and there's no reason for you to believe me," said Anna.

Glenis still did not speak; she appeared to be held fast by the earth. Anna had the sensation that Glenis had turned into a hard drive from a massive computer, and her brain was spinning, searching back through every moment since Anna had washed ashore.

"This is where you should say something. I won't be able to stand it if you keep staring at me," said Anna.

Glenis shook her head a bit as if to clear off debris that had settled on her. "Well, you'll need to give me a moment. I'm trying to fathom all that you've said, and I'm leaning in the direction of a very big blow to your head that we didn't rightly account for in your troubles. The future? That's a grave matter if it's true and not one that I've ever run into. How far into the future do you reckon you're from, and how do you know it's the future? And can I have a look at your head please, because there could be a scabbie gash that we've long ignored."

What could Anna say that would make it clear that the problem was not a brain injury, a traumatically induced delusion about the future? And would Anna ever in a million years have believed someone from her own time who'd said they were from the future?

"I don't understand how this happened, how my nephew and I were ripped from one time and tossed into another. I'm missing too many pieces. Here's what I do know: I know that my people come from Ireland, that they immigrated to America some time after the Famine. Scratch that, I shouldn't tell you about the future, your future here in Ireland. Everything in me says that telling someone about the future is wrong."

"What now, you mean about there being a famine? We've had famines all along. Crops fail, that's the way of it. We had a famine when I was a babe; my mother said it was the result of too much bitterness in the world, too much greed and so forth. She was a bit old-fashioned. Tom said it was because there was too much damp and cold at all the wrong times," said Glenis.

Anna had to be more careful about blabbing things about the future. She simply had nothing to show Glenis to prove her story, not even the scraps of fabric that she'd had on when she'd been found. The waistband and the scrap of T-shirt were odd, but they weren't substantial enough to prove time travel. And telling Glenis about the disasters that were in store for Ireland would do nothing to help. Nor would explaining to her about airplanes, rockets, computers, or cell phones.

Then Anna had an idea. She spit out the pebble. "I want you to look into my mouth and look at my teeth. Tell me what you see," she instructed Glenis. She opened her mouth wide and bent down so that Glenis could take a proper look.

"Like I've said before, you have abnormally straight teeth. As if someone straightened them for you. And most remarkably, you have all your teeth and not a bit of rot on any of them."

"Right. And I'm thirty-four years old. Do you know anyone else with all their teeth and not a black spot on any of them?"

"Not a grown person, no. And for women, we lose a tooth for every child that we bear. I've lost two teeth already, so I'm due to lose another any moment. And you do have the most starlit teeth, not a stain on them, and all lined up like fence posts, straight fence posts. But none of that means you're from the future, dearie."

Anna had to break her own rule, which, she imagined, was a universal rule for time travelers. It had to be. If she was going to make Glenis understand (and now she almost wished she had never started down the road of telling her about the future), then she would have to prove it. If she told Glenis most things about the future, Glenis would fall down laughing.

"In my time, in America, most children go to special physicians, called dentists, and if their teeth are naturally crooked, the teeth are straightened with metal bands that force the teeth into line. Not all children, you must have something called health insurance. Well, let's skip that part. And all children brush their teeth several times a day and almost none of the kids get cavities and almost everyone gets to keep all their teeth. This is all greatly simplified, but you asked me to tell you one thing about the future. Your knowing that one thing probably won't turn the universe inside out."

Glenis said, "Let me look inside your mouth again."

This time, Anna sat down on the ground, crossed her legs,

and opened her mouth. Glenis got on one knee and looked and looked while Anna patiently kept her mouth wide open, turning this way and that as Glenis requested. When Glenis was fully satisfied, she sat back on her haunches.

"Tis a grand sight in there," she said.

Anna rubbed her stiff jaws. "Can you consider the possibility that I am from some other time, a time other than this one?" asked Anna.

"And you're telling me this confabulation to explain why you can't help us smuggle our goods to American ships?"

"No, I mean yes, partly yes. I can't help you find markets for your goods because I'm not from the America of right now. Don't you see? I'm from a time so much after this and I'm telling you because I trust you and I need your help. There must be someone who understands how this has happened, someone who can help me. Once I find Joseph, we have to go back, or forward. I'm like anyone else, Glennie. I want to go home."

"Whether you're from today or tomorrow, we can't sit in the dirt all day debating it. We've got to find a safe house on this side of Clonakilty before dark. I expect they know we're coming. And it's another day to Skibbereen, where we can unload."

The two women dusted off their skirts and returned to the wagon filled with thatch, as well as goods to be smuggled off the Beara Peninsula. O'Connell the horse started up the moment Glenis released the brake handle.

"God, he is like Daniel O'Connell, like the uncrowned king of Ireland," said Glenis. As if to prove her point, the horse tossed his head and stepped smartly.

* * *

Glenis gave the reins a smart snap and the horse strained against his harness to set a good pace. Then Tom's perfectly hammered, spoked, and balanced wheels began to roll and O'Connell the horse settled into a steady pace.

Anna turned to look back at the bound thatch that overflowed from the back of the wagon.

"Should I ask what we carry in the thatch?"

"It's nothing so bad that you can't know," said Glenis. "We're not running guns, if that's what you mean. We're trying to survive, that's the way of it. But if you don't know, you'll never be able to tell the English if they capture you and threaten to imprison you or hang you or worse. So I leave it to you. Do you want to know or not?"

"Not," said Anna, turning to look forward again, her left leg pressed against the right thigh of this young woman, wife, mother, smuggler.

But she was unable to stop herself from knowing; the lawyer in her spoke up.

"What is it that you trade for with the French and the Americans? I want to know."

"Often what we receive is whiskey, I'm sorry to say, and the market for whiskey is without ending. Besides, with the thumb of England on us in all ways imaginable, whiskey is one thing that the men crave. In all their fiery animal anger that cannot be set loose, there is always whiskey."

That night, Glenis and Anna rode through Clonakilty aware that O'Connell the horse badly needed food, rest, and water, although he'd given no sign.

"We've many places along the way where we're welcome," said Glenis.

They stopped at the western edge of the village, turning up a hill to a stone cottage that had a vigilant vantage point. Anna's exhaustion from riding a full day in a wagon hit her hard, pulling the shade down on her brain. Glenis pulled the wagon behind the cottage and under the protection of a three-sided barn. She unhitched the horse.

"Go inside, Anna. They'll put food down for you and show you where to bed. I can see you're done clear through to the bone."

Anna wanted dearly not to speak, not to explain. Not even her constant hunger could motivate her to join in with the family of children and grannies and parents who stood expectantly by the hearth as she entered.

"Is there a place to sleep?" she said. She sounded abrupt and rude, so unlike the Irish.

"Oh, yes," said the woman of the house. "Himself and I will sleep outside with your wagonload, and you and Glenis will take our bed, such as it is. That's the way it shall go. We'll keep a good eye on the horse as well. Now sit down; I can see you think you're too beyond to eat, but that's all the more reason to fill up. You've a far way to go tomorrow."

Anna obeyed and sat down in front of a bowl of potatoes and buttermilk. To her surprise, she devoured it, tilting the bowl up to her lips to gain the last of it. When she placed the bowl back on the table and wiped her mouth with her sleeve, she paused with wrist in midair as she looked up to the astonished faces of the family. The woman stirred to action, breaking the spell.

"There's never such a fine compliment of a woman's cooking," she said and graciously ladled more into Anna's bowl.

* * *

Anna was so grateful for the bed, the memory of her own mattress at home now only a hazy image, a fable from another time that even she found difficult to embrace. She took off her boots and her outer skirt and blouse, down to a light shift. She heard Glenis's voice in the main room of the house, the murmur of it, the sureness of Glenis, Anna's constant companion since slipping through time. And now, everything depended on Glenis. Whether Glenis believed her or not, thought her insane or not, she was the one person Anna had trusted enough to tell. Glenis the smuggler, Anna the time traveler.

But more people than not were smugglers, links on the perilous black market under England's iron fist. A worm of fear started low in Anna's belly, wrapped itself around her spine, laid eggs along her heart and throat. What if Glenis discarded her, tossed her out, what if she was worth nothing to Glenis in the brutal black market trade? Was she worth anything at all to Glenis and Tom now? Her head smoked and sputtered, giving off electrical charges of panic.

Glenis opened the creaky door and stepped into the dark room. The ever-present scent of peat smoke followed her. She let her dress fall to the floor with a hiss and climbed into the small bed with careful movements.

"I'm awake," said Anna. She rolled onto her side to face Glenis.

They looked at each other, nose to nose, eyes glowing in the dark. Had Anna ever dared look this far into someone, let them see into her?

"It's all right now," said Glenis, using her hand to wipe a gush of tears that had filled the pocket of Anna's eye and run along the edge of her nose. "We'll reckon our way through this. It's a fantastic story, truly it is, what you've told me today. I can see you're thinking I'll toss you back into the ocean with the fish guts. We're survivors here, we survive anything. Give me a few days of thinking. You're all right, Anna. Go to sleep now."

Chapter 22

They had one more night before they reached Skibbereen and their weary wagonload could be delivered. They misjudged, however, so that by dark, they were nowhere near a village.

"I've traveled this road so many times that it's a wonder I need to keep my eyes open. Yet I've left us without a safe haven for sleeping. You're shattered from this journey; I can see it, sister," said Glenis. She stopped the horse and stood up in the wagon. It was the dark of the moon, and Anna could see nothing at all. She couldn't imagine that Glenis could see beyond O'Connell.

"We can't leave the cart, that's the main thing. But I promise you if we go on a bit longer there's a lane that will take us up the hill to an abandoned place. We can pull behind it and not be seen," she said.

She was right. Glenis and the horse worked as one, each responding to the path beneath them. Glenis's touch was light on the reins as she nickered to O'Connell, letting him take the lead.

"Carry on, O'Connell. You've been this way before, that's

it. I know you're far wearier than we are. Take us in, you great beast."

And O'Connell did. Anna saw the stuttered black outline of a ruined building, massive hunks of stone revealing a door, then a window, and small section of roof. When they stopped, she heard the light trill of water, and her own thirst awakened with a lurch. After they unhitched the horse and let him graze with a long tether, both women sank their faces into the spring that bubbled beyond the ruins.

"There is nothing so sweet as the sacred springs," said Glenis.

Anna wiped her mouth. "What makes them sacred?" She was hungry, and they had no more food, having counted on supplies from the next village. Her irritation crackled.

Glenis answered straight on. "There are many such springs all over Ireland. Drink more and see if this one doesn't fill your hunger. You've not had as much practice with hunger, wherever and whenever you've come from. What makes them sacred? The centuries of wearied travelers seeking them out, the life of them, unwilling to bend to invaders, all the faith that we put back into them. And the fairies live in and around them. You're telling me you don't have sacred springs where you're from?"

Anna had to think. Had she ever heard of a sacred spring in Massachusetts?

"No, no sacred springs, and definitely no fairies," she said.

"Well then, it can't be much of a place that you come from. The land gives us sweet reprieve from all our troubles. What place can be worth living in that doesn't wash away the strains of living?"

Anna had to ask herself the same question.

* * *

They slept amid the ruins, huddled together as tightly as bark and tree, sleeping on a mass of grasses and dried plants, anything to keep their bodies off the cold slab of stones. They put one blanket beneath them, one on top of them, and both their capes on top of that. Anna waited for Glenis to fall asleep, which she did almost instantly, issuing a deep sigh and giving a jerk with her legs, as if she entered sleep by falling off a cliff. When Anna was sure that Glenis was asleep, she drew even closer to her, pressing herself into Glennie's back, letting her right arm fall across the woman. Anna held on for dear life. If she could keep hold of Glenis through the night, then she'd be brave enough to sleep. But she could not let even Glenis know how afraid she was of traveling the road at night, the possibility of getting caught with the black market goods, of never finding Joseph, of her brother wrangling with traumatic brain injury in their time. She breathed into Glenis's neck and fluttered into sleep.

The dream. *Oh, she was pregnant again, and when the baby came out, it was as small as a kitten. No, it truly was a kitten, a dark tabby with eyes squeezed shut and tiny claws in the limp paws. She had nothing to feed it, no milk in her breasts. The kitten was weak and hungry, and Anna fled to find a grown cat to feed it, to keep it breathing.*

Anna was jolted out of her dream by a deep, guttural howl that vibrated her ribs. Glenis threw off the covers, bumped Anna aside, and sat up.

"Oh, Jaysus! Oh, only a dream," Glenis said, rubbing her face.

"What? You had a dream? You howled like someone about to be killed. What did you dream?"

"Dreams are a jumble of nonsense," said Glenis unchar-acteristically. Under all other circumstances, Glenis willingly saw omens, spirits, and troubles carried on the breezes and every other thing and place. Anna doubted her lack of inter-est in dreams.

"Tell me," she said, stretching her legs out as her racing heart began to slow. "Then I'll tell you mine."

Glenis stood up, shook out her considerable hank of hair, and brushed her skirt.

"Well, it makes no sense, but I was so awful afraid that my heart felt ripped open. There was a man, see, and I loved him, not that I don't love my own dear husband, Tom, because you know that I do, but in this dream there was this other man and his eyelids were so swollen that I could only see the center dots of eyes through these slits, and he was looking directly at me like he knew me stem to stern, like he'd seen me naked. And he had snakes or something awful coming out of his head. More like black ropes and from his heart too and right out of his arms. Oh, it was a frightful sight. He couldn't speak and I knew that, yet I could hear him in my head. He said, 'Trajectory.' I've never heard this word in my life or said it or know what it means."

Anna stood up and placed a roughened hand on the stone sill of a window. That's what Patrick had looked like all bun-gled up in the ICU, wires flapping out of his head, chest and arms. And a trajectory was like a path or a flight. Maybe like time travel.

"Glennie, here's my dream. I dreamed I was pregnant and I gave birth to a sick little kitten."

"If anyone is pregnant, that would be me. I thought as much. I wondered if I was, but this didn't feel like the other times. But I'm quite sure there are no kittens in here," said Glenis rubbing her belly.

The women stared at each other, silently exchanging dreams, letting them settle back where they belonged.

"And who was I dreaming about? Don't tell me you know this monstrous fellow?" asked Glenis.

"He's not monstrous. That sounds so much like my brother, Patrick. Remember, I told you he'd been hurt."

"Yes, you did, but I don't know how much of what you told me was true, given the fantastic story that you told me a few days ago. If I recall, you told me that you and your nephew were on a voyage to France to care for your ailing brother. Was that true?"

"Part of that was true. He was horribly injured in an accident with broken bones and such. But it's not the broken bones we're worried about, it's his head that was bashed. And I told you what was true. I'm from the future, Glennie. Just forget the part about the story I told you about France. It was the best I could do back then. I was afraid to tell you the truth. I'm still afraid, but I'm not alone now."

They reached Skibbereen by midday, making the journey a good deal longer than Glenis had promised. Any painful memory that Anna had of inadequate airline seating was now overshadowed by two days on the wooden plank seat of a horse cart. She thought that some of her bones might be so shaken that they could now be lost in her body, floating in a confused grid of arms, legs, neck, spine, ankles, and toes. Anna had a compelling desire to go for a run, just for a few miles, to put herself back together again. Could she? She'd have to test out the idea. This could mean that her leg injury was healed, her muscles knitted back as they should be.

Glenis drove the wagon through the village and then along a tiny lane, badly rutted, until Anna's sit bones could stand it no longer.

"Stop, for God's sake! If we're going to the cottage that I see, then please stop and let me walk, or I might become paralyzed."

Glenis, who had been singing, continued to do so, but she pulled up the reins. O'Connell reluctantly stopped; Anna jumped off and rubbed her butt. Glenis drove on, singing a tale of disastrous love, and the ribbon of notes floated back to Anna.

By the time Anna reached the house, she realized that it was far larger than she had imagined from down below. Thatched like nearly every house she had seen, this one extended to twice the size of Glenis and Tom's house. A large stable sat to one side. O'Connell was already being tended by two men, who walked him and the cart into the stable. Somewhere, another horse neighed to O'Connell, offering a greeting of familiarity. From the squeal of voices inside the whitewashed house, Anna surmised that Glenis had received a riotous welcome.

Anna walked along the path to the house and noted several cows and chickens. This was a house of abundance compared to most. As Anna neared the last few steps, the door flew open and Glenis emerged, her face stretched into a wide grin and her cheeks flushed.

"Anna, come in. They don't believe that you're from America. Say something so they won't think I'm making up a tale."

Anna flinched, worried that she had already been betrayed, but no, this was the playful Glenis, just wanting to shock a roomful of people with Anna's strange accent. Glenis grabbed her by the hand and fairly dragged her into the house. Two little girls hid behind an older woman, who stood on one side of a table, nearest the hearth. An older man rose from a chair and offered her a ready smile that announced the absence of several prominent teeth. At the very moment that Anna stood gawking and adjusting her eyes to the interior, a younger man filled up a doorway leading to the back of the house, backlit by a window. She saw the silhouette of a loose shirtsleeve pinned up. He had lost an arm and she could not pull her eyes from the armless sleeve. Glenis must have followed her gaze.

"Donal, come meet Anna. She's about to thrill us with her American accent. And whatever have you done with your arm? I think you've lost it."

One of the girls squealed with laughter and ran to the man, who scooped her up with ease. "Kathleen, have you taken me arm again? I can't find it anywhere."

Anna recognized the familiarity of family, of unbridled teasing—not that her own family had been riddled with it, but she had witnessed it enough at her girlfriend's house when she'd sought refuge.

"Go on, Anna, say something," said Glenis.

Anna felt like a child being prodded to name all the states or presidents. She felt a deep blush rising.

"I'm very pleased to meet you all," she said.

After a lengthy pause, the old man said something in Gaelic, and they all exploded with laughter.

"Careful now, she can say a thing or two in Irish and probably understands more than that," said Glenis. Then she turned to Anna and asked, "Can you mind yourself for a bit while I work out the barter with Donal?"

That's what Glenis called smuggling: the *barter*.

After eating a warm custard pudding that only partially addressed her hunger, Anna said she wanted to walk along the hillsides. Maura, the old woman of the house, directed Anna to a path that led to a view of the bay that was reportedly magnificent. Maura put her hand over her heart when she recalled the lookout point.

Anna had explained to Glenis that in general, she needed more breathing space between people than the Irish did. Over the weeks, her walks had grown longer and longer so that she could think.

"My family is smaller than yours and we don't crave all smashing in together in a small space like you do. I'm not saying one is right and the other wrong. I'm saying that ten people in a room with a peat fire and four pipe smokers is too much for me," Anna had tried to explain to Glenis during their ride.

"But be sure to stay on the path. The bogs are still terrible. You'll sink in to your knees and we'll have to haul you out with the horses," Maura said.

Anna stayed on the path, fortified by the egg pudding. She felt the protein run through her body like a sentinel, ringing bells and declaring a holiday on hunger. She immediately felt energized and walked for hours until coming to a vantage point, a blunt plateau where sheep, cows, and people had flattened the tough grasses.

She hadn't thought to ask Glenis what would happen next now that they had delivered the wagonload of black market goods hidden within the thatch. Would they immediately begin their journey back to Kinsale? Anna decided to campaign for at least one day of rest, one day of not bruising her tailbone on the wagon. She stretched languidly along the flattened grass. She was grateful for these moments of privacy, of not being observed, of her careful suppression of twenty-first-century words and phrases. In a flood of relief, she shouted a list of words from her life that had remained chained to the back of her skull. She stood in the center of the lookout and yelled:

Subway

Fast food

Superconductor

Email

Text message

Super Tuesday

Hurricane Katrina

Fucking A

Clean Water Act

Atkins diet

Boston marathon

Health club

Fitness guru

Investment broker

Bar exam

Hybrid car

Caribbean vacation

Red Sox

Divorce court

The list went on and on until she had spit out all the words that had pounded for release. She had known a kid in high school who'd had Tourette's Syndrome. He'd said that he'd been able to contain his ticks and barks during school, but they'd accumulated all day until he'd gotten home, and then he'd had to empty them out in their two-car garage, barking and twitching his head, touching the doorway one hundred times.

"They never went away," he had said. "But I could make them wait. I sort of housebroke them."

Now Anna understood. She got up and scooped up her skirt in one hand and galloped her way down the hill, taking the path that kept her safe from the suck of the bogs. As soon as she saw the house, she adjusted her skirts again and walked empty of all the twenty-first-century words and her need to run.

As she approached the back of the stable, she heard angry voices from fifty yards away.

"You shall not! Have you lost your mind? I'll not be saddled with her."

This had to be Donal. Although she had spoken very little with him, she recognized his full-throttle voice. She stopped immediately, fearing that they were arguing about her. If this was true, she wanted to get into the fray, especially if she was the one to be saddled upon someone. If the argument was about another, then she could press into the background. She saw Glenis and Donal emerging from the stable.

"You can't go, and you can't take a good horse like O'Connell. He's the best horse here, and we need him to haul the goods," said Donal.

"Yes, he's a fine horse indeed, and that's why I need to take him to Dromore Hill. He'll keep a fine pace, you know he will, you know I'm right about this. Give me a saddle and stop your blathering," said Glenis.

Glenis was leaving? Anna tilted her head to one side. Had she missed something that Glenis had told her? Were they both to ride O'Connell?

"Glennie?" she said.

Glenis and Donal whipped their heads around to face Anna, suddenly seeing her. Glenis looked startled and suddenly younger than she was, like a schoolgirl caught in a lie, eyes big, lips parted, hands open.

"Anna, there is someone who lives past Limerick, a ways out on Dromore Hill, who I've heard of all my life. I think she can help your, ah, your delicate situation, and help you find your boy Joseph if there's anything left of him to find. I'll take O'Connell by myself, taking the old roads, and I can be there in two days," she said, reaching for Anna's hands.

"By yourself? You mean leave me here? Glenis, don't do it; I won't hold us up, I promise. I won't utter one word of complaint."

"No. I've thought and thought about this, and it is a golden plan. You can stay here for a few days, help deliver the load to Glengariff, and then Donal can bring you back to Kinsale. I'll be riding into the village the very same moment that you arrive, see if I don't."

Donal's chest radiated with rage, expanding it, exploding with red-hot blasts of air. "Have you forgotten the risk, have you forgotten what we're doing here? Sure you've got one woman who lost her way and can't find her lad. How does that stack up against all of us who face the gallows if we are caught? What the devil is wrong with you?"

Glenis's chin shook and puckered, and she fought off tears. She faced her cousin, looking up at his angry face.

"I'm sick to death of living to run whiskey, smuggling the

barest of things that keep us alive, staying forty paces ahead of the troops. Have you ever felt like you had a choice, that for once in your life all the stars turned just so and the sun and the moon lined up to light your way to do something that truly mattered? Because that's how I feel at this very moment. I have a chance to do something more than smuggle, so that my children can grow up to be something other than smugglers. I'm not a foolish woman. You've known me since I was born and you've never known me to do anything but what was right for my family. You must trust me."

"And just who is it that you must see, who is so almighty important?" he asked.

"Why, Biddy Early, of course. If there is help to be had, it is the great Biddy Early who can help us."

Chapter 23

Glenis's euphoria could not be hampered by Donal's grumbling. When he finally relinquished a suitable saddle for her to use, Glenis grabbed the unhappy cousin and kissed him. She prepared O'Connell, who immediately picked up her air of adventure. She spoke constantly to the horse in Irish, and his flanks quivered in conspiratorial excitement as she cinched the saddle. Glenis stroked his neck and his long face. Anna could have sworn that the horse understood every word that Glenis spoke. She wondered for the first time if her own sister-in-law Tiffany had been able to speak a secret language with horses, if she had been able to tell the horse of Patrick's growing anger toward his only son, as if some drug, or a curse, would overcome him when he shouted caustic words that would burn young Joseph. Anna prayed that Tiffany's horse had listened as keenly on her last day of life as O'Connell listened to Glenis.

Two leather saddlebags were filled with flat breads, along with grain for the horse. The day was bright and warm, so Glenis folded her cape tight and rolled it behind the saddle. She stepped away from the horse and turned to Anna, placing her hands on either shoulder, looking up into her face. Anna could smell the fresh sweat that pumped from Glenis.

"We'll be back home in Kinsale again, you'll see. We'll have worked our way through all this, and the worst that we shall face will be Tom pouting for the first two days," she said. "And if he's alive anywhere in Ireland, we'll find your nephew."

Anna latched onto her hands with an iron grip. She drew her close and whispered, "I don't think Donal likes me one bit. And who could Biddy Early be that you'd place such faith in her?"

"Just the most powerful seer in all of Ireland. Even the Catholic priests and the British call on her when they think no one is looking. There's no one else who can help you the way she can."

"Then why can't I go with you?"

They had been through this discussion several times, and Anna knew she sounded like a whining child.

Glenis tested the saddle, giving it a tug. "O'Connell and I can travel light and fast. I don't want to have to worry about taking care of you on a journey like this. Now, I've nothing new to tell you and I won't tell you this again. I'm leaving you with my most trusted cousin, who truly is a cousin. All I ask is that you take my place in helping him. Just ride with him for a few days. It won't be so hard, I promise.

"Don't be put off by Donal," Glenis went on. "You've seen how gentle he can be with children, and those children are not even his; they're Maura's grandchildren. The girls' parents died from consumption and he took in this lot. He's furious at me right now, but it has nothing to do with you."

"Yes, it does. I distinctly heard him say that he didn't

want to be saddled with me. Do you know how horrible that feels?"

Glenis's cheeks were flushed, and a light gleam of moisture on her face and neck made her glow. The sun danced off her hair, with its strands of red, brown, and ebony twined together in one harmonious blend. Glenis mounted O'Connell as if gravity held no claim to her. Already she and the horse were one creature, a two-headed animal that was glorious to behold, exploding with energy. Anna was sure that she had never seen anything as beautiful as Glenis at that moment. And she could not recall being more set adrift, abandoned, and angry.

As Glenis rode off, Donal and Anna were left with the silence of her exuberant departure. Anna cleared her throat and said, "Well, there she goes." She did not face Donal full on but stood at an angle to him. She stole a glance at his profile, waiting for the "now what" to happen. She had been in sight of Glenis since she had arrived nearly six weeks ago. An uneasy fear began to grip her, freezing the tips of her shoulder blades. She was suddenly exposed and naked without Glenis. Anna had not spoken one full sentence to this man since she'd arrived, and now she was left in his charge. How could Glenis have done this?

She watched his Adam's apple slide up a notch and then down again as he swallowed.

"She was always like this," he said, more to himself. Then he turned to Anna and said, "Glenis wouldn't tell me exactly, but I have a feeling that she is going on your account. I hope you are worth the risk."

Anna was shocked out of her sadness. "That was the rudest thing I've ever heard. You don't know one thing about me.

And I had no say in Glenis coming or going. If I had my way, I'd be with her right now and not with you. If you're related to her, it is not through your good nature."

She glared at him, refusing to stalk off. His eyes were darker than brown, and he looked down at her from an advantage of half a foot. His shirt caught a breeze and expanded like a sail, like an animal making itself bigger, with the extra sleeve suddenly coming loose from its pinning and snapping like a flag.

"If you're not using that extra sleeve, you could at least stop it from flapping," she said. She held her ground until Donal turned and headed back to the house.

Without Glenis, Anna was a free-floating boat, no oars, no sail, and not much of a rudder, just a vessel subjected to the whims of currents and wind.

If Anna had thought she could talk Glenis out of her leave-taking, she had been wrong. Glenis was gone, and Anna was left standing between house and stable. She straightened her shoulders. Donal had been the one to stalk off, which had pleased her in the tiniest way. He had promised Glenis that he would take Anna back to Kinsale, so she only needed to occupy herself for a few days, then ride into Glengariff and back. She was confident that an extra set of hands was welcomed, even her unskilled hands. She walked into the house and sought out Maura, the matriarch of the group.

"Can I give you a hand with anything while I'm here?"

Maura glanced at Anna but returned her attention to her husband, with whom she was sitting knee to knee. He looked considerably older than Maura. His face was deeply lined in a pattern that looked designed by the wind, as if the old man had stood on the cliffs facing out to sea and allowed the northwest winds to wear away at him. Anna detected a scowl, the tightness of his lips, the stare past Maura's shoulder, shunning his wife momentarily. Maura sighed and patted his gnarled hand.

"Look now, this is the way it will be, and I'll be back before you can forgive me for leaving." Maura stood up and turned to Anna, saying, "Anna, there is something you can do here. We need to take the thatch to Glengariff . . . and . . . well, Glenis said she explained a few things to you. It would look so much better at this time if you joined Donal and me. An old woman accompanied by her son and daughter, that's what we shall say. And you being the quiet one, if we are stopped. Can you do that? Oh, better yet, you'll be the fevered one, that should keep the curious at bay. With a smear of dark ashes around your eyes, we can make a perfectly pathetic fevered one out of you."

"Oh, I've already promised Glenis that I would help. I'm pleased to hear that you'll be coming also. Where is Glengariff? Are we going further west?"

"Quite a bit more, yes. And it's a stronghold of the English. They're fond of the castle, the forest, the hunting, but with a sickly traveler, they should give us a broad pass. No one wants to examine someone with the fever," said Maura.

"And once we deliver the wagonload, then we can come back here? Then Donal will drive me back to Kinsale?"

"Oh, he shall. Aye, our return journey will be lighter. There's others to take over on the far side of Glengariff."

Anna did not see a vast array of choices. She looked at the old man with the foul dark mood, the children who would need tending, and gained clarity.

"When do we leave for Glengariff?"

Maura smiled. "In the morning, dear, and not at the first light of dawn, but after my bones have warmed."

Midmorning the next day, Maura seemed to take some pleasure in dabbing Anna with soot around her eyes.

"I think she looks poorly, don't you?" the older woman asked Donal.

"Poorly indeed, as if the plague itself was set on her. Quite poorly. And could you scratch your head as if you had a goodly amount of lice?" asked Donal as he hoisted the last of the provisions to the front of the cart. They expected to be gone for two days.

Anna bristled at Donal's too quick assessment of her sickly looks, which had been designed to repel a close inspection by troops.

"Perhaps you should be the sick one. And the quiet one who doesn't speak."

Something like a smile, the beginning twitches around the edges of his lips, formed. He turned his head away for a moment, then said, "I'd not fit nearly as well as you do, stuck behind the bench seat on your own sick pallet. Come on now, hop aboard, my dear sister, while I sit next to our sainted mother."

Donal extended his arm to Anna as she stood contemplating her travel strategy.

"Tis a great honor to have you aboard. Now could you give us a show of your phlegmatic cough?"

They had agreed that the most unquestioning configuration was for Maura to be their mother, with Anna and Donal as the devoted siblings. Anna did not imagine that the total trip would last long, since Glengariff was not but twenty miles. And if law school had taught her anything, it was that she could endure the most excruciating circumstances as long as she knew there was an end. She could easily see the end of this mission.

They had fashioned a small nook for Anna directly behind the bench seat, where she could either lay crossways with her head behind Maura's generous rear, or she could sit up with her knees crammed hard into the bench seat. She had tried both options as they'd packed and prepared for the journey.

Anna gathered her skirts in one hand and accepted Donal's hand to climb up. She noticed that his arm held her steady, as if it had been a banister, firm and carved, burnished from use. Did all of his strength from two arms run into his one arm? Glenis had told her that he'd lost his arm as a child, in a skirmish with the British.

Anna glared at Donal, knowing that she looked nothing short of hideous with her eyes dramatically hollowed by Maura's application of peat soot.

She settled into a position that allowed her to sit sideways with her hips squashed between the canvas-covered thatch in the back and the bench seat. Donal and Maura climbed up, and the procession to Glengariff began. Maura talked on about people they knew, their children and their desirable and not-so-desirable traits. Anna heard more than once, "What is the world coming to? Those children! I never could have carried on that way when I was a child."

Had every generation since the beginning of time despaired over the younger generation? Perhaps there had always been some perception of children as some alien species, one devoid of social graces. Anna had to admit that she thought this was absolutely true of her nephew. How could he have been arrested? But she considered Maura's commentary as convincing evidence that perhaps every generation really wasn't worse than the former because it just wasn't possible. She pictured herself behind a podium in a lecture hall, perhaps Boston College. A PowerPoint presentation glowed in back of her, showing an Irish family in 1844. "When I was in Ireland in 1844, people were already complaining about the ruin of civilization because of their children. So you can see that this firsthand knowledge of historical/social mores leads one to see this pessimism more as a stage theory of adult development. At some stage we all despair of the next generation. Are there any questions?"

No, nothing that she heard or saw could be mentioned if she ever found her way home again. If she made it home, she'd be muzzled. This very bumpy journey to Glengariff would exist only in her mind. But what about Glenis, Donal, and Maura; surely they would remember her? There would be no one to tell, except for Joseph, if he was alive. If she could find him.

By nightfall, they were within five miles of Glengariff. Donal unhitched the horse and allowed her to graze.

"It's not a good thing to drive a horse into the ground," he said. "This draft horse will do anything I ask her, but in return, I shouldn't ask her to go beyond her mark."

Anna wondered why she had been asked to go ridiculously beyond her own mark. Donal arranged the camp for the night. Anna watched his movements. Had he done this one thousand times? Was setting up camp as normal to him as getting in her car and driving to the Cumberland Farms was to her? He flipped open the carefully rolled canvas that had protected her from the rough thatch. She noted the muscles in his neck popping to attention as he focused on a project that as yet made little sense to her. Then, as he pushed and pulled and arranged, she suddenly saw their accommodations. He'd set sturdy rocks on either side of the wheels and draped a long swath of canvas from one side of the loaded cart to let it flow to the ground.

"There. That should keep the mist off you throughout the night."

Anna peeked under the wagon and saw that he had extended another layer of canvas to cover the earth. Anna sighed as she pictured how hard the night would go, sleeping on the ground, catching scraps of sleep on her side until that went numb, then turning over to try the other side, then on her back until her tailbone howled, then some variation on her belly. All of this would have gone better with Glenis. They would have leaned into each other, somehow relieving the pain. Now she imagined all three of them flip-flopping through the night, with chances for sleep dramatically remote.

"Please tell me you don't snore," she said to Donal.

"I'll tell you nothing of the sort, and you won't be finding out on this night if I snore like a foghorn from hell. I'm walking into Glengariff over the hills to make sure our next man along the way is ready for us in the morning."

"You're leaving us?" asked Anna, suddenly alarmed.

"There's nothing to harm you out this way. A few hedge-hogs might sniff at your toes, nothing else. Oh, the magpies will screech you awake with their complaining, but I should be back before then."

After a supper of potatoes heated in a small fire, Maura and Anna crawled beneath the cart and arranged themselves.

Donal had disappeared into the darkness, setting out at a crisp pace. Maura arranged herself like a dog, turning, sighing, and farting over and over until she was satisfied.

"Tis a good thing for an old married woman like me, grandmother to seventeen already—seventeen who lived, I won't count the dead ones—to run off now and then to let Himself grow a little fonder in the heart, if you take my meaning. Old men can, if they live long enough and if the drink doesn't take their minds, get stiffened and unnoticing like old trees; the birds nest in them and they forget to say please and thank you kindly."

Maura had loosened her white hair, which was accented with a few brilliant reminders of red, a combination that Anna realized would have been lost to the twenty-first-century obsession with looking young and using hair coloring to hide any signs of aging. Maura was soft in the hips and breasts, and Anna caught a pleasing scent from the older woman that was nearly hidden beneath the strong unwashed odor that permeated nearly everyone. Beneath all that, Maura smelled of fresh air and simmering potato soup, a combination that could stop armies in their tracks and make them fall to their knees and moan with longing.

Maura spoke again. Anna had been sure that the older woman had fallen asleep.

"I'll head home tomorrow, and the whole way I'll picture his craggy head as he holds a blade to the grinding wheel or tightening a door pull in the cupboard. It is a sweetness missing someone you love, a privilege from the heavens. Good night, Anna."

Had she ever missed her husband Steve like that, before the miscarriages, before the affair, the divorce? Or had they been two automatons working 80 hours per week at their respective jobs, clamoring for their lawyerly ascent? Could she remember his head, the bristle along his closely shaven neck? As Anna dropped off to sleep, she recalled the way that Donal had snapped the heavy canvas, shaking it hard with his arm, making a long arc from his legs past the tips of his fingers.

The night passed more quickly than she'd imagined it would. From her vantage point between wheel and canvas, she periodically noted the clockwise turning of the stars ticking across the canopy of sky. Maura snored in a soothing way, with puffs of exhalations that came rhythmically, like the ocean.

It was Donal, not the magpies, who woke them.

"Come awake, Maura, there's trouble. Come on now."

Anna heard the tang of urgency in his voice, and she rolled out from under the wagon into a crouch.

"What's wrong?" she said, standing up and dusting off her skirt. She slipped on her jacket.

Donal's eyes betrayed a night without sleep; a shock of jagged red lines stared back at her.

"We've lost two men in town. One was killed outright, and the other is on his way to Cork to the almighty new prison. He'll wish he was dead. Maura! For God's sake, come out from under there."

The glint of mist hung on Donal's cap, and his shoes were muddied up to his ankles. The magpies began their morning song, and their gleaming black bodies soared over the camp. He ran to the slight rise where the horse was tethered and brought her back, injecting his sense of impending danger into the animal.

"Help me, Anna. We've got to get this wagon into Glengariff and beyond. We've got to drive straight through to the far side of Beara Peninsula."

Maura crawled out from her sleeping nest. Donal paused in his labors to extend a hand and pull some grasses from Maura's long nest of hair. Anna watched as Donal gently picked out the debris with care. An abandoned place in Anna's throat swelled and sweetened, tasting of light maple syrup. Maura grabbed Donal's hand for a quick pat and began to twist and wrap her hair.

"You know I can't go that far; I've got to go home. I promised I would. The old man is waiting, and all he has left are my promises."

Donal backed the horse into place to be hitched to the carriage. She threw her head up to catch even more of Donal's fear-laden scent. The horse's eyes were wide. He murmured to her, soothed her with some Irish words that Anna could not understand, but the sound of them coated her rising adrenaline as well. What ancient words could do that?

"Then you're in luck, because the stage from Glengariff to Skibbereen runs three days a week and today is one of them. We'll put you on it; no promises to an old man will be shattered today," said Donal.

They were silent for the ride into Glengariff. Only the brisk trot of the horse marked time. Once they crossed a small bridge, Donal brought the cart to a halt by a whitewashed inn. Two men and a boy waited outside with rucksacks. Maura immediately brightened.

"Look now, if it isn't John Murphy and his sons waiting for the stage. I'll have a fine ride to Skibb with the likes of him. I'll learn all the gossip that's true and all that's storied up by John."

They said their good-byes to Maura and left her at the stage stop, already engaged by the alleged storyteller. Glengariff was dominated by the presence of English soldiers, who looked eerily like every other occupying army: proprietary, disdainful, vigilant, and armed. Anna rode next to Donal. Anyone would assume they were husband and wife, but neither of them had spoken of it, neither of them had said they would pretend to be so. After they rode through the town, Anna wiped all the soot from her face; they had decided that it had only made her look filthy, not sick.

"Where exactly are we going?" asked Anna from her perch on the horse cart.

Donal took up considerably more space in every way than Glenis had. When he sat on the bench seat, he spread his knees wide, immediately carving out more area, the way men do, with legs, shoulders and elbows. He lifted his right elbow to give a lazy snap of the reins and nearly smashed into Anna's face.

"If I told you exactly, what would it matter? You don't know the Beara Peninsula in any way. If I said three miles inland from the boggy glen, would you know where I meant? And this is for your own protection. You are protected by your lack of knowledge," he said.

He wore his cap, a brown wool weave, from which came a scent of damp wool, body oil, and peat smoke, all sent steaming from his head. Anna's nostrils flared slightly to make room for the size of this particular smell, then she caught herself and rubbed at her nose with her fist, as if she could rub him away. Donal turned to look at her.

"You have no bonnet. Don't the ladies wear them in America?"

This had been a concession to living in the past that Anna had refused. She didn't like to wear hats, even though she realized that there were perfectly sensible reasons why other women wore them: they wore them to keep their infrequently washed hair clean and to demonstrate their modesty. Covering hair put a visual cap on their sexuality. Glenis had scolded her on several occasions and had even refused to walk along the cobbled streets of Kinsale unless Anna had put a hat on, at least for the day. Now that Anna was traveling with Donal, she was not going to accept fashion mandates from him.

"That's correct. Women do not wear hats with the same rigor as they do here in Ireland. And do not think that you can advise me otherwise," she said.

"It's only that you'll come to the attention of people, and I don't want either of us to come to attention. You'll be the odd bird, the one with the wrong-colored feathers, if you get what I mean. So I'm not making a request of you; it is something that you must do and it goes far beyond your peevish preferences. Now, do you happen to have a bonnet in your satchel?"

Clomp, clomp, tick, tick, the wheels, the wood of the cart creaking, the full brightness of the midday sun making Anna squint. She pictured a neon sign hanging over her with a flopping arrow pointing down at her bare head for all to see her otherness. If she'd been advising a client about how to appear in court, she would have used the same logic as Donal, except she would have said, "Ditch the tongue stud, cover up the tattoos, wear a skirt of a soft pastel shade—a tasteful, kindergarten teacher outfit."

She grabbed her satchel from the floor of the cart and found a wrinkled cloth hat. She shook it out and ran her hands over the wrinkles, pressing them and staring straight over the haunches of the horse, until she put on the hat. Donal said nothing, but he straightened his shoulders a bit and began to whistle a tune.

Late in the day, they arrived at the exact middle of nowhere, as near as Anna could tell. It was lined with sharp and un-yielding gorse plants, which hampered Anna's efforts at peeing discreetly. There were no houses, and the path they were following placed them perilously close to the edge of the cliffs. Donal guided the cart under a canopy of ever-green trees, well hidden from the coast and from what traffic might chance by. They made a small fire and ate potatoes that Donal had purchased along the way after their supplies had run low. They sat across from each other, with the fire glowing between them.

"I know you like to understand where we're going. Tomor-row, if all things go in our favor, we'll stay at a little bit of a cottage where you can sleep in a bed. Near there, we'll trade our goods with a French ship. Ardgroom is the name of the town."

"What would happen to Glenis and Tom and all the people who, uh, barter with them if this load is not smuggled out to the French ship?" asked Anna. She wiped her hands on the hem of her skirt, which was already miserably dirty.

Donal stood up and moved to the cart. He took the op-portunity to tighten the rolls of bound thatch that had come loose. She spun around on her rock seat and watched him.

"It was four months of work inch by inch, this one and that one bringing what they had to trade by the dark of the moon to Glennie and Tom. Then you came along and slowed down the flow of things. Glennie let it be known that she wouldn't make the trip until you were clearly well enough from your mishaps and were fully mended. If something goes wrong, they would start over, that's what. We are born knowing how to start over," he said.

Donal strapped on a peg of an artificial arm. "Meet my stabber and poker."

It was a perfectly straight stick. At the end, where a hand should have been, was an imposingly sharp iron point, rather like a large letter opener, attached by screws. "What's it made of?" asked Anna.

"Bone. The femur bone of a horse in this case. I had one made of wood, but I didn't like it as much. I rather like another animal attached to me, and I'm fond of horses. Glennie and I have that in common."

Donal stabbed at the thatch with his horse bone arm, while he used his good arm to tighten the hemp rope around it.

Anna pictured all the artificial limbs that she'd ever seen, the hi-tech versions that could produce movement in perfectly sculpted waxen fingers, the viciously sharp hooks and all the less technologically advanced prosthetics. But Donal's horse bone arm with an iron point at the end looked effective enough. Once an arm was gone, any replacement wasn't ever going to look like an arm again; it was another thing entirely. She watched the rhythm of his work. He turned slightly with his left side and jabbed at the thatch, then yanked hard with his powerful right arm, cinching the hemp rope where it had come loose. Stab, cinch, pull out the sharp pointed arm, and start again.

No one had expected this expedition to take longer than three days, and now everything seemed to be fraying, even the thatch. Donal had told her that they were on the out-skirts of Ardgroom, but she had no mental picture at all of where they were, as if her sense of directions had been short-circuited. The discomfort of this created a sense of helpless-ness that she dreaded.

Anna would do anything for Glenis, even help Donal travel to safer access points with the black market goods. Glenis had sworn that if there was help to be had for Anna and Joseph, then Biddy Early was their truest hope. And if Glenis could ride for three days to Limerick, surely Anna could do her part by supplying the labor that Glenis would have provided to Donal. Surely she could do anything for a few days.

"You sound like you know every crevice of the coastline," said Anna.

"And well I should. Oh, you think it's the smuggling made me wise. Did not Glenis tell you two wits about me? I'm a cartographer. After my arm was cut off as a lad, my father found a way to send me to France to go to school. I was smug-gled myself. I was there for seven years, bundled off like a firkin of butter when I was twelve or so. There's many Irish in France. Some say all the old Irish royalty left, abandoned the rest of us and left for France. I can't say if that's true or not, but I was given safe passage, and good haven while I studied. And here's the precious thing; I was a mapmaker for the British in Cork, or I was until two years ago."

Cartographer? Muscles along Anna's neck relaxed; she hadn't known that they were pulling her up like a mario-nette. Donal was the pilot of this aircraft; she didn't need to keep straining to see where they were going. He did know every inch of the coastline.

"The village that we're going to, Ardgroom? You won't see

it on a map, not any map that I've drawn. I've left off places that the British are not deserving of."

Of course: the cartographer has the ultimate power of knowledge over the occupying forces. And an invading country was always at a disadvantage; no one knew the landscape like the people who'd grown up on it.

"And I suspect that there are other places you've left off your maps," she said. She swatted at the smoke, urging it out of her face.

"Aye. Only with the greatest care. I've left off a cove or two, but that's the best I could do. Anything too glaring and I'd be convicted of treason."

"Are you married? Do you have a family waiting for this trip to be over? This is so strange that I know almost nothing about you," said Anna.

"Until now, you didn't care to know about me. You were only able to see Glenis and think about finding the lad and going home. You are most like a hunting dog, oh, not so much in looks, not at all. But true in the way you stick your nose in the air to catch a scent and you hear nothing else, see less, and only taste your prey."

"Thanks for the comparison to a four-legged creature with fur and fangs. I notice that you didn't answer the part about marriage."

The firelight spun off his dark eyes. Donal pulled a final rope hard and looped the end of the rope around a peg on the side of the cart. He put one foot up on the step of the cart in a resting pose. He rubbed his right hand along the length of the bone arm, and she heard the sizzle of his callused hand caress polished bone. Her eyes followed the line of his thigh, bent at ninety degrees.

"I see Glenis neglected to tell you. One more day on the ride with her and my entire history would have been splayed out. I was married and we had two children. I think of them still as wee ones, but when it was all over, they were not so small. Two years ago, the fever ran through Cork. That's where I had lived all my life, when I wasn't a student on the Continent. My wife, Peg, and the boys were blasted hard by the fever. First the boys were struck down, and then when she had nursed them through their deaths, Peg collapsed and the fever dove fiendishly into her. I wished she had not seen her sons die . . . " Donal's breath caught, and he exhaled hard in jagged bursts.

Anna felt the uncomfortable sting of tears fill her eyes. His loss slammed into her and pressed hard to be released. She knew that death from disease had been common in the nineteenth century. Glenis had recounted the deaths of scores of children, mothers in childbirth, loved ones deemed too young, taken by diseases that were all but eradicated in the twenty-first century. If she had ever thought that death was tolerated with greater ease because of its prevalence, Donal's pain disavowed her of this belief. She'd been wrong; she felt the crash of it resound in Donal, echo from side to side within his torso.

Anna stood up. She took a step toward him and stopped. She felt the heat from their small fire lap at her back.

"I'm sorry. There are no words for me to say . . . "

"Don't try. It was god-awful, and it still is. But that's the way of life. We get a swift life here and most of what we are left with is the remembering of times gone by that we can't relish enough when they're happening. But I will tell you this. I loved my wife every day and loved my boys so much that I can smell their necks right now if I let myself."

The skin on her inner arms began to vibrate, as if a tiny flock of butterflies had been struggling right beneath the epidermis, hoping to lift off. There was the unsettling sensation of a breeze on her nipples when there should have been no breeze at all, tucked away as they were beneath two layers of thick cotton, stitched and overstitched to make a firm bodice, and over this a washed wool that kept out all but the most vicious rain. A light mist began to fall on them, nothing that anyone who slept indoors would notice, but for those unfortunate enough to be outside, it was an indicator that their night would be long and cold.

Anna pulled her hood up and tightened her cape around her. "I can't imagine a father loving his sons. That just didn't happen in my family. My father acted like he was possessed by demons, wanting to love my brother and loathing him in the same moment. I know that love does happen between fathers and sons, but I only saw the opposite. And then my brother carried on with the same rage even though he had hated every second of it as a boy."

"What of you? Did your Da treat you the same?"

Anna flinched. She never liked it when the questions focused on her. But there was something different about Donal.

"I was the one who got in between them. I was sure that they'd kill each other, and they very nearly did. I came home one night when I was twelve and there was an ambulance, I mean all the neighbors were there, Patrick was bloodied and hurt, taken out on a stretcher, and my father was gone. I don't ever remember a time when I wasn't on alert, trying to do or say something that would stop my father."

Donal put his foot back on the ground and took one step closer to Anna. "What became of your Da? Did he soften in his old age? Men do that, the hard ones sometimes soften."

"After he nearly killed my brother, he left. Abandoned us. But that was over twenty years ago." Anna paused and shifted around in the future and the past. "He never contacted us again. But now he's sick, or so I hear." Anna didn't know how to tell Donal that she had hired a detective agency to find her father when he was in Thailand and that he was now in California, diagnosed with the early onset of Alzheimer's. She decided not to try.

"And how did your brother fare with his son, the lad that you're searching for?" Donal was close enough that Anna could see his lips as he spoke, even in the dark.

"That's the awful part. He can't seem to do any better. He can't touch Joseph, can't wrap an arm around him, can't laugh with him, can't eat a meal with him when he's not glaring at the kid like he's a criminal. But Patrick is tormented, I know he is. I understand my brother, and I know he wants to love his son more than anything."

" If Glennie was here I know what she'd say. Have you not told her this pitiful bit?"

"No, not this part."

"She'd say to look for a curse."

Anna prepared to catch her breath and she found that her breath could not be caught, that her lungs pumped and labored at the sight of his moist brow, his black hair beneath his knit cap. Her organs jerked around in her torso like breakdancers, her stomach twirling, doing a one-handed push-up ending in a dazzling back flip. She wondered if she could still speak; if she did, would words come, or would they emerge as smoke.

"A curse? Do you mean like, well, a curse? I don't think I can accept that. I've never known anyone who was cursed. I've known people who seemed to live beneath a dark cloud . . . "

"Aye, and no matter what they did, what crop they planted, who they fell in love with, what sweet child they bore, everything turned to maggoty rot. You've known them. Only you didn't know they were cursed, and neither did they," said Donal.

The rain had just gone from mist to the next stage, something that had more weight to it. Donal looked up, squinting into the sky. He reached behind the seat of the cart.

"But don't be thinking we are cursed, you and I, by a series of poor accommodations. This will be our last night sleeping under this cart. Come now, help me roll out our canvas."

As Anna prepared to make her way under the cart once again, she slid her hands into the deep pockets of her skirt to catch a reassuring feel of the twenty-first-century cloth that she kept with her at all times. Gone. The scrap of blue silk was gone. She thought back and realized that she must have left it when she and Glennie had slept out. Or had it been last night with the old woman? No matter, she'd never be able to find it now. She smiled at the thought of whoever might find it.

Anna thought she would never be able to sleep near this man she had met only several days ago. How could she? And she still wondered this as she fell asleep almost instantly, lulled by the rain pattering on the cart, curled against the back wheel. The last thing she heard was the throaty snore of a man.

They had been at the isolated one-room cottage in Ardgroom for two days. The air began to turn cooler, then sharp at night. Donal had left stacks of stones arranged in piles of three on the eastern outskirts of Glengariff, alerting those in the smuggling route that Donal was now at a different location.

"We'll divide it into three loads with the drink being its own separate box," said Donal. "The French sailors find some use for our poteen, but they should take care that they don't go blind from drinking it. If all goes as planned, men should come and take the loads, and then our part is done."

Poteen was the local white lightning, a home brew that had scorched Anna's throat when she had tested it in Kinsale.

Together they had unloaded the thatch from the cart and unpacked the goods from within each bundle of thatch. There were tight bolts of linen, beautiful tatted lace, whole firkins of butter, everything that Ireland had been forbidden to export. Except to England; they could always export to England, which would pay the Irish one-tenth of the goods' worth.

"We've been here for two days," said Anna, picking painful bits of thatch from her fingers. "Why hasn't anyone come to get these things?" The two of them had grown increasingly edgy, bumping into each other, ricocheting like dancing molecules, saying, "Sorry, oh how clumsy of me." Anna wanted out. She wanted to be back in Kinsale when Glenis rode in with the news of how to find Joseph, how to go back home.

"The rocks that I left as a sign only mean that someone

may be at any of a dozen places with goods to smuggle out. Those who take them to the sea must look in each location, each shed, stable, abandoned cottage, until they find us."

They had stacked the goods in the darkest corners of the cottage, under canvas tarps. Donal's restlessness, mixed with her own, made her want to scream. He had repacked the grease in the wheels, poked around with horse's shoes, tethered the horse here or there for grazing, oiled his boots, oiled her boots, and found a sharpening stone to sharpen two knives that appeared from his leather satchel.

On the third day, Donal announced a change in plans.

"The killing in Glengariff has put off the lads. We'll miss the French ship if we don't take the crates down to the beach. And we'll lose their trade if we don't deliver as we swore to."

Still groggy from sleep, Anna was just sitting up in bed, amazingly left behind by the former tenants. She tossed off her cape, which had covered her in the night.

"Did you say 'we,' as in we will take the crate? You and I?" said Anna.

Donal pulled open the door, and the hinges protested with a deeply metallic whine. "This may be a poorly hatched plan, and if it is, I'll pay dearly with Glennie. She'll have my hide if anything happens to you. Not to say that I want anything to befall you. . . . "

Anna leaped from bed. "How hard can this be? Let's go."

Chapter 24

She walked in front of Donal, climbing up the path from the bay. They had had to wait all day and into the night for the ship. The moon was new and the sliver of light gave them only the hint of illumination, so Anna was reduced to walking with her hands in front of her, as if she'd been newly blind.

They had met the French sailors in the tiny rowboat, the emissaries from their ship, and the exchange had been swift. Donal had passed two tightly packed boxes of poteen, a major currency of smuggling, which was now traded for what Donal truly wanted: grain and meat, the breath of life that would be parceled out to those who needed it the most. The next trade would be for other items, the finer things. But Donal hid the bounty as soon as the tiny boat was out of sight, saying it needed to be recovered by someone else.

"Who?" asked Anna as she stumbled and caught herself.

"Oh, here," he said. "Let me go first and you place your hand on me back, right on the point of me shoulder blade, or we'll be creeping along this coastal path when the sun comes up. We don't want that."

Anna stood still and Donal stepped past her.

"What now, who, you ask? Now why would I tell you that? Don't ask me such things."

And he began to walk with Anna's anxious hand pressed against his back. Already their pace picked up. She wanted to grip his shoulder blade, hold it like a steering wheel. Sweat sluiced down the center of her back and between her breasts. Twice she ran smack into him when he paused. He turned to face her.

"I'll not drive us off the cliff. You've no choice but to trust me. Try this again. Do you ride, Anna?" he asked.

Her twenty-first-century brain focused on her glorious bike, which she rode on weekends, training for the triathlon. A cross-trainer, good for trails or the road. But of course he wasn't asking about her bike. He meant horses.

"No," she said. "I don't."

"Strange. I took you for a horsewoman. Aye, I took you for that fancy group. Well, my story won't help you as much, then. But consider if you and I are horse and rider. A good horse reads the slightest movement from your legs, your arse, your hands. If you moved your head to the left, a good horse would know it, and he'd know before you fully knew that left was the way to go. And I can't quite say who is horse and who is rider here, but I want you to put your fine brain to rest and let your hand read my body so that we can get up this bloody trail."

Anna could not help but notice that in his directions, he had mentioned her legs, ass, head, hands and even her fine brain. He had just articulated more parts of her body than her ex-husband had noticed in the last six months of their marriage.

.

He continued. "Put your hand on my back again, my shoulder blade, and I'm going to turn. What did you feel?"

"Your shoulder blade pointed back toward me."

"Good. Now I'm stepping over a rock here, a good big one. What happened with my shoulder blade?"

"It moved up, and I think the other moved down a bit."

"Right. You should be picking your foot up, searching for whatever I just stepped over."

As he said this, Anna let her eyes sink down to the soles of her feet, and she lifted one foot and let it glide along a rock. She read his back all the way to the crest of the trail, where the horse and cart waited for them.

As they settled into the bench seat, and the horse began her steady pace back to the shelter of the cottage, Donal said, "Tomorrow is the last day for the other French ships destined to come to shore. You have just advanced in the smuggling trade. You'll be handling one trade at a spot very much like this one while I take the last batch across the peninsula."

"Am I moving up in the ranks?"

"Aye, lassie, you are moving up. To what rank is unclear, but you are moving up. And I must be losing my mind."

The shore along Rockport could be wild with storms. But unlike now, she could always go home, take off the rain gear and jump into a hot shower.

Now, Anna tried to remember what dry felt like on her skin, what warm had been. The invention of Gortex, more than 100 years in the future, whispered a distant song to her. Her job was to wait on the dark coastline, squatting on the rocks until she spotted a flash of lantern from an oth-

erwise darkened boat. She was determined to get her part
of this right. She had to light her small lantern in response,
using her cape as a tent to keep out the wind. Then, after
two minutes, she was to douse the light again. She had reas-
sured Donal that she could do this, and that she would not
panic, not fail, not flub the whole flipping deal. She had not
counted on the blistering severity of the cold, despite having
been here in the increasingly icy days of fall for two months,
despite knowing that cold and water and hypothermia could
be fatal assailants.

She had grilled Donal earlier in the day, after she had
convinced him that she could handle one of the clandestine
meetings by herself while he managed the other rendezvous
on the bay side of the peninsula.

"What if the boat that came ashore was English and not
French? Where will you be? When will you return? Tell me
again what to say if they offer less than the agreed-upon
amount?"

He had answered all her questions, all that she had dared
to ask, because if she had asked more (as she'd dearly wanted
to do), he likely would have denied her this chance. She'd
seen that he'd been on the edge of saying that she was too
much of a risk, and more than anything, she wanted to prove
her worth. He had shown her the spot on the beach, they had
walked it out yesterday, and today he had helped her drag the
cache to the protection of the rocky cove. Then he had driven
off with the cart, heading straight for the other side of the
peninsula to make a similar transaction.

She squatted to offer less of her body to the dense wind
and mist that billowed ashore like an advancing army. She
reminded herself that this sort of weather was hardly called

rain by the Irish; just mist, or the strange word *mizzle*. Only her booted feet had contact with the rocks as she made the rest of her as small as possible, keeping her knees tucked tight, head low. But even so, the cold sank into her bones so that she was raw from her spine out to her skin. There was no hiding from this elemental tyrant.

She saw a light and lit her lantern, dousing it two minutes later. She waited for a response, three blinks of light in answer to hers that said French, that said we are rowing ashore, be there, be quick. There, there it was. Anna had squatted too long; her knees were frozen in place. She willed her once triathlon-trained body to obey her. "Stand up," she commanded. She stood up, keeping a firm grip on the lantern. There was only one place for a boat to come ashore—there was no mistaking the spot. Anywhere else, a boat would shatter on the imposing rocks on either side of the cove. Her job was to show the men where it was and to accept the exchange, the bottles of the gracious items that the slim mercantile class would be willing to readily buy. How hard could the transaction be after working in a law firm?

Walk, she told herself. She had practiced this walk several times, over the slippery, steep rocks and trail, and as her chilly brain insisted, she only had to go down to the cove, which was far easier than climbing up. She didn't have to worry about climbing up just yet. Down, down to the slope of the beach, where she stood, waiting, as the dark shape approached, the men slicing through the water with their oars, looking all the while like a slinking pterodactyl, rising up to greet her.

The sailors delivered their crate a little ways up the beach, just far enough so that the high tide wouldn't wash it away. Anna was helpless with the French language. She wanted to ask them to help her drag the crate up to the rocks so that it couldn't be seen, but she was shivering too much by the time they arrived, and her teeth were chattering, and she only knew a few words of French. She tried to remember her high school Spanish because surely there would be similarities, but the more she shivered, the more her brain decelerated.

There were four sailors and they moved quickly, leaping out of the rowboat, slamming their crate on the sand, taking hers, saying something about her, laughing, one shaking his head and barking an order, all before Anna could do anything. The rain had become steady, rain that needed a special name, rain for which, she suspected, the Irish had a name. She'd have to ask Glenis. The winds had diminished, for which she was grateful, but the rain increased and was tinged with ice.

She had promised Donal that she'd stay with the cargo until he came back. He said he'd come and get her, and she wanted him to know that she could do this just as well as Glenis. And she wanted Glennie to know that her word was good. And now she felt like sleeping; she could close her eyes and the rain and the night would be gone. She sat down next to the crate and leaned her head against the rough wood, pulling her woolen hood closer, making a condensed version of herself, an elixir.

From her huddled position, time was foreshortened. Her knees pulled into her chest, her left side pressed against the crate, and the ice came down in pinpricks of hot, hot, hot. *Oh, that's the hypothermia*, she thought with a steady calm. Now, at last, she'd be warm again.

What did painters do before they learned about the techniques of foreshortening? How did they explain distance and the perception of tiny cows far away, of long hallways that disappeared into smaller and smaller spaces? This must have had something to do with time travel, she could feel it; if she could no longer feel her body, at least she could feel this certain connection with time, back where she started, back on the shore, freezing again. She deduced that this must be the case and looked for causality. She strained to stay awake, because foreshortening had something to do with time travel, and if she could keep thinking, she'd figure this out. As she sat freezing on the beach, Anna was fueled by the tenacity of lawyer-speak, opened by the rain, stroked by the rhythm of the waves, and pushed by the sand beneath her feet.

Foreshortening. She had walked through the Boston Museum of Fine Arts and had stood puzzled before the great flat artists of the twelfth and thirteenth centuries. Couldn't they tell that something wasn't as it should be? Or had they collectively agreed that the world of painting must be flat, that the way our eyes saw the distance was a trick, not to be spoken or replicated? That's it, there was something about time that was right in front of her, and she had to stop seeing in the way that everyone had collectively agreed to. She was sitting—squatting, if she recalled correctly—on the coast of Ireland, having just concluded a black market business venture with French sailors, awaiting the rendezvous with Donal. Yes, all this—the rain, her thickening thoughts, the sodden wool cape, her head resting against the crate, the agreed-upon year of 1844, looping from the twenty-first century, her brother's head bashed in with a Ford truck—all coming together as flat. If she could see it all foreshortened, the way the first great renegade artists who let their gaze run off the tiny horizon dared to show us a large hand, followed by a small body, then she could understand the whole thing.

And there was nothing more important than understanding the foreshortening of time.

What was this painting? What overly large image was the foreground? There, it was Joseph, her nephew, in his absolute mathematical value, not the monosyllabic, sixteen-year-old version. The painting was all about him. All oversized and waiting for Anna to see him. And look, behind him, the road that had started wide grew more narrow as it flew off into the background, all streaming to the past. She thought she saw tiny bits of people: Glenis, Donal, other people standing on the spongy tundra of hope, waving. Keep going; this was making perfect sense.

She suddenly jetted back to her body. Something had sliced her back. A hand, an arm, a voice, someone urging her up. Donal. He was crying something like tears and she knew this without opening her eyes, yet she had to tell him about the painting before she forgot. His face came close to hers. She said, "Foreshortening." But with the rain she wasn't sure that he heard her.

She felt lifted, and he carried her the only way a one-armed man could carry her, over his shoulders, her upper torso bobbing along, hanging upside down. Ah, perfect. Foreshortening, she nodded to herself.

The rusty hinge of the door screamed open, audible over the rain and through the fog of her too-chilled brain. Donal kicked something out of the way; wood skidded across the room. Before she could wonder what had merited his urgent entry into the cottage, she was on the bed sitting up. Donal untied her hat and her waterlogged cape. While she sat, oddly immobile, he unfastened her boots. The top of his head fascinated her as he bent over her feet, working frantically to relieve her of her dripping shoes.

As soon as the shoes hit the floor, Donal flung a quilt and a wool blanket over her, wrapping her tightly. He struck the flint into action, lighting the peat fire. Her chest filled with a delicious gratitude for the fire, which surpassed anything that she could remember. Is this what it was like for all the Irish? Did the fire mean this much to everyone?

With the fire sending tendrils of heat to her face, her body began to relax and the shivering moved down a notch. Donal took two steps from the fire to stand in front of her. Anna felt obliged to try and sit up. She had so much to tell him about the French sailors, about the foreshortening, the painting, but what was all that?

"Listen to me," Donal said, grabbing her chin, then letting go too quickly, as if the oval end of her jaw had jolted him. "You've nearly killed yourself. Don't you know enough to seek shelter? There was nothing so precious in that crate worth dying for. Oh, Jaysus, if you had died. . . ."

Donal stopped. Anna's teeth had begun to chatter again as she warmed, reversing the process of hypothermia. She was so grateful that the rain was not running down her neck, and the wind off the Atlantic was not slamming into her. She wanted to tell Donal that she'd understood something about time while she had been huddled on the beach guarding the black market goods, but even now it made less sense to her. Wait, it had been so clear in the way that dreams are clear in the seconds of waking in the middle of the night, only to be left shardlike in the morning. But if it had been about time and Joseph, she'd have to save that for Glenis, who understood everything.

She wiggled an arm from the quilt and reached out, still shivering, for Donal, whom she had not touched in the way she was about to touch him. Both of them watched her arm as if it heralded a proclamation. She found his hand, still hot with rage and fear, and pulled as best she could, pulled until he understood that she wanted him to come down to her. He sank to his knees while she kept her eyes on his face, saw his brow soften, his eyes close. Still unable to keep her teeth from chattering, she moved her hand up to his shoulder, working her fingers along until they came to his moist neck. Ah, there it was, that's what she was looking for, the vast epidermal covering of this man. Her fingers sank into the back of his neck, pulling his head to hers.

"Come here," she said, with surprising clarity, not chattering at all.

Chapter 25

Joseph was shocked at how strong his body had become by practicing every day. It wasn't as if he hadn't practiced in high school. This was what he imagined it was like to take testosterone. His coach in high school had been so dramatic at the start of each season.

"If I catch any of you taking performance-enhancing drugs, I will immediately throw your ass off the team. So if you double in size between now and November, get acne the size of tomatoes, and growl like a rabid dog, that's going to be my clue that you're using and you'll be busted. No negotiating. This is wrestling, not multimillion-dollar baseball."

But Joseph was not in high school, not on the wrestling team. He was no longer the lowest life-form, a social throwaway, and he no longer had to tangle with his father every day and wonder what he'd done wrong. His father had had a list, which had started in the morning and grown to an exhausted heap by bedtime. It was better not to think about that part of his life.

Or maybe this is what sixteen was like, with his shoulders swelling up and his forearms hardening. The manservant who dressed him said that his shirts were now too small for him, and his neck was larger. His grandmother would call this a growth spurt. She'd told him once that his father had grown four inches one summer. She'd said it had been like watching a science experiment, or one of those tiny sponges that turned into Scooby Doo when you put it in water. He did wish his grandmother could see him—that much he missed.

He'd won four wrestling matches and was scheduled for another with the champion of Cork. The colonel had his new wrestling career mapped out; all the local parishes, and Dublin. Then he would have beaten every Irish man who called himself a wrestler. The colonel said that wrestling was a gentleman's sport and the Irish had no business in it. He intended to prove it.

The matches that Joseph had observed here sometimes took as long as thirty minutes. All of his matches in high school had been over in less than five minutes. Joseph's coach had trained them in building sprinter-type muscles designed to give maximum power for up to ten minutes. Ten minutes was an extraordinary length of time for a match. By his second year, Joseph had been able to take down every opponent before he knew what was happening.

Only one tiny thought, niggling around in the back of his brain, troubled him. All of the men he wrestled were endurance athletes. They were farmers who plowed fields for ten hours, fishermen who hauled nets until their muscles popped up along their arms, and they could all just keep going. If Joseph couldn't pin a man in his sprinter's time, it might get difficult. So far, his speed and ferocity had beat out endurance. He had superior training, his reflexes were faster than those of any of the men he had challenged, his balance was fantastic, and, most of all, he had been trained to read an opponent's body from the moment he first saw him. He looked at the walk, the flexibility, and, most telling of all, the initial handshake.

Joseph practiced wrestling all morning with Sean, who was gradually becoming a better opponent. Owen was mercifully given other duties by Deirdre and no longer had to return for practices. More often than not, Madigan liked to watch the wrestling practices. The huge dog seemed to think that his part in the whole production was to run into the melee when one of the boys was pinned and to pound his two front feet on the loser's chest. *Take that*, the dog said.

Joseph had taught Sean the fundamentals, the rules, how to watch his opponent, how to place a hand on a shoulder, a thigh, the place between the shoulder blades. Even though Sean complained bitterly that he would never be as good as Joseph, he was clearly improving. Once he'd even surprised Joseph by flipping him to the ground. Sean had been so startled by his success that both of them had broken out in spasms of laughter. Since then, the practices had gone easier, as Sean had a ray of hope that his destiny was not just to be used as something for Joseph to fling about.

Sean trotted off to the kitchen to find whatever Deirdre had put out for the groundsmen. Madigan went with him. Joseph took a few moments to stretch after the practice, which he could not convince Sean to do. As he headed off to the comforts of the kitchen, he heard a familiar *ching* of hardened metal on stone. He followed the *tap, tap* to the construction site of the garden wall. He felt the pull, felt time tugging at him, dragging him by his ears.

When he had been a little boy and his father had just begun

to build stone walls and fancy garden terraces, his father had taken him to work with him on weekends. Not often, because his grandmother had clamored for him to come with her, or Anna had said it was time for him to learn rollerblading, rock climbing, kayaking, swimming, or any of the things that Anna had thought were good. That was before Anna had gone all mental and gotten divorced and then gotten even more mental. But when Joseph had gone with his father, his father had given him firm instructions.

"Take your Tonka truck and stay over there, not close to me, because I'm splitting Goshen stone and you could get hurt. Got it?"

And Joseph had tried to be a good boy, had tried to do as his father had told him, but somehow he'd never been a good boy. One time, he had picked up his yellow truck in both arms because the dumping mechanism had broken, and he'd taken it to his father who'd been tap, tap, tapping on a giant rock, and it had all happened so quickly, so many things converging. Joseph had held up the Tonka to his father, his father had swung the hammer on the rock, the rock had split, and Joseph had fallen, the truck popping up into the air and making a yellow-and-black spiral. Joseph had landed on the sharp edge of the rock, his hand coming down on the newly exposed, surgically sharp edge of stone. A red river of blood had poured from the side of his hand. His father had dropped the hammer.

"Can't you stay out of trouble for two minutes? For two lousy minutes? What good are you?"

Joseph wondered if everyone was dragged around by memories the way he was. He couldn't shake the bad memories of his father, and at the same time he knew he was missing something important that should be remembered about his father. What was he missing?

He made his way to the stonemason, who held a stout pole under one large rock, ready to move it.

"Can you give me a hand here, lad? Can you put some of your fine wrestling arms to moving some stone?"

Oh, yes, he could do that. If only his father had asked him in the easy way of the stonemason. And if only his father had winked and smiled, and if only he had tousled his hair. If only.

Deirdre stirred a pot of sauce. Its aroma was enough to make Joseph pass out. He'd never really seen anyone pass out from pleasure, but he had never tasted anything like Deirdre's cooking. She cooked a lot of things that were a cross between cakes and puddings mashed together. There were a few things that Deirdre made that he couldn't eat, but only a few, and they all had to do with the organ meats; at those moments he did the best he could to beg off.

Joseph had hazy memories of his mother pouring ingredients while he stood on a chair, eager to mix with a spoon. But how much could he expect to remember, when he was just four when she died? From then on, it had been just the two of them, his father and him. His grandmother had provided a neutral zone, and she'd enjoyed cooking on the weekends, but for the rest of the time, his father would stop at Burger King for a soda, burgers, and fries and bring the whole thing home. Or pizza, or maybe they'd stop at Subway. None of that had prepared Joseph for Deirdre's cooking. And Taleen, nothing in his entire life had prepared him for Taleen. If Taleen walked near his food, it tasted even better, her scent lingering like a spice.

The only history about Ireland that Joseph knew was something about a famine, but he didn't know when it was. From all indicators, there wasn't a famine happening in Tramore. The gardens at the estate were lush and crammed full, or they had been crammed full; it was late fall and the harvest had come and gone. The trees were bare.

"Here, sit down. I'll give you a dish of this so that you don't die on the spot from wishing," said Deirdre. She spooned in some moist cake, then covered it with a ladle full of the creamy sauce.

Joseph dove into it and ended by running his finger around the bowl, wiping up every crumb, down to each rivulet of cream. Madigan lay at his feet, with his head resting on Joseph's boots. The dog followed each movement of the spoon.

"What sort of food does your family eat? I can't tell if you devour this because it reminds you of home or because it is the thrill of eating a new and rare delight," said Deirdre.

"My mother died when I was four. She had a riding accident; she was thrown by a horse." They would understand a riding accident here.

"The death of a mum is a terrible thing," said Deirdre. "Did your father marry again?"

Every time Deirdre mentioned his father, Joseph felt something big and powerful squeeze his skull, threatening to crush it.

"No, he didn't remarry. There's something about my father that I should remember, but I can't," he said and pushed his palms into the sides of his head.

"Sorry, lad. Let's keep to food then. Here now, it grieves you to talk about your mum. Or is it your father that gives you the pain?"

"It's my father. You're right. Let's keep to the food."

She dug out a spoonful, tested the pudding, made a squeezed-up face, and looked skyward as she considered.

"The cows have gotten into the cabbage again. Turns the milk in a sharp way. I'll send Con out to tell them that cows are not pigs. Pigs can turn the sharpness of cabbage to muscle. What has come over the lads looking after the herd? Nodding off, that's what I think."

Joseph couldn't find one thing wrong with the pudding and thought Deirdre, despite all her strengths, might be a little too fussy. He reached across the table to a pie and tried to nudge a bit of crust that was perilously loose along the edge. Deirdre slapped his hand.

"Away with you," she said.

Joseph smiled. Is this what it was like to have a mother—the firm swat on his knuckles, the persistent inquiry into his welfare? He stood up and looked down at the formidable woman, whose jarring green eyes always startled him. Madigan scurried to stand as well, as if he'd heard someone calling him.

"I don't remember much of my mother, but you're like a mum to me. Do you mind if I think that?" He had never said *Mum* before, and the way it sounded pleased him.

The late afternoon sunlight caught Deirdre's face from an angle. "Think it if it gives you comfort, lad; we need all the comfort we can get." Both of them looked toward the door, where Madigan stood impatiently.

"She's not back from school yet," said Deirdre, as if she could read his mind.

"I wasn't thinking about Taleen," he said, letting the lie fall off his tongue.

Deirdre took him by the hand and led him outside. "You're a lad and lads are not very complicated, if you don't mind me saying so. I know you find my cooking to your liking, but even my fine cooking is not reason enough for you to wander down to the kitchen as often as you do. You feel the pull of her."

Deirdre let go of his hand as they emerged on the courtyard that overlooked the kitchen garden, the bare fruit trees trellising up the garden walls, and, further still, the stables.

"You'll need to find one of your own, not from the servants. It would go badly for Taleen if the colonel knew that you fancied her."

Joseph kicked at the remains of a dried pit from one of the trees.

"What would happen to Taleen?"

"He'd forbid it. He is very much against gentlemen taking up with Irish. He could send her away."

Just then a gate squeaked, the sound carried by the moist air. From the upper pasture, Taleen came running, a book in her hand, the book that Joseph had taken from the colonel's library. Nothing that Deirdre thought mattered nearly as much as Taleen gliding over the pasture, her hair spreading out like dark wings. Madigan ran to meet her and danced circles around her.

This is my life now, thought Joseph, *and this is how it was always meant to be.* Living in the twenty-first century had been one big mix-up.

Chapter 26

Anna and Donal did not emerge from the whitewashed cottage for three more days, except to stumble out to pee, or to haul a bucket of water and pour it over their sweat-soaked bodies, gleaming in the November glare of midday light. Once Anna stepped outside naked, her hair damp and frizzing, rubbed into a tangled knot at the back of her head, just to breathe the cold air back into her lungs. Donal opened the door and pulled her back to him, wrapping his one arm across her chest, as a lifeguard might.

"Do you think we'll catch on fire?" asked Anna, already dissolving into his chest, as if she'd been doing the backstroke and he'd been the ocean.

"Aye, we could go up in smoke. People have, you know. There are certain places where saints ignited and their ashes ascended to the heavens."

She twisted her head around to catch a glimpse of the dark stubble on his face. "Are we being saintly? Do you think that people will remember us and that they'll canonize us with sainthood?"

"I've no interest in saints, nor in what shreds of us will be remembered. Come back inside, Anna, and see if we can rise in our own smoke."

What common language could they unravel? Anna had the language of technology, speed, the law, and sarcasm. And trickery, a thick layer of trickery that submerged her twenty-first-century world so that it did not peek out, embarrassed and naked in Ardgroom.

Donal had the language of the land, secret and submerged as well, used as a language that the English didn't understand. The price for speaking it within earshot of the English was severe: loss of job, loss of the right to rent or worse. Anna continued to learn it, although her head threatened to burst from the effort.

She had learned that children had a saying for every day in school, when they were allowed to go to school. "Tell me again a saying for the day in Irish," she asked him, running her finger along his collarbone. His shirt hung from a peg, trying to dry itself near the small peat fire.

"Molann an abair an fear," he said. "The work praises the man."

Anna was befuddled by the daily sayings, until she sat quietly, letting an ancient light shine in her brain. Then they became like Aesop's fables or Celtic fortune cookies.

She wore a light linen shift, an underthing that months ago would have been too rough for her skin, but everything about her had grown firmer, as if even her skin cells had been lifting weights, tiny cells pumping iron. Anna knew she had lost weight, but for the first time in her life, she couldn't run to a scale to determine how much weight. Instead she ran her hand along his chest, his shoulder, and the place where there should have been an arm. He did not flinch as she wrapped her palm around the thick stub just inches down from his shoulder.

"You're drawn to it. How can that be? I could not bear to look at it when I was a boy, thinking that half my world was gone. A man builds a life, work, a family with two arms."

Anna ran her fingers over the knotted scar tissue, the line of notches where thick stitches had once held his life together and saved him.

"Tell me how it happened," she said, bringing her lips to his scar.

As she waited for him to speak, she loosened her hair, letting it fall around her shoulders.

"Thirty years ago, I was a lad of eight when the British troops ran through the streets of Cork to smash a suspected uprising. Me mum had sent me to a safe house outside town; she and all the others knew that the troops were coming. But I doubled back. I sensed something big was happening, huge like a storm and there was nowhere else where I wanted to be. I came around a corner and was trapped, surrounded by troops. I reckon the soldier was not fully grown himself, but proving himself, hardening his heart. With one buttery stroke of a sword, me arm had flew off, thudding in the street. I didn't feel the pain of it for a long time, but I was shocked to see my very own arm laying so far from me, I'll say that. I felt someone grab me up, and a woman took me into her arms and she ran down a little space between the houses and she took off her shawl and stuffed it around the stub of me arm. I can't say why I lived or how they found a midwife to sew it tight enough to keep me from sending every ounce of my blood back into the earth. I remember her smell, crushed apples, and even as a boy, I took in her scent. It was the last thing I remembered for weeks."

Anna got up to stir the hearth fire. She added more peat. She could now manage a peat fire flawlessly.

"Hurting children is a way to break the spirit of a people," she said, as much to herself as to Donal. She settled back in next to him on their pile of clothes and blankets.

"But there is nothing broken about you," she said, rubbing her palm in a circular motion on his belly.

Donal rolled to his side and pulled her close.

"You're fixing everything there is to fix. If you don't stop, I'll sprout another arm."

Later, when her leg escaped from the heat under the blankets, he ran his foot along her scar.

"So you've been marked by the sea," he said, glancing over at her lower leg with the racing stripe of a scar running from knee to ankle. "Nearly all of us here are, in one way or another."

No one else had seen the scar except for the midwife who had stitched her leg, and Glenis and Tom. Anna had never seen a scar as vivid or as large as this one. She rubbed her leg.

"It will get lighter as time passes; it won't look as angry and bright after a year," she said. A wool blanket only partially covered them. Their bodies still warm from sex, neither wanted more heat. Anna rolled into the side of him and stretched with abandon, arching her spine, pressing her belly into him, forming a C with her body.

"Anna, I think you like sex as much as a man. And I'm not complaining even the smallest amount, but I didn't know it was possible."

She realigned her spine and rose up on her elbows, pushing long ropes of hair off her shoulders. She looked at him, this pre-AIDS, pre-genital herpes, pre-papilloma virus man who had only had sex with the one woman who had been his wife and given birth to their children. What could she tell him that would explain growing up in the culture of the twentieth and twenty-first centuries?

She folded her arms on his chest and laid her chin on her arms so that she could look straight at him. "Most of the time a woman worries about getting pregnant while having sex, especially if she doesn't want to be. That takes away from the enjoyment and she feels alone, rather than with her husband, at the moment of greatest pleasure. Or if she wants to be with child, then she can only think of that, and not what's happening, not the wonder of all the elements of two people fusing into one."

He sat up, and Anna tumbled off him like a cat. "Is that what it's like for you?" he asked. "Did you feel my elements fuse with yours? Because whatever happened for you was so very large and shocking."

In law school, the word was all-important; each word had to carry an exact weight and meaning. Words meant everything. But she had never tried to put words to an orgasm before, so how would she do it now, using only nineteenth-century words? She wanted to use words about trains with happy cars rushing along the tracks at incredible speeds, exploding with crackling energy, then chugging happily into a warm station, sighing. No. She also wanted to use analogies of sky diving, hang gliding, all the over-the-top sports that she had tried on vacation in Cancun. No, these would not do.

"It's like this, like you and I are riding down a river, floating at first, hand in hand or hand in foot, or any other body parts that we would perhaps least expect in contact with another body part, here there or anywhere, and the river's current picks up speed, sends us careening around heart-stopping rapids, and you and I must hold onto each other and our insides turn molten. Not hot like a blacksmith's fire but hot as if the smallest bits of ourselves have expanded and with each expansion we see the most dazzling spectacle of colors inside our brains shouting directly from our sex parts (a term that Anna had settled on after considering all possibilities) and we hurtled down the rushing river with something both excruciating and near God-like, and when we don't think we can bear it one more second without destroying ourselves in a celestial explosion of stars, we hear the roar of a massive waterfall ahead and there is no possible way for us to stop. The current grabs us and jerks us this way and that and suddenly we are over the top of the waterfall, and we are airborne, not knowing if we will live or die, entwined with each other. Gravity pulls at us and we spin, topple, head earthward and a pool of water catches us, dizzy and breathless as we are, struck dumb. We sink below the surface and finally come up for air and drag ourselves to a sandy shore, only able to stare at each other and gasp for breath. That's what it's like."

Donal put his hand on the back of her head, pulling her toward him. "Well," he said. "I thought so."

Chapter 27

It had been more than a week since Anna had wondered if her family and friends had forgotten her or if her law school buddies had stopped calling. Had anyone filed a missing person's report about her and Joseph? Had she been accused of kidnapping Joseph, irritating minor that he was?

These thoughts had pressed so hard on her in the first few months after barreling through a time chasm, a slippery slide that had dropped her off in 1844. Now they were softening and losing their urgency. She stopped trying to calculate quantum physics and the string theory of time. Cleary, time had its own validity, and just because she couldn't explain it, there was no reason to deny it. Anna no longer had the desire to see the exact formula. It turned out she had plenty of desire, bubbling over, erupting, undulating spine desires. But not for formulas; instead, she had desire for this man seated next to her on the bench seat of the cart, giving the horse a lackadaisical snap of the reins, more of a leather nudge. They were way off schedule—not that the Irish would adhere to any schedule, but they had stayed days longer than planned at the cottage in Ardgroom. But smuggling did adhere to the shipping schedules, which were also given to the whimsy of ocean and wind. They were all ultimately guided by the sea. Still, here she was, a smuggler.

Anna was used to defining herself by her ability to tolerate pain, which she knew was the best possible quality for a new lawyer in a large law firm that was ready to expand. She'd overheard one of the partners talking about her during the first year. "Every company has its workhorse, and that's just what Anna is." Despite having felt ruffled by being associated with a farm animal, Anna had secretly been proud, and she'd worked even harder. Her seventy-hour week had slid into eighty. Somewhere between the first and third year her husband had fallen in love with a woman who'd been perfectly happy being a receptionist manager in a dental clinic, the clinic where Anna and Steve had gone twice a year to have their teeth cleaned and where Anna had had her wisdom teeth extracted. The office manager's name was Rita. And Anna had to admit that Rita had been vivacious, positive, and attractive, with the potential for moments of vulnerability and helplessness. Just enough to get Steve's attention. And coincidentally, Rita had needed an attorney for her divorce.

The horse cart met a sharp dip in the lane and jolted Anna back to the here and now.

"Is there a man waiting for you in America? Do I have a rival who I must pummel?" asked Donal.

Anna wondered if her thoughts had been bleeding out on her forehead.

"I was married once. He left me."

"He's gone for good then?"

"Yes."

"All the better for me. And what a horse's ass he was. Clearly your taste in men has taken a turn for the better."

"Clearly," said Anna.

They continued on their way to Kinsale. And with each step of the horse, she left behind the disappointing life of almost-babies and wandering husbands, and expanded into the space next to Donal. Now she was fresh from the passions of love, and although she had not called it love and neither had Donal, she did not want to leave this man.

Growing up, her ability to read a room instantly, to spot signs of danger, had been as essential as breathing. If she was to be successful at smuggling, to help Donal and Glenis, she still needed to be this acutely aware of her environment.

But she was slowed by culture and time, and she had to concentrate on more carefully understanding the social cues of 1844 if she was to protect them, as well as the rest of the fine smugglers. She was sure that she missed the majority of non-verbal language, and she wondered if this feeling of being unable to catch critical interpersonal nuances was what it felt like to have Asperger's.

What did it mean when she and Donal stopped at a blacksmith to water the horse and three men in the barn stopped talking when she walked in? Was there something odd about her behavior? Or was she like a true outsider—was there something so inescapably different about her that everyone sensed it?

When the horse was rested and watered, they continued on.

"Why did the men stop speaking when I went in?" she asked him.

"I suppose they were surprised that a woman went into the blacksmith shop, and more so, that they didn't know you, or your family. That's all," said Donal. He was clearly not as impressed with their behavior as Anna had been. He shifted his weight on the plank seat.

Being in the past felt as if she'd been dropped off in Madagascar without a tourist guidebook. Time held its own customs and language, inside jokes, and longings. Her only advantage was historical hindsight, and she wasn't always sure that her hindsight was accurate. There was the gender stuff, things that women were not expected to do, and she would need to be more observant, but surely her ability to scope out a situation—the way she could walk into a roomful of lawyers, defendants, and prosecutors and tell who was going to make the first move—surely that would defy time.

The future began to lose its hold on her, drop by drop. Anna swore she would find Joseph, but she was no longer sure what would happen when she found him. As if she had ever been sure.

They spent four days in all, traveling from the Beara Peninsula back to Kinsale, sleeping snugly beneath the cart each night. They avoided the coastal road for fear of roving militia, especially after the capture and killing of smugglers in Glengariff. By the time they rode into Kinsale, night had taken hold. Donal had not fully stopped the wagon when Anna leaped off, sprinting to the door of Tom and Glennie's cottage.

"Glenis? I'm back! Where are you?"

As soon as Anna opened the door, she smelled the brittle

vibration of fear. The children were too quiet, their spines too upright in their soft bodies, their jaws clenched shut. She looked for their father.

"Where's your father, Michael?"

Michael clenched one hand around a hoe, while the other hand dragged a sharpening stone across the metal edge. The boy didn't look up.

"He's in with our mother. She's taken sick in the stomach."

Anna stepped as quickly as she could through the thick atmosphere of illness to the one room off the hearth room where Glenis and Tom slept. She heard the murmur of voices; she recognized Tom's voice but not the other. She tapped on the door. Not waiting for an answer, she pushed it open even as she knocked with the knuckle of her forefinger.

The only color remaining in Glenis's face was gray, the color of blood gone wrong, lack of oxygen, of dread. Her eyes had sunk deep into her skull. Tom stood on one side of the bed, while a woman pulled the quilt tighter around Glenis's shoulder.

Glenis rolled her head to one side to look toward the door.

"Anna," she said, letting the name expel from her lungs as if the effort lacerated her throat.

Anna looked quickly at Tom, who bravely met her eyes with a heavy, unblinking language reserved for disaster. "Tell me what's happened. She was strong and fit when I last saw her. It's only been ten days."

"This is Mrs. Eveleen O'Donohue, who births babies for all the women. We've sent out a word for the parish doctor, too, but we've been told he's too far off, tending to people a full day's ride from here."

Anna nodded to the woman by the bed.

"There's a poison of some sort in her belly. She's with child, but something's terribly wrong. I've seen this before; the baby has taken hold outside the womb. From the color of her, she's bleeding inside. The body can't shake it, and fever has taken over."

Ectopic pregnancy; Anna knew they'd have no way of dealing with the catastrophic medical emergency. It would mean surgery to remove a burst fallopian tube. In the course of Anna's three miscarriages, she had studied up on all possible calamities that could rob her of a full-term pregnancy. The worst was an ectopic pregnancy because of the fatal threat to the mother.

But not to Glenis, this couldn't have been happening to Glenis, who had defended Anna against dangerous rumors of spy, traitor, outsider. Not Glenis, who had braided Anna's hair, helped her wash it despite Glenis's admonitions against frequent bathing, who'd laughed uproariously at Anna's size nine feet. Not the Glenis who knew where Anna was from, when she was from. Not this Glenis.

Tom stood next to the bed and picked up a cloth. He dipped it into a jug of water, wrung it out, and placed it on his wife's forehead. Then he dipped a finger in the water and let a drop of water land on her lips. Her tongue sought out the water, emerging like a fattened sow's tongue, but dry and hard. Anna could see a crack in her tongue from eight feet away. Eveleen put her hand on Anna's arm and guided her out of the room, closing the door behind her. They edged into a corner as far away from the children as possible.

"She won't be with us much longer. It will be a miracle if the morning finds her alive," she said.

"She's dying? There was nothing wrong with her when I left her. She did say that this pregnancy felt different. But then each of the babies had come differently, had felt different." Even though Anna knew what the outcome of this was going to be, she could not bear to speak it.

Eveleen was six inches shorter than Anna, and she spoke softly, which forced Anna to bend her knees and pull her head closer to her. Both women looked over at the children. They lowered their voices even more.

"Even if a doctor were to come this moment and cut her belly open, there would be no saving her or the baby. The womb is the only place for a baby to grow. Misguided ones try to set up on the outside of the womb or in the most confounded places. This is the worst thing that could happen to her, nearly as terrible as bleeding to death after a birth. I can smell the infection; there's a smell that I'm attuned to, a sweet and putrid scent, and once it gets started on the inside of the body, there is nothing that I can do." The midwife hung her head and pressed her palms to her eyes. A shudder ran through Eveleen's body, then she continued. "Glenis told me that she had to speak to you. So you need to go back in there now, very close to her. Tell her you're here. She's in a horrid amount of pain, but I've known the lass since she was a baby; she was born into me own hands. She'll not die until she speaks to you."

Tiny dots of black flicked across Anna's vision. She nodded and willed her feet to move, in the boots that Glenis had bartered for her, the dress she had altered for her, and the shawl she had knit for her.

Eveleen stepped in the room and said, "Give the two

women a moment, Tom. Your children are frightened half to death out here."

When Tom left, Anna moved to the bedside and dropped to her knees. She heard Donal's voice as Tom greeted him in the outer room. She placed her head close to Glenis and said, "I'm here, Glennie. It's me, Anna. I know what's happening, the midwife told me." She found Glenis's hand, cold and already waxen, and covered it with her hot fist. Glenis rolled her head toward Anna.

Glenis focused with the greatest effort and parted her dry lips. Anna dipped the cloth in more water and let a few drops fall into her mouth. Glenis spoke with excruciating slowness. "You've. Got. To. Go. Back," she said.

This is not what Anna had expected. "No, I don't know how to go back, I told you that. And if I could, I don't want to. That's what I wanted to tell you. I want to stay. I'll keep looking for my nephew. If he's survived the travel from my time to here, we can make a life here . . ."

With shocking strength, Glenis emphasized every word. "It's wrong that you are here. Go back, Anna. For all of us, you've got to find a way. Find the coin . . ."

Glenis gasped, and her head fell back on the bed.

"Glennie! Tell me why. Is this what Biddy Early told you? And how, you've got to tell me how. What about the coin?"

But Glenis could not catch her breath, and her eyes rolled white. Anna rushed to the door and said, "Eveleen, please, she can't breathe."

And from there, the midwife guided them all through the reckoning stages. The three children were led in to say goodbye. Their brave properness nearly killed Anna. Michael held the hands of his younger sisters and walked them to the side of the bed. When the youngest, little Nuala, began to crumble, he picked her up, and she wrapped her arms and legs around him. From that point on, Glenis's breath took on a rasping nature, as if dragged over stones, and her eyes remained closed.

"It won't be long now," Eveleen whispered in Glenis's ear. Tom knelt by the bed, folding his frame at the knees and hips, and laid his head on his wife's breasts.

"Oh sweet breath, sweet breath, stay with me," he said as the breaths grew further apart. Everything about Tom grew softer—his lips, his hands, his voice.

Is this it? thought Anna. *Is it this simple and this horrible, that breath leaves in a sudden screech and that's it?*

The pause between breaths grew longer, punctuated by Tom's murmur of *"sweet breath, sweet breath."* Then, as if caught in midsentence, Glenis exhaled and did not inhale; there was no more breath, and Glenis was still.

Anna had never seen anyone die before. *I'm only thirty-four years old,* she thought to herself, as if being thirty-four had been a safety net that precluded death. She suddenly wished to be younger still, to feel an elusively protective family around her that had never quite been there in the first place.

Women prepared the body; Anna was asked to help and she did. When the older women began to weep, she truly knew how alone she was. She knew the sound that they made was keening—she'd heard the word before—but why did they wail so hideously and tug at their hair? One woman rubbed dirt on her face, and her tears ran muddy down her cheeks. If Glenis had been there, Anna would have whispered to her,

"What are they doing? Why are they screeching so?" She would have asked her friend, her chosen sister, the one person who'd known that Anna was not from there or then.

After washing and dressing the body, binding the jaw with cloth, and weighing down the eyelids with coins, the women set Glenis on a plank in the center of the cottage for one day and night. The crush of mourners was constant. Anna pressed her back to the wall and stayed there, vowing not to leave Glenis for an instant. Donal rarely left Tom's side; if he did, it was to take the children outside to walk.

When the sun set, a group of young men came in, stinking of whiskey and singing a song best suited for a pub. Tom rose up and fell on them like a lion.

"Not here, not at Glennie's funeral, you drunken bastards!"

The flush-faced boys were shocked into sobriety. Tom threw the closest one against the wall, and the entire house shook. Two men laid hands on Tom, wrapping their arms around him, saying, "You know it's the way, Tom. It's not their fault."

Chapter 28

Anna and Donal stayed in the barn behind the cottage for a week after the funeral. In the days immediately following Glennie's burial, Anna wanted to reach out to Donal, but her own sadness kept her paralyzed. She had known Glenis for only a few months, but Donal had known her since she was born. Glenis had been his cousin, his lifelong mate, and she could smell the anguish of grief coming off him.

Losing Glenis was too much. Each circuit board of her brain was steaming with the sharp smell of burned wires, anesthetizing the part that went to her vocal cords. Anna tried to speak, but the memory of speech had gone missing. She could still ponder, and she wondered how odd, how strange it was that here in 1844 she could smell electrical wires burning while no one else could because they didn't exist yet. Donal could not and Glenis would never, ever sniff electrical wires.

So this was what it would have been like to have had a sister. She'd had no idea, before sluicing through time and waking up under the care of Tom and Glenis, that having a sister was like being in a walnut shell. Glennie had been one half, and she was the other half, connected by small but essential tendrils. She'd had girlfriends before, but never someone who had stood up for her the way Glennie had when she'd ridden off on O'Connell, leaving her husband, children, and thriving smuggling enterprise behind. There had never been anyone like Glenis, not in law school, and certainly not in the gut-clenching work at the firm.

Anna was not sure what Donal did when he left the barn during the day; at night, he returned and slept with her. They held each other in the barn without making love and breathed in the warm scent of the cow and the horse. O'Connell, Glennie's heroic steed, had such a restless night after the funeral that Anna slipped Donal's coat over her shoulders and went to the horse, cooing to him as she had seen Glenis do, touching and talking. She finally pressed her head into his neck and wrapped her arms around him. Tom found her sobbing and hugging the horse.

"When O'Connell brought her back, she was gripped with pain. Glennie said she felt the pain hours after leaving Biddy Early. She rode two days in stinking misery," Tom revealed.

"O'Connell is truly Glennie's horse?"

"Aye. The two of them could barely stand to be apart. She only trusted one neighbor with her horse. You do remember that we can't acquire too many horses, don't you?"

Anna remembered. There was much she didn't know about Glenis.

On one of these days, Anna emerged blinking into the sunlight and found Donal and Tom coming back with a load of dried peat. The two men loaded the dark bricks off the cart and into the house. When they were done and Tom was surrounded by his three sad children, Anna walked shyly up to Donal, as if speaking to him for the first time.

"Would you tell me about Glennie? Would you tell me what she was like as a child?"

Donal wiped his hand on his pant legs. He paused for a moment, and it looked as if he was watching a flash of images and he was trying to pick one.

"Oh, she was a thorny babe, all spiked hair and shrieks."

Anna pictured a baby Glennie. For the first time since returning to Kinsale, something like a laugh gurgled out of her. Donal took her hand, and they walked back to the barn, where they nestled into the loft that they had made their own.

"What did she tell you?" asked Donal. "Tom thinks she stayed alive until you got here. After she spoke to you, she never spoke again."

The days since the funeral were a soggy blur. Anna had not eaten since she'd returned, or at least she couldn't remember eating, couldn't remember how she had ever eaten, how anything had slid past the clotted sorrow in her throat.

"She said that I had to go back to my home, that's what she said."

Anna knew she had to be careful about how she phrased all of this to Donal.

"That's all. She told me I should go home," Anna repeated. She left out the part about the coin.

Donal pressed something into her hand, some version of roasted potato that he had pulled from a covered jug. He guided it to her mouth and she took it in. Saliva, seemingly absent for days, rushed to meet the spud. She ran her tongue over it; it tasted the way Glennie had smelled when they had slept side by side in the open, like fresh sea air and earth and a burst of surprise.

Anna knew what Glennie had meant, that she had to go back home to her own time. Her presence here could be altering the present and the future. Glennie was the only person who'd known, except for this Biddy Early whom Glennie had ridden off to see in Limerick. Somewhere out there, a woman knew Anna was from the future. And she knew how desperately Anna was searching for Joseph.

Donal slipped another piece of roasted potato into her palm as soon as she swallowed the first bite.

"She didn't know about us, Anna. If she'd known, she'd not have told you to go home. I've known Glennie all my life, and if she had but seen my face, she would have known. . . . "

Both of them stopped, suddenly awkward. Anna swallowed the spud and looked at Donal. She placed her hand on his chest, where she thought his large heart sat nested under his ribs. He placed his hand on her loose dress, under her breast, letting it sit like a bird in his palm.

"Glennie was for the living. When my wife and sons died, it was Glennie who kept me from slitting me own throat, or turning to drink. She told me to honor them by living. She said the dead, the fairies, and God, all of them grow sad when we throw away the sights and smells of this life. When we sing, they sing. When we love, they love."

They fell back on the blanket-covered hay.

"I always knew that it would come to talk of fairies. Should we make them all happy? Will you make love with me?" she asked.

For the first time since the funeral, they lay down in their perch above the animals and made love, shyly, as if everything was happening for the first time now that the world was different, now that Glennie had left them. Donal's fingers traveled along the buttons of her spine, opening her from back to front, charting her from thigh to throat.

"I can't imagine what it would be like to make love with you if you had two hands," Anna whispered.

He continued his methodical journey along her earlobes as he replied. "I would not be as exact. I'm a cartographer, and we chart all landscape, name all the nooks and crannies, the quiet bays, dangerous outcroppings, and the places where riptides will carry you away." He traced one jaunty nipple. "See here, if I was a ship and trying to come to port and this fine nipple was the bay, I'd most certainly need to know when the bay was soft and shallow, spreading wide and filled with tricks. And just as surely, I must know that if I touched it so . . ." He placed a firm tongue along one side of the nipple and it rose to ever greater attention, a brown column rising to the dusty roof of the barn. "Then I must know how to navigate at this time as well."

Anna liked being a map. She raised her head and looked down past her breasts, considerably smaller than they had been two months ago. She turned on her side and Donal placed his hand on her hip, placing his thumb on the front and his palm on the backside. He kept going, measuring, mapping her, leaving no place uncharted.

The next day was a Sunday, and Anna began her school lessons once again with Michael and Mary. She even let little Nuala sit on her lap. Glenis would have wanted her to do this. After two brisk hours of doing fractions, Michael smiled for the first time since his mum had died.

"I think I love mathematics almost as much as I loved me mum. Not that they are the same, mind you, but these numbers set the world right again."

Anna stopped midstream and looked hard at Michael, hearing the echo of her mother's words when all the calamity of their family had been tearing them to ribbons. She knew her family came from a long jumble of Irish. What were the chances that she had dropped a mathematical seed into her mother's side of the family?

"Your mother was proud of you," said Anna, with a wavering voice. "Let's get back to the numbers."

Kinsale was carved right out of the hillside. Every street, except those that ran along the port, was steep and narrow, designed originally for cloven-footed creatures. The cemetery—the Catholic cemetery—was far above the town. The British landowners, the Protestants, were buried right in Kinsale, tucked behind the Church of England, which lavished Irish earth on them even in death.

Anna went to the cemetery every day, sitting next to the freshly turned dirt that blanketed Glenis. *This is what old people do,* she thought. *They huddle around gravestones, bringing flowers. This is not what a young woman does.* She wanted Glennie to burst out of her coffin to tell her what to do.

Anna stood up and dusted the dirt off her skirt. She walked down the hill from the humble cemetery, past Tom and Glennie's house, and kept going toward the village. After several miles, her feet met the cobblestones of Kinsale, where the sounds of commerce began to jostle her—the cobbler, the stables, the ting of horses being shod, a boy rolling a barrel down the hill, the tinker's wagon clattering as pieces of tin collided into each other.

She continued down the curving streets, careful to miss the fresh piles of horse dung, until she came to the port, with its lapping sounds from the sea, its air thick with gulls calling for hunks of fish tossed off by the fishmongers. The steady presence of the troops, some leaning against the strong timbers of the piers, made her wary. She welcomed the blistering distraction that the village offered.

She looked at the ticket station. One could buy a passage to England or the Continent. As if she truly could leave, as if she could book passage home. For no reason at all, she approached the ticket station, with its massive doors. Suddenly she was caught off guard for a moment by a dog chasing a set of gulls that had been savagely ripping strips of flesh from the discarded hunks of fish. Everyone wants to live, she thought, we all want life when given the option. Glenis had been right.

She looked up and reached for the door. Tacked to one side was a sheet of paper, an announcement.

Wrestling Match. Canadian Champion, Joseph Blair challenges Cork Champion. Cork City Centre. Saturday Afternoon.

Her hand rested on the gleam of the door handle. Wrestling? Joseph? No, she didn't want to make connections where there were none. Joseph? She paused and remembered her first law class. "Keep it simple," her professor had said. "Don't ignore the obvious." She spun around and grabbed the notice, ripping it from the wall. She rolled it tight and held it in one hand. She began to walk back up the hill, then she walked faster, then she loosened into a run, not caring that grown women did not run here. Then she pounded the cobbled stones, her legs stretched long, a bit of her skirt held in one hand.

By the time she reached Tom's cottage, the late afternoon sun had just plunged below the horizon and Donal had just returned from wherever he had gone. When he saw her coming, he halted in midmotion, his hand on the wooden gate. Anna had the notice about the wrestler from the Canadian provinces, a Joseph Blair, rolled tight in her hands. She snapped it open before Donal. Her skirt had been gathered up in one hand.

He read the poster and looked at Anna, whose chest was still heaving from her run up the hill.

"These boots are giving me fits," she said between gulps of air.

"You've taken a sudden interest in wrestling. It's a fine old sport, but why now?" Donal asked, one eyebrow lifting.

"Not sudden. This could be my nephew. He could be using another name. I can't explain why. But I've got to find out. How far is Cork from here?"

She let the edge of her skirt fall in place again and it fluttered around the tops of her shoes. She knew he could tell her precisely how far away Cork was. He was the cartographer.

"Twenty-three miles from the center of Kinsale if we travel inland a bit. The coastal road is full of vistas that will tear at your heart, but the way is longer. Did you know that you look like a ten-year-old boy when you run?"

"I have to go to Cork. This is for Saturday. What day are we on?" Anna asked. She had lost track of days although she had sworn she would not do so.

"Friday. The match is tomorrow," said Donal.

"I've got to go. I've got to see if it's him. Have you ever heard of this wrestler before three months ago?"

"I can't say that I have, but I can't say that I've had my mind on the lads who wrestle. And I'm not eager to travel to Cork City. I've not been back there since my wife and boys were taken by the fever two years back. I left my work, I left everything, you see. I'm not eager to go."

This was the first time that Donal had backed up, hesitated. She had not allowed the full weight of his loyalty to his dead wife and young sons to register. They were still foremost in his heart. Of course she would never compare; the dead were the real ones for Donal. She would forever be Other, an add-on. Even if she stayed with him, she'd be the secondary one. Who had she been kidding? She should have recognized his hesitancy instantly. Instead, she had been waiting, panting like a teenager. Anna straightened her shoulders and steeled her abdominals, the way she'd done so many times at the firm. The way she'd done when Steven had left her.

"There's no need for you to come with me. I'll ask Tom if I can take O'Connell to Cork. The horse has had a good, long rest, and I can find my way there," she replied. People did not stay with her; she needed to carve this into her palm. So this would be good-bye. She should not have leaned so far into this man, should not have taken the taste of him into her mouth. First Glenis, now Donal. She understood being alone. She would have to forget the brief respite of feeling attached to Donal. It had been an illusion. She would just find Joseph and go from there.

Donal's dark eyebrows pulled together as his cartographer's eyes measured her.

"You jump from rock to ledge like a bloody rutting ram! I said I'd not been there in two years. Where did you leap to? Cork is filled with spies and thieves and militia, and you'll not go there alone. And O'Connel shall have to carry the two of us."

Anna's shoulders softened minutely, her belly relaxed with an exhale. She pushed away the thoughts that had cascaded over her, so ready to destroy her.

" 'Bloody rutting ram'? Would you say that again? I've never been called that before. And is that the worst you can think of, or is there more?"

"Oh, there is much more for the likes of you. Rascal, scoundrel, smuggler, wild woman. Beloved."

They rose in the hours before dawn. As Tom lent them the powerful O'Connell, he said stoically, "Never let a horse remember the ride of the dying. They've got to ride forward into life."

Michael solemnly handed Anna her walking stick. "You should take this along with you."

Anna stopped her preparations. "Michael, I want you to keep this for me until I get back. Will you watch over it? And will you keep doing your computations?"

The boy nodded and moved closer to his father as Anna and Donal completed saddling O'Connell.

Anna had never ridden farther than a trail ride along the beaches north of Puerto Vallarta in Mexico, where she'd gone on spring break. When their trail guide had called out, "Let's let these guys gallop!" she had nearly fallen off.

Donal let her step on his thigh to launch herself on the horse's back, then he swung up behind her.

"I've never ridden much," she said.

"Both the horse and I have noticed," he said.

Anna felt her back enveloped by Donal, her legs shadowed by his. An unfamiliar sensation came over her. *This is what it feels like when someone has your back*, she thought. *This is what love feels like.*

Donal stopped every few hours to let Anna get off and stretch her legs, but only long enough for her to do some unladylike squats and hamstring stretches.

"Do you have an ailment? Can I help you in some way?" asked Donal after he returned from a discreet visit to the bushes.

"No. This is preventive; this will keep my muscles from tightening up." As soon as she said it, she wondered if everything that she did looked slightly out of whack. He had already noted her tooth flossing.

"You look like you're eating your own fist," he had said when she'd flossed after stopping for a bite to eat.

On their third rest stop, Anna lifted her skirt and peered down at her knees. The skin on her inner thighs had turned bright red from rubbing against the saddle. She tried every way imaginable to wrap her skirt around her legs, but by the next stop, the skin on the inside of both knees and thighs had gone from a blossoming red to angry blisters.

"I could lay you across the backside of O'Connell," suggested Donal.

"How about this? How about you slip off those pants and I'll give you this skirt. Let's see who gets blisters then. This is exactly why everyone should wear pants."

Donal put a protective hand on his belt and backed away from her.

"I can't say that I've ever seen a lass with britches on. But it is a pity about your legs. We'll get them attended to in the next village. Lard will do the trick."

They arrived in Cork City in early afternoon.

"You must have a lifetime of friends here," said Anna, glad to be off the horse. She refused to leave O'Connell until she saw that he was properly stabled, wiped down, and given all that he needed. She had seen some horses treated badly in Kinsale, and she wanted nothing bad to happen to Glennie's horse.

They walked along a river path that led to a college. Anna noticed the absence of women but said nothing. Or at least she intended to say nothing; that would have been the wiser thing to do, but instead she said, "We have colleges where women attend."

"Oh, do you now? That seems as good an idea as any I've heard. Do they not mind being tossed in with so many lads?"

There, she shouldn't have said anything; it was just PMS stalking her. She could feel the prickly belligerence, the vigilant search for injustice that rolled in with the monthly changing guard of hormones. No, if she said any more, she'd say too much and she'd drag Donal into her world—the future—and he couldn't be there. He'd never be there; he'd never see the view from an airliner, never sit in front of the TV in his underwear mindlessly surfing from one basketball game to another, never drive a car or receive a vaccine. And yet here he was and here she was.

"The men and women did all right together at college," she said, capping the topic. "Where will the wrestling tournament be held?"

Lowering his eyes, Donal followed two British soldiers

without turning his head, keeping them in his field of vision as long as possible.

"Past the college, up the slight hill there, as far from the church as they could make it."

They walked briskly, propelled by Anna's belief that her nephew Joseph might truly be alive, be a wrestler going by another name, but alive all the same. As they approached the plateau, the bustle of people, men and women, pressed into the atmosphere of a country fair. The day was sunny, an aberration for late fall, and warm enough for her to unbutton her jacket. A bank of thick clouds approached from the sea.

She was taller than a good many people, but she still had difficulty seeing into the center area where the wrestling took place. There was one noticeable difference with this crowd that surprised Anna: it was thick with British militia. She quickly assessed the women's footwear—fine kid leather— and their ornate hats and realized that these were part of the wealthier strata of the population. As if acknowledging her understanding, Donal shook his head and gave a slight shrug of his shoulders. They had already established a shorthand language of lovers.

They inched their way forward, stepping between wagering men.

"Who's holding the bet? No, not Paddy, he'll make off with it."

"Put it all on the Canadian lad, he's not lost one match."

"I'll put mine on the big fella. He's a fine specimen of a man."

Anna felt the skin along her neck prickle. It couldn't be this easy. Could Joseph suddenly appear after nearly three months? If he was here, she'd simply grab him and go. And then what? She'd think of that later.

Donal's lips brushed her ears.

"Be careful now. Something is off the boards here."

A stout man came to the center, and his voice resonated with a practiced bellow.

"We've one more elimination round before the main event. A lad from Waterford has come all this way to contend with our own Walter Downing. They are goodly matched. The rules stand. They must stay within the boundaries at all times. The first man pinned is the unfortunate loser. Gentlemen?"

"Something is wrong here," said Donal in a whisper. "Either I've been away from Cork for too long, or there's a new wind blowing. The crowd is too massive for a wrestling match. Would you stay put, Anna? Can you be proper and still while I look around?"

Anna stood directly in front of him, looking as demure as she could as she pressed into him and slid her palms up his thighs.

"Is that proper enough for you?" she asked.

He grabbed both of her hands and brought them to his lips.

"Aye, properly wicked. But stay put, I beg of you."

Donal pulled out of the crowd and moved to the perimeter. He was judging differences, politics; he understood the players and she did not. There was little point in Anna's trying to assess the political climate. She had eyes only for the wrestlers, and she did not see Joseph anywhere. Anna had never intended to stay put. She stood on her toes, twisted her body to the left and to the right, straining with her neck. She collected fragments of conversation as she wove among the crowd.

"He's turned the matches into his own bloody war."

"Irish against English. Why did they have to poke into our wrestling?"

Anna began to observe the simple obvious details. She stood among people whom she could now easily identify as Irish. The men's hands were thick with calluses, their shoes were patched, and the woolen vests were threadbare in places. The few women wore dresses and skirts that were as sturdy as her own, made of rough buckram cloth.

Somewhere there was an invisible dividing line where the crowd turned English, heavily dotted with militia. There the women's hats were richly fashioned with burgundy laces, ribbons, and feathers. They wore finely woven jackets. The men wore boots, and their jackets buttoned smartly. *Oh, I get it,* she thought. *We've got the home team and the visitors, only this time the Irish are the home team.* But there was a problem, and it was a big problem: the English thought they were the home team, the rightful heirs to this land.

She looked to see where Donal had slipped off to. She couldn't see him, which hopefully meant that he couldn't see her. She made her way as nonchalantly as she could to the English section of the crowd. As she did, the announcer stood on a box and declared the next match. "A fine wrestler from Waterford, Paddy Murphy, and Mr. Walter Downing from Cork shall square off. Into the circle, men."

The buzz of a fresh competition pulled the attention of the crowd to the center, a perfect time for Anna to amble among the British. She peeked at the wrestlers, checking to see, just in case, if Joseph stared back at her. No, no Joseph. The two men grappled with each other. What had brought the gentry out for this match of grunting men?

As Anna pressed into the English crowd, she suddenly saw herself through their eyes. She had dirt beneath her fingernails, and her dress had not been washed in weeks. She had just ridden in from Kinsale and she smelled of horse and road dirt. Not that body odors were subtle in the nineteenth century, but the gentry had floral scents to mask the offending smells. The bottom edge of her green skirt was dirty, and she noticed that the hem had gone ragged.

Everything about her clothing screamed plain and poor. She pulled her shawl tighter around her shoulders, straightened her spine, and adjusted her dreadful bonnet. As she approached two women, she noticed that they drew in toward each other and observed Anna as if she had already done something wrong, as if she'd been ready to pick their pockets. One of the women said, "What can you expect? They'll never be able to aspire to a better life."

The two women rotated away from Anna with the practiced air of their class. The wise thing to do would be to observe, catalogue the facts, and not take anything personally. That would be so prudent, so reasonable. The main priority was finding her nephew, if he could be found. Let the two women go on their way thinking whatever class-laden stereotype they believed. Instead, Anna stepped in front of them and flashed her dazzling twenty-first-century smile.

"I'm American, and we can help ourselves just fine, thank you. And we can aspire magnificently."

She saw the flash of anger move across both women, the slight narrowing of their eyes, the tightening of the lips, followed by a well-practiced control.

"It is so difficult to tell the difference between you and the

Irish. Perhaps it is all about your, shall we say, harsh circumstances," said the taller woman.

Anna wanted to lash out at them, wanted to tell them that their descendents would witness the shrinkage of their colonial empire and the twentieth century would offer them two devastating world wars. But she didn't. She corked her bitter, vengeful self and got back to the task at hand.

A fine mist began to fall, nothing that would halt a wrestling match among these hardy, damp-weather people. She continued to weave slowly through the English crowd, giving the red-coated soldiers a slightly wider space. The two men had been grappling each other in a standoff for longer than Anna had ever witnessed in her nephew's high school matches, or long ago in Patrick's. All eyes were on the two men wrestling, and shouts of encouragement rang out.

"Snag down the Waterford lad. Show him what you're made of, Wally!"

But all the shouts came from the Irish section of the crowd. The English were attentive enough, but lacking in passion. She logged the simple, obvious facts: the crowd had about two hundred people total, more Irish than English; Donal had stated that something was different and worrisome; she was hungry; her skirt had a heavy ledge of mud along the ragged hem; the mist was turning to mizzle. Or had it already been mizzle and now it was turning to mist? She'd never get that straight.

A largely baritone roar went up.

"Down with him. That's our lad, Wally. Pin him, pin him!"

Wally must have pinned his opponent, because a shout went up. The stout master of ceremonies stood on the box again and announced, "Walter Downing of Cork wins the round."

Anna craned her head around to find Donal. She saw him far to the outer perimeter, crouched on his heels under a tree. He was talking to another man. It was impossible to see their faces; their caps were pulled low and they faced away from the crowd. Nevertheless, by now she could easily spot the familiar turn of Donal's head and the shift of his torso. He listened to the other man intently, giving the slightest nod. Should she join him? Before she could decide, the next match was about to begin.

"Ladies and gents, here's the match that drew you from your fires today."

Anna felt a ripple go through the crowd. The English had snapped to attention.

"The wrestler who has challenged every Irish wrestler from Kincaid to Kilkenny and won every match is here with us today. He's been called the next British victor of wrestling, but I'll let you see that for yourselves. He is the undefeated Joseph Blair, a young man sponsored by Colonel Mitford."

The English crowd cheered. One soldier pulled out his bayonet and punched it toward the sky.

Anna's heart sped up. Oh, God, what if this was him? Maybe they could make some sense of what happened. What if he truly had survived?

She couldn't see the two wrestlers, so she pressed urgently into the mass of bodies. Without thinking, she tried to nudge a man out of her way and instantly regretted it. He was an armed soldier, but even his red uniform had not slowed her. He shot his arm in front of her to block her way. With a firm nod of his head to the right, he indicated that she should move to the Irish side. His nose had been broken once and bore the crooked remains of his injury. Anna had to bite her bottom lip to keep from speaking, but she could not keep from glaring at him.

"Get off with you," he spat, as if she'd been a stray dog.

He was a waste of time. The agitation of the crowd seeped into her like a shot of caffeine, and she struggled through the forward press of people to get back to the Irish side.

"And his opponent, our own undefeated Walter Downing."

The Irish cheered.

"Keep your bets to the side, bets to the side."

Anna worked her way toward the front.

"Take your places, lads, feet inside the circle. First man thrown out of the markings or the first man pinned is the loser."

Anna gained sight of a profile of one of the wrestlers. No, not Joseph. She shouldered her way more forcefully past men jingling coins. Then she stopped breathing. It was the hair, the rich brown hair, hanging over his ears, then the profile, and his twenty-first-century high school wrestler's crouch. But something else seared into her. A smile, a burst of assuredness she'd never seen in her nephew. She had to catch her breath, she had to keep breathing; all the love that she had felt for Joseph since he was a baby washed over her. She forced her diaphragm to push the air out of her lungs and take in a fresh gulp. The crowd closed in again, blocking her view.

It was her nephew, there was no doubt. She shoved as hard as she could, and amid bellowing shouts, she saw a flutter of legs in the center ring. The two wrestlers were down on the ground, a tangle of limbs entwined and flipped like snakes. Torsos heaved against each other. Joseph was the smaller of the two by far, but he maneuvered his opponent as if he'd been a cat playing with a doomed mouse. And the wide smile never left his face. First one of Wally's shoulders was down and then another. She caught a wide-eyed look of disbelief and anger on Wally. Joseph had pinned him.

The Irish section was darkly silent while the English gave hearty shouts. The announcer grabbed Joseph's arm and held it high.

"The undefeated Joseph Blair!"

Anna had the odd sensation that all the people were extras in a movie, all except for Joseph, so that it didn't matter what the others said or did. Suddenly only the two of them were on the knoll overlooking Cork College, only Joseph, who was as alive and vibrantly handsome as only a sixteen-year-old boy could be, and Anna. For a moment, she pulled both of her palms to her face, as if resting her head on a dock after a long and arduous swim. The search was over. He was alive; he had survived their violent cascade through time.

Anna couldn't find words large enough to fit the occasion. The English fans surged around Joseph, slapping his back or pumping his hand. One shouted, "Long live the empire!"

Joseph was paired with an older man who was exquisitely dressed. His dark blond hair was slicked behind his ears, his jacket pulled in smartly at his waist, his buttons gleamed, his black riding boots had been polished so intently that the mist beaded and rolled off them. He kept a proprietary hand on Joseph's shoulder. And he was congratulated as heartily as Joseph. Anna had the sense of jockey and owner. Or horse and owner.

She pushed ahead, waiting for whatever was to come from reuniting with her nephew, ready to accept whatever they must face together. Anna was victorious.

"Joseph, Joseph," she yelled, cupping her hands around her mouth. She was still four layers of people back from the epicenter.

"Joseph, it's Anna, I'm here." She jumped up, waving an arm the same way she would have done if she'd been greeting anyone on a busy street, or at a party bulging with people. Joseph followed the sound. He saw her, and the muscles along his mouth flickered. Anna knew that he was shocked. Of course he was; he had believed she was dead or that he was alone without any family. She would have to be gentle, which was not generally in her nature, but in this case, she'd try.

She slid in closer, turning sideways to slip between two more people. Finally she stood within arm's reach.

"Joseph, I thought I'd never find you. Are you all right?" She took a step closer, wanting to pull him into a hug, not caring that he was a teenage boy who dreaded hugs. Finally something was working; they were going to be OK. The universe was beginning to make sense again. As she stepped in, Joseph stumbled back.

"What's this? What have we here?" said the man with the gleaming buttons. "Joseph, do you know this woman?"

Anna gave a knowing laugh, waiting for the man to discover that she was the boy's aunt—family—and thus due an equitable share of the adulation that was going around. Joseph was clearly in shock at the sight of her. Who wouldn't be? She couldn't wait to get him alone to hear all the details of his arrival.

"Ah, no, sir. Well, she may have been on the same ship, but

I don't know her. They let steerage passengers come up for fresh air a few times, and she might have been in that bunch. No, I don't know her."

"It's Anna," she said more slowly. She turned to the colonel. "I'm his aunt," she said with a serious nod to her head, as if the boy had been a patient on the psych ward.

"He doesn't know you, miss. I doubt very much that he would know you at all."

She felt the tilt of the situation, the swirl in her intestines, and she scrambled to keep up. She looked past the man to her nephew.

"I need to talk with you. Right now."

The man placed a finger delicately in the air and a soldier appeared.

"Trouble with the riffraff, sir? Off with you. This is the second time I've had to warn you. Off, I say." He nudged her with the butt end of his bayonet.

"Joseph, for God's sake . . ." She turned to the boy, even as she was being pushed away. A sudden hand gripped her, and she whirled around. It was Donal.

"Oh, here she is, me darling foolish woman. Come now," he said. His grip was tight and urgent.

"Donal, this is . . . ," Anna stuttered.

"There, there. Come home with me and we'll make things right," he said.

Donal turned to the colonel. "Pardon us, sir. She has suffered from a great illness and is still troubled from time to time. I hope you've not been disturbed."

Donal put all his weight into pulling Anna away to mingle with the flow of the downcast Irish, who headed down the hill. Anna craned her head around to catch sight of Joseph.

She saw the back of his head as he was swallowed by the crowd of British well-wishers.

"That's my nephew. And when I get my hands on him, I'm going to kill him," said Anna.

"You'll find it difficult to get your hands on that one. He's under the thumb of Colonel George Mitford, and he's not to be trifled with. He's the most powerful landowner in this part of Ireland. And he's vicious, Anna, more vicious than you can know."

Chapter 29

The colonel and Joseph went directly to a tavern with an entourage of back-slapping men. The colonel was in high form, clanging his glass with everyone within reach, letting the foam linger too long on his golden moustache. Joseph began to wonder if wrestling was more about betting and raking in coins.

But he could think of none of this; he no longer cared that he had won the match. Anna was here, he had seen her. She was like a rusty needle bursting his balloon of a fantastic life. He had earned everything that he'd gotten here. He was the colonel's champion wrestler. This was the life he was meant to have. He was meant to have Taleen, and he had promised her that he'd never leave her.

He knew how Anna was; she'd never stop until she convinced the colonel and all of Ireland that she was his aunt. And so what if she was, just so what? Why did she have to come and ruin everything? His eyelid spasmed. Anna had looked awful, sort of skinny and tired, not at all the way he remembered her. She looked different in some other way too that he couldn't quite reach. And who was the dude she'd hooked up with?

The colonel held court across the room, standing in front of the fire with his fine friends. Joseph was truly impressed with how much they could drink. The colonel had switched to an amber brandy, his favorite drink.

If Joseph could slip out and find Anna without anyone seeing him, he'd tell her what the deal was. Here they were, tossed back in time for who knew what reason, so they should enjoy it. That's what he was going to do. He'd tell her, "Just go away. I don't know why I'm here or why you're here, but I've got the best life ever, so don't screw it up for me. For once, can I please have something without it getting trashed?"

Anna would want to tell him what to do, how things should be, act like the boss of him. As far as Joseph could tell, that was over and done with. He wasn't some kid in high school; he was the man.

"Eat up, lad. I'll have the coachman take us back to Tramore this evening. We won't get home until midnight. Eat up. Barkeep! Roast beef for the champion. You'll need your strength for the next match in Kilkenny."

Good, he would be with Taleen again all the sooner. Should he tell her? Tell her what? That he was from the future, that he couldn't leave because there was no home for him to return to, that this mental woman would probably come and ruin his life in Tramore?

The barkeep set down a very well-cooked hunk of beef, surrounded by potatoes and rich gravy.

"Well done, sir. The wrestling match was splendid."

"Thank you," said Joseph.

"Aye, you're well on the way to becoming the best in Ireland."

Yes, that would secure his position. He'd become the best in Ireland.

As promised, they took a carriage and headed for home after the colonel finished celebrating the victory. Joseph watched the colonel doze, as impossible as it seemed to sleep in a coach that rocked violently along the earthen road. But maybe the colonel could sleep anywhere because he was so sure that there was nothing to challenge him; even the impenetrable blackness and the ruts in the road did not challenge him. Joseph stayed awake and thought about Anna.

As the carriage pulled into the sloping hill of the estate, the hounds barked. Joseph could recognize the sound of the three older dogs and the occasional deepening yip of Madigan. Everyone on the estate was alerted to their arrival, and he was glad for it. He wanted Taleen to know he was home.

They were greeted by a sleepy-looking Mr. Edwards.

"Welcome home, sir. You'll find the bed warmed for you by the time you retire."

This did feel like home, his wonderful new life. The bustle of servants had sprung to life at their arrival. Yes, this was as it should be. Lights were lit along the stairway.

"Something to eat, sir?" asked Mr. Edwards.

"Nothing for me, but the lad should eat. He remains undefeated. He's the champion. I've an eye for greatness, and I saw it on him right off," said the colonel in a not entirely sober mumble as he headed up the wide stairs.

"Good night, sir," said Joseph.

"Good night, my fine young champion. Sleep in a bit tomorrow. Your next match is important. Kilkenny . . . ," he said as he disappeared along the second-story passageway, his heels tapping on the floors.

Joseph barely heard anything that was said. He could think of nothing but Anna, that she had survived, right here in his Ireland. He knew Taleen was awake somewhere on the estate; everyone in the manor was awake.

Mr. Edwards produced a plate of cold ham, sliced eggs, and bread. The meal at the tavern had not diminished Joseph's appetite. The servants in the kitchen were up and bustling, and by now they had already heard of his success.

"Well done," said Mr. Edwards, standing by the table.

Joseph was startled by what sounded like a genuine compliment. He couldn't figure this guy. Mr. Edwards treated him with the exacting politeness that was part of his job. Yet there was something different about him. Maybe it was that Mr. Edwards was English, and he clearly lorded it over the Irish servants. Deirdre had explained to him that being an English servant was about a thousand times better than being an Irish servant.

"I've looked into the next competition in Kilkenny on the assumption that you would win this last match," Mr. Edwards informed Joseph. "The wrestling champion is from Tipperary. His reputation is that he's no gentleman. He's never lost a match. And he's an unusually large man."

This was the most that Mr. Edwards had ever said to Joseph. Was he warning him, or trying to get him off his game?

"Big? How big? Bigger than the stonemason? He's a good-sized man. I wouldn't try to wrestle *him*," said Joseph after washing down a mouthful of ham with the hard cider.

"Think of our master stonemason and add yet another half man."

Joseph had too much to think about to worry about a big clumsy guy who wouldn't know much about wrestling. He had been wrestling far beyond his weight class since he had arrived, and his speed had won out each time. No need to worry.

"Thanks for the warning."

"It's more than a warning. He's inflicted damage. You'll need to prepare for him. The colonel is preparing to wager a staggering amount on this match."

Why would Edwards help him? Joseph had figured that he was just extra trouble for the guy. He pushed the empty plate away.

"You're right. I need to prepare," he said.

Mr. Edwards nodded in his inscrutable fashion, picked up the plate, and departed.

After the wrestling match in Cork, Joseph noticed a slight tingle in his calf muscle. Three days later, as he practiced with Sean, his calf muscle seized up in a cramp that dropped him to the ground. Sean ran off for help and brought Deirdre.

Hugging his knee into his chest, both hands grabbing the throbbing muscle, Joseph looked up at her from his flattened position in the courtyard. She looked different from this angle; not so tiny. The way the morning light was reflected in her green eyes and the offshore breeze caught at her skirt made him think of seaweed and ocean.

Deirdre rubbed her hands together, then blew into them with a humming song. She bent down beside him, placed her hands on his, and gently unwrapped his grip on the spasms.

Her hands were hot to the touch, and he willingly released his grip. She closed her eyes and placed her hands on his lower leg.

Her hands grew hot, then icy cold, then hot again. He'd never had this exact perspective before, and he noticed that her skin was oddly smooth and young, not like a mother's should be, a mother of so many children, all of whom were far older than Taleen. The hot and cold ran along the back of his leg from his ankle to his butt. Then a warm, wet breeze blew along his leg on the inside, under the skin, running circles around the muscles, skimming over his kneecap. His entire leg was sucked into something like a tornado, and all the hot, tight places were extracted and blown away. Not once was Joseph afraid, not once did he doubt that this small, dark-haired woman could extinguish the pain in his leg.

"Deirdre?" he said once, but the Deirdre that he knew, the mother of his true love, the woman who managed a gigantic kitchen, who cooked roasts, puddings, and sauces that made all the men weep, that Deirdre was not present. Sean said, "Be still, man, and let her do her work."

Joseph laid his torso back but kept his head raised, let his young and powerful neck hold his head up because he had never seen anything like Deirdre, eyes closed, hand on his leg, giving him something, taking away something. If he squinted, it was possible to see a rosy light all over her and his leg.

"Let the hounds come now," she said to Sean. "Off with you to the stables."

Sean ran off, and before Joseph imagined it was possible, the three adult wolfhounds arrived. The gray giants sniffed his leg, looked once at Deirdre, then again at Joseph with their amber eyes. The wolfhounds still spooked him. Joseph was the first one to look away.

Deirdre jerked her hands off his leg and said, "Run!" The hounds sped off, heading for the pastures. Joseph rolled to his side and saw all three of them outstretched, their long, narrow faces pointed into the wind, their powerful lungs bellowing and their legs all but invisible.

Deirdre flicked her hands at the wind and suddenly looked like her old self again.

"That was a growing injury. You were graced with good fortune to take ill here and not in your next wrestling match. But you have a spot where you are weak, not terrible, but weak, and you'll be wise to treat it tenderly and not let it be worsened with wrestling," said Deirdre.

"What did you just do?" asked Joseph. He felt a delicious warmth in his suddenly painless leg.

She patted his shoulder. "Only what I do for everyone."

"What did the hounds do? Why did you call them?"

"I acted on inspiration. They'll only help with the Irish. Is there something you'd like to tell me, Joseph Blair from the Canadian Provinces? The hounds don't lie. They're dying out, refusing to continue, but they've no ability to lie."

Even under the triple stare of monster dogs and the green eyes of Deirdre, Joseph made himself lie.

"Looks like there's a first time for everything," he shrugged.

Joseph retreated to the main house—the "big house," as the Irish called it. He was sure of two things: the colonel thought he was a champion, and Taleen was in love with him. What else mattered? He waited for Taleen and Madigan to return from her lessons.

* * *

After the manor grew quiet and all those within had taken to bed, Joseph and Taleen met in the laundry room, far from the ears of upper levels and other servants. Madigan lay wedged against the door. His creamy, oatmeal color had darkened slightly since Joseph had first arrived. His new color was shot through with serious threads of dark brown, and his tail and ears were thoroughly tinged with the deeper shade. He lay on his side, his legs twitching in slumber.

Joseph and Taleen had made a bed of the soiled bed linens that were destined to be washed the next day. They lay side by side, facing each other. His white shirt was unbuttoned, and Taleen's small hands grazed his skin as a reminder of the sex that had just consumed them. She had lifted her skirt and revealed, once again, the entry into her body that consumed so much of Joseph's attention.

"We must keep on some clothes," she had breathed heavily, "in case someone comes. Madigan will give us enough warning to run off, but we should run off with our clothes, not naked."

Although Joseph longed for the freedom to be completely naked with Taleen, to see every inch of her, he understood the need to protect her as well. He remembered Deirdre's warning about the colonel; remembered, but disregarded.

He kissed her wrist. "Your mother helped me when my leg cramped today. I've never seen anything like it. I didn't know she could do stuff like that, you know, like a doctor."

Taleen pushed him away, far enough so that she could look directly at him without her eyes crossing. "She's a healer, just like I will be someday. It comes down through our line. We don't speak of it to the colonel, but all the local Irish come to Mum for the ailments."

"But how does she do it? I mean, she sort of put her hands on my leg, called for the hounds, and poof, my leg was better. Can you do that?" Joseph asked, pushing up on one elbow.

"I'm still young, and the sight—that's what it's called—doesn't settle down in young ones until we are fully ready to use it. Mum says it should happen soon for me."

"What does it feel like, this sight?" asked Joseph.

"Every day it is different. Sometimes I see a bit beyond today, mostly about sickness. I can see if someone will take ill. I don't know what to do about the sickness, so I don't know what the point is. Or other days, I can see a shadowy glow rising from people, the way you can see heat rising from a candle in the right light. Mum said that was their strength of spirit and not to worry about it. Other times I can see colors around people when they talk. The colors change if they are afraid, or happy, or sad."

As incredible as this should have been to hear, Joseph accepted every word as easily as he would have if Taleen had said that she was particularly good at roasting a chicken. He was so completely in love with her that if she had said she could fly, he would have believed her.

"Can you make something happen? Could you make someone go away?"

"You mean make a person do something they didn't want to do? Do you mean a curse? Mum tells me we are pledged never to curse, and if we find a curse, we must heal the poor soul who is taken by it."

Joseph slumped in disappointment then.

"Me mum says that love is mixing in with my sight and causing an uproar, making the sight slower to settle into its proper place with me. She said I must be careful."

"When people are old, they always tell us to be careful, to pay attention, to go slow. They have no idea what real love feels like," said Joseph.

"Aye, and I love you, Joseph. You and I were meant to be."

Madigan stirred. He clattered to standing and trotted over to the lovers, nudging Taleen's hand with his nose.

"My wondrous sight, as well as this grand hound, tells me that the sun is a few hours from rising and that the wrath of God will be on us if we are found here."

They stood up, returned the bed linens to the basket, and crept back to their respective beds.

Chapter 30

The shock of seeing Joseph left her rudderless. Everything had hinged on finding him. She had searched for the boy, terrified that he could not survive the hardships that the common people of Ireland endured, until finally Glenis had joined in the quest by seeking out Biddy Early. Was all this worth Glennie dying? No, she wasn't thinking clearly; Glennie would have died no matter what. Ectopic pregnancies were efficient slayers.

Why couldn't she think straight? Joseph had looked unbelievably healthy, but something had been profoundly different about him. He'd filled out more with an evident growth spurt. But it was the way he'd stood, with his chin out, sure and ready. He'd been Joseph and not Joseph. And he had shunned her.

Anna had been unseen by him. He was family and he had turned away from her. All the space inside her reserved for the boy, the memories of rollerblading on the bike trail, reading to him when he was a toddler, all the thinking of him, all the fiberoptical connectedness had dissolved and turned her lopsided with empty spaces. The gaps filled instantly with shame, for which she was equally unprepared. The shame was hooded and certain, adding jet fuel to the spark of having been abandoned by her father. The internal explosion was spectacular. Anna wanted to hide from herself.

Then she got mad. She said, "I'm gonna kill that kid when I get my hands on him."

Anna and Donal took refuge in a friend's house. Donal had lived in Cork, mapmaking for fifteen years. He seemed to know every Irish man and woman in the town, and hearths sprang open to him. He accepted the hospitality of Liam and his aged father, who lived on the east side of town, on the way to Cobh, one of the largest ports in Ireland, and the site of intense military wariness by the English, according to Donal.

Anna and Donal shared a meal with meat in it, bits of sweet pork, and Anna felt the shock of meat in her mouth, the undeniable fleshiness of it.

"God, this is wonderful," she said, tipping the plate up and licking it. "Your friends here eat quite differently from the west."

Donal positioned himself so that he faced the door. "The farther east that you go, the better the food. The land is richer here. It's the west that must live on air and water. By the time you go as far as Tramore, where Colonel Mitford lives, the countryside is fairly bursting with food: fruit trees from Spain, thick larders, butter, cream, meat. . . ."

Anna pictured the arrival of the potato blight and the resulting famine killing millions. The west coast would be hammered, because they had no reserves; even their smuggling might not save them. She calculated the months until the next potato season would be harvested. They had eight months before the devastation began.

"I want you to stay here for a few days," said Donal, inter-
rupting her thoughts. "You'll be a welcomed guest in this
house."

Anna whipped her head around. "Do you mean that you're
leaving me here? Where are you going, and why can't I go
with you?"

"Your legs are in no shape to travel. Your lovely thighs are
too raw from riding. I can take O'Connell and make my way
to Tramore. I'll find out why your nephew is under the grip
of the English colonel."

They had just rubbed her legs with a generous slather of
lard. They were red and raw from the full day's ride from
Kinsale. Anna knew he was right, and she hated it. She
slouched in her chair and spread her legs wide, making a dip
in her skirt.

"How long?"

"Two days. And I can't return to this house, because it
would make it too dangerous for Liam. You must meet me
at the Passage West Tavern. The place is well worn by the
smugglers. You'll be expected."

"Wait a minute. You used to live here. You worked for
the British in Cork. Why do you have to duck around the
corners?"

"If by ducking you mean keeping my face in the shad-
ows, I do so exactly because I worked for the English. No one
walks away from the employ of the British. I was their cartographer, and they didn't fancy that I made off with every
map of Ireland in my head. I am a smuggler's dream. Glenis
and Tom were persuasive."

"Then you shouldn't have come here. You never should
have agreed to come with me." Anna stood up.

"And let you step into this viper's nest alone? You don't know the ways here, my Anna. You don't know the half of what goes on around you. Cork is the most frightfully dangerous place, so it is best if you don't speak when you are out. You'll draw too much attention." He sighed. "As if you didn't draw all the sight out of a man's eye even when you've slept on the ground and woke with sticks in your hair and lard on your dear legs. I shall meet you at the Passage West in two days. Liam will be glad of your company. Nothing could stop me from coming back to you."

Anna spent the few days without Donal in a feverish fit of reading. She discovered that even the poorest Irish houses had books, and she worked her way through local newspapers to understand the tenor of the time politically. She also read one volume of Charles Dickens, a young British author whose political satire was hugely admired by the Irish. In fact, when she arrived at the pub, she was still daydreaming about the full-throttle nerve of Dickens to challenge the status quo. She imagined twining herself around Donal in a nearly warm bed, feeling the scratch of his legs, talking about the political impact of authors like Dickens. But first, Donal would tell her how to extract Joseph from Colonel Mitford. She didn't particularly care if it meant tossing the boy into a sack and hauling him on the backside of a horse. Such were her thoughts when she pulled open the door of the Passage West.

The pub was everything Donal had promised; a small slip of a storefront that opened to a larger pub, nestled into the poor side of town, as close to the bay as one could go without falling in. Cork was famous for its massive and complex bays and coves, which made it a haven for ships seeking shelter from the wild forces of wind and sea. Donal had picked the Passage West precisely because it was in the poorest part of town, with the fewest militia. The pub was a stopping place for smugglers and those who yearned for an Irish home rule.

"You'll be welcomed there. If you find the drinking and the singing too much for your liking, the barkeep will let you rest in the back of the pub. They've quiet rooms," Donal had said.

The smoke assaulted her eyes and nose, quickly filling her lungs with the gritty residue of a poorly ventilated peat fire and smoke from the clay pipes that half the men sucked on. A soldier at the far end of the bar stood out like a beacon, his red coat rakishly open and his hat on the bar. Even from the door, she could see that he was drunk and that the others in the pub offered him a wary, yet genial, distance. A fiddler played near the hearth and tipped his head sideways to Anna as she entered. This meant that she should do something, but what?

The British soldier caught her eye, and she looked quickly away. She recognized the crooked nose immediately; he was the soldier who had twice shoved Anna away at the wrestling match. Recognition slowly dawned on him as he pushed away from the bar. Something was wrong. Where was Donal? He had said that he'd be here. Wasn't this the place? She turned to look in the far right corner, remembering how Donal liked to sit facing the door.

Taking quick strides that Anna heard rather than saw, the soldier was on her before she even took off her wrap. His hand latched tightly to the back of her neck. No one had ever touched her like that before, gripping her neck, trying to guide her like a dog. Her reaction came from the don't-kill-me part of her brain.

"Get your hands off me," she yelped. She had wanted to snarl with deep, resonant tones, but her voice came out high and shrill with fear. The breath of the soldier was thick with alcohol and smoke, but her words rattled him to a sort of sobriety. She recognized the look, the blur of passion and humiliation, followed by the decision to inflict damage and take possession. She did not have long to ponder, only a fraction of a second to look at the barkeep whom Donal had said could be trusted.

The fist burst into Anna's jaw like a car crash. There had been no attempt at slowing or swerving to avoid the collision. With the shatter of light and sound, the crunch of her teeth, she felt not the pang of nerve endings insulted but wonderment. Had her mother forgotten her, had her brother forgotten her, and had her father long since forgotten her? No, she knew they hadn't. The bolt of light that illumined her brain confirmed her connection; she mattered to the people in her time, to her family, even to her rascal of a nephew.

She spit the broken teeth into her hand, wanting to save them, just in case she was spirited back to her time again. She wanted the teeth put back in her mouth, reinstated. The commotion in the pub screeched to a thick silence, and the only sound was the scratch of her boots along the floor as she tried to right herself.

He dragged her to the door, his hands dug deep into her long hair. Her boots scraped furiously along the stone floor. She gripped the bits of her teeth in one hand and thrashed about with the other arm, trying to reach any part of the man. He pulled open the tavern door, and her feet bumped over the threshold as he dragged her to the street.

Anna was suddenly enraged that she couldn't stand up. Even the smash to the jaw was not this bad. She rallied with a surge of righteous anger. Adrenaline fueled her, running mostly to the large muscles of her thighs. Her legs, that's what would save her. What good was all the triathlon training, the running, bike riding, and the swimming if she couldn't use it for something that truly mattered, like saving her life? She willed her abdominal muscles to engage. Her legs pulled under her and she stood, racing to keep up with the man who held her hair.

She knew he would expect her to pull away, but instead she charged straight at him, reaching for his eyes with one hand and his throat with the other. It meant letting go of her precious teeth. She caught sight of them for a moment, as they arced behind the soldier, catching light from the streetlamp.

He was still drunk, and that was both her advantage and the unpredictable danger. If she could force him to let go of her hair, she could escape him by running. She knew she could outrun him.

The street outside the pub had one circle of light. The two of them thrashed beyond it as they skidded along the wet cobblestones. From the corner of her eye, she noted a small crowd of people. She heard a man's voice say, "Get off her, man. She's not for you."

The soldier turned his head and yelled, "Piss off with you! Or the lot of you'll be arrested."

She was on her own. Her fingers searched for his eyes, but he turned his head. With his other hand he grabbed one of her arms and pulled her close to his body. They scuffled into an alley that reeked of urine. Anna tallied up her remaining options. He meant to beat her, rape her, kill her, or a horrible mixture of all three. She had to use anything; her remaining arsenal was her voice, her teeth, and her legs. She lunged into his neck and bit hard. At the same time, she brought up her right knee and slammed it into his balls, hitting off center, not giving the full gut-blasting pain that she'd hoped for. Still, he grunted and let go of her hair.

The release was so gratifying. It was the one thing that she had wanted. Anna pulled away, but to her amazement, the man still held her arm despite his pain. As she pulled away, the force of her movement toppled them to the ground, with the soldier on top of her. His face, contorted in a grimace, was close to hers. She breathed in his heated scent of thwarted propriety.

"You're nothing but trouble, not worth the bloody effort," he said.

She felt his arm moving along his side. He was a slender man, wrapped with sinewy muscles. The glint of a knife caught her eye. He moved one hand up to her throat and pushed her chin to the side. Anna understood with excruciating clarity that he meant to slit her throat. For a slice of a second she realized that an observer would think they were wrestling and that the soldier was close to a takedown; one of her shoulder blades was on the dirt and the other hovered inches above it. This is just what Joseph would do, transfer the energy to his legs, disrupt his opponent's balance and establish his. Anna pumped her legs hard, hoping at least to ruin his aim, to do anything that would keep her from dying in a stinking alley.

The response was better than she imagined possible. His head lurched backward and his body shuddered, falling forward. Anna jerked her body quickly to the left, missing the impact of the man. She scissored her legs out from under him and rolled.

Her success had nothing to do with her improvised kick. The soldier had a knife in his back, dead center. Blood flowed out. She stumbled to a standing position and saw two men.

"For Christ's sake, get a wagon and take him out to the bay. Wrap him and weigh him down with stones. Quick, before every dog in town smells his blood."

Anna could not quiet her breath. The soldier had been killed, and the toxic coating of death spread out like a stain, running up her legs. She didn't know which man had killed him. One of the men took her arm and gently pulled her into the street again.

"Here, take my arm like you're my sweetheart. Donal has been delayed and we must take you away from this mire of misfortune. Are you hurt? Can you tell yet?"

He was the barkeep; she recognized him, or, more truly, she recognized the way he had his shirtsleeves rolled up. Anna trusted him as soon as he said Donal's name.

"My jaw. I don't think it's broken, but two of my teeth are gone," she said.

Once they were beyond sight of the Passage West, he set a faster pace.

"Can you keep up, lassie? Donal tells me you're bloody strong."

"Yes. What's your name?"

She let go of his arm and they broke into a run. Somewhere a dead British soldier was being wrapped in a canvas tarp, weighted with stones, taken into a boat, and slipped into the black waters.

"It's best if you can't say my name. You'll think poorly of

me manners, but under bludgeoning distress, you'll never be able to tell the militia my name. D'ya see?" he said, beginning to huff.

"Yes. Thank you for saving me. I just wanted to know your name, but I understand why you can't tell me. I've never been saved so many times since coming to Ireland. You are my hero," she said. Anna knew this sounded stilted and silly, but she meant it. She didn't know who had put the knife into the soldier, and she would not ask.

"Aye. We are all heroes and most of us are doomed. A frightful conflagration of circumstances."

They continued running, Anna with her skirts gathered up in each hand, turning corners, following a trail that was purposefully complicated.

"Here now, slow down and give me your arm again. Lean into me a wee bit, like I'm sodden drunk and you're the good woman taking me home."

As they walked, streetlights appeared again, the houses were suddenly grand, and there were cobblestones again and not just mud. They had emerged into the section of Cork that cloistered the well-to-do. Anna immediately understood where they were—the Protestant neighborhood, more English than Irish.

"We've loyal friends here. Nothing is ever so black and white as it seems. And even if we didn't have one friend among the English, the best concealment is to be in the center of the invaders. Given our history, that puts us in the center of a good many places."

They came to a whitewashed cottage surrounded by a waist-high stone fence in front. A tiny glow of yellow light came from an upstairs window. The barkeep rapped the knocker on the thick front door. Anna noticed that the iron knocker was a dog with a long snout, racing with the legs extended, as if the animal had been a rocket. A man appeared in his nightgown; his hair was ruffled, and he had sleep creases along one side of his face.

"Good evening to you, John. This is a friend of Donal's," said her companion instantly. "And she's been hurt. Donal will come for her."

A flicker of fear crossed the man's face, an involuntary contraction, the basic desire to run from danger. He recovered and said, "Please, bring her in. Welcome, miss."

"You're English?" said Anna, forgetting any caution as she stepped into the house.

"Quite so. Don't look so shocked. There are more than a few of us who disagree with our government. We are loyal to the death to our people, but in grand disagreement with our government."

They took her to a bedchamber upstairs. A young maid brought water for the washbasin and helped Anna out of her torn clothing. The young woman put her hand on Anna's jaw and concluded that it was not broken. While Anna washed, the maid put a warming stone between the covers. She tucked Anna in bed like a baby, murmuring, "There, there. No, not a word from you until morning."

The last thing Anna heard was the low rumble of men's voices recounting the night. She heard only " . . . bastard . . . vermin . . . good riddance . . . take courage," then she sank into a dreamless sleep.

She woke, with the sun sending a sharp rectangle of light on the wall across the room. And snoring, soft snoring that was rich and rumbling. Anna opened her eyes and saw

Donal, legs stretched out in the chair, a blanket thrown over his chest and his head tipped at an angle sure to make his neck muscles angry.

Anna pushed up in the bed and groaned. Every muscle in her body protested and blared distress. Donal roused immediately. He threw off the blanket and came to the bed.

"Anna. I am so sorry. This is the fault of mine. If I'd come back sooner . . . "

They clung to each other, arms wrapped around necks and ribs, faces pushed into hair and tender ears. They rocked and swayed, matching heartbeats, finding the harmonious refrain of lovers. They crooned to each other, Donal singing soft songs in Irish and French.

"Don't let's talk yet, my love. We've all the time in the world for that. I'll tell you all about my journey and you'll tell me yours. But not yet. I only want you in my arms," he said.

They did not budge from the room, only answering a shy knock on the door when the maid brought them hot bread and soup, then sleeping again as if they had never slept.

Chapter 31

Anna woke to a red-hot bolt of pain in her mouth, the center of which pulsed like a drum. She placed her hand on her cheek and met a hard and swollen knot. They had slept through the afternoon and early evening.

"Donal, wake up," she said, suddenly finding her tongue too large and too dry. "Something is wrong with my mouth."

Donal sat up and placed his hand on her distorted cheek. "I feared this. You've got to have the stubs taken out of your mouth. You can't let the poison kill you, I'll not let that happen."

She ran her tongue over the stubs of what had been her left incisor and the next tooth, which she thought was called a canine. She decided to call them number two and three from the center. As her fever rose, she was grateful that the soldier had not slammed out her two middle teeth at least.

It was just after midnight; a set of church bells, impervious to the sleeping masses, rang out the hour. In spite of the time, Donal arranged for the procedure to happen quickly, before Anna could rise to a stubborn protest. She suspected that not only had two of her teeth been broken off but something else had gone wrong as well; a nerve had been severed or damaged. This was her worst fear, that she would succumb to a malady of 1844 and perish long before her time.

Anna sat her feet on a stool and held a wet cloth on her face. Ice, yes, ice would be just the thing for a hot, swollen jaw. But there was no ice, no dentist, and no antibiotics.

"The blacksmith must have been held up," said John, who glanced anxiously at Anna. "It's a pity you must suffer so."

No sooner had he said this than the door fairly blew open to frame a man, hat pulled over one eye, a leather satchel in his hand. Two other young men followed him. This had to be the blacksmith. He nodded to John, then Donal, and glanced at Anna.

"This be our patient?" he asked with such warm humor that Anna forgot for one nanosecond what was about to happen.

"Have you a few glasses of whiskey? Or better yet, to get the job done, poteen?" he asked.

"I'm not much of a drinker," said Anna.

This was not entirely true. She had tried both poteen and whiskey, and neither one of them had tasted anything but hot and revolting.

"That may well be the case, but some moments call for drink, the way the night calls for morning. Tell me, lass. How has it gone for you when you've had teeth pulled before?"

"I've never had a tooth pulled," said Anna.

In fact, Anna's teeth were nearly pristine, a product of fluoride, orthodontics, dental visits twice a year, and obsessive brushing and flossing.

The blacksmith set his foot on a chair.

"I see. So this shall be your first. Well then, all the more reason to drink up."

Anna looked at Donal and he nodded. Drinks were poured, and the men all sat down as if it hadn't really been past midnight, as if they'd had all the time in the world.

"Should you be drinking?" Anna asked the blacksmith after choking down several sips of the burning poteen.

"Oh, don't worry about me. And don't try to keep up with me and the drink. It steadies my hand," he said.

Anna worried that her new dental practitioner was drinking the local white lightning, something her own dentist had never done in the gleaming world of stainless steel, soothing music, and pastel walls. She also worried how very much this operation was going to hurt without anesthesia of any sort. She tipped her glass and opened her throat as she had learned to do at freshman drinking parties. She downed the entire glass.

"There, that's the way," said Donal, pouring more into her glass.

Anna watched the glow of the fire shimmer in a more welcoming dance. She opened a few buttons of her blouse until her collarbone felt the air and the first blush of heat rose from her torso and raced to her head. She managed to open her mouth and poke her finger along stubs where two lovely teeth should have been. The poteen began to taste better, with hints of hot pepper, cinnamon, and cheap vodka.

"You drink up, dearie, I'll step out for a bit with my lads and gather a few things together. A little of this and that," said the blacksmith.

"Wait," said Anna, feeling more festive. "I want to make a toast to you."

She stood up and held her third glass of poteen.

"To the best damned blacksmith in all of Ireland."

"Let's wait until the night is over before you toast me with accolades," he said.

Anna drank another half glass, and her knees felt squishy.

"Donal, my knees feel squishy," she announced.

"That often happens," he said, moving closer to her side. "I should tell you that this will go better if you are dead drunk, much better."

"Okey-dokey," said Anna, tipping her glass up and pouring the lava liquid down her throat. "Wait just one minute. Will this make me go blind?" She held her glass out to Donal for a refill.

"On every other occasion when you have been offered this drink, you've turned your nose up. You're in no danger of going blind from this one night of indulgence," he said.

"That's good. When I get back home again, I can have these teeth replaced with perfect white teeth. You'll never know the difference, never, never, ever."

Anna felt a powerful euphoria building up like a geyser. She spun around and wrapped her arms around Donal's neck.

"I have a secret, a teeny secret. Do you know where I really come from? Donal, I'm from the future. Far, far away." Anna convulsed into laughter. "Have you ever heard of anything so hilarious? We mustn't tell the others. Sshhh. "

From a distance, she heard the men return. She felt herself lifted up, felt her feet leave the ground, and suddenly she was on the long table. She tried to move and saw that one of the young men held her legs and another held her head. Donal climbed up on the table and straddled her, placing a knee on each arm.

"She's very particular about her teeth. And I do believe

she's had as much drink as she can stand," said Donal, looking at the blacksmith.

Anna looked up at the ceiling, and it wiggled like cottage cheese. The room itself began to bob around, as if it had been floating on the ocean.

The blacksmith put his face close to hers. "This can go quickly. I'm famously fast. I want you to let me do my job here, lass, and you'll be all the happier for it."

Every instinct told Anna to clamp her jaws shut. She wanted to be far more inebriated; Anna prayed for unconsciousness.

"I'm not drunk enough. I can feel everything. I'll just wait until I get home and go to my dentist. He's a nice man who doesn't drink on the job, and he'll give me a beautiful bridge."

The picture of a bridge in her mouth, a stone bridge, a hanging bridge, a suspension bridge was irresistibly funny. And when Anna laughed, she opened her mouth wide and squeezed her eyes shut.

The blacksmith seized the moment. Anna couldn't see the implement as it went in; the man had kept it strategically out of sight. She felt an enormous tug, as if he'd been extracting her entire jawbone from her head. She imagined her skull shattering from the force. And then a jolt of fire, a blast of lightning that flashed neon from the tail of her spine to her head. Her eyes flushed with tears. She smelled something dreadfully foul, a combination of raw sewage and rotting flesh. The blacksmith quickly turned her head to one side and wiped her mouth with a liquor-soaked rag.

"We'll have you smelling like a rose in no time. The pus

is the worst part; you can't believe that something so vile can build up in us. I've got the first tooth. It came out whole, which is how we want it to come out. No need to go fishing for bits. Now the other one," he said.

Anna couldn't see Donal clearly because her eyes were thick with salty tears, but she could feel him straddling her chest and she could make out his outline. An epithet was rising up out of her, a guttural threat to life and limb. But before she could spit out the words, the blacksmith was back in her mouth again, the tug again, the spine-splitting shock. The burst of pus and smell was repeated on the second extraction. She heard the man at her feet cough into his sleeve.

"There, the stubs of your teeth are out. You've got a big gash. We'll make a little stitch and then turn you loose," said the blacksmith.

"No stitches!" shrieked Anna. Donal hadn't told her this part.

"Shouldn't we let the gap bleed freely? We want the infection to drain out." Donal was sounding less confident.

Anna began to buck and writhe.

"Get the fuck off me!" she bellowed.

A moment of silence followed.

"Great glory. Do you suppose all the women in America talk like that? I'll never be sending me daughters there," said a fellow from the safe distance of the kitchen doorway.

"I don't like leaving her this torn open. But if you both want no stitches here, then that's the way it will be. Make sure she keeps this poultice on it for as long as she can stand. A good famous healer sent this along. Biddy Early. I've heard of her, but this is the first time I've ever laid eyes on her. She made a point of it, she did. Not just everyone is sent a gift from Biddy Early. There now. A little swish with the liquor."

Anna shrieked again.

She heard the blacksmith step away.

"Now lads, this is how we turn her loose. We want to keep all of our parts, and she's drunk enough and mad enough to rip out your hearts as well as parts south. First I walk out. Next, you there, Timothy, let go of her head. Gerry, let go of her legs. Lastly, we'll leave Donal to contend with the furies of his sweetheart. You'll pray she wants to go to sleep. A few more drops of drink at this point could turn the tide in your favor."

The three men left, beating a retreat of self-preservation. Donal remained. John had disappeared.

"Anna, you were brave. Shatteringly loud, but brave. I hope you remember none of this. I'm going to get off you now, and I don't want you to kill me straightaway."

Donal lifted one knee off her arm and then the other, slipping each foot to one side of the table. Then he stepped back quickly.

Anna rolled to her side in a limp heap, exhausted from the pain, from screeching, from crying. A mighty drumbeat had taken up residence in her jaw. When she pushed up from her horizontal position, Donal was there with a glass of the clear liquid.

"Sip a wee bit more."

He handed her the poultice and said, "Press this in the gap." She pressed the sodden cloth and found that it didn't hurt any more than it already had. *Good*, she thought, *I have gone through the worst of this. I'm surviving this. I should be getting medals.*

She woke the next day with a wretched taste in her mouth,

as if mice had camped out in her cheeks. Ah, the poteen: a full-out, white-lightning hangover. Anna desperately wanted water. She rolled over and felt the immediate lack of red-hot pain in her jaw. The pain was a dull throb, a manageable dull throb. She sat up and touched her face with both hands.

She rose up on her knees and shouted, "Donal, wake up. The big lump on my jaw, it's gone. Or it's mostly gone and it's no longer red hot."

"Anna, you'll wake snakes at this hour. We Irish like to sleep if we can." He reached up with his arm and circled her waist, then tugged her back to the bed. His eyes were etched with red lines. "Let's get all on one stick about something."

"Oh, yes, let's," said Anna without knowing what he meant.

He rubbed his legs against hers until they were well braided together. He placed his hand on her jaw.

"The blacksmith did a magnificent extraction. May I look, please?"

Anna opened her mouth and gently pulled up her top lip.

"God bless Biddy Early. I've heard her name more in the last weeks than in all my life. This is going to heal well."

Anna waggled her tongue in the gap where her teeth had been.

"I've an idea. Now that your face is no longer swollen up like a blowfish, this is a perfectly good time to tell you."

Anna pressed her nose into his neck and smelled the scent of hope.

"Anna, once we latch your nephew, once that part is done, and once he is released from that Mitford chap, well, what I'm coming to is that I want you to come back to Skibbereen with me. Or to Kinsale if you've taken to Kinsale more than Skib. But let's say we go together. We are both free to marry."

Donal twisted so that he faced her, nose to nose on the bed.

"You fit with me. When I look at us, we make this thing that's altogether new from either you or me. Me old mum would have called us a huckleberry above a persimmon, but she was old-fashioned, she was."

Anna was open and soft all over, and she had never been both at one time before. Her body was new and rearranged by what passed between them, by the third thing they created from her breath and his skin. She had never been more scraped, terrified, battle scarred, toothless, hungry, and hungover from home brew than now. And more loved; she had never been more loved.

"The last words on Glennie's lips told me to go home. The first words on your lips tell me to stay here forever. I'm going to pray that our Glenis was wrong."

"What do you mean?"

"That means that I want more than anything to stay with you. I may not be able to go home, even after we rescue my nephew. Is that what we're calling it, a rescue?"

She heard a hard rain and wind crash into the house.

"Tell me we don't have to smuggle anything, meet sailors on frozen beaches, or find each other at smoky taverns today. Please tell me that we don't have to go out in this rainstorm."

"There are two beautiful kinds of rain in Ireland. One is the mist, which keeps the isle green, gives us flowers and crops of potatoes. We call it liquid gold, and we all praise it. The other is a rain like today, hard and forbidding, that makes it impossible to venture out the door. All who can will find excuses to stay inside. And that is just what we shall do."

Anna relaxed deeper into the bed.

"Now tell me everything about my nephew and your journey," she said, changing the topic slightly, pressing close to him, swinging one leg over his.

"We have an insider working on the colonel's estate. I met him at the docks in Tramore. Don't ask me his name; it is all the better that his name remains unspoken. There is no telling what any of us will say under the force of capture. Even under the foolishness of drink, we'll tell the most horrendous tales and someone will think they're true. You thought you were from the future after four glasses of poteen," he said with a wink.

"No kidding? Imagine that," said Anna, wrapping a stand of hair around her finger.

"So his name remains unspoken. He said the colonel's father was awarded the entire estate by the English for his service in the military, gobbling up an immense amount of Irish land and running people out of their homes, tumbling their cottages. The great irony is that the estate is now run by Irish cooks, stonemasons, servants, farmers, stablemen, and a host of other Irish who, for the most part, keep the colonel from causing a fearsome amount of trouble. For years, he has hunted with his English mates, bet on horse races, and traveled to England more often than not, leaving the Irish be. Until your nephew washed up onshore."

"Glenis never thought to search that far away," she said.

"Aye. He came ashore a good seventy miles from where you were found. She never would have thought that was possible. The colonel is using the lad as his wrestling champion as further proof that Irish men are inferior. He has plans to take him to England and promote him. He may even give up betting on horses. And he had no qualms about your nephew's life and limb. The fellow I talked with said that Joseph is valuable to him, but no more so than a good racehorse."

"So how do we get him?"

"We're going to book passage out of Cork and go to Tramore. If he'll come willingly, we could simply meet him and make off with him for Cork, then Skibbereen. But there's a complication. The lad is in love."

Anna sat up. "He's sixteen! How much in love can he be?"

She knew the answer to this as soon as she said it. Horribly, impossibly, over the top in love, that's how much.

"Do you mean that he won't leave because he's in love?" she asked.

"The fellow I talked with said there is tragedy brewing; the lad is in love with an Irish girl. The colonel is violently opposed to the upper class fraternizing with the Irish."

For the rest of the day, while the rain pounded along the southern edge of Ireland, Anna and Donal planned their approach to Tramore and shared a grateful meal with John. Anna drank a thin soup, nursing the absence of two lovely teeth.

Chapter 32

By the time Anna woke, Donal was already gone, having left word with their obliging host that she should meet him at a small church.

"Where has he gone?" asked Anna.

"Booking passage for the two of you to Tramore. It's far easier than by land. He says you have family there—a lad," said John.

"Should I be prepared to leave directly from the church?"

"Aye. And our maid has located a skirt and a jacket that is not torn to shreds. She left it for you."

Anna could not imagine the sacrifice that had gone into acquiring a skirt and a jacket for her. The jacket fit too snugly across her shoulders and the skirt truly needed to be let down, but they would have to do. Her boots had been polished, and they were greatly improved. She let a freshly laundered linen shift fall over her head and slide along her body. She paused to take stock. She had a glaring scar on one leg, which was well healed but still plum; her inner thighs had healed nicely from a full day of riding with a skirt on; she was shy two teeth; and the swelling in her jaw was all but gone. Not bad, she thought, trying to cheer herself, not bad at all.

Leaving John's house swiftly was the kindest thing she could do for him.

"You are a saint of a man. And I have never loved taking a bath as much as I have at your house," she said as she solemnly kissed his cheek. She knew people thought baths were an extravagance, or at least frequent bathers were suspect. But Anna had left frequent bathing behind and was now on to infrequent bathing.

"The English are good people," he said. "We don't all agree with strangling the Irish and their trades. . . ." His eyes reddened, and Anna saw his passion flare. She took his hand and nodded.

John had hired a coach for her, another extravagance that she gratefully accepted.

The small Catholic church was hardly a church at all, but it was a building of sorts, and someone had filled a tray with sand to hold a few candles. There was no fireplace, and the inside was like a cave: damp and cold. The barren walls and altar were just as the church's young priest explained.

"Our churches are as plain as we can make them; it is all the better for us to deny attentions to the church and put our attentions into our people and the liberation of our country," he whispered to her, guiding her to a rough pew.

Anna knelt in the unforgiving pew, waiting for Donal to appear. She knew that she might have to wait an hour—or perhaps she might have to wait four hours. Time was more fluid here, less tethered to a glowing, digital clock. To occupy her time-constrained thinking, she got up and walked to the far side of the altar to light a candle in memory of all who were going to die between now and when she was born. She lit one candle for all those destined to die in the Famine. She knelt in front of the candles and rested her head on the bar, polished to a dull gleam by the palms of many. Another woman knelt beside her.

"Hello, Anna," said the woman.

Anna looked sharply at her, taking in her rich mahogany hair, her firm skin dusted with freckles, her diminutive frame, and her confident air.

"Excuse me?" Anna said, dodging for time.

"I've been sent by Donal. Well, not exactly, but on his behalf. Excuse me manners. I'm Biddy Early."

Anna's heart leaped, and a sound like a mewling kitten escaped her lips. She didn't want to make another mistake. There was already a dead man in the ocean because of her. She was losing her grip; she had to be careful. She cleared her throat. "You've mistaken me for someone else."

"I know a bit about you. And it is not safe for us to stay here. You must come with me."

Biddy paused, and Anna saw an appraising look come over her, not unlike one a good lawyer would exhibit.

"There are too many ears in this church. Walk away from the others and step into this alcove." Biddy nodded with her head to a darkened nook.

Anna stood up abruptly. When she did, she towered over Biddy. The two women moved to the privacy of the alcove. Even in her panic, Anna noted the tiny creases around the woman's eyes, which were deep ocean blue, and the corners of her mouth. Anna imagined that Biddy was in her forties, although it was not easy to judge age in the harsh world of uncertain food.

"Did Glenis not tell you about me before she died?"

At the sound of Glenis's name, Anna crumbled and held her hands up to her face.

"Give me a reason to trust you, because I long to trust another person," said Anna. "She was unable to tell me anything." This was a lie, but one that Anna decided to keep tucked inside, with all of the precious parts of Glennie.

"I'll tell you about dear Glenis," said Biddy, pressing a shoulder lightly against the cold slab of stone in the alcove. "I can tell you that she loved you like her sister and that the two of you dreamed each other's dreams, sleeping out by a sacred spring. Is that enough for you?"

Anna swallowed hard. "Yes. Thank you."

"Glenis said you were from another time, that you had traveled from the future. You're searching for another, a lad, who came with you. I've seen and heard more than you can imagine, so take heart; I believe you. And Glenis brought this with her." Biddy pulled a bit of cloth out of her pocket. It was the shred of silk marked with the Man Silk tag.

Anna gasped and shot out her hand to grab the cloth. She pulled it to her face.

"When Glenis showed this to me, I was struck hard by a thing that had only been flimsy vapors, a memory. I know this cloth from somewhere, I've had it in me hands before. And the second I touched it, I heard a man's voice, as clear and pure as any voice I've ever heard. 'Mine the coin,' he said."

Anna gasped. That's why Glennie knew, Biddy had told her.

"My brother said something about a coin right after he

was hurt. But it was the last thing that he said, before . . . I don't know if he'll survive," said Anna.

"Time is pockmarked and fluid to be sure, but if you're here, there's a reason. And I know part of what it is."

Anna sank into Biddy's assuredness. Finally.

"It's a curse as sure as I've ever seen. They can last for centuries, starting like a bad speck of dust and once they start rolling, they can pick up fearsome speed, and a hundred and sixty-four years later you have trouble that is thick and deep as stone. I don't know what's become of people in your time that you can't tell a curse when clearly you're living every day under its ugly breath."

"And that's why I'm here? But there's nothing special about my family, we're not world leaders or famous in any way. We are the plainest people around. Why us?"

Biddy rolled her eyes and sighed.

"You and I will not have time to say all that needs be said about curses. In the world of healing, we are taught that to save a single life is to save the whole world in time. These are the truest and the most ancient words that I know."

Anna nodded, unable to take her eyes off the woman.

"I am a seventh daughter, and that is how the sight passes in my people. But for all those who touch skin and know it as skin, we touch skin and know it as sound and story. Here, give me your hand."

Anna instinctively pulled her hands back, as if she'd felt the flame of a torch. With a jerky movement, she held out her right hand.

"Aye. You and the boy are from the same line. Wait, I can't decipher this, hold still, woman, you're shaking. There is a turning, a spiral where a direct line should be. You are from here and not from here, and yet he precedes you. He stands in front and you are behind him in the distance. . . ."

Anna snatched her hand away. She suddenly remembered the strange vision of Joseph from her frozen night on Beara.

"Donal and I know where Joseph is. Donal is booking passage for us to go to Tramore this very day. He's meeting me here," said Anna.

Biddy Early took Anna's hand again, and welcome warmth spread up her arms.

"I've saved the worst for last. Donal has been taken by the British. He's in Cork prison for murder and treason. There was an informer in the Passage West who somehow connected Donal to the death of the soldier."

Anna's knees gave out and Biddy caught her.

"Here now, lean against me."

"Donal wasn't even there! Where is the prison? We need to get him released. I can speak on his behalf."

"I feel time dwindling. We can try to salvage Donal or find your nephew. I'm not at all sure we can do both."

"I'm not losing either of them. If time is dwindling, then tell me what to do."

Chapter 33

"Get me a dress, the finest dress you can manage. And shoes. Get me shoes that a lady would wear," said Anna.

It was December, and even along the southern shores of Ireland, the air did not warm during the fleetingly short hours of daylight. Anna had full faith in Biddy Early's stealth empire of subversive power and sight. The two women had taken over the priest's meager quarters behind the church.

Biddy took time to examine Anna's gums where the two teeth had been extracted. Or where the stubs of her teeth had been extracted.

"That's sterling work by the blacksmith. And you took good care with the poultice. I don't like to brag, but it could have gone far worse for you. Would you care for a cup of poteen? It could settle your nerves," she said with a smile.

"I never want to taste poteen again. Let's get this done, and then I need to think quietly about meeting with the governor of the prison."

"Don't let your nerves run off with you. You'll be no help to Donal or the boy in an agitated state of mind."

Within hours, a dress appeared, fresh from a British estate in Cork, delivered by a chambermaid, who gave it to the kitchen help, who packed it in a crate for a gardener, who delivered it to a stonemason, who appeared in the doorway and handed it over without a word. Biddy pried the crate open.

"This will do. This will make a titled lady out of you."

There were no undergarments for this dress (an unfortunate omission) except for a corset. Biddy made quick work of the corset, placing a knee in Anna's back and yanking hard on the ties. Then Anna let the finely woven wool dress pour over her head, a disarming blue, with a tightly striped bodice, flaring below her waist, coming to a provocative point below her belly button, directing the eye downward. The dress had a jacket with slightly puffed shoulders and a velvet blue collar of a darker, richer blue.

Biddy helped her brush her hair out, then arranged it in a tight design of twists and braids that Anna could never replicate. A hat, the thing that irritated Anna more than the corset, was the final touch, pinned through her hair, a conglomeration of satin, velvet, blue wool, and feathers. The shoes were too tight and the two women fretted over this.

"You have god-awful large feet," said Biddy.

"So I've been told," said Anna.

When she was dressed and cinched, her feet stuffed into soft leather shoes far too small for her, and with no underclothes on at all (an oversight, but they all agreed that if she stayed upright, no one would be the wiser), she was ready to call on the governor of the New Cork Prison. She had one hour to prepare. Biddy had already arranged for a meeting with the governor through one of her grateful former patients, a British lord.

"You're sure he's not going to connect me with the death at Passage West?" asked Anna.

"His dinner was dusted with herbs that will soften his memory. But his true nature will not be altered. He is still ruthless and small of heart. Like all men of his profession, he has convinced himself that his prisoners are less than human. Are you prepared to offer him something that will be worth one Irish man? There is no room for error; it must be something that he cannot refuse."

"I am prepared to offer him anything," said Anna, "as soon as I think of it."

New Cork Prison overlooked the city, with a majestic view of the River Lee leading to the bay. Biddy and Anna stood at the gate. Streetlamps offered yellow pools of light.

"He's just had his dinner and is expecting you. He's been told that you are a wealthy woman from America, nothing else. Are you sure you can do this?" asked Biddy.

Anna rapped firmly on the massive door bookended by stone pillars.

"I've never been more certain of anything," she lied.

Two British guards opened the gates and escorted her, one on either side. The walkway was long, passing through gardens, newly planted the past season. If Anna hadn't known this was a prison, it might have looked like a castle from storybooks, all stone and small windows. A wooden platform stood to the right. Of course, the gallows. Prisoners were hung for their crimes, especially traitors.

The governor's room was immediately to the right. The cold quickly seeped from the stone floor to her feet.

"Your guest, sir," said one guard.

The remains of dinner had been pushed to one side of his massive desk. There was one chair in front of the desk. He pushed back in his chair and rose halfway before sinking back down, looking slightly buzzed. *Oh, thank you, Biddy,* thought Anna.

He was younger than she expected, close to her age, narrow-lipped, with a small, dark beard, tightly trimmed.

"What a pleasure," he said unconvincingly. "Please sit down, Mrs. Flemming. That is correct, Flemming?"

Flemming had been as good a name as any, as long as it hadn't been Irish.

"Thank you, Governor. May I come rudely to the point of my visit? I am departing Ireland tomorrow and I have so little time."

Anna was already sweating. Biddy had said that the effects of the herbs lasted less than an hour, and it took so blasted long for conversations here.

He leaned back in his immense chair. He twirled his hand like a conductor.

"Please. I have not had a rude question from a beautiful woman all day."

She had known from the beginning what it was she had to offer him. She had information about the future, but she had quickly decided against that as a bargaining chip. Anna was sure that he wouldn't believe her. She was prepared, fully prepared to fuck like a monkey with this guy to get Donal released. It just couldn't be that bad. She'd get over it and so would Donal.

"I need to ask for the release of a prisoner, Donal Mahoney. He's been falsely accused of murder and treason. I'm willing to offer—"

Tilting his head to one side, he held up his hand to stop her.

"Please say no more. I can grant this," said the governor of New Cork Prison. "I ask only that you relieve me of an odious task this evening. I am suddenly feeling the need for diversion from my responsibilities."

Anna was, for once, speechless.

"He will be known as a traitor, and the great masses will believe that he has been executed. At dawn tomorrow, another man will be executed. We have no shortage of traitors, madam. I can select randomly from a large group of men and women who are dangerous to the empire. But it would please me if you would relieve me of this burden. You shall select who is executed in place of your Donal. Come, there is no time like the present," he said, offering Anna his public smile composed of gun barrels and darkish oil. He pushed back his chair.

"No. I cannot . . ."

He sat down.

"Then I cannot help you. Then Donal shall be executed in the morning. Is this too complicated for you?"

She had not bargained on this. Anna had been ready to endure anything to get Donal released. But not this. Not naming a man, pointing out the next to be executed.

The governor walked to the front of his desk, took her hand, and pulled her elegantly to her feet.

"They're going to die no matter what you say. Your selection is only about timing," he hissed into her ear.

The bile rose shockingly unbidden in her throat. She turned her head from him and wretched, the vomit splashing on the stone floor.

"Such dramatics, my dear lady."

Anna wiped her mouth on her sleeve.

"What will happen to Donal when he is released? Will he be allowed to leave with me?" she croaked, her throat stung with acid.

The governor clasped his hands together as if in prayer.

"You will not get everything that you want; so few of us do. We have a tunnel that runs below the prison that emerges downhill in a private home. It is the tasteful exit for British spies who have infiltrated the traitors. He shall be escorted the moment after you select his replacement. He will be held one day until he can be taken aboard a ship for Australia, a repository for our most undesirable commoners, and it is there that he shall serve out his days. He will never see Ireland again. Shall we?"

He took her arm, and they walked out of his office, through the entryway, and directly into a vast prison warehouse of cells, two stories tall, brimming with fear, sickness, and human excretions. The governor patted her hand, which was resting on his forearm.

"Dreadful smell. I should have warned you."

They walked half the length of a football field and came to a stop in front of one of the many wooden cell doors.

"Guard, please open this door," said the governor.

As the door opened, Anna put her hand to her mouth in a failed effort to squelch the sound that came out. Five men were packed into a room no larger than eight by eight. Donal was in the midst of them. He looked at her and quickly looked away.

"Here we are. Gentlemen, this is Mrs. Flemming. She has agreed to select which of you will be hung tomorrow morning. Truly an honor, don't you agree?"

The governor pressed her forward to the doorway and she stumbled slightly, catching her hand on the doorframe. Five sets of hollowed eyes looked back at her. Behind their legs, she saw canvas stretched over hay for beds. A wood bucket capped with a plank served as a toilet. She was suddenly aware of the silence in the prison. She looked at their feet and saw that all of them wore felt shoes. The only noise was the metallic sound of the guards, their boots and sabers.

"Don't do this," whispered Donal. "Don't become part of it."

"There is silence in the prison. There is no speaking, only contemplation. Remember that," warned the governor.

Time was not on her side. She shuddered to think what the governor was like when he was not softened by Biddy's concoction. She scanned the cramped cell. Two of the prisoners were boys, not more than teenagers. Anna skipped them. She skipped Donal. Another man had been beaten about the head; his face was so swollen on one side that only one eye looked back at her. She chose the oldest man in the group, offering time back to the rest of them. Anna pointed her gloved hand to the man who stood in the back.

"Him," she said.

The appointed man closed his eyes and nodded.

"Very good, delightful," said the governor. "Guard, bring along our Mr. Donal Mahoney. He'll be leaving us this evening. Come with me, my dear."

He took her arm again and they walked back the way they had come. She looked back to see two guards on either side of Donal, who walked soundlessly between them with his felt shoes. They came to the entryway.

"Gentlemen, escort him through the tunnel," the governor instructed the guards. Then he turned to Donal.

"You'll be leaving on a ship for Australia. If you ever return to Ireland, you'll be hung within the day. And you, Mrs. Flemming. You have offered an unexpected diversion to my banal life here among criminals. It has been my pleasure."

Something worse than panic set in. Was this the last that she would ever see of Donal? The two guards guided Donal to a doorway tucked under the staircase. Was she just expected to walk out the door and go away?

"Governor! May I accompany the prisoner through the tunnel?" she asked.

Keep it simple, don't embellish, just make the request.

Without turning around, he fluttered his hand, signaling her to go along with them.

"Yes, yes. Send the boy to clean my floor and tend my fire. I shall be resting in my office," he said and closed his door.

The tunnel was lit by infrequent torches. Anna walked first with one guard, while Donal and the other guard followed. The tunnel followed the same decline as the streets outside. After a few minutes of the parade, Anna stopped and said, "May I walk with him? I've a message of farewell from his mum."

Most people responded to messages from mothers, and these guards were no different. They shrugged, and Donal stepped forward to walk next to Anna. She already saw a stronger light that marked the end of the tunnel. She tilted her head to his and whispered.

"I have never loved anyone as much as I love you. I am from the future. Please forgive me for what I've just done."

They were twenty feet from the thick door that marked the end of the tunnel.

"Anna—"

"That's the end of it now. Come this way, miss, the guard will show you to the street. And you, traitor, will spend your last night in Ireland on a dry bed that you don't deserve. Your ship sails for Australia with a hold filled with vermin just like you. Begone to rubbish," said a guard.

As the door opened, Anna was pulled through to the street, and Donal was hauled into an innocuous-looking stone house. Perfect camouflage. Anna was alone on the street. She fell to her knees, covered with the filth of prison degradation, and sobbed. That is where Biddy found her, after pounding on the prison gates, demanding to know where she was.

Biddy squatted beside her. "Come now, tell me everything, tell me all of it."

Chapter 34

Joseph drank in the colonel's adulation, feeling satisfied for brief periods before needing more of the thin drink. The dogs and the horses had not had benefit of the colonel in weeks, other than the treks to the wrestling competitions. Then, one day, the colonel canceled a trip to England to attend a family celebration.

Joseph and the colonel were dining in the echo chamber of a dining room. Huge portraits of solemn relatives hung on two walls.

"Sir, did you cancel a trip?" Joseph asked.

A lock of blond hair had fallen over one eye, and the colonel brushed it back.

"Yes, I most certainly did."

"Was it a party?"

"Yes, an engagement party, in fact."

"Was it the engagement of a close friend?"

"It was my engagement party."

Joseph stopped in mid chew and considered this. He had no experience with engagement parties, but still, to cancel one's own engagement party seemed wrong.

"You canceled your own engagement party? Does that mean that the engagement is off? Isn't that the sort of thing that makes ladies upset?"

"Engagements can last so very long, years and years, and my family can arrange a party at any time. But far more important is your latest challenge. You have been given the challenge by a champion from Tipperary, and I happen to know the ruling gentleman from the area quite well. He bested me in a hunt once and I haven't forgotten it. I've sent word that you shall accept the challenge," the colonel replied.

The two of them continued to eat their supper in the large room, overlooking the portico and the vast acreage, dotted with horses, cattle, and sheep. Joseph finished masticating a particularly tough piece of pork, then washed it down with two mugs of hard cider, more in an effort to soften it than for the extreme love of the drink. But he was swollen with alcohol, his winning streak, the drumbeat of romance, and the first reach at camaraderie with the colonel. He pushed the empty mug away from his plate, placed one forearm on the table, and cocked his head to one side.

"Sir, I don't think I'd be ready for another match so soon after Cork. We've had a steady run of matches, and as my coach would say—"

The colonel's knife hit his plate with a loud crack. Joseph felt the temperature change in the vast room.

"Did I ask you if the timing was to your liking? Because I don't need to know. My honor is riding on this match, as well as a fair wager. I've cancelled my own engagement party in England. You cannot imagine that I care about what a wrestling fellow in the Canadian Provinces has to say."

Joseph shrank back, sniffed the change in the air. He saw

the line being drawn, heard the declaration that Joseph had dared to step over the line and that further trespasses would not be allowed.

"I'm sorry, sir. Yes, you know I'll do my best."

"No, lad, you'll do better than your best. You'll win the match and I'll win my wager."

Joseph had an impulse to run from the room, from the Big House. Things had taken a sour turn. He wanted to escape from the dread that bore down on his shoulders, the feeling that his wretched destiny had searched him out and found him in the past. He caught a movement in his peripheral vision, near the door, and he was sure that Mr. Edwards had been listening.

The colonel smiled again. "I understand that you had a leg cramp. Nothing painful, I hope?"

"No, sir."

His appetite vanished; he pushed his food around his plate until the colonel finished his dinner and said goodnight.

Joseph rose early the next day, planning to walk to Tramore to sit by the ocean, but an aroma abruptly stopped him. He smelled the fish cooking in the pan before he saw it. He rounded the corner of the stable, running his hand along the cornerstone, felt the places where chisels had left decorative thumbprints in the stone. And there was Con with his father, the master stonemason with broad hands and thick fingers. Both of them squatted near the small pit of fire, the father holding the fry pan by the handle, shaking it so that the fish, covered with something like oatmeal, sizzled in the pan. In the second before the two turned their heads to see Joseph, he saw a touch pass between them, the natural skin on skin never formalized by hug or handshake. Joseph took it all in, the way the father placed one hand on Con's shoulder to press himself up to standing, the way Con steadied himself to push into his father's calloused palm, as if the question of being any other than father and son had never occurred to them.

Joseph had seen this affection before with other fathers and sons, the thing that had never passed between his father and him. Joseph knew it was his fault, some inherent failing as a boy, that had made him unqualified, unlovable, a disaster of a son. He tried not to hope anymore, like he used to when he was a kid. Now, at sixteen, he knew better than to think that his father could love him. Not like when he was eight years old, not like the fishing trip with his father.

When Joseph had been rolled under his red plaid comforter in his bed, protected by the dark of night, he had overheard his father on the phone. His father's rich voice had caught him by surprise.

"We're not working this Saturday. No. I'm taking my son fishing. That's right. I want to spend the day with my boy tomorrow. I can't wait to show him my favorite fishing spot. No, I'm not telling you where it is. Get your own."

Joseph had been giddy with a steady warm tune; his father wanted to spend time with him, show him something secret, important. Joseph had fallen asleep with the feeling of being wanted, and he'd prayed that he wouldn't spoil it by being bad again.

His father had woken him early. Joseph had smelled the coffee on his father's breath, mixed with the outdoor air that had hovered around his father's shoulders like a cape. His father had put a hand on his leg and shaken him.

"Get up, Joey. We're going fishing."

Joseph had slid out of bed, gotten into the jeans laying on his floor, pulled a long-sleeved shirt over his head, then socks, and tied the laces on his shoes. Would the good father still be in the kitchen when he opened his bedroom door, or would the other Dad be there?

The door had creaked as he'd pushed it open. He'd walked down the hallway, through the small living room, into the kitchen, where his father had put hooks and lines into a mustardy yellow plastic box filled with little compartments.

"Come on Bud, eat some cereal or slap some peanut butter on this bread. We can't be fishermen on an empty stomach."

It had still been the good Dad. The vigilant part of Joseph's brain had yawned and gone back to sleep, nonetheless keeping one eye open, like a cat. He'd been glad that he'd done everything he'd had to do the day before. The dishes had been put into the dishwasher. He'd taken a shower and plucked all the hairs out of the chrome filter in the bottom, because that was one of the things that could make his father turn into the bad Dad. If he could just remember all the right things to do and say, the good Dad would be with him always, and he loved the good Dad.

Who knew that fishing line tangled so viciously in the trees when a boy tried to cast? Who knew a father would careen from good Dad to raving maniac, tossing the tackle box into the river, kicking the beach chairs into mangled aluminum junk? Who knew a father could slap a boy so hard that he'd hit the earth and bounce?

One week later, the colonel, Joseph, and Sean prepared to leave for the wrestling tournament in Kilkenny with the reportedly ass-kicking guy from Tipperary. This was the last wrestling match before going to Dublin and then on to England. At the last minute, the colonel decided to go by horseback rather than travel by coach. "We'll leave today and be there long before supper tonight; plenty of time for our champion to rest. We need to ride into Kilkenny like warriors, not baggage. I've missed my splendid horses," he said with a toss of his head.

As the horses were prepared in front of the portico, stamping their hooves, eager for the run, Deirdre appeared with a small cloth bag for Sean.

"Some extra bits of food for the day," she said loud enough for the colonel to hear. As she walked past Joseph, she whispered, "There is a salve for your leg if it takes a turn for the worse."

"Where is Taleen? I thought she'd see me off?"

"I have her working in the kitchen. You're growing foolhardy. The colonel can have no idea that you are in love with her. For her sake, you must think of her," said Deirdre.

"I think of nothing else," he whispered fiercely.

They mounted their horses and clipped along the long lane of the estate, coming finally to the road leading north to Waterford and then north to Kilkenny. As they rode past the last of the estate, Joseph saw Taleen and Madigan on the crest of the hill. He knew that she had stolen away from the kitchen so that the last thing he'd see would be her. The colonel followed his gaze.

"Do we still have that runt dog? Sean, remind me to get rid of the dog. We can't have a runt breeding. Have it killed so that Deirdre thinks the dog ran off; I can't have the cook turning sour," said the colonel with a wink. He dug his heels into the well-groomed horse and trotted off.

The day was clear and cold. Sean stopped his horse for a moment and let Joseph come even with him.

"What are we going to do about Madigan?" asked Sean, his eyes filled with panic.

Joseph had never seen Sean panic about anything.

"We've two days to think of something. I'll win the match tomorrow. The colonel will have won more money and he'll be in the mood for me to ask a favor. I'll ask him if I can have Madigan. I'll think of a good reason; I'll tell him the dog is good luck," said Joseph.

The colonel bellowed, "Come on, lads! We've a wrestling tournament to attend and forty miles to ride." Joseph and Sean rode on.

Joseph spent a sleepless night at the Kilkenny Wayside Inn. The tournament was held on the grounds of Kilkenny Castle, a massive place, all curving walls and imposing spires. The day of the wrestling tournament was filled with the same festive atmosphere that all the matches had inspired. Wagers were made, the lesser matches were won and lost by young wrestlers trying to work their way up, by impulsive boys who just that morning decided to try their luck, and by some of the more impressive wrestlers of Kilkenny. Sean was absent most of the morning. Joseph caught sight of him once, talking intently with a woman, their heads together, alarm registering in her eyes.

Joseph's stomach curdled the contents of his breakfast into a sour mash. The pounded earth of the courtyard, often used for livestock, today served the wrestling championship. He took off his shoes and rubbed his feet into the dried clay, hoping for a superstitious connection with the dirt.

The announcer stepped lightly onto a box. "If there is anyone here who has not heard—and I doubt that—our champion fromTipperary, Padriag O'Brien, has been challenged by Joseph Blair, the lad who is sweeping across Ireland. It's a fine day in Ireland for wrestling, a fine day for reckoning. Step forward, contenders."

Joseph had seen O'Brien across the courtyard. The man had remained seated, a blanket on his shoulders, an indecipherable expression on his face. He was big, but Joseph had wrestled big before. Big had always been trumped by speed, precision, and balance.

Joseph stepped into the circle, claiming it as his own, trying to shake the feeling of unease that hovered over him. He pumped his legs, running in place, and a tingle from his calf telegraphed him. He disregarded it; he could do anything for five minutes, and that was all he ever needed.

O'Brien entered the chalked ring. He glided along, as light on his feet as one of the wolfhounds. And if a man could be a sight hound with amber eyes, O'Brien fit the bill as he honed in on his prey. He was a challenging combination; big, muscled, and agile. Joseph still had advantages, despite the difference of seventy or so pounds. He was prepared to win and to do so quickly, before the big man had a chance.

O'Brien's hair was a smoky haze, an early gray that Joseph had seen in many of the Irish. *Don't be deceived into thinking he's old, he's not,* Joseph thought to himself as he balanced on his feet in the center of the ring. O'Brien came to the center, shook Joseph's hand, and drained all the win out of the boy, excising it like a vampire.

"Glad to meet you, lad. Call me Paddy, if you can call me anything."

Shit, thought Patrick. He glanced down at Paddy's feet, balanced perfectly, each foot turned equally out a few degrees from center, a martial arts stance. Paddy gave an easy tug with his hand that pulled the boy off balance.

"Pardon me, the match hasn't begun, and look what I've done."

But Joseph knew that the match had begun and nothing would ever be the same again.

He exhausted his sprinter muscles in the first ten minutes, while Paddy danced around him, touching him here and there with a taunting hand. Ten more minutes and the leg cramp reminded Joseph of its presence, not badly, but clearly. With a sudden strike, Paddy pulled Joseph's right arm from the shoulder socket while he pressed his chest on the boy's back. He clasped his lips to Joseph's ear and said, "Shall I pull out one or two?"

Joseph heard his arm rip and pop; if he hadn't already been on the ground, he would have fallen. He screamed into the dirt. Paddy flipped him over like a fish and, with one hand, pressed the boy's shoulder blades to the ground.

"Paddy O'Brien, our own, undefeated champion!"

The Irish crowd carried Paddy O'Brien off to a tavern to celebrate his continued stature as champion, while Joseph sat in the dirt. He hung his head, refusing to seek out the face of his benefactor. A doctor in town instructed two other men in how to reinsert the arm bone back into the socket. Joseph had screamed when Paddy O'Brien had ripped the arm from its socket; he screamed when it was put back. When he stood up, he sought out the eyes of the colonel, who looked at him in much the same way he had looked at Madigan—as something to be culled out to strengthen the stock.

"Come along, now. No need for us to stay in Kilkenny after a disgrace. Sean, get the horses."

"Sir, I'm not sure that he can ride. He's as gray as a rock," said Sean.

"Then he'll have to do a better job of riding than he did of wrestling. Get the horses," said the colonel.

The colonel set a blistering pace, and the riders were spared any conversation. Every inch of the ride ground into Joseph's arm, where the nerves were still sizzling and hot. He dug in hard with his thighs and concentrated all his focus on his legs, letting his pelvis operate as a shock absorber. He had never been injured before in wrestling, and the severity of his injury left him filled with shame. What had he done wrong?

The hounds roused Edwards and most of the house staff when the men arrived after nightfall. Clearly they had not been expected until the next day, when the champion was to have triumphantly returned home.

The colonel swung off his horse. Without a backward glance at Joseph, he stomped into the mansion. Joseph slowly edged off the horse. Both Sean and Edwards came to his side.

"I'll take him," said Edwards. "See to the horses. Were you trying to ruin the best horses in Ireland? Send for Deirdre; tell her to meet me in the lad's room."

Mr. Edwards put his arm out but hesitated, not knowing where to touch the boy.

"It's best if I walk on my own," said Joseph. "I've already

disappointed the colonel. I don't want him to think that I can't walk."

Edwards clenched his jaw. "Very well then. I suppose tossing you into a match with a giant wasn't enough. I'll be right behind you."

Deirdre brought soup and a hot cloth that smelled revolting. She wrapped the cloth around Joseph's shoulder and arm.

"You'll need to sleep with this wrapped tight. There's no permanent damage. But you can't wrestle, lad. Your arm needs time to heal. Jaysus, I should have been able to hear you scream from Kilkenny. There's few things that cause more pain than an arm yanked out of its socket. Well, birthing babies, but men never believe me when I tell them, so I should stop trying. Go to sleep, lad. I'm sending in one of the old hounds to sleep with you."

"Not Madigan. Oh, God, Deirdre, the colonel said—"

"We know, lad. D'ya think we were all born yesterday? Go to sleep," Deirdre murmured, bending over him to kiss his forehead, placing two hands on either side of his face. Joseph heard the clatter of claws on the floor, then a fluttered sigh as a hound came to rest beside his bed.

The first sound that he heard the next morning was the colonel's grumbling.

"Get the carriage! Take that food away from me." Crash. "I'm going to Waterford. I can't bear to look at the lot of you."

The old wolfhound was gone by the time Joseph rose. He dressed, treating his arm gingerly, testing it by lifting it level with the horizon and sighing deeply with relief that it worked at all. He pressed his back against the cold wall near the window, taking peeks around the edge until he saw the carriage pull away. Even the mansion itself heaved with relief at the colonel's departure.

More than anything else he wanted to find Taleen. He splashed water on his face, noticing for the first time the thickening of the fuzz along his upper lip. Joseph made his way downstairs; he was walking out the front door when the ping of hammer on rock caught him by the throat.

Con was slowly walking away, as if he'd been in a wedding procession. He was balancing a steaming crock of tea; Deirdre never failed to remember the stonemasons with early morning tea. The stonemason was at work, fitting rock into rock, and the sound of it filled Joseph with a longing for the very thing he'd never had. If he'd been at home, in his time, he would have been a kid with a police record. And here, in this time, everything he thought he'd had with the colonel was slipping away.

Dreamlike, he walked to the new wall, where the stonemason worked with his crew. The new garden wall was massive, five feet tall.

"Dig the first course and fill her with rubble stone. Then we'll sort out the other stones," the stonemason said to his crew of three men. Then he saw Joseph and Con at the same time. "You've brought me a wrestler. I could use one this morning. The cap stones cry out for a tussle," he told Con, squeezing his thick eyebrows together as he took an appraising look at Joseph.

"And how are you this morning? You took a terrible beating. Can you hand me that quoin stone? We're ready for it." He pointed to a perfectly smooth stone that was going to fill the gap where two walls met at right angles, then stepped two rungs up on a ladder.

"What did you call this stone?" asked Joseph.

"Quoin. Have you never seen one before? It's where the whole wall comes together, both sides. It's where we leave our mark. See here, I took this one home last night and worried it with my chisel by the fire."

Joseph's neck and arms prickled. The quoin stone had a spiral chiseled neatly into one edge. Flickering black dots filled his vision, and he leaned hard against the wall.

"Mind the quoin! You shouldn't be out and about so soon lad. Here, let me take it from you. Did you not like my insignia?"

Joseph slid along the wall to the ground.

"It's not that at all, sir. It's my father. I just remembered about my father. He's been hurt; I should have gone to him. How could I have forgotten; what's wrong with me?"

"Con, pour him some tea. The brute in Kilkenny knocked all the sense out of him."

Con poured tea into a tin cup and handed it to Joseph. The stonemason sat on a pile of stone nearby.

"Now what made you think of your father? Sure, we've all wondered why you don't speak of your family beyond a few words."

"My father was injured in a huge accident. The last thing he said was, 'Mind the quoin,' or that's what my aunt told me when she came to get me in . . . when I heard you say it, this whole part of my brain got bright and clear. My head feels like it's going to explode."

Joseph dropped his head into his hands. The stonemason reached down with his thick hands and pulled the boy up.

"You're like one of me own, and we take care of our own. When me wife and I took in Con, we said he'd be ours as sure as he'd been born to us. Consider yourself one of the family."

Joseph looked at Con and the stonemason. "Con isn't your son?"

"Oh, he is now. But he was born to my sister and she married an O'Shea, so rightfully he's an O'Shea. They both died of cholera the summer he was born. But in answer to your question, he's my son now. A man couldn't ask for a better son," he said as he winked at Con.

O'Shea. He couldn't be. No, there was no way that was possible.

"I've got to attend to the wall, lad. Now go back to the Big House and go directly to the kitchen, where Deirdre can tend to you. You had a shock yesterday, and your mind is turning about and can't be trusted today. Will you be a good lad and do as I say?"

Joseph shook his entire body, and then his head, to help clear his thinking.

"As soon as I find Taleen. I need to talk to her."

Chapter 35

Taleen despised laundry work more than anything. Even with the colonel gone for the day, this was washing day and there would be no school at all for her whether the colonel was here or not.

"I hate the soiled linens! I'll learn to do anything but this," she had complained to her mother.

But Deirdre had held firm. She had told Taleen to assist with the bed linens on washing day no matter how much she hated the job. Every element of the process was a pestilence to her—the boiling hot water to kill the bedbugs, the scrub boards, stirring the linens with the large paddle until her arms screamed, the bloody potato water for the starching. Her mother had told her again and again that she wanted her to know how to perform all the functions of the estate, including the cooking, cleaning, putting up preserves, salting meat and fish. Deirdre wanted to enhance Taleen's usefulness to Colonel Mitford.

Madigan came with Taleen and offered an air of sympathy, batting his eyelashes and tilting his head. The dog rarely sat down. His preferred position was standing, leaning into

Taleen, but the steam from the hot water tested even his loyalty. He sulked, and stretched out his long body on the stone floor with his head on his paws. Taleen sweated and cursed at the laundry.

"Aren't we a pair, Madigan," she whispered to the dog during a break between rounds of sheets. "I'm the seventh daughter of a seventh daughter and you're the keeper of the soul of the ancient Celts gone by. Right here in the depths of the laundry room. But soon, my gorgeous beast, there will be more of us, one more."

Madigan obliged her by pressing his huge head into her small hands. If Taleen truly was a healer in training waiting for her specialty to settle in during her young years, and if Madigan, perhaps the last of his reluctant breed, was so awful important, then surely they should be given some worth.

Joseph stuck his head into the steamy room.

"Taleen, can you come out?"

Madigan galloped to Joseph, giving him a sniff and greeting him as usual by taking the lad's arm in his mouth, surrounding it with warm saliva.

"Do I look like I can come out?" said Taleen. Her thin arms struggled to lift the bedclothes for their final rinsing. Her dark hair was tightly bound today. She worked with two older women, whose sleeves were well pushed up. Their biceps muscles popped.

"Oh, go on, Taleen," one of them said as she muscled out a hunk of sheet. "You've been suffering too much for all of us today. We could use the peace. Go on now."

Taleen did not pause for polite refusals. She jumped down from the risers around the massive kettles and ran from the room with Madigan, eager to be released.

"You lost the tournament. I already heard all about it from Sean. You've only had this one loss; no need to fret," she said with a tone of forced gaiety.

"I need to talk with you. I've started to remember about my father," said Joseph.

They walked to the pear trees, now bare and without a hint of leaf or bud. The garden walls gave the two lovers what passed for privacy.

"What made you remember your father?"

"It was the stonemason. He said he was getting ready to put in the quoin stone," Joseph told her.

"Well, yes, I suppose he should be ready by now. Con tells me that two whole sections of the wall are done."

They continued walking while Madigan pranced lightly beside them.

"Quoin. That's what my father said, the last thing he said after the accident. Anna told me that. And now I'm remembering what else she told me, that he's in a bad way in a hospital."

"And why would they put your ailing father in a hospital? My mother has told me that they are dreadful places, filled with disease and sickness and certain death. Is it that your family can't do any better? You can tell me, my love, I'll not think any worse of you, and I know you've been holding a secret. I've known it since they pulled you from the ocean."

They sat with their backs against the garden wall and soaked in the thin bits of warmth the walls had absorbed. Madigan's jaw fell open in a relaxed smile; his snout was already sprouting the whiskers that would give him an old-man look.

"I'm not from where you think I'm from. I've only ever

been to Canada once. I'm from America, near Boston. And I'm Irish, all my family is, both sides, as my grandmother says." He took in a breath in jagged starts.

Taleen rubbed her hand along the rough flank of the dog.

"Did you pretend all this to give yourself a leg up with the colonel? More than a few Irish have done so, but most do it by turning Protestant. Jumpers, we call them. They get much better work, the wee ones go to better schools. Is that why?"

She had stiffened her neck, but only slightly.

"Yes, but my reason was more than that." He changed positions so that he faced her. He got on his knees, then let his butt sink back to his heels. "I'm from the future, one hundred and sixty-four years from now. It sounds crazy, and if someone had ever told me this story, I would flat out say they were liars. But it's true. And I swear that I will never lie to you ever again."

Taleen stopped stroking the dog.

"I didn't know that I'd fall in love," he continued. "I've never been in love before, and it changes how everything matters. Oh, I'm not saying this right." He brushed dog hair off his pants. "My aunt is here in Ireland. Anna. Somehow we came together and I don't know why either of us traveled through time. There's nothing special about us, we're ordinary people. I'm a boy in school. I have a father, a grandmother. We're the least special people you could imagine."

Joseph stopped moving. He looked like a gull, catching a tail wind with wings outspread, seemingly still of all effort.

"When the colonel finds out his fine prize is Irish he'll—" began Taleen.

"Don't you see? I'm not his fine prize anymore. And there's

more. There's the future part. Did you hear what I said about the future?"

"Aye. But I don't know how to reckon it. How can such a thing happen? My mother knows close to everything, and she never once told me about people traveling from now to tomorrow." Taleen tried to say more, but the words were stuck in the pocket of her throat.

"It just happened," Joseph tried to explain. "Anna and I were at her house. She tried to help me after my father was hurt, and I was an idiot. Oh, God, I remember everything now. It was some dream about my father needing me and I got out of bed and tried to find something in a package. Then Anna woke up and she grabbed at the little package. It was just cloth; I didn't get why she was so upset. Just cloth, like nothing, then the world broke loose. We were sucked up and the air roared and you'll never believe this part. We were pulled underwater, so far underwater that I heard whales singing and then I came apart and lost Anna. I came back together again, I don't know how, but then I don't understand any of this. And then I was here."

He reached for her hands and she rose up on her knees. She let her hands be covered by his before she spoke with a solemn expression. "There is something I must tell you as well. I'm with child. We have a bairn, Joseph, whoever you are, whenever you have come from."

The full shock registered on his face, and Taleen was suddenly terrified.

"Taleen . . . " Her name sounded like a wave breaking from his soft mouth.

She wanted very much to hear him say something, to let

her know that this baby would have a good father. She waited and didn't know if what he'd say would be enough to stop her lips from trembling, to smooth the twitch in her eye. Agitated footsteps crunching along the garden path jarred her from his face. Mr. Edwards, his prim jacket open and flapping, approached with an Irishman, a one-armed man.

Mr. Edwards scanned the area. "I thought we'd find you here. Joseph, you need to leave with this gentleman. Hurry. He'll take you to Tramore. Taleen, you must stay here. You must do as I say."

Chapter 36

Anna and Biddy had boarded a small sailing rig from Cork to Tramore. The seas had been atrocious. They now sat hip to hip amid the coiled hemp ropes, wool shawls pulled tight around them.

"Why did he send Donal to Australia?" Anna asked, already knowing part of the answer. Her eyes were swollen from crying.

"You saved his life. Donal will live with thousands of other Irish who were sent away from their homeland against their will. At this moment, he's breathing the last of Irish air, but he's still breathing. There was no other way, and it's a fair miracle that your performance worked at all."

Anna wiped her nose on the sleeve of her jacket. She had returned the impossibly fancy dress to the priest at the church. He'd promised to get it to the rightful house without detection.

"And that is one of the many problems; you taking the heart of someone here in our time. I can see that you love him. This will be neither simple nor painless. Love never is," said Biddy Early.

"I didn't know what love was. I had no idea . . ."

"It is always shocking when we first taste it," said Biddy, rubbing her hands together. After piecing certain facts together, she had confirmed the scent of a curse, but her demand for specifics was exhausting Anna.

"Tell me again what led up to you hurtling through time? And no matter how much I beg, please do not tell me what the future holds. Nothing grand has happened for the Irish in two hundred years, and I don't think I could survive hearing of a future that is worse. Promise, even if I beg you in a moment of weakness, and Lord knows I have enough of those."

"Yes, I promise," said Anna.

Anna repeated what she had already told Biddy.

"My brother, Patrick—Joseph's father—had been in a terrible accident and my mother sent me to find Joseph, who had gotten into trouble with the law," said Anna.

"Oh, had he now? That makes him the same as every Irish lad I know," said Biddy, as if she hadn't already heard this twice before. "And he's no Canadian. He's an American, just like you. And from Irish stock. He's a pitiful liar, at least to my ear. Let's hope his deception holds with the colonel a bit longer. Now, keep going, tell me more."

"I gathered up my nephew and we drove—I mean we traveled—to my house. It was very late when we arrived, so we planned to go to the hospital the next day to see my brother," said Anna.

Biddy shuddered. "I cannot fathom that you took the poor fellow to a place like a hospital. Have you no midwives or physicians to tend to the sick? Don't answer that. I'll not peek into the future."

Anna continued. "And here is the part where it gets muddled for me. I heard Joseph get up in the middle of the night.
I got up to see if anything was wrong. When I saw him, I
thought he was going through my luggage looking for something to steal. This was a crazy, middle-of-the-night thought;
he's no thief, never was, never will be. But I had just come
back from a journey, and the moment I returned, I saw my
brother with his head split open, and I wanted nothing more
than to tend to him and be by his side with my mother. And
then I learned that my nephew had to be collected from the
police—and quite far away, may I add. I think I was near
insane from lack of sleep, so that when I saw him flipping
through my luggage in the middle of the night, holding
something of mine, I yelled at him and startled him. Then
I grabbed onto whatever he was holding; I remembered our
fingers touched and he looked terrified. I immediately regretted screaming like a banshee at him. But that was when
I heard the loudest sound, like a waterfall, and it was as if we
were pulled beneath the ocean and very quickly pulled apart.
And the next thing I truly remember is crawling along the
beach near Kinsale."

Biddy said nothing for a moment but sat with her eyes
closed. "No, no, I don't have it yet. There's a piece missing, at
least one piece, possibly more. What was it that he found in
your luggage?" asked Biddy.

It wasn't as if Anna hadn't thought of this, although her
efforts to remember had dimmed when Donal had slept with
her and her legs had wound around him like so much ivy.

"Was it your wraps, skirts and such?" asked Biddy Early.

"No, it was something small. When we held it, it was small
enough that our hands touched. Oh, and he had nearly un-

wrapped it. The thing was wrapped in paper," said Anna, as if a flashlight shone on the scene.

"Such extravagance the future holds," sighed Biddy. "Tell me, dear, name the things that were wrapped in paper in your luggage."

Anna once again tried to picture the contents of her luggage, and while she did, Biddy asked, "You've never mentioned where your trip was. Where had you gone on this terribly long journey before your brother's mishap?"

Anna was such an idiot. Of course, the trip to England, Scotland, and the impulsive side trip to Ireland that Harper had insisted they take to see one more castle. "I had been in Ireland," she said.

Biddy straightened her back and swung her head around to look at Anna. "Well, why did you never say so?"

"We were there for less than a day. We took a . . . well, never mind how we got there from London, but the important part is, we were only here for the smallest bit of time. It was some castle near Limerick. Believe me, Ireland was not the cause of our trip. I was with a friend who writes about places to travel, and we had been in England and Scotland for weeks."

"Can you remember the name of the castle?"

"Ratty something. That's all I can remember."

Biddy shivered. "Was it Bunratty? It's a wreck of a castle, but a castle all the same."

From where they huddled, their faces whipped by the wind and salt, they saw the lights of Tramore, and a long white strip of beach came into view.

"I think it was Bunratty. And the woman outside the castle

said she'd been waiting for me. Did I tell you that part?" asked Anna.

"You did not. Tell me about the woman outside Bunratty Castle. This is coming together. Bunratty Castle is an easy day's walk from where I live." The ship rose up on a swell and bumped the two women together.

"Well, I had just been inside the castle and someone had toured us through, telling us about the castle. And here's where you might be interested, because this has the ring of something in your expertise. The guide showed us a Fairy Flag, made of silk. She said it was good for three times to save their clan—"

"Oh, rubbish! There's no such thing as a Fairy Flag, and if anyone would know, I would," said Biddy.

Anna was stung by the rebuke. "If you put two and two together, the old woman outside the castle, who seemed to know me, and the talk of the Fairy Flag inside the castle . . . ," started Anna.

"Forget the Fairy Flag, I said." Biddy let an edge of impatience bleed through.

"Sorry," said Anna. "I haven't understood anything about landing in the past. I thought for a moment that I could offer you these bits and because you are so famous for healing and whatever else you do, that you could make sense of this in a way that a mere mortal like me could not."

"Oh, there now, you've gone peevish on me. Don't try to upstage me with your peevishness. I've lived through four husbands already and I've seen and heard everything. Let's try this again. We'll not be landing at Tramore for another hour or so."

Anna told Biddy again about the woman who had startled her at Bunratty, how the woman had said she'd been waiting for her, that Anna had needed to take the package. The woman had said she'd known that things had gone badly in America and that this was all that had been left to help. The more Anna repeated, the more she remembered.

The ship could not have been colder, even though Biddy and Anna were huddled together. They combined the two blankets they'd been given, spreading them across their knees.

Biddy went silent for a long time, much to Anna's relief; the intense questioning had exhausted her. She was wedged between a stiff coil of rope and Biddy Early. Her eyes gave in to the irresistible demand of sleep. She jumped at the sound of Biddy's voice.

"And the wee package, did you open it?"

Anna was still astounded at the infinite pauses between sentences among the Irish.

"No, I told you. It was all a jumble. Then I went back to America, picked up Joseph, don't ask me to repeat that part, and it was Joseph in the middle of the night who went through my luggage and found the package. He was opening it when I grabbed it, and then, well, that's the last thing that happened before we were transported here."

Silence again.

"Biddy, are you going to keep asking me questions, or should I go to sleep?"

"Ah, so the lad knew to go to it. The wee package, that is."

Silence, another pause long enough to insert a sermon.

"If someone was waiting for you outside Bunratty Castle, I think I know who sent them," said Biddy.

Anna turned to face her, now wide awake.

"Who?"

"It was me. Or it will be me. It's so blasted hard to tell with time." She put her hands on either side of Anna's face. "You've done well, lassie. But what is ever more clear to me is that you've been sent to stop a curse."

"And how do you stop a curse?"

Biddy shook her head. "With a blessing, of course. We are doomed if the future is filled with people who can't tell a curse from a blessing. Come, they'll set anchor soon and take us by rowboat to the shore."

"And where are we going in Tramore?"

"To a bookbinder's shop. A lovely spot," said Biddy. "We have a friend among the English at Mitford's estate. They don't come better than George Edwards."

Chapter 37

Anna woke stiff and sore after having curled in an exhausted heap on the floor of Thomas Fitzgerald's Book Bindery. Biddy looked perfectly serene, laid out like a smiling corpse on the plank bench with a wool blanket tucked around her chin. An east window showered the floor with a direct hit of sunlight. It had to be late. Anna wrapped her cape around her and went outside to the outhouse. She had taken only two steps in the fresh, sea air when the nightmare of Cork Prison and Donal latched onto her with sharp talons. She'd sent a man to his execution and Donal to a British penal colony. She opened the door to the stinking outhouse, pulled up her skirts, squatted and peed. She had ruined everything she had touched.

Anna stepped outside and wiped her hands on the bark of a damp tree. She heard the clopping of hooves out on the street and suddenly remembered O'Connell. O'Connell! Oh God, O'Connell had been left in the stable in Cork. She ran into the shop to wake Biddy.

"When we get back to Cork we've got to collect O'Connell. He was Glennie's horse, and I won't let harm . . . "

Anna skidded to a halt. An exhausted-looking Donal stood

next to Biddy. Joseph sat on the plank bench. Donal pulled off his cap and smiled.

"Is that all you can think of, the horse? And you just now remembered him? Remind me to never put you in charge of the livestock." His smile dissolved her into a gasp.

Anna was stuck in place, a pivot point between Donal and her nephew, and her head turned from one to the other. In two giant steps, she had surrounded Donal's neck with her arms. She shoved off him long enough to stroke his arm, then his face.

"How could you have possibly escaped? You're a magician. God, I thought I'd lost you."

"Did you forget more than the horse? I'm a cartographer and a smuggler. The combination makes me a poor candidate for exile. My lads had me out before the Governor had farted. O'Connell is getting a well-deserved rest at Colonel Mitford's estate. He'll be returned to Tom in good time."

Anna was suddenly rich with all that she had desired and she scurried to understand. She whirled around to the bench where Joseph sat. He put up his hand before she could speak.

"You probably won't believe me, but I didn't remember part of what happened to us. I didn't remember about Dad, about the accident. I only remembered that I had gotten into trouble. I'm sorry."

Anna's eyes filled with tears. Donal cleared his throat.

"So you'll not have to strangle him as you said you would."

Anna sat down on the bench next to her nephew.

"Are you all right?" she asked, putting her arm around him and shaking him like a rag doll.

"After what I've heard from Donal, I think I'm in a hell of

a lot better shape than you are. Until yesterday, that is. I can't stay at the colonel's estate anymore. I lost a wrestling match and he lost a ton of money. But I've got to tell you something. There's a girl . . ."

From the corner of the room, Biddy clapped her hands together.

"Aye, there's a girl you love; we know. It's written all over you," said Biddy.

"Excuse my manners. Joseph, Donal, this is Biddy Early, and she's been helping us."

Donal nodded. "Everyone in Ireland knows of Biddy Early. That was a masterful poultice that you sent to Anna," he said with a nod to Biddy.

"It was just a bit of this and that. And I'm afraid everyone in Ireland does know of me. Now, I'd love to chat and visit, but I've left me home because of a curse, and now we have added an escaped criminal—please pardon me for saying so—and an angry English chap who's lost money on the lad. I'm going to step outside and think for a few moments. The sea air will clear the fog from my mind. The three of you need your private words with each other."

Biddy wound her long dark hair and pinned it up. She wrapped her cape around her. "We are in for a blue sky, sharp, and crisp. A good December day," she said as she went out the door.

Donal dragged a chair near Anna and Joseph.

"The man in prison . . ." she started.

"We were all slated to be hung, Anna. The bastard governor took pleasure in your agony. All four of those blokes are hung by now. You caused nothing to happen that was not already destined."

Anna grabbed hold of Donal's hand, then Joseph's. They sat together, without speaking until Joseph's hand grew sweaty.

"That's enough hand holding for me," said Joseph, trying to discreetly wipe his palm on his pants.

"I don't understand how the two of you traveled from one time to another, but I've given up thinking you're daft. I don't know the depth of it, the reason," said Donal.

Anna knew what she had to do, what Biddy told her must be done. *This cannot be about love*, thought Anna, stiffening her spine, preparing for her heart to be splayed open on the rocks. Real desire had taken her by surprise. If she thought too long about Donal, the soft skin of his inner arm or the scent of him directly behind his ears, she would weaken, turn back and hide her face in his shirt. The easiest thing in the world would be to stay with him and forget the dry desert of the future, where life had been bloodless corporate law seasoned with the prospect of online dating.

Biddy opened the door and a fresh wave of morning air rushed into the book bindery.

"Come sit with me, lad. Your auntie has recited every inch that she remembers about the night that you left your time and came to ours. Now I need to hear yours. Start with coming to Anna's house."

Biddy and Joseph sat in the chairs near the bookbinder's desk.

"Anna's house had her luggage all over it. Some was open, some was still zipped. I just wanted to go to bed. We were going to leave really early the next morning for the hospital. When I went to sleep, I had a dream that my father said I had to find something, that Anna and all of us needed it. When I got out of bed, it was like I was pulled to Anna's suitcase. I put my hand on some little paper packages and I picked one up and opened it."

Anna was spellbound, hearing the boy's version, hating that she had yelled at him.

"That's grand, Joseph. What was in the wee package?" asked Biddy.

Joseph laughed. "That's what's so stupid. It was a ripped-up pair of old boxer shorts, the silky kind. They even said something stupid on them, like *Man Silk*. Then Anna came in the room and she sort of shrieked and grabbed on to the package and that's when we did it. We, ah, time traveled."

"Aye, the silken cloth," said Biddy. "Anna, will you show the boy the slip of cloth in your pocket?"

Anna heard the drum of waves pounding in her body. She stood next to Biddy and pulled the blue cloth from a deep pocket in her skirt.

"Would it be this?" asked Biddy.

Joseph reached his hand out and took the scrap of fabric. "Like this, except older. But yes, just like this."

"Holy shit," said Anna. "This is what the woman outside Bunratty Castle gave me? The shred of clothing that I arrived in, that I wore one hundred and sixty-four years in the future? I'm trying very hard to understand this, but this is making my brain hurt," said Anna, taking the familiar blue silk back into her hand again.

"Jaysus. One hundred and sixty-four years. You told me you were from the future but you failed to mention just how far," said Donal.

"Anna and Joseph are here because of a curse. Curses have a copper scent, and all of us in the room reek of it. Anna, we tried to fix the curse before in another patch of time. We

failed, which made for years of suffering, with poison dripping in the veins of this entire family. We've been given another chance, and we must get it right."

"How could we have already tried? I've never time traveled before," said Anna.

"Stop thinking of time like it was a straight line; it never
was and it never will be. I don't know the half of it, but you
met a woman outside Bunratty Castle who'd been waiting for
you. If she recognized you, then I must have sent her; she'd
be one of my own descendents. She said she couldn't leave
Ireland, did she? She was a seventh daughter all right. I must
have made sure that someone would meet you there. We live
famously long; we go through husbands like water, outliving
them all."

Donal and Anna stood closer together, their fingers reaching for each other.

"But why didn't it work? Why am I back here, and why
Joseph?"

They all startled at the sound of the front door unlatching.
A man poked his head in the doorway.

Donal said, "Thomas, you're a good man to let us take over
your shop. This is the fine owner of this shop and our host,
Mr. Thomas Fitzgerald."

"You've some visitors outside. There's no trouble, only
Deirdre's lass and her dog," said Thomas.

Joseph stood up and ran outside.

"Taleen! You shouldn't have followed us."

Anna followed to the sea-slick cobblestones of the street,
and instantly saw the spurt of adolescent love that surrounded
Joseph and the dark-haired girl. Only the blind could miss the
cord of light, as thick as a sapling emanating from the solar

plexus of the two of them, powering through all misgivings, seeking one another. If only this had been about the powder keg of desire when first it lands in the hearts of a boy and a girl, then the decisions would not have been so devastatingly hard. If only.

Taleen took in the scene with fear in her eyes.

"Were you leaving me? Were you running away without me?"

Taleen placed a protective hand low on her belly. Anna's radar for pregnancy saw the instinctive hand guarding the uterus, the way all women do, whether they are fourteen or forty. Here were the DNA generators, a young girl and a sixteen-year-old boy, dizzy and stupid with impossible love. Anna looked at her nephew and saw him for the first time as the man he would become, the kind of man who could love a son or a daughter. Or he could be, without the curse.

Here was the strange foreshortening of time. Joseph, the father of their clan from this point onward, standing front and center, and there in the faraway future was Joseph, heir to generations of a curse. *No wonder we have flipped over in tendrils of time.*

Taleen was pregnant. What would come of this babe from twenty-first-century sperm and a nineteenth-century ovum? One very notable thing was Anna, her brother Patrick and their wild, brilliant, tyrannical father and his miserable father before him. Was the whole story about one boy and one girl given over to the force of tender love and fumbling sex? Joseph and Taleen looked like babies, all soft around the eyes, and flushed around the cheeks.

Taleen had been crying and her eyes were dashed with red. "I've seen it! You're leaving me Joseph. I see ahead and you've gone. Did all of this mean nothing to you? Is she taking you away?" she said pointing to Anna.

Joseph looked as though he'd been struck by a sandbag. The massive dog at Taleen's side trotted to the boy's side. The dog took the boy's forearm in his mouth and wagged his tail.

"Not now, Madigan," said Joseph, as if the dog had been an old friend.

"Biddy, she's pregnant . . ." started Anna.

Biddy saw it first, took a step toward the girl, but she was too late. The wolfhound stepped neatly between Biddy and the girl. A swirl of rejected love took its dark slide into wrath and covered Taleen. Her uncontrolled powers of healing ignited into tattered spits of rage. The tenor of her voice grew deep. A sharp wind blew her skirt. If life existed beyond Joseph, or if the entire world incinerated, Taleen would not have noticed. She exploded in her shattered grief.

"I curse you. All grace will stop its flow from father to son from this day forth, down through every generation. You, Joseph, will beget a lineage of fathers with their hearts shriveled and torn. Not one father from this time forward will be able to love their sons," said Taleen, her lips pulled back, her ebony hair wafting around her head.

Taleen suddenly swiveled to Anna, taking her in for the first time. "And your womb will be barren, dry as stone!"

Joseph froze in place, all the glass shards of the curse already cutting through his heart. Anna gasped and stumbled. She had been cursed by a child. The devastating miscarriages came from this moment; the almost-babies had never had a chance. She turned to look at Biddy, imploring her. "Biddy, please . . ."

Anna took in the curse and saw it spinning through time,

sucking under every good man in her lineage who fell in love and bore a son. Anna saw the Y chromosome of maleness embedded with the sly dark tinge of the curse that had followed every father and son. No matter what their hopes and dreams, no matter how totally in love they had been with their young wives, the men could not love their tender, sweet sons. And Anna would never, never have a child, never hold a newborn in her arms. If she had dared to want anything in life, it had been this.

Biddy Early pushed past the dog, who dropped his tail under Biddy's glare. She grabbed the girl's wrist.

"You are too young, too fresh at our craft to understand. And like all the young ones, healer or not, you are blinded by the wind of love. You don't know what you've set in motion. Taleen, it has already happened. You've had your revenge, years of beaten sons, alcohol sodden fathers, women who have seen their good men go mad with rage. Joseph is the product of your curse. Is this what you wanted for all your sons? You've cursed your own baby."

Taleen's hair floated back down again.

"Anna, the blessing. Before it's too late!" said Biddy, releasing the girl's arm.

"I don't know how to make a blessing or who to bless."

Anna fingered the tattered shred of fabric in her pocket.

"A blessing is all about alchemy, it transmutes the poison of a curse, but do get on with it before the curse takes hold good and solid," said Biddy, looking uncertain for the first time since Anna had met her. "It must be either you or the boy. That must be why you're here."

Biddy had been right about the sky; the morning fog had burned off unusually early, giving way to a blue sky with scratches of high clouds. Anna could see the long beach that started in Tramore and seemed to go forever. Thomas hung in the background, looking continually startled. Taleen and Joseph had edged together. Donal stood beneath the shadow of the shop sign.

Anna grabbed Biddy's arm and pulled her a few steps away and whispered urgently. "Before I try to make a blessing, which could be a complete mess because I've never blessed anyone, you have to promise me something," said Anna. "And I must tell you one thing about the future."

"I wish you wouldn't but go on, dearie, quickly."

"There will be a famine. The potatoes won't grow for years. I want you to make sure that Tom and his children move here. They must need a blacksmith. And Donal, will you look after him?"

"I can help with Glenis's family if you insist. Sure, we've had famines before," said Biddy.

"Yes," said Anna, with the specter of the Great Famine staring at her. "But not like this one."

Anna felt it first in her lungs, the sense of sweetness being drained off. Crows descended on the roof of the book bindery. Donal had called them hoodie crows. Donal stepped out from the shadow of the book bindery sign that caught the bright glare of the morning light. The air crackled with the taste of copper. The sun hit the side of Donal's face and even from across the street, Anna saw three days worth of stubble.

He put his hand along his brow to keep out the sun. "You've found the lad. Let's take him and go, if he'll come along with us. But you've seen that he's unharmed. Biddy can undo the curse . . ."

Anna shouted at him, "You must let me know that you've

lived a life . . . that this all meant something, that I meant something . . ."

"What are you saying, woman?" said Donal.

Anna saw a woman in the distance, running down the street.

"Now, Anna!" screamed Biddy.

Anna went to Taleen and awkwardly got down on her knees in front of her, the way she used to do in church when she was a child, before their family blew apart. She cleared her throat.

"I bless this child inside you and all the children who come from this child. I forgive you for all that you've said in anger. I forgive you for not knowing, for being young and in love. I bless you and all the generations to follow," said Anna, looking directly into the face of the long ago matriarch of the family. "I forgive you for cursing me and my family. And yours. Ours."

Anna stood up, expecting something to happen.

"Biddy, how will we know if the blessing works?" said Anna.

Everyone turned as the woman running down the street came closer.

"Madigan, come here," commanded the woman.

"That's me mum," said Taleen. "She'll be furious with me. I've uttered a curse and she said that I must never."

"That's right. You must never and yet you did what you must never do. It's the way of the young ones. And your mum's name?" said Biddy.

"Deirdre," said the girl, gulping hard.

"Aye, lovely name. I've heard of her from time to time. We are about to have three seventh daughters coming together with an Irish wolfhound and in all my years, I've never seen the likes of it."

The dog galloped off to Taleen's mother who stroked his head and put her lips to his ears. Anna reached out to touch Joseph and he jumped back as if her touch had scalded him.

"I'm not leaving her!" Joseph called out.

Anna did not hear the huge, strange dog. In fact she only saw it the moment that it took flight, some twenty feet beyond them, aiming for Joseph's back. She reached out to grab the boy and the cloth burned hot in her pocket. She suddenly knew what was happening before Joseph did. She had a sense of things stirring, of rusty cogs beginning to shift and reverse. She had time to pull the blue silk out of her pocket, clutch it, and brace herself as the dog launched into Joseph and slammed him into her.

Anna tried to turn her head to see Donal but the gut-inverting sensation had already grabbed her and the roar of the deep ocean filled her ears and the ability to move began to fall away from her. With supreme effort she twined her fingers into Joseph's hair. The last thing she saw before the water took them was the dog, with his great long jaw clamped around the boy's arm.

"I bless us, I bless us, I bless," she thought as they dissolved among the depths of the ocean.

Chapter 38

Arthur Jones collected cans and bottles from the garbage cans along Rockport's beaches and craggy seaside. He no longer slept past 4 a.m.; his Gulf War PTSD required an early-morning vigilance. He started downtown and worked his way south along the little nooks of beaches where the town crews left the fifty-gallon drums lined with black plastic bags to slow the tide of trash. A few houses still had their Christmas decorations up.

Arthur outfitted his bike with large plastic crates on either side of the back wheel. He knew what he looked like—one of the mentally ill, homeless Vets. Except he wasn't homeless; he had a furnished apartment behind the library and his own cell phone. He wasn't sure about the mental illness part.

The cove was his last stop before the sun came up. Stuff washed up on the beach all the time and sometimes he checked it out and sometimes he didn't. He was almost always disappointed with what he found. This morning a ruby blade of dawn had just hit the watery horizon and he saw a dog, one of those huge dogs. He ran the names: mastiff, Great Dane, Bernese mountain dogs. No, this was an Irish wolfhound. He'd seen one on the Animal Planet. The dog guarded something, a big pile. Oh no.

Arthur had been a medic, and his PTSD relaxed. True disasters were easier for him to handle than the imagined ones. He got off his bike and walked across the sand, his feet sinking in with each step. The dog didn't look so great. The animal hung its head and weaved a little, like he was forcing himself to stand up.

Arthur pulled a granola bar out of his pocket, opened it, and placed it on his palm to let the dog know he was a friend. There were two bodies behind the dog, covered with sand and seaweed. One of the bodies moved, rose up on an elbow, and shook long hair off her face. It was a woman, her breasts bloodied and raw, and her eyelids swollen from saltwater. She turned her head toward him.

"Donal?" she croaked.

He slipped his other hand into his inside coat pocket and pulled out his cell phone and called 911.

Chapter 39

Two days after Anna and Joseph were spotted by Arthur Jones, they were released from the hospital after being treated for hypothermia and abrasions. Anna had lost twenty pounds and Joseph had gained fifteen since their disappearance. They told the police that they didn't remember anything. They told them again and again and finally the police stopped asking.

As they walked out of the hospital with Mary Louise O'Shea, Anna stopped on the sidewalk.

"We remember everything. We have to tell you what happened but you may not believe us. We're not the same. We've both lost something unimaginable," said Anna, twitching from the noise of cars, buses, and cell phones. She was jumpy around the crush of twenty-first-century sounds and inundated by the smells of shampoos, lotions, conditioners, and most offensive of all, room fresheners.

"I thought that I had lost something unimaginable and I'll spend the rest of my days counting my blessings for your return," said Mary Louise. "I can hear the worst that you have to tell me. Just don't disappear again."

"I want to see my father," said Joseph. "And Madigan, I've got to see him. He won't understand it here."

"Madigan is at home with Alice and he seems to have taken a liking to her. The dog is adjusting," said Mary Louise.

The two women turned to him. He'd been nearly silent since they were recovered from the beach. Anna said, "Let's go see your Dad, and we'll tell them as much as we can."

They went directly to the rehabilitation center where Patrick was finishing his treatment. Anna and Joseph rammed a chair against the door in Patrick's room and told them all the parts that mattered—the time travel, Glennie and Biddy Early, and even Donal and Taleen. And the pregnancy. They said enough to make them understand. They didn't tell them about the curse. Not yet.

"You've got to be shitting me," said Patrick.

"I'm inclined to say the same thing," said Mary Louise.

"Look at me," said Anna. "I'm missing teeth, I've got a scar on my leg that you can see from across the street. And look at Joseph."

She hadn't meant to say the last part. Patrick was still in bed, but was able to get up with a walker. He'd lost muscle tone in his arms and his hands looked uncharacteristically smooth. Patrick swung his legs over the edge of the bed and painfully pulled himself up, pushed into the walker and took halting steps toward Joseph.

"I thought I'd lost you, Joey," said Patrick. His chin quivered. The walker clattered over and Joseph reached out to steady his father.

"I've got you now, Dad."

The room vibrated with newness and miracle. Anna didn't want to talk more. She wanted to go to her mother's house and pull the drapes and unplug everything electrical. She sank quietly to the floor.

Mary Louise squatted next to Anna. "You're coming home with me, both of you."

"Madigan too," said Joseph.

Anna noted the lack of question, the firmness in his voice.

"Yes. When we leave here, we'll go straight to Alice's house and pick up Madigan. I only hope my car is large enough," said Mary Louise.

Anna's mother refused to leave their side and took a leave of absence from the school.

Chapter 40

Three months later

Patrick's left foot still lagged slightly when he walked. The doctors said with brain injuries, you never knew how things would turn out. Still, they hadn't expected him to live, never mind walk unassisted seven months later.

Anna, Joseph, Patrick, and Madigan walked single file through the double doors of the long-term care facility, code name for the Alzheimer's ward. Madigan, who loved Science Diet, now weighed one hundred and forty pounds. He had adapted to the twenty-first century with surprising grace—with the exception of cars, which he loathed but would tolerate if Joseph insisted.

"I told the nurse supervisor that we were coming today. She said they'd have him dressed and up. There's nothing wrong with him physically. I mean all his body parts work. Alzheimer's is selective," said Anna.

"We know what Alzheimer's is," said Patrick.

Joseph had refused to go back to school. His grandmother arranged for a combination of home schooling balanced with the promise of classes at Greenfield Community College in the fall.

"I want to be a stone mason. I want to work with my father," he'd said. "The name of our company has to be Quoin Stone."

Negotiations were in progress.

Oscar's grandmother had long since dropped charges when she realized that her grandson Oscar had taken her car. Oscar spent four weeks in drug rehab. All other charges had been dropped.

Anna had looked everywhere for evidence that the curse had been lifted. And indeed, Joseph and Patrick were learning to get along better. But she decided on the unthinkable— a visit to their violent, brilliant father who had nearly killed Patrick and then abandoned them. When their mother had learned that her ex-husband had Alzheimer's, she had him moved to Massachusetts.

Joseph stopped at the receptionist's desk. Madigan stopped with him, the dog's tail thumping loudly along the side of the desk.

"This is as far as I go. I've never met my grandfather. He won't know me anyhow. You two go ahead," he said.

Anna and Patrick followed the social worker down the corridor to a yellow room with vinyl-covered chairs and a piano.

"I'll go get him," said the social worker. She had short gray hair and clear blue eyes.

"I'm not sure this is a good idea," said Patrick.

Anna heard the boy in him, the terror in his voice that he had tried to hide for their entire childhood.

The squeaking wheels along the linoleum announced

Charles's arrival. Only one wheel of the chair needed oil to still the one bit of friction that shrilled with each rotation. Anna had stopped breathing and she wasn't sure if she could start again. The wild father of their youth was slumped over in a wheelchair; his thick Irish hair was gray and severely cut. He wore a Red Sox sweatshirt.

The social worker stopped near the coffee table and set the brake.

"Charles, you have visitors," she said, touching their father on his shoulder to get his attention.

Someone had just shaved him and his cheeks had the shine of soap and blade. Anna sucked in a breath. She couldn't move. This was a mistake. She couldn't do this.

Patrick stepped forward, his left foot taking one half second longer than the other. Charles O'Shea looked up and focused hard on Patrick. Their father's face began to contort into open fear.

"I'm sorry, Daddy. I won't do it again," said Charles, gripping the handrails of the chair.

The social worker said quietly, "They often see their children as their parents or someone else from that generation."

Patrick came close to the wheelchair and knelt down on one knee. Anna put her hand over her mouth to keep from crying out. Patrick eased his hand near his father's hand. Both hands were trembling.

"You're a good boy, Charlie, a very good boy. I'm sorry if I scared you. You are the best son a father could hope for. I'm so proud of you."

The terror melted from the older man's face. Madigan, who had slipped past a group of adoring elders, pressed into Anna's side.

"And that is how you make a blessing, you great hound. Come meet another lost Irishman."

Madigan walked lightly to Patrick's side and looked directly at Charles O'Shea, politely sniffing his hand. Madigan's head was slightly higher than Charles. Even from behind, Anna saw that the dog was offering his goofiest look, head tilted, one ear up, jaw relaxed and open.

Charles brightened and said, "He's a big dog. Can we keep him?"

Patrick reached out to scratch the hound behind his ears. "He's part of the package now. We're keeping him and he's keeping us."

Chapter 41

Anna sat in the first-class section of Aer Lingus, the flight a gift from her mother, who said it might be the only time Anna ever rode in first class, so enjoy. She ran her tongue along the two newly implanted teeth. She missed the gap, the canyon where her tongue explored for months.

Anna was more terrified to return to Ireland than she had been having teeth pulled out by a blacksmith, or going toe-to-toe with the governor of New Cork Prison. This time she had to find out if love mattered.

Joseph had said, "You're not going without me. I've got to know what happened to Taleen. I know she must have married Con. But I've got to find out if she was happy."

Even his desperate plea had not dissuaded her. "Next trip. Take your father when he's up to it. You two can become our genealogists."

The plane landed at Shannon Airport. Anna rented a car just as the sun was rising on Ireland.

She looked at the map for the one hundredth time as she sat on a side road outside the airport. Where should she go? Back to Bunratty Castle, Skibbereen, Kinsale? It was April and the trees along the side road had buds that threatened to burst open any second. Two hoodie crows landed on a branch, caught their balance, and turned in unison to look her way. One tilted his head.

"Of course," she said to them, with the certainty of it coursing through her. "Tramore."

She drove south to Cork, considered touring the New Cork Prison and thought better of it. It had not been used as prison since the 1920s, but she could not have faced it. She drove east to Waterford, skipping the scenic coastal route. She cut south to Tramore. How would she know where to look? Should she start with church records or a cemetery?

The beach along Tramore was still long and magnificent. Later she would walk along it, imagining a boy tossed out by the ocean, imagining a man she had loved and thought of every day.

The part of town that used to be the busy port had been turned into a vast amusement park, just waking up from the winter, with fun houses and Ferris wheels. She walked uphill, into the heart of the old town, where no building was newer than the nineteenth century. The tiny streets remained the same. Anna wondered if she had turned into a ghost.

She walked up two streets, then over for one. This should be it, the old book bindery would be right here. The sign read FITZGERALD BOOK SHOP. Her spine tingled and her hands shook when she pressed the door open.

A young girl behind the counter thumbed through a box of books. She was not classically bookish. Her black hair was cropped short in a ragged cut that emphasized her heart-shaped face.

"I'm looking for something," said Anna. "Something old."

"The shop's been in our family for over two hundred years. If old is what you want, you've come to the right place. What sort of old thing are you after? I do hope it's books."

"I'm not sure . . ." started Anna. She turned toward a door when she heard the clatter of claws along the floor. A wolf-hound peered around the corner and caught Anna in his sights. The amber eyes startled her.

"Oh, don't be alarmed by Fergus. He's a gentle giant. The worst thing about him today is that he doesn't smell good a'tal. He rolled in a dead fish along the beach."

"It's not his size," said Anna. "It's their eyes. I'm never used to their eyes."

The wolfhound loped past the shopgirl and came straight for Anna with a relaxed and easy mouth. With a wet grip, he took Anna's forearm in his massive jaw. She placed her other hand reflexively to her abdomen. She was four months pregnant and the gentle swell of her uterus felt huge to her but she knew it was only now truly showing.

"Here now! Let go of the woman, Fergus," she scolded.

"I'm quite used to this. He's no bother."

"He only does this with the people of the village. Truth be told, he only does it with the Irish."

The dog wagged his firm, nearly hairless tail and released her soggy arm. Fergus pressed his head into Anna halfway up her rib cage and she automatically stroked the dog, noting that his fur was coarser than Madigan's. She wrinkled her nose at the powerful scent coming from the happy dog.

"You'll want to wash your hands now. There's a sink in the back room," said the girl as she pointed to the far end of the shop.

Anna saw it above the girl's head, the walking stick held

horizontally on a rack, the letter A carved dark and heavy near the top knob. Anna froze.

"Oh, that is quite old and not for sale, I'm sorry to say."

The wood had darkened over the years.

"Would you care to see it? Fergus here has given you a good recommendation. The carving along the length of it is worth a look. And I've a soft spot for women who are pregnant." She was the first person outside the family to say the word.

The girl used a broom to nudge the walking stick from its rack. She caught the top knob and passed it to Anna.

"Look carefully and you'll see it's a map. See, it starts here up by the letter A, then keep turning it slowly, that's right, and the map travels on. The topmost is Glengariff, then all around Beara Peninsula. Keep turning it. Can you see Skibbereen? If you're not familiar with the southern coastline, it will seem a jumble to you. But it keeps on going, all the coves and inlets, and ends here at Tramore. There are some who say the entire thing is truly a woman, her body with all the nooks and crannies. Now who would take such time today to do all this?"

Anna turned the stick over and over, hope and love spinning forward and back in her hands.

"A cartographer," she said and pressed the darkened wood to her cheek.

Acknowledgments

Time travel explodes the complexity of plot and the need for information in multiple realms. The following people were generous with their time and expertise. Cheryl McGraw and Pam Murphy allowed me to spend time with their gorgeous Irish wolfhounds. Justin Mooney, an Irish stonemason in Connecticut, and Joel Strate, an American stonemason in Massachusetts, shared their love of stonework and the intricate history. Ted and Eilis O'Sullivan of Cork, Ireland, opened their home to me and led me down the right paths of nineteenth-century Irish history. Cathal Cavanagh, an Irish historian, did his best to inject a fresh take on the political shenanigans of the time period. Brian Cahillane, Esq., and Thomas E. Maloney, Esq., gave me insights into law school and the laws of New Jersey. Martha Sheehan graciously traveled with me along the routes of my characters in Ireland, no matter how tiny the roads became. Charles MacInerney, a superb yoga teacher from Austin, Texas, gave me all his high school wrestling secrets. Lisa Drnec Kerr allowed me to write in Owl Cottage. Diana Gordon expanded my equestrian knowledge.

My life is infinitely better due to my membership in The Great Darkness Writing Group. They are: Marianne Banks, Jeanne Borfitz, Jennifer Jacobson, Celia Jeffries, Lisa Drnec Kerr, Alan & Edie Lipp, Patricia Lee Lewis, Christine Menard, Patricia Riggs, and Marion VanArsdell. My Manuscript Group provided good cheer and insightful critiques. They are: Anne Kornblatt, Rita Marks, Brenda Marsian, Elli Meeropol, Lydia Nettler, and Dori Ostermiller. Morgan Sheehan-Bubla was an enthusiastic and skilled editor from start to finish.

The team at Avon/HarperCollins is made up of people who love books, and I am grateful for their expertise. The team includes Carrie Feron, editor, and Tessa Woodward, assistant editor. And lastly, I thank my agent, Jenny Bent, for being the best.

Joann Berris

I grew up in Connecticut and live in
Massachusetts today, where I divide
my time between writing, teaching
writing workshops and yoga, and
running a small psychotherapy practice. But I spent twenty years living
in western states: California, Oregon,
and New Mexico. For most of my childhood, I lived in a single-parent home,
after the early death of my father left
my mother with five kids. My siblings
were 8 to 13 years older than I was
at the time, so they really had a different childhood, complete with two
parents. My mother was a nurse by
day, but she had the spirit of an artist.
My first memory of her was watching
her paint at her easel on her day off.
She was one of the most fascinating

Jacqueline Sheehan

people I've ever met and even as a child, I was aware of my good fortune to have landed in her nest.

Which is not to say that childhood or my teen years were easy. They were not. I was impulsive and wild, slipping out of my bedroom window at night to meet friends, smoke Newport cigarettes, and drive with boys in fast cars. After unsuccessfully attempting to rein me in, she wisely took another approach and gave me a very long leash, which was what I needed. At the end of my second year of college, a girlfriend and I hitchhiked across the country and to her amazing credit, my mother actually drove us to our first highway entrance and dropped us off.

At college in Colorado, I studied anthropology and art, preparing me for few jobs. During the summer I worked at an institution in Connecticut for people with mental retardation. This was truly the Dark Ages in how we regarded people with developmental delays and we clumped them all together under the umbrella of mental retardation. People of all ages were warehoused in large buildings in awful conditions. College students who worked there in the summer were acutely aware of the injustices done to residents and we plotted many small and not so small rebellions on behalf of the residents.

My career path after college did not lead straight to writing, but instead took a sometimes dizzying route. Among my more illustrious job choices were: director of a traveling puppet troupe, roofer, waitress, recreation worker and lifeguard for handicapped kids, health-food clerk, freelance photographer (the low point was taking pictures of kids with Santa, the high point was photographing births), substance-abuse counselor with street kids in Chicago, freelance newspaper writer, and something about baiting sewers for rats in Oregon, but that one is always too hard to explain. After the birth of my daughter, I returned to graduate school to study psychology, eventually earning my Ph.D. and working at university counseling centers.

As soon as I settled in with psychology, I began to write fiction. Short stories, long stories, novellas, novels, essays. I woke at five A.M. to write before I left for work, spent part of every weekend writing, most holidays, and parts of every vacation that I could squeeze out of my very full life. I have now switched the balance; writing is my primary occupation and private practice is my part-time job.

When people ask me how I find time to write, I am always puzzled, because finding time is not a huge problem. Pat Schneider, a wise writing teacher, once said, "You would find time for a lover, wouldn't you? That is how you find time for writing." And possibly the image of my mother, happily painting at her easel on her day off made an imprint on me that said, here is what you do with your life, do those things you love.

I have a backlog of stories and novels that are yammering to come out and I am doing my best to keep them in an orderly line.

www.jacquelinesheehan.com